Books By Chris Broyhill

Fiction
The Colin Pearce Series
The Viper Contract
The Cabo Contract
The Satan Contract
The Shadow Contract
The Bronco Contract
The Enteron Contract

Non-Fiction
Business Aviation Leadership:
From the Traits to the Trenches

The Satan Contract
Colin Pearce Series III

Chris Broyhill

SECOND EDITION
Published by
Citadel Publishing LLC
Dover, Delaware, USA
2017

ISBN-13: 978-0-9994183-8-3
ISBN-10: 0-9994183-8-6

Paperback

Cover Design and Text Formatting By:
Welhaven and Associates

This is a work of fiction.
The characters in this book are fictitious and the
creation of the author's imagination.
Any resemblance to other characters or to persons
living or dead is purely coincidental.

Dedication

To all my fellow knights of the air.
You know who you are.

Acknowledgements for the Second Edition

The Satan Contract marks the third and final transition of a Colin Pearce adventure from a former, more traditional publisher to my own company, Citadel Publishing, LLC. Like both The Viper Contract and The Cabo Contract which preceded it, this second edition of Satan has been reformatted, proofread and has had minor changes to correct errors and improve readability.

Acknowledgements for this edition would not be complete without the recognition of the technical experts I consulted in the initial manuscript. I have received many complements on the authenticity of the flying sequences that I write. My obsession for technical accuracy required me to review all the non-classified material available for both the F-16 and the F-35 at the time I wrote the this book. My F-16 knowledge was rusty and I knew little to nothing about some of the features that were just coming aboard when I retired and now are standard in the jet, particularly NVGs, the Link 16 datalink and the joint helmet mounted cueing system. Where the F-35 was concerned, I only knew what I read in aviation publications and not much of it was complimentary. I'm indebted to Casey "Fletch" Richardson, Mike Young and Moon

Milham, all active or former Viper drivers and F-35 observers for their superb critiques of the initial manuscript as well as their recommended improvements to the technical aspects of it. The realism and the "grit" of the aerial scenes is largely due to their input. Any opinions about the performance of the two aircraft is mine and mine alone as are any errors or inaccuracies about the details.

A final note of thanks is to you, my faithful readers. Since I originally wrote this volume in 2013, Colin Pearce has journeyed into three more adventures and now has a total of six to his credit. More will follow. Colin Pearce has many fans, both male and female, who are always eager for his next foray into the unknown. I am deeply appreciative for each one of you and for your support of both Colin Pearce and me over the years.

Tailwinds Always,

Chris Broyhill
Arlington, TX
March 2020

Prologue

Back in the Viper again. Back in my cocoon again. Ready to kill again.

I raced along the desert floor at over six hundred knots, just under the Mach. The sleek jet sliced through the torrid July air of southern Arizona, pushed with as much thrust as the giant Pratt and Whitney PW-220 engine could provide without afterburner under the harsh environmental conditions. The sweat beaded across my forehead and ran down my face as I scanned the cockpit through the HUD-like display in the helmet-mounted cueing system I had been issued. The soft plastic of the oxygen mask cupped my face, and the reassuring hard plastic of the sidestick controller and throttle made my hands feel alive, even electric.

I had a mission: stop two pilots who were trying to steal a pair of Lockheed Martin F-35A Lighting II's, the USAF's newest jet fighter. The jets were marvels of modern technology and here I was, chasing them in the Viper, a product of the 1970s.

Some might call it suicide. For me it seemed typical.

One of the pilots was someone I thought was my friend. The other was a former boss from my USAF days, a man who treated his people with such malice we nicknamed him "Satan." Both men were working for Miguel Hidalgo, the Mexican drug lord who had placed a ten-million-dollar contract on my head. And it was my job to stop them.

But their luck was running out and mine seemed to be holding.

I had help. A fellow pilot from my class at Luke Air Force Base was going to play decoy, and I was going to sneak up behind them and ram a pair of AIM-9X Sidewinders up their asses. I had them on radar, and my wingman was tracking them. All was well.

But then, suddenly, the fireball of an aircraft explosion appeared in the Arizona sky.

And everything went to shit.

Chapter One

Monday, June 21, 2010
1100 Hours Local Time
Pearce Townhouse
Wilmington, Delaware

Déjà vu sucks.

I glanced over at the BlackBerry vibrating on my desktop and heard the strains of AC/DC's "Highway to Hell" piercing the silence of the room. While the lead guitar riff comprised the ring tone, my mind filled in the lyrics with Bon Scott's voice providing the vocals:

Living easy, living free
Season ticket on a one-way ride...

I shut my eyes involuntarily and felt myself transport back in time. The Highway to Hell seemed to be the road I was on. A few months ago, before I had taken a fateful phone call in November, life had been simpler. Now there was a woman I loved, a daughter I wanted to hold, and a contract on my head, which made being with them impossible. They were in a government protection program, and the odds were high I'd never see them again. Particularly if the powerful Mexican drug lord, or one of his hit teams, managed to find me and put a bullet in my brain.

The scary thing was that a part of me longed for that outcome.

But another part of me did not.

"No way," I said aloud to the empty room as Angus Young's guitar repeated its familiar riff, "I'm not touching the fucking phone. That's how all this shit got started."

I was sitting at the desk in my living room/study, wading through the stack of paper work that had amassed since the last time I had been there. There were bills to pay, statements to file, and chores to be done. Regardless of whether I was to continue to function as bait for one Miguel Hidalgo, the Mexican drug lord in question, I still had things I needed to do. And answering a phone call and getting involved in someone else's business was simply not on the menu.

Bing!

The BlackBerry alerted me that it had downloaded a voicemail. I picked it up off the desktop and thumbed over to the screen to delete it. But my thumb seemed to be on autopilot, and it pushed the button to play the message instead.

"Hi Colin, it's Bob Barnett. I don't know if you remember me, but we were classmates at the Zoo, CS 27..."

I didn't hear the rest of the message because the neurons in my brain were firing in a frantic attempt to remember the man attached to the name. *Bob Barnett? Robert Barnett? General Robert Barnett?* His face floated out of my memory and appeared in my mind's eye: short guy, friendly face with dark hair. He was serious but smiled easily. I occasionally skimmed through the USAF Academy alumni updates, and so I knew about his promotion to brigadier general and assignment to some important-sounding post at the Pentagon, but I couldn't remember what it was. I replayed the message.

"Hi Colin, it's Bob Barnett. I don't know if you remember me, but we were classmates at the Zoo, CS 27, back in the good-ole days." There was a quick but forced laugh. "Anyway, I have a…a thing I'd like to talk to you about. It's pretty important." I could hear a woman's voice in the background saying something that was unintelligible but didn't sound complimentary. "Can you call me as soon as you get this? I'd really appreciate it. Thanks, Colin."

I sat at my desk and looked down at my BlackBerry incredulously. *Why in the hell would a classmate I barely remembered want to talk to me? And a one-star general, no less.* I could feel the curiosity beginning to seep into my brain along with an equal measure of good old Pearce skepticism. There was no need for me to get involved. It was none of my business.

So of course I hit the send key anyway.

"Goddamn it," I cursed to the empty room. "What the fuck, Pearce?"

The phone rang three times before I heard him click on. "Bob Barnett," he replied crisply. It must have been his personal cell phone and not his government issued one, or he would have answered with his rank.

"Bob, Colin Pearce. You rang?"

"Colin! Thank God!" There was an audible sigh of relief, and I could hear him call to someone in the background. "It's him, honey."

I found myself shaking my head. *What the hell was going on and who was I that I deserved this quasi-notable status?* He didn't even bother with small talk or banter. There was obviously an agenda.

"Colin, I know you live in Delaware somewhere. Is there any possible way you could drive down to the DC area and meet me for about an hour or so? I'll pay you for your time."

Well, this was a little awkward. I had worked numerous times for wealthy individuals, aircraft management companies, and even the US Government, but never for what I'd consider a regular person. I knew that general officers in the USAF made a decent salary, but I knew he still made less than I did.

But there was something about his voice. It didn't sound like the typical, confident voice of a general. There was a distinct element of emotion in it.

"Is there any reason we can't discuss it on the phone, Bob?"

There was a discernible pause, and it told me everything I needed to know. He thought someone might be listening.

"Never mind, Bob," I said before he could answer. "I had some business down there anyway. Let me make a phone call or two to move some things around. When and where would you like to meet?"

"Tonight if you can do it, about two hours before they used to play taps at the Zoo."

Okay, so that was pretty cryptic. I thought back to my cadet days. I thought taps was played about 11:00 p.m. or 2300 hours. So he wanted to meet at about 9:00 p.m.

"I can make that happen," I replied. "Whereabouts?"

"Remember that squadron classmate of ours who passed away very young? The guy who had the great singing voice? There's a restaurant where the squids come from that has a name just like his. I'll be in the bar there."

That one came a little more quickly. The guy's name was Ray Francisco and cancer had claimed him way too early. He was a man of color and one of the most genuinely selfless people I had ever met. He also had a fantastic baritone voice and could belt out R&B. The world was a poorer place without him in it. The restaurant where "squids came from" meant the place was in the town of Annapolis, Maryland, where the US Naval Academy was. We Air Force Academy types called them squids; and they called us "zoomies." No doubt who got the better end of that moniker contest.

"I do," I said. "And I'll be there."

"Thanks, Colin. Thanks so much."

He broke the connection and I was left staring at my BlackBerry again. High emotion. Apparently high pressure. A refusal to discuss details over the phone and an encoded time and place for a meeting. I didn't waste any time at all before I called the people who were watching me.

"Hello T. C.," said CIA Operations Officer Dave Smith as he picked up his phone.

"Hi Dave," I said.

"Does this have to do with the phone call you just made?"

"It does. Your tech guys will have the transcript of both the voice mail and my conversation with Bob Barnett in short order, but I'd like to know if you guys would have any issues with me heading down to Annapolis tonight? Specifically to a restaurant called Francisco's."

"I don't see any problem with that," he replied. "We have no indication that Miguel has anything going on where you're concerned. He seems to be extremely busy in Mexico these days. Maybe he's put you on hold for a while."

"Busy?" I asked. "You guys never told me anything about him being busy. What's going on?"

Smith paused and I could almost hear the cogs in his brain turning over the phone.

"And don't pull any of that need to know shit. This is a secure line and if anyone has a right to know what's going on in Miguel Hidalgo's mind, it's the guy he's marked for death."

"You're right, I guess," Smith said. "Although Amrine will shit if he hears me telling this."

"I don't need a full briefing. Just a sketch," I said.

"Well, the sketch is that there is this large Chinese bank that is buying up all the manufacturing space around Mexico City and moving people and equipment in like crazy. Evidently Hidalgo is using his influence and a lot of his cash to bypass the government red tape to make this happen."

He stopped speaking and I waited, expecting more. After

a few seconds, I realized he was finished.

"And?" I asked. "That doesn't seem illegal at all. Miguel might actually be helping the economy with that. Joe Sanchez, the deep cover DEA guy, said he does the philanthropist thing from time to time. That's one of the reasons why the support for him inside the country is as high as it is."

"We're doing more research right now. We have assets on the ground in China and Mexico, but we haven't turned up anything substantial yet."

"I see," I said as my own mental gears turned. "Based on what I know of the guy, I don't think he'd rest all his chances on buying the goodwill of the people. He'd have another tactic as well."

"We agree," Smith said.

"But hell, if it keeps him away from me for a little while, more power to him."

"Well, we don't think he has anyone shadowing you or monitoring you. That's one of the reasons we ran you through those different locations for your aircraft initial courses and other training over these last few months. If someone is really trying to shadow a target, they'll reveal themselves if the target goes through multiple location changes. Like they did in Dallas."

"Well, I'm glad that you chose to do that. I've wanted to get checked out in the Falcon 2000LX and 7X for a long time. Being able to do it on government expense at Dallas and Teterboro was just a bonus. I needed something to help me forget about Sarah and Colleen. I'm glad it was something constructive."

"You know, you might actually get to see them again at some point."

I shook my head unconsciously. "I'm too dangerous, Dave. We both know that. I told Sarah she needed to forget about me and move on with her life. You guys have given her the opportunity to do that and I'm grateful."

The anguish that lived inside of me rose up again as I thought of the lovely red-haired woman who had wanted to marry me and whom I had almost gotten killed. And then I saw the cherubic cheeks of the baby she had named after me—the baby that had my eyes.

Damn. I thought as the tears burned my eyes once again. *You need a distraction Pearce, and this might be the ticket.*

"So I take it that I'm good to go south tonight then?" I asked after a long moment.

"Sure. Do you want to drive yourself or would you like us to provide a car and driver?"

"I appreciate the offer, but I haven't had much windshield time recently. I'll drive."

"No problem. But we'll need you to provide an exact route and itinerary."

"Seriously?"

Smith was patient with me. "It's the only way we can make sure you're covered, Colin. Regardless of what Miguel may or may not be doing in Mexico, he still could have a team or two looking for you. And in spite of all the weapons and hand-to-hand training we put you through when you weren't learning to fly new airplanes, you still get backup. We have a rule: never fight fair."

"I get that about you," I said. "I'll leave here about six in the evening and go down the Eastern Shore of Maryland."

"The Eastern Shore? Taking the scenic route?"

"It's just much more predictable, and I'm not in a hurry," I replied.

"OK," Smith said with a sigh. "I guess that will work. We'll have a team deployable if you need it. We'll contact you if your GPS tracker isn't working. Have a good time tonight, Colin. We'll see you on the satellite."

I laughed. "Have fun with that, Dave."

"Oh we do," he said. "You know we're not always just looking at you. Often times we have to examine the activities going on in cars around you, and you'd be surprised what we can see. The resolution of those cameras is impressive."

"Really?" I replied. "And just how good would that be?"

"Well," he said, with a note of humor in voice, "while the pixel count is classified, let me tell you this: you'd be surprised at how many women aren't wearing panties under the skirts of those designer business suits."

"The things you learn," I said.

Chapter Two

Monday, June 21, 2010
1900 Hours Local Time
US Highway 301
Somewhere between the Delaware Border and Centreville, Maryland

There was nothing like a drive along the Eastern Shore of Maryland to clear one's thoughts. I didn't travel between Wilmington, Delaware, and Annapolis often, but when I did, I preferred the Eastern Shore route to Interstate 95. Delaware Highway 1 to Delaware 896, 896 to US 301, and then 301 until it joined US 50 and on into Annapolis, either across the Severn River Bridge or, more likely tonight, south on Maryland 450 and across the Naval Academy Bridge and into historic Annapolis. Sure the distance was longer and the speed limits were lower, but it was predictable and peaceful. It allowed plenty of time for the mind to wander, and it seemed that was what I needed that tonight. A few hours away from my townhouse, a few hours away from my life for that matter, would provide a nice respite.

The phone call with Smith had reminded me that the last few months had been a whirlwind to say the least. After ejecting from a jet at high speed last November and enduring the agonizing damage that had been done to my body, as well as the ten weeks in a drug-induced coma that had been required for my body to heal afterward, the recovery and rehabilitation process had been excruciating.

Then there had been all that followed.

I shook my head and sighed as I eyed the lonely highway in front of me through the windshield of my Ford Explorer. People who have lived the life I've lived and done the things I've done don't get offered the chance to change their destinies very often. But I had been shown a woman who cared about me and wanted to spend her life with me and a daughter that was the nearest thing to perfect beauty that I had ever seen.

And then it had all been taken away.

The ones who had tried to kill Sarah and little Colleen had been Arabs, but the voice on the phone a few days later had made it clear, in his nearly undetectable Mexican accent, that the next ones who would come for me would belong to him. And that they wouldn't fail. Having seen Miguel Hidalgo in action, I didn't doubt him for a moment.

So rather than subject Sarah and Colleen to a life with security teams guarding them 24/7/365, Smith and Amrine had pulled some strings and simply made them disappear into the general population. They were living new lives in a new city with a new home and all the money they'd need, thanks to the work I had done for the CIA.

And all I had to do to keep them safe was stay away from them.

For a person who had done his best to hide from his emotions all of his life, the mere thought of never seeing them again touched a nerve very close to the surface for me and filled me with a mixture of longing and sadness that I had no frame of reference for—even after losing both parents and seeing people I cared about die in front of me.

"Someday, Colin," Sarah had said over the phone that last

time we had spoken, months ago, "someday we'll be together again."

And now, with the wetness in my eyes again looking out at an empty road again and being alone again, I didn't believe a word of it. I was born alone, had spent the vast majority of my life alone, and was destined to die that way. The rest was just details.

But to Smith and Amrine's credit, they had done the best they could to keep my mind off of all of it for the last few months. I had spent a month in Teterboro, New Jersey, learning to fly the Dassault Falcon 2000 EASy, and had enjoyed immersing myself in the advanced business jet, and learning the systems and avionics. Then several weeks just outside of Las Vegas, Nevada, at a complex called First Sight, I learned more than I had ever thought there was to learn about handling firearms, particularly handguns. Then there were the lessons in hand-to-hand combat, not the sort of thing you see in movies or even at tournaments, but the sort of thing that can kill or permanently disable a person in just a few moves.

Finally, it was on to Dallas, Texas, and about a month learning how to fly the Dassault Falcon 7X, a bigger brother to the other Falcon I had learned to fly, with three engines, a digital flight control system, a lot of thrust, a sidestick controller, and a heads-up display—I had felt like I was going home to the F-16. While I had enjoyed all the training at the government expense, as well as sumptuous hotel accommodations, meals, and nice rental cars, a part of me knew there'd be payback for all of it at some point. The government never gave you anything for free.

And now here I was, headed south, possibly to get involved in yet another matter that I had no business in and maybe even hoping I'd get killed in the process. I've never been anything if not self-destructive. I watched the pastoral farmland of the Eastern Shore go by and listened to the strains of Celtic music seep through the Explorer's Bose speakers, feebly hoping to snag a few moments of peace.

But it was not to be.

My BlackBerry beeped with an incoming text message, and I held it up so I could read and drive at the same time.

The message came from Dave Smith's cellphone. CALL ME ASAP, it said.

I keyed the send button and called Smith's number, putting the phone on speaker mode as I did so. His number rang once and he answered.

"Hi Dave. What's so urgent?"

"Look in your rearview mirror," he said, interrupting me.

I don't like speed limits, so I look in the rearview mirror a lot anyway, but I did so again at Smith's request. I saw nothing except for a few cars far behind me in the distance.

"Nothing there, Dave," I said. "I mean there are some cars way back there but nothing really."

"Look again," he said.

I glanced into the mirror again and was rewarded with the same view I had seen previously; cars traveling the same highway far behind me. But then I saw it. A dark-colored pickup truck with its headlights on, aggressively weaving in and out of the cars and apparently moving at high speed.

"What an idiot," I said unconsciously. "They patrol the shit out of this road. The Highway Patrol is going to notice him for sure."

"Not him. Them," Smith said. "There are at least four of them and they're heavily armed and apparently coming after you."

While I shouldn't have been surprised at that revelation— we had been planning for it for months—my brain was having trouble processing Smith's words.

"How the hell did that happen?" I asked after a few seconds. "Who are they?"

"We don't know," Smith answered. "We just picked them up on the satellite and confirmed it with a traffic feed. It's one of Miguel's teams. All we can think of is that they were backup and just trying to stay out of sight. When you stopped for gas in Middletown, Delaware, someone must have noticed you and called them."

"Noticed me and called? Who would do that?" I asked.

Smith signed audibly. "Delaware is mostly farmland, Colin. Who do they pay to work farmland?"

I thought for just a second, and then the implications of his words hit me.

"Migrant workers," I said. "Hispanic migrant workers. Miguel has connections here?"

"Of course he does," Smith said. "He has connections everywhere, especially where the population speaks Spanish and drugs might be sold."

I instinctively pressed the Explorer's accelerator pedal to the floor. The V-6 engine responded with a low growl and the transmission geared down to provide additional speed.

"Speed is life," I said, unconsciously. "More speed, more life."

I looked in my rearview mirror again. The pickup was definitely gaining on me.

"So I'll interrogate you later on how all your monitoring shit didn't notice these guys until now, but the immediate questions are: Where's my backup and what the fuck do I do until they get here?"

"The one ground unit we had on you is too far back. We've got another ground unit coming over the Chesapeake Bay Bridge just now; and we've just tasked the alert helo ops team from Langley, but we're concerned none of them will reach you in time."

I looked in the rearview. I could see detail on the truck now. It wasn't more than a few miles back. I glanced at my speedometer. The Explorer was accelerating to ninety-five miles per hour. It wasn't going to get much faster.

"Do you have a recommendation?" I asked, trying to keep the apprehension out of my voice.

"Not particularly," Smith answered. "The road is pretty straight. We were hoping you could just keep moving until one of the ops teams can make it to you."

"If I was driving a car with a little more heat, that might be possible, Dave. But these guys are going to catch me. And odds are high that they're going to start firing shit at me as soon as they get in range."

As if on cue, I heard a "clink" sound and a bullet hole appeared in the windshield to my right. I looked in the rearview and saw the corresponding hole in the lift gate window and beyond, a huge man standing in the bed of the pickup truck behind me with a long-barreled rifle, firing over the cab at me. I was amazed that the rear window hadn't shattered.

Jink! The thought occurred to me immediately; a jink—a random change in flight path. I began weaving, unpredictably, between the two southbound lanes. My speed began to decrease, which was undoubtedly what they were hoping for.

"Shit!" I said unconsciously as I turned the wheel again. "They're shooting at me, Dave. Probably with something big. I'm jinking to avoid getting shot. They're definitely going to catch me."

REST AREA. 5 MILES.

The sign went by on the right side of the divided highway, and my brain quickly pulled up a mental sketch. It sat in the middle of the divided highway between the south and northbound lanes. Since places to turnaround and reverse course were infrequent in this part of the highway, it might offer me the opportunity to create some sort of ambush. Although I hadn't come terribly prepared, I had a Colt 1911 Commander in .45ACP and four spare magazines—a total of some twenty-nine rounds of ammunition. I was sure they had automatic weapons of some sort. It wasn't going to be a fair fight unless I did something to even the odds. I did some mental math. I was averaging ninety miles per hour. The rest area was about two and a half minutes away. I hoped I could last that long.

"I'm going to stop at the rest area that's coming up on my left, Dave."

CRASH! My rear window exploded and a large round thudded into my dashboard. Apparently my jinking tactics weren't working out well. I floored the gas pedal again and looked in the rearview. The pickup looked to be about half a mile back.

REST AREA 2 MILES.

Just over a minute now. A lifetime.

"Can you alert the Maryland Highway Patrol?" I asked. "They've got a barracks just south of here. If there's anyone at that rest stop, this could be a blood bath."

"Done," Smith said.

"Did you tell them what I look like so they won't shoot me? Assuming I'm still alive to shoot?" I added.

He didn't answer.

REST AREA 1 MILE. KEEP LEFT.

About thirty seconds. I reached into the Explorer's center console, retrieved two spare magazines for the Colt, and stuffed them into my right pants pocket. Then I looked at my rearview mirror in time to see it explode in a blur of plastic and glass. Small shards embedded themselves in the right side of my face. My Ray-Ban sunglasses vibrated slightly as they repelled the pieces of glass headed toward my eyes.

I didn't even notice.

"This guy is good," I said to myself, thinking of the shooter. And then something occurred to me that gave me hope and filled me with dread at the same time. *Miguel wants me alive.*

This guy isn't missing me at all. He's deliberately trying to fuck with me.

REST AREA 1/2 MILE. NEXT LEFT.

As soon as I saw the turnoff for the rest area, I slammed on my brakes and turned across the empty left lane, putting the Explorer into a full skid as I did so. The larger pickup truck was still about half a mile back, and I hoped I might have a few moments out of sight of the passengers before they arrived. Additionally, if they valued the life of their marksman standing in the truck bed, I was betting that the driver wouldn't maneuver so radically or he'd eject the marksman from the truck.

The rest area consisted of a long, rectangular building between the north and southbound lanes of the highway and parallel to them, with entrances and parking lots on each side. I turned onto the access road for the rest area then made the second right, not the first one, so I could park on the far side of the building. I skidded to a stop between a blue Volvo station wagon and a red Nissan Altima and hoped like hell that their occupants would stay out of the line of fire. I leapt out of the SUV the moment it stopped and ran around the south side of the rectangular building away from the two entrances and into a small tree grove. Then I hid behind the biggest bush I could find and waited.

I saw the large pickup speed off the highway and onto the access road. The man standing in the bed was no longer visible. Within seconds, the truck skidded to a halt on the same side of the building where I had parked. I heard its doors slam. As they came into view around the side of the building, I got my first look at them—a crew of four men, all wearing khaki slacks and black windbreakers with the letters ATF in yellow on the back.

That's fucking cute, I thought, *posing as agents from the Bureau of Alcohol, Tobacco, and Firearms.* It was an agency that no one knew much about or cared about. And it was one that would give casual observers the impression that the wearers were US Government agents and also allow them to engage anyone with a gun who was foolish enough to try to take them on. In other words, someone like me.

Marvelous, I thought as they dispersed into two, two-man teams with military precision. *Just fucking marvelous.* I texted a quick note to Smith.

THEY'RE WEARING ATF JACKETS. TELL HP.

Even from a concealed position, I didn't see how I'd be able to engage two teams that professional without being cut to pieces, even if they did want to take me alive. I watched as the teams worked a quick clearing search pattern around the building and then took positions at the entrance to each of the restrooms. They would go through the restrooms and the main lobby, find nothing, and then do a more thorough exterior search and find me. It was just a question of time, which was the one commodity I didn't seem to have.

Then I saw the maintenance ladder next to my side of the building and had an idea. As both teams entered the restrooms with a scream or two of surprise emanating from the ladies' room as they did so, I ran to the side of the building and dashed up the ladder onto the roof of the facility as quickly as I could.

"Shit," I muttered when I got up there. There were no cooling units to hide behind. But the roof had small gables on both sides and a large pointed section in the center. I hoped the gables would provide enough concealment. I lay down behind the nearest one, drew the Colt, checked the magazine and the chamber, and trained the sights toward the edge of the roof from where I had just come.

In the distance, I could hear sirens that sounded like they were getting closer. There was a rapid discussion in Spanish from the direction of the restroom doors a few moments later.

I could hear the team members moving all around the building now, much more deliberately than they had the first time. I didn't understand the Spanish they were speaking, but the words were crisp and unemotional, like commands on a battlefield. These guys were very well trained, and had apparently worked together before. I hoped I could stay alive long enough for the cavalry to arrive. Whether it was HP or CIA, at this point it didn't matter.

And, I realized suddenly, I actually did want to live. I wanted to see Sarah and my daughter again, whenever that might be. And no one, not even one of the most powerful drug lords in the world, was going to keep that from happening. I clicked off the thumb safety on the Colt and waited.

There was a scratching sound, like the movement of metal on concrete.

Someone on the ladder, I thought. *So here we go.*

And in a moment, the training kicked in and any conscious fear I had of the upcoming events was gone. I had experienced the same phenomenon in my flying career. I was trained so well to perform myriad tasks under stressful conditions that when situations arose where those skills where necessary, there wasn't much thinking or feeling required. The training kicked in and there was only performance. I knew that as targets presented themselves over the next few minutes, I could engage them and probably do so successfully. How many targets there would be and the associated conditions surrounding them were still variables in the equation, but there was one constant; if I could get the Colt Commander's sights lined up with a target, that target was going down.

I smiled to myself as I recalled a classic line from an old Clint Eastwood movie called Magnum Force, where Eastwood had portrayed a relentless cop named Harry Callahan who wielded a .44 Magnum revolver. "There's nothing wrong with shooting," Eastwood's character had said, "as long as the right people get shot."

I was going to shoot the right people.

A few seconds later, a head emerged over the edge of the roof. He was a handsome young kid. He didn't look like a hoodlum at all. But his dark eyes were cold and hard and they gave the Hispanic features a somewhat weathered look, as if the person inside was being used up at a far greater rate than normal.

For a moment, I wondered if that's what people saw in my face. But then I centered the Colt's front sight on the bridge of his nose and slowly pressed the trigger. I watched the cold eyes work their way around the rooftop and finally detect me, then the mouth began to open just as the trigger reached its aft stop; the sear inside the frame moved, the hammer fell, and two hundred grains of hollow-point lead closed the gap between us at eight hundred feet per second. A geyser of blood erupted from the middle of the handsome face, and it disappeared over the edge of the roof.

One down, three to go. But it's still three to one.

The next thing that appeared over the side of the roof was a dull-colored metal canister about the size of my fist. It flew a lazy arc trajectory to land on the roof on the other side of the gable I was hiding behind.

Flash bang, I thought. *Neat trick.*

A flash-bang grenade does just that. It generates a quick, intense flash and a quick burst of overpressure and is meant to disorient the occupants of enclosed spaces before a tactical team performs a forced entry. But these guys had two things working against them. While flash bangs can generate intense effects in enclosed spaces, in open spaces, without walls to contain the blast and reflect the sound waves, the effect is much less profound. The rooftop area was small, but it was not an enclosed space. The second thing they didn't take into account was that I was trained—and ready. I shut my eyes tightly and placed my hands over my ears while I ducked below the edge of the gable.

THUMP!

I felt the vibration of the explosion pass through the roof. Then I raised myself over the edge of the gable and trained the Colt off the edge of the roof where the first guy's head had made its appearance. Apparently they either overestimated the effect of the grenade or underestimated me, because the second guy's head appeared very quickly. And just as quickly, I put two hundred grains of lead into it and it went down.

Two down. Two to go.

A few moments of silence followed. I could almost hear the gears in the heads of the remaining team members turning as they formulated a new plan. One of the things I had learned from working with the Army in the early part of my USAF career was not to continuously fire from the same position if that could be avoided. And a little voice inside my head told me that it was time to move. I got to my feet, and crouching as low as I could, I made my way to the middle of the roof. I eased myself over the center of it and just to the other side so I could use the apex of the roof as concealment from the area I had just occupied.

They didn't keep me waiting long. Two more flash-bang grenades cleared the side of the roof and landed near my previous position. I was farther away, but I still closed my eyes and covered my ears.

TH-THUMP!

The two grenades detonated nearly simultaneously. I recovered quickly. I got the Colt out in front of me, over the roofline, and readied it for engagement. The sounds of sirens were very close now, and I expected the Maryland Highway Patrol to arrive at any moment. It occurred to me that Miguel must have scared the shit out of these guys if they were willing to risk a shootout with the state police to get to me. But then again, he was pretty fucking intimidating. And death at the hands of the MHP probably paled in comparison to their fate in Miguel's hands if they arrived without the required prize.

A head appeared at the edge of the roof but at a different spot than the first two. Apparently they had moved the ladder to a place behind my former position, around the side of the roofline.

Flanking maneuver, I thought. *Well played.*

The head and the body attached to it scrambled over the side of the roof very quickly. The man's eyes fixed on my former position and apparently he was unable to discern the fact that I wasn't there due to the residual smoke from the multiple grenades. As I aligned the Colt's sights on the dark-clad figure and my finger tightened on the trigger, something told me to wait for just a moment. Sure enough, another head appeared over the edge of the roof. I sighted in on the head, pressed the trigger, and watched the head disappear. Then I pivoted to the figure on the roof, firing my remaining four rounds in rapid succession. Another body went down.

Tires squealed in the parking lot below as the Maryland Highway Patrol arrived, and I found myself breathing a sigh of relief as I replaced the magazine in the Colt and released the slide to chamber a new round.

And then I heard the shot.

It was a low but impossibly loud BOOM sound unlike anything I had ever heard. The tire squealing stopped abruptly with a crash of metal and glass. Instinctively, judging by the size of the rifle I saw in my mirror earlier and the huge holes it had made in my car, I realized that I'd heard the report of a Barrett .50 for the first time. I also realized that I had been wrong about my initial count of the number of Miguel's team. There were five. And number five was the sniper.

Part of me wanted to stick my head over the edge of the roof and engage him. But the part of me with common sense told me that showing my head to a sniper armed with a Barrett .50, at this range, was like waving a flag and yelling "Shoot me" at the top of my lungs. But I needed to engage him and do so in a way that placed him at the disadvantage.

I crawled over the center of the apex of the rooftop to the one team member I had downed and who I could get to. He had the M-4 version of the AR-15 strapped to him, and I relieved him of it as quickly as I could. I grabbed a few magazines as well. Then I heard the sound of the pickup's engine starting and the sound of tires squealing. The pickup then appeared in view as it backed up to the farthest point in the parking lot away from the building, and I realized what was happening.

Holy shit! I thought. *He's trying to get a line on me!*

Time to move. I leaped over the center of the roof as I heard the pickup's door slam. Then I crept to the side of the roof and eyeballed the distance to the ground. It was about twelve feet. Without thinking, I swung my legs over the far side of the building, lowered myself over the side until I was hanging by my hands, and dropped, grateful that I had chosen the Johnston & Murphy shoes with good arch support for the evening's engagement. My legs absorbed the shock better than I thought they would, and I moved quickly around to the end of the building so I could attempt to engage the sniper from a different position. I didn't have any illusions about my capability. The sniper had a weapon that was several times more powerful than mine, and I was sure he was a much better shot than me. I had no idea what I intended to do. I just wanted to stop him before he killed anyone else in his effort to get me.

I reached the south side of the rest stop building, squatted down, and carefully peered around the corner to survey the landscape. I was rewarded with a view of an impossibly huge man standing in the bed of the pickup truck, his eye glued

to the telescopic sight on top of the receiver of a Barrett
.50 rifle mounted on a bipod that sat upon the roof of the
pickup. His hair was jet black and fashioned in a long ponytail
that ran down the center of his back. His arms were heavily
muscled and covered with tattoos. He was clad in blue jeans
and a sleeveless leather vest, studded with silver knobs that
glistened in the decreasing sunlight. He looked like some
kind of character from a Mad Max movie. As I viewed him
from around the corner of the building, I felt my usual, blind
confidence ebbing. He was unbelievably large, powerful, and
proficient. For just a moment, the somewhat ethereal sense
of Miguel's power seemed embodied in this incredible man.
And in that same moment, I felt a sense of hopelessness.

And then the sirens of another highway patrol car blared
and sounds of squealing tires filled the air. I saw the sniper
pivot to the right to engage the arriving car, and I picked
that moment to raise the M4 and opened fire. I didn't count
on the M4 being set to the full auto mode, though, and it did
what most full auto weapons do in the hands of inexperienced
people: the muzzle rose while I was firing it. The first few
rounds of my burst hit the side of the pickup and one or two
more hit the shooter, but the rest went harmlessly into the
sky above him.

Impatiently, I tossed the M4 aside and drew the Colt.
Then I did what the instructors at First Sight taught me. I
aligned the sights, pressed the trigger, waited for the gun to
fire, released the trigger just to the point that I felt it reset,
and then pressed it again. Over and over—seven times. I could
see the bullets impacting the huge man's torso repeatedly;
and while his body moved in response to the force of the
projectiles striking him, he stayed on target, firing the Barrett
repeatedly at the MHP cars that entered the rest area. I ejected
the magazine as it ran dry, inserted another, and continued
to fire upon him as I left my concealment behind the corner

of the building and advanced upon his truck, shooting as I walked. The rounds continued to strike home but he remained unfazed, firing upon the highway patrolmen and not turning to deal with me. It was as if I was a fly that was not even enough of a nuisance to swat.

But then the third magazine went dry. I replaced it and looked up in time to see the huge man and the huge rifle pivoting toward me. As I raised the Colt to engage him, I found myself looking into the Barrett's gaping barrel, the ugly muzzle brake defining the end of it. I could almost picture the long .50 caliber round sliding into the chamber and the large 600-grain, steel-jacketed slug poised to split my skull. As I raised my pistol and braced for the impact, the huge man suddenly, inexplicably, fell to the ground. Like he was thrown there by an invisible hand.

Then I heard the roar of the helicopter behind me and the sound of large SUVs pulling into the parking lot on the other side of the rest area. The cavalry had arrived. I looked upward and back to see a dark-colored Sikorsky Blackhawk helicopter skidding into a hover. The door on the near side of the helo was open, and I saw a CIA sniper sitting in the doorway, hat backward on his head, and telescopic sight pressed to his eyes. As I watched, he lowered the weapon, and I saw a puzzled look on his face. He pointed toward the pickup; and as I returned my gaze to the vehicle, I saw what he was pointing at. The Barrett .50 rested on the cab of the pickup with smoke still visible as it wafted up from the muzzle.

But the large man was gone.

I blinked in disbelief and closed the remaining distance to the pickup, Colt at the ready, as members of the CIA ground team reached me and ran alongside me to the vehicle. We got there mere seconds later, and my suspicions were confirmed. He was gone. There was a little blood in the bed of the pickup, but otherwise, there was no trace of him.

"I fired 14 rounds at him," I whispered in disbelief. "I know I fucking hit him."

"The black vest he wears is Kevlar," one of the team members responded. "And between that, the steroids, drugs, and muscles, he might not have even felt it."

I looked over at the guy who had spoken. He was as young as the Hispanic man I had shot earlier. And while he was blond and Caucasian, he had the same empty eyes.

"Jesus," I said. "You know who this guy is?"

"Ramon Pétreo," the familiar voice of Dave Smith said from behind me, "or Ramon the Rock. He's one of Miguel's top enforcers. You're lucky to be alive, T. C."

I turned to face him as I engaged the Colt's thumb safety and holstered it.

"I guess," I said. "Without trying to sound ungrateful here, Dave, can I ask what the fuck happened to all the coverage and surveillance?"

Smith hung his head as he led me from the group. The ops team members had spread out and were systematically searching the terrain around the rest area, while the helicopter had climbed into a low orbit. Three highway patrol cars were on scene now, and MHP officers were closing the rest area and dealing with the traffic. What had been a no-name rest area on a lonely stretch of highway would undoubtedly make the news tonight. I wondered how the CIA public affairs machine would spin it.

"Damn sorry about that, T. C.," Smith said. "We had you covered until you reached the Delaware-Maryland Border. Then we had a five-minute gap in satellite coverage and the ground team following you had a flat tire. Before we knew it, Ramon and the gang were on your tail. We'll do better. I promise."

I was shaking now as the adrenaline worked its way out of my system. "Well, if it happens again," I said, "there may not be much of a next time. I'm happy to fight anyone in a jet, but this ground shit is definitely not my forte."

Smith smiled grimly as he looked at the crews cleaning up the bodies next to the restroom building and on the roof. "Looks like you did okay to me," he said. "You did okay in Dallas too as I recall."

"Luck," I said. "Both times luck. And I know I'd rather be lucky than good; but if this keeps occurring, my luck might run out at some point."

Smith nodded unconsciously as he continued to survey the scene. "We need to get you something with a little more firepower that you can handle without much training. We'll have a compartment for it installed in your Explorer after we have it analyzed and repaired." He looked at me. "When you did the automatic weapons demo at First Sight, what weapon did you like the best?"

I shrugged. "Easy choice," I said, "especially after I spewed bullets all over the countryside with that damn M4. I like the H & K MP-5, great rate of fire and easy to keep on target. In .45 ACP, if I can get it that way."

Smith nodded. "We'll make it happen," he said. "Now let me get you to a medic and get you cleaned up."

I had totally forgotten about the glass embedded in my face. I unconsciously reached up to touch it and felt several small shards sticking out.

"Damn," I said. "There go my movie star good looks."

Chapter Three

Monday, June 21, 2010
2100 Hours Local Time
Francisco's Steak House
Annapolis, Maryland

It had been several years since I had been in Annapolis, but I fondly remembered the town, one of the most quaint and historic places in the United States. It took me a while to find Francisco's Steakhouse since it wasn't in the main town area but south, in Eastport across the harbor, and nestled into an area among several upscale condominium complexes. I cruised around the block twice in the rental car provided by the CIA, in opposite directions, to ensure I wasn't followed, and then I parked in the designated lot next to the restaurant. As I walked to the door of the steak house, I slowly but purposefully let my eyes roam over the surrounding landscape, ever mindful of the odd parked car or bystander who looked out of place.

The rich wood and glass doors of Francisco's loomed in front of me. I entered the restaurant and nodded politely at the attractive brunette hostess in the formal black dress with the plunging neckline. Ever the image of the multitasking businessman, I retrieved my CIA-issue BlackBerry from its holder and clicked on an application icon that would provide the features Smith had recommended for the upcoming conversation.

"Good evening, sir!" The hostess said brightly. "Welcome to Francisco's!"

"Thank you," I replied as I reholstered the phone, making every effort to look her in the eye and not stare at her large breasts, which were bared nearly down to the nipples. This restaurant was obviously geared toward male clientele. "Where's the bar?"

She motioned to her left. "Through here. Just down and to the right."

"Thanks again," I said, nodding and damn proud of myself for keeping my eyes on hers.

I walked through the archway where she had directed me, took several steps, and found the bar in an open area to my right. It was all done in a nautical motif with highly polished wood and brass fixtures and featured a beautiful view of the harbor through several bay windows. The bar was doing a decent business for just after 9:00 p.m. on a Monday night, particularly when the entire brigade of midshipmen at the Naval Academy wasn't in town. I looked around the dimly lit bar and only saw one person who even slightly matched the mental picture I had of Bob Barnett but dismissed him as the one I'd be meeting because there was a woman at his table.

And then he looked up, stood, and motioned me over, nodding to the woman as he did so.

He was a little shorter than I remembered, about five feet nine inches, and the hair was now more salt and pepper than dark, but the blue eyes were still friendly, and the smile was still easy. He looked trim and fit. The woman with him turned as I approached, as if to take me in. She was blonde and well maintained for her age, which I estimated to be in the mid- to late-fifties range, a little older than Bob and I. Her body, what

I could see of it, was highly toned—no doubt the product of many long hours in the gym. As I neared the table, I could sense a definite element of tension between the two of them.

"Colin," Bob said softly but warmly as I approached, "it is damn good to see you." He extended his hand and we shook firmly. He nodded toward the woman at the table. "This is my wife, Kristin."

I extended my hand to her and she took it, but her shake was tentative. The look on her face showed wariness and skepticism.

Bob motioned for me to take the seat at the square table on the side between them and I did so. I saw Bob's eyes quickly glance inside my jacket as we sat and be smiled grimly.

"You've got a good eye, Bob," I said.

"Too much time in overseas places with a security detail around me. You learn what to look for. Glock? Nine millimeter?"

I shook my head.

"Model 1911-style Colt Commander .45 ACP. I could never get used to the trigger on a Glock. Plus, I like the way the Colt feels in my hand better. And the .45 actually knocks people down instead of going through them." I remembered the bullets striking Ramon the Rock with no apparent effect. "At least in most cases," I added.

"Nothing wrong with a little constructive paranoia," he said. "I just wish I could do something about mine." He looked at me, and I could see tinges of both anger and frustration in his eyes. "If I act paranoid, in the slightest way, then they may know I'm on to them."

"Well, your time and space coordinates for our meeting tonight were pretty enigmatic," I said. "And I assumed you didn't want to talk on the phone because you were afraid you might be overheard."

He nodded. "I didn't want to make it too easy for someone

to follow us here. But the truth is that Kristin and I come here regularly," he said, "just not usually during the week. Besides, Kristin's son went to school here, so this is one of her favorite places to have dinner with him."

I nodded respectfully to her. "Naval aviator?"

"He was," she said flatly, "until someone in the Air Force killed him."

I swallowed hard as I settled into my chair. *All righty then.*

"Which is why you're here, Colin," Bob said, obviously trying to divert the conversation.

But Kristin wasn't having any. She nodded at her husband dismissively. "He's come up with this harebrained scheme to find out who did it, and he needs you to carry it off." She looked me over again, and when she spoke her tone was as bitter as a squirt of straight lime juice. "I mean I've heard these stories about things you've done, but that doesn't mean shit to me when it comes to finding out who killed my boy. So I'm sitting here wondering who the hell you are and what so-called special abilities you have."

I was a bit taken aback. *Harebrained scheme? Special abilities?* I looked over at Bob. His eyes had the gleam of knowledge, and I wasn't sure how much of it he had shared.

"How much do you know, Bob?" I asked.

I could see the hesitation in his eyes. Need to know was undoubtedly what he was thinking. I knew enough about his career to know that he was a rule follower, like most of his fellow transport pilots. Thinking outside the box wasn't really his strong suit. But meeting me here tonight obviously fell outside of his comfort zone, so he was making progress.

"Let's move back a few steps," I said. "It's obvious that you know some history about me. How do you know it?"

"I'm the J-34 on the Joint Staff, the Deputy Director for Anti-Terrorism and Homeland Defense," Bob said quietly. "I actually had a few of my people assisting the CIA at Edwards when you shot down all those terrorists over the high desert of California last year. But the whole plot against the president thing that you foiled was a closely guarded secret in spite of all the media coverage it received. I only found out you were involved a few weeks ago, which is why we're talking." He smiled thinly. "You recovered pretty well for a guy who ejected from an airplane at nearly the speed of sound. You set a good example for us fifty-something types."

I could have told them about what it felt like to have your body twisted at impossible angles and then hit the water at nearly fifty miles per hour. I also could have told them about two months in a drug-induced coma and months of physical therapy. And I could have mentioned that my body now had so many metal rods and fixtures on the inside of it that I couldn't pass through an airport metal detector without setting it off. But I didn't bother. The fact was that I was damn lucky to be alive.

"Apparently I'm pretty hard to kill," I said, looking at his wife.

She slowly nodded back at me. The look on her face wasn't quite as skeptical now.

"So Bob," I turned back to him. "Why am I here?"

Bob opened his mouth to speak, but it was apparent that he didn't know quite where to begin. As he struggled, I turned back to his wife, suddenly remembering my manners.

"I don't have any idea what it's like to lose a child, but I do understand the pain of having people you care about taken from you," I said. "Three people I cared about were killed last year. Two of them actually died in my arms. There are two more I'll probably never see again. I know what it's like to feel your heart ripped out."

Her expression softened somewhat, and she looked directly into my eyes. "What did you do about the ones who were killed?"

"Lived up to my nickname," I said quietly.

Bob must have told her what it meant and it must have taken her a moment to recall it. But after a second or two, her eyes got very wide.

"Let's just say that the people responsible for the killings got to see a demonstration."

She leaned back in her chair as a look of cold satisfaction crept onto her face. Then she looked over at her husband. "What are you waiting for honey? Tell him!"

Bob took a drink of his water.

"Well, it's probably easier to begin with Kristin and me," he said. "We met each other about two years ago, before I went to Iraq for my year of mandatory fun. We both worked at Headquarters USAF on Warfighter Systems. She was a civilian analyst, and I was the Deputy Director. We spent so much time together that our professional relationship developed into a friendship and then something more. We got married very soon after that. We had known each other about seven or eight months. Most people thought it was very sudden; but at our age, when something seems right, it's better not to waste time."

I nodded and thought of my time with Sarah. We had known each other for a mere few weeks several years ago and it had left an indelible impression on both of us. Most recently she had stayed by my side through the recovery from my ejection wounds and the ensuing physical therapy. It was apparent then that our feelings for each other were very strong, and we felt like we'd been given a second chance. I asked her to marry me when the moment presented itself, and she had eagerly accepted, playfully asking me what took me so long. After what we had been through, we realized life was too short to wait for the things and people you love.

Of course, Miguel Hidalgo forced us to give it all up, but that was another issue.

I reined my mind back into the conversation.

"Kristin and I both had kids from previous marriages. Kristin's eldest was Thomas, who is the one we're discussing. He was a Navy F-18 driver on an exchange tour at the 56th Fighter Wing at Luke Air Force Base, flying with the 310th Fighter Squadron at the time of..."

"When he was murdered," Kristin interrupted.

Bob hung his head and sighed. Apparently this was a sore subject with both of them. Kristin seemed to hate the USAF as a result of the incident, and Bob didn't know what to say to deflect her ire.

"The 310th was the squadron I was assigned to when I retired," I said, hoping to lighten the moment. "Great bunch of guys there."

Kristin fixed me with a hateful glare, and I could feel the tension level rise between the three of us.

"Bob, can you just continue please?" she said.

He nodded slowly. "So Thomas was killed in a midair collision that occurred during an off-target maneuver on a four-ship, air-to-ground sortie."

"Low-altitude tactics?" I asked. Four aircraft attacking the same target or targets near to one another required detailed choreography during the attack and post-attack maneuvers to avoid issues with fuse arming or fragmentation damage from the bombs the jets delivered and, of course, for the attacking aircraft to avoid hitting one another. Typically four jets would be on and off target in about ninety seconds. Most of the time it was less. Much less.

Bob shook his head in frustration. "Yes, and it was just a ride to fill training squares for instructor pilots. Most of the stuff they do these days is with JDAMs or Laser Guided Bombs from medium altitude. This was a low-altitude attack using dumb bombs. What was the point of it?"

I smiled grimly at him. "Because sometimes technology

doesn't work. But also, because it's fun," I said. "So what did the accident report say?"

One of the few things the USAF does well from an administrative perspective is investigate aircraft accidents. When a mishap occurs involving the loss of an aircraft, the death of a crewmember or more than one million dollars in damage, a safety investigation board or SIB is formed and is typically on scene within twenty-four hours. Normally a colonel or brigadier general leads the board and is charged with determining the cause of the accident and writing a thorough report within thirty days. The goal of the board is to prevent future mishaps; and since testimony given to accident investigators is privileged, there is little motivation for a witness or participant to lie. Nearly every accident report I had read while I was active duty had been direct, insightful, and accurate, often disturbingly so.

"Pilot error," Bob said. "Both Thomas and the guy who hit him theoretically screwed up their spacing on the attack and the subsequent off-target maneuver. So where they should have arrived over the same place with time separation, they arrived in the same piece of sky at the same time."

"Wouldn't be the first time that's happened," I said. "Unfortunately."

I could feel Kristin tensing. She wanted him to get to the point.

"The problem is the timing doesn't work," Bob said resignedly.

"Excuse me?" I asked. "What timing?"

"The timing of his wingman's ejection," Bob explained.

I shook my head. "I'm not sure I understand."

"According to the sequence of events in the accident report, the collision occurred, and then Thomas's wingman ejected.

I nodded. "That makes sense."

"But that's not what happened," Bob said. "I had a guy

who worked for me on the accident board as the safety officer member. He supervised construction of the animation of the collision. Once all the data elements and eyewitness accounts were consolidated, it became clear that Thomas's wingman didn't eject after the collision; he ejected before the collision."

I searched for an explanation that made sense and couldn't find one. Unless. I looked across the table at Bob and Kristin. "You're thinking he collided with Thomas on purpose?"

Kristin nodded forcefully, and Bob nodded more slowly.

"It seems to be the only explanation that jibes with the data," he said.

"Well, what did the board president do about it?" The accident board president was like God in the accident investigation process. He was beholden to no one other than the convening authority, the four-star commander of the major command, which owned the asset lost in the mishap. In this case, it would have been the commander of Air Education and Training Command.

"Nothing," Bob said quietly. "They completely ignored it. It was like it never existed."

"Did it even appear in the final report?"

Bob shook his head.

"But how?" I was finding myself becoming a bit disillusioned.

"It was altered. By someone very close to the investigation," Bob continued. "That's the only possibility."

"Well, this should be fairly easy to remedy," I said. "Let's talk to your guy on the board."

"We can't," Bob said. "He's dead."

I guess my eyes must have widened in surprise.

"One week after the report was published. It was a hit-and-run accident. That was six days ago."

"Jesus," I said. "But what about the guy who hit Thomas's airplane? The guy who ejected?"

"Dead as well," Bob said. "An apparent suicide. The safety board never even had a chance to interview him."

I sat back in my chair and exhaled slowly.

The waiter, an athletic-looking older man with salt and pepper hair and a pale complexion, took that opportunity to ask us what we wanted to drink; and as Bob and Kristin placed their orders, I let the information I'd just learned circulate through my brain. After a moment or two, the waiter turned to me for my order.

"Sapphire martini, please," I said, looking up at him. "Up and very dry with a slice of lime. And ask the bartender to shake it as hard as he can, please." He wrote my drink order down and then raised his blue eyes to look back at me. He kept them on me for just a few seconds too long before he caught himself and looked back down at his pad. An alarm bell went off somewhere in my head.

I watched the waiter thoughtfully as he scurried away, and then I allowed my brain to return to the matter at hand.

"So it would seem that somebody killed Thomas," I said, "or had him killed. I guess my first question would be, why kill him this way? It's big, it's public, it's noticeable, and it's going to be thoroughly investigated. Even if a potential murderer was going to try to create an accidental death scenario, it seems like it could have been done a lot more quietly."

"He was going to the OSI that afternoon, after he got back from his flight," Kristin blurted out, "to record a formal statement. And the bastards knew it."

I bristled at the mention of the OSI, more properly the AFOSI, Air Force Office of Special Investigations. My career had ended largely because of the witch hunt the local detachment of the OSI had conducted on me at my final base, which, coincidentally, happened to be Luke. While they considered themselves "credentialed federal agents," the IQs of the agents I had encountered were well less than average.

As a rule, every member of the USAF despised, hated, and feared them.

I looked over at Kristin. Her eyes were glistening with unshed tears, and I could tell they were generated by a combination of sadness and rage. I decided to swallow my opinions on the OSI for now. I shifted my gaze to Bob to see him regarding the wood grain of the table idly.

"Why was he going to meet with the OSI?" I asked the two of them.

"The 56th Fighter Wing had recently taken delivery of its first F-35," Bob said. "You're familiar right?"

I nodded. The F-35 Lightning II was the USAF's long-awaited new multirole fighter, the follow-on to the F-16. It was stealthier than the Viper but slower and uglier. I had also heard, since the USAF had not opted for vectored thrust, it wasn't nearly as maneuverable as the venerable Viper.

Bob continued. "The aircraft was assigned to the 310th, Thomas's squadron. Thomas was in the squadron one night, finishing up the paper work after a night flight, when he overheard a conversation he wasn't supposed to hear between the wing commander and the squadron commander. The conversation involved a mission in which the F-35 would disappear south of the border."

I scowled. "What the hell would the Mexicans want with an F-35?" I asked. "They can barely deal with the aircraft they've got."

"Well, that's where the plot thickens," Bob said as the waiter arrived. The man placed our drinks on the table and seemed to be anxious to take our dinner orders. His efforts not to look in my direction too often were excruciatingly obvious, and the realization of what was going on seeped slowly into my brain.

I nodded mentally to myself and acted nonchalant. After Bob and Kirsten ordered their meals, I settled on a New York

Strip steak, grilled asparagus, and fried potatoes and onions. I also ordered us a bottle of red wine to share.

After the waiter departed, I took a long, slow sip of my martini and allowed the warmth of the day's first alcohol to course through me.

"You guys come here a lot, right?" I asked.

They both nodded.

"And the last time you were here was?"

"About a week ago?" Bob said, looking at his wife.

She nodded at him. "That seems about right." Her eyes narrowed. "Why?"

I ignored her question. "The waiter. Don't look over at him, but try to picture his face in your mind. Have you ever seen him before?"

There was a moment as the two of them looked at each other, and then they shook their heads slowly, nearly in unison.

"Didn't think so," I said. "Give me just a quick minute." I picked up my BlackBerry and typed a brief e-mail to Smith and Amrine. When I looked up, Bob and Kristin were both looking at me questioningly.

"It's probably nothing," I said to them. "I'm just indulging my paranoia a little. So," I continued, "you were saying. Did Thomas hear something else?"

Bob looked at me grimly. "A name," he said. "Just a name. But it's a name you know."

I looked at him with curiosity.

"Miguel Hidalgo," he said softly.

I leaned back into my chair as the questions began to collide in my brain.

"Jesus," I said, looking up at the ceiling and shaking my head. "What the hell would Miguel want with an F-35?"

Bob was shaking his head. "It didn't make sense to me either."

But suddenly, as I recalled my earlier conversation with Dave Smith, I found a stream of logic that led me to a viable possibility. It was far-fetched, no doubt, but viable.

"Holy shit," I said, thinking aloud. "It actually could make sense. It actually could make fucking sense."

I suddenly remembered my manners. "Sorry about my language, Kristin. I forget myself sometimes."

She actually smiled at me, shaking her head. "My son was a fighter pilot," she said, her eyes welling up slightly. "I'm used to it."

"Comes with the personality," I replied.

Bob was looking back and forth between the two of us. "So continue your thought," he said. "How does this make sense?"

I shook my head at him, indicating that I couldn't elaborate.

He nodded, obviously disappointed but resigned. He knew about the compartmentalization of intelligence.

"So when did Thomas decide to go to the OSI?" I went on.

"That night he talked to us," Bob said. "I convinced him to. They are a bunch of clowns and cowboys, but it was the only conduit we had."

"You should have gone to the Agency," I said quietly. "They're the pros here. I've never heard of an investigation the OSI has been involved in that they didn't fuck up."

"Well, it might go beyond incompetency," Bob said. "Thomas met with the OSI detachment commander, a light colonel by the name of Lorna Dahlke, that morning before his flight and related what he had heard. The commander told him to come back that afternoon and sign a statement. But obviously he never made it."

I knew what he was implying. "You think the OSI commander is in on this," I said.

"It's the only thing that makes sense," Bob said. "Thomas goes to see this woman and he dies the same day? A formal statement must be witnessed by two agents and entered into their system. If that had happened, a record would have existed. As it is, no one at the detachment even remembers he was there."

"How do you know he saw the commander?"

"Thomas called me and told me," Kristin said. "He felt good about going. He felt like he was doing the right thing."

"Damn," I said. "Well, that explains the public nature of his accident. They had to make sure he never went back, and they had to do so quickly. That means that there are people in the squadron who are involved, as well as the squadron commander."

"It goes higher," Bob said. "Obviously Thomas overheard the conversation between the wing commander and the squadron commander, and while the OSI det commander isn't responsible to anyone on the base, there is one person in the chain of command she would interact with and that would be the wing commander."

"Jesus," I said. "So who is the wing king out at Luke these days?"

Bob actually smiled at me then. "I think you used to work for him. He was the commander of the 310th when you were the ops officer there. His name is Mark Tappan."

I slumped back in my chair.

"Great," I said. "Yes. He was my boss. For a while. Probably the worst commander I ever saw. We all hated him. He treated everyone so poorly, we gave him a derogatory tactical call sign. He found about it later; and rather than getting angry, he used it."

"What did you call him?" Kristin asked.

I looked back at her evenly. "Satan," I said, "because he was evil. He loved it."

***

Dinner arrived a few moments later and the conversation lightened as we ate. Bob and I exchanged our career stories, and I learned more about the relationship he had with Kristin. It was apparent that they were very much in love with each other. And it was also apparent that this business with the death of her son was eating him up. They also had an air of uneasiness about them, as if they knew they were being watched and monitored. After the ever-watchful waiter took our after-dinner drink orders, I asked the obvious question.

"You think this goes up even higher than Tappan, don't you?"

He nodded. "Someone is conducting surveillance on us. The military taught me what to look for because I've spent so much time overseas. The signs are subtle, but they're there. I work in the Pentagon. So for something that happened at Luke to have ramifications here means that quite a network is in place."

I nodded. "You know, I have some friends in the Agency who might be able to find out what's going on."

Bob shook his head. "That's not the important part right now," he said, "especially since we could meet up with you." He took Kristin's hand in his and kissed it. "We need to know what happened to Thomas and who is responsible. That's the important thing."

I nodded in agreement. "I get that," I said. "I just don't know how I can help. I'm not in the Air Force anymore, and I don't see how I'm going to get any answers without a way onto Luke Air Force Base."

"Actually," Bob said, smiling. "That's the easy part. One of our classmates is the Commander of the Air Force Personnel Center right now, and she's a really good friend. What you don't realize is that while you think you've been retired, you've actually been on a staff tour in the reserves. Now you're returning to active duty to attend the F-16 VIP checkout course at Luke before assuming your new job as an air attaché to the Belgian Air Force."

The waiter arrived with our drinks and brought me a nice tumbler of Lagavulin, neat, the way all good single malt Scotch should be served. I raised the glass to my nose and inhaled its aroma, relishing the hints of sherry and mild smokiness infused in it. Then I drank and enjoyed the complex mixture of fruit and peat on my tongue, followed by the rising peat flavor of the finish. Finally, I looked back across the table at the two of them, both of whom had bemused smiles on their faces.

"Air attaché," I said. "Isn't that an O-6 billet? A job for a full colonel?"

Bob nodded. "Your promotion orders are on the Personnel Commander's desk." He raised his glass and nudged Kristin to do the same. "Congratulations on your promotion, Colonel Pearce. You'll need to get some eagles to replace those silver oak leaves on your flightsuit."

Chapter Four

Monday, June 21, 2010
2245 Hours Local Time
Francisco's Steak House
Annapolis, Maryland

Bob insisted on paying for the meal and I didn't protest. My head was still spinning with possibilities and permutations. I scanned the bar area around us as nonchalantly as I could. We were one of three parties remaining at the tables in this section, and there were two couples sitting at the bar. None of the people sitting there attracted my attention, but I did notice that there was no sign of our waiter. I also noticed that a particular woman who had lingered at the bar for nearly our entire dinner was no longer present. I nodded unconsciously as I returned my gaze to Bob and Kristin, both of whom were eyeing me warily.

"What?" Bob asked in a low voice.

"Well, your instincts about being under surveillance are dead on," I said. "I'd be willing to bet my next paycheck that our waiter isn't a regular member of the staff and that he was here tonight solely to keep an eye on you two and possibly pick up whatever snippets of conversation he could."

I let that sink in for a moment.

"Why do you think that?" Kristin asked. Her face had lost some of its color. It's one thing to discuss the possibility of being watched and quite another to encounter the watchers directly.

"He recognized me," I said. "He looked right at me, and I saw it in his eyes. He's either new and inexperienced or not trained very well, both of which indicate the involvement of a particular agency that we're all familiar with."

"The OSI?" Bob asked, indignantly. "The OSI is surveilling us? When Thomas was the one who brought this to their attention?"

"You're surprised? They're not the sharpest tools in the shed."

He shook his head in disgust. "Idiots," he spat. Then he looked at me intently. "Do you think they have some kind of listening devices in place?"

I smiled wryly. "Wouldn't matter. My BlackBerry has some special features in it, one of which is a wireless signal jammer that operates in the range of most listening devices."

"So it keeps the mic from hearing us?" Kristin asked.

"No, the mic can still hear us but any transmission from the mic to a collection point is jammed. In essence, it makes the mic useless."

Bob grinned at me. "You, sir, are a suspicious man."

"No, just careful. That's one of reasons I'm still alive. And speaking of careful, we need to make our exit cautiously. I'd like to walk the two of you out to your car if you don't mind. Where are you parked?"

Bob inclined his chin toward the side of the restaurant. "Out in the side lot. We always park there because on the weekends we eat outside on the deck."

I nodded and rose. "Then out the side door it is."

"But the deck is closed during the week," Kristin whispered. "Won't someone try to stop us?"

"Only if we let them," I said.

We walked purposefully over to the side door; and before the bartender or a member of the staff could stop us, we exited the restaurant and found ourselves on a nice wooden deck with a stunning view of Annapolis Harbor. Rows of sail and motor craft were tied up neatly at the docks in the foreground, while the buildings of the town square loomed beyond and the lighted rotunda of the state capitol building glowed in the distance.

"This is a beautiful place," I whispered under my breath.

"Kristin and I are going to retire here one day," Bob said in an equally low tone. "We love it here."

We stepped across the deck, down some steps and into the parking lot. The lot was only two rows wide and neatly tucked into a small rectangle of land between the harbor, the deck, the side of the restaurant and the street. Much to my relief, most of it was brightly lit by a pair of simulated gas lamps and while there were several cars in the lot, there were no people meandering about.

"There's my car," Bob said, pointing to a red Jaguar XKS at the far end of the lot, near the water. A large, black SUV was backed into a spot a few spaces away from it in the shadow of a large oak tree. The dim outlines of two figures were visible in the front seats.

"Perfect," I said with a sigh as I eyed the vehicles, "we've got company."

Bob reached into his pants pocket and produced his key fob. "Any chance they're friends of yours?"

"Nope," I said. "If my friends were here, you'd never know it unless they wanted you to." Even as I said the words, the BlackBerry vibrated on my hip. I smiled to myself. The cavalry had arrived again. "Let's just play this by ear and see what happens."

As we approached Bob's car and he hit the unlock button,

the doors of the SUV opened and two people got out. One was male, one female, and both were as I had seen them before; the male in his waiter ensemble and the female in a business-style pantsuit. They carried standard government-issue credential wallets in their left hands, but their dour expressions identified them before they raised their creds or uttered a word. I felt myself tense, and I found my right hand yearning for the 1911's rubber grip. It was an effort to keep my hands at my sides and relaxed.

The male agent was a few inches shorter than my 6' 2". He looked fit, but his upper body was unimpressive. His dark hair and pale complexion made him appear slightly vampiric in the night, and his features exuded the arrogance of official power. The female was a little older than he was, and she was the one I remembered nursing a drink at the bar earlier. She had blonde hair pulled back from her face into some kind of ponytail at the back of her head. She was almost as tall as her male counterpart, and her business attire couldn't hide the fact that she was slim and exceptionally well proportioned. I could see her regarding me intently. Her right hand was resting just to the right of her belt buckle. She was obviously expecting trouble, and apparently she was expecting it from me.

"General Barnett," the male said, "I'm Agent Shaw and my partner is Agent Otenski. We're from the OSI and we need you to come with us, sir."

"What?" Bob asked indignantly. "What for?"

"We'll discuss it in a secure location, sir."

"I don't think so," I said.

"You have no right to interfere in an official investigation, Mr. Pearce," the female agent said, looking directly at me.

They knew who I was, and they knew I was here. This wasn't good on so many levels.

"Or perhaps," Agent Otenski continued, "you'd like us to

have you recalled to active duty so that we bring you in for questioning as well?" The timbre of her voice didn't match her words. She was trying very hard to sound official. But it came off as uncertain.

"You guys haven't changed your act in ten years," I said in a bored tone. "General Barnett isn't going with you. So you'll have to tell the idiot you work for, that he or she can go find someone else to fuck with."

Agent Otenski's hand was moving slowly back toward her right hip. Her partner had also assumed the foundation of a Weaver stance and his hand was making its way back toward his hip as well.

"I wouldn't do that if I were you two," I warned. "Your hands go back any further and it's going to make some people very nervous."

"And who's going to stop us?" Shaw asked disdainfully. "You?"

"No," I said, inclining my head behind them, "they are."

"Do you think we're that stupid?" Otenski actually sounded disappointed.

"No, I don't. I think you're that unobservant."

Otenski was about to utter a retort when she was quickly and efficiently relieved of her weapon and laid out horizontally by a large figure in black tactical gear. Her partner suffered the same fate as she, and in mere moments, they were both face down on the pavement with their hands zip-tied behind their backs and their feet tied together. Standing around them were the ten members of a CIA operations team, clad in their typical black garb and bristling with weapons.

"That wasn't even a challenge," Dave Smith said as he removed his mask. "Makes me ashamed to think I used to be one of these guys many years ago."

"Took you long enough," I said. "I thought I was going to have to start reciting sonnets to keep their interest."

"Couldn't find a place to put the damn chopper down," Smith said. "They build the houses way too close together down here. We finally had to rappel down in a parking lot over by 6th Street."

"Troubles all over," I said.

One of the other figures pulled off his mask and revealed the blond hair and surfer-like complexion of John Amrine, Smith's partner.

"Good tip, Colin," Amrine said. "What gave them away?"

"Numb nuts over there," I said, indicating the male agent. "When he was playing waiter, his eyes lit up nicely when he first saw me. He obviously knew who I was, and he spent the rest of the evening trying to not look at me. It couldn't have been any more obvious."

"Fuckin' amateurs," Amrine said in disgust. He turned to the men behind him. "Stand 'em up," he commanded.

Two ops team members each grabbed both Otenski and Shaw and effortlessly placed them both on their feet. Amrine stood in front of them with his hands on his hips and an M-4 assault carbine strapped to his chest.

"I know what you're thinking," he said in a tone that was utterly devoid of expression or emotion. "You're thinking that because we're not the FBI or someone who looks like you that we don't have any authority here. You need to understand that we don't give a shit. We're going to find out what you know. You can either tell us now, voluntarily, or we can pump you full of drugs until you tell us or we can plug you into a Taser until you tell us. The point is that you're going to tell us. You know who we are and you know we don't bluff. Make your choice."

Amrine turned to Bob and Kristin.

"General Barnett, you and your lovely wife are going to get an expense-paid vacation. We're going take you out on the chopper and drop you at our hangar at a nearby airport where one of our jets will take you away."

"But," Bob began.

Amrine held his hand up.

"I'm sorry, sir. This is for your safety. If these nimrods are following you then just about anyone can do the same. Based on what we learned from you tonight, we need to keep you somewhere no one can find you for a while."

"What you learned?" Bob asked.

"I have a small confession to make, Bob," I said. "My BlackBerry doubles as a databurst transmitter as well as a jammer. Dave and John here had a transcript of our entire conversation before you even paid the check. When our waiter made himself so obvious, I emailed them and told them they probably needed to get you out of here. That's why the team showed up."

He looked at me as if seeing me for the first time. "All this? From a few words and an e-mail?"

I nodded. "It's the name you mentioned. It tends to get a lot of attention these days."

"But what about my boss? My job?"

"Our boss, the Director of Intelligence, will handle that, General Barnett," Amrine answered. "He's making a call to your boss telling him that you've been called away on a classified assignment. Fortunately, your job title gives a little room to play with there."

"But we've got no clothes or luggage or anything," Kristin said, obviously bewildered by how quickly events were moving.

"No worries, ma'am," Dave Smith replied. "The safe house comes stocked with quite an assortment of clothes and personal items. For the amenities it doesn't have, there's plenty of shopping nearby that you can make use of. At government expense of course."

"You guys have thought of everything," Bob said. "This is amazing." He raised his car keys. "Do I need to leave these with anyone?"

Even as he spoke, a platform tow truck turned into the parking lot and made its way toward us.

Bob's jaw dropped.

"You can keep the keys, General Barnett," Amrine said. "Our man here will deposit the car in your numbered slot at your condo. It will be there when you get back. Now, if you don't have any further questions, we'd like to get you out of here. Ready to move out?"

Bob and Kristin looked at each other for a moment with stunned expressions on their faces. After a moment, they both nodded.

"Harold. Charlie," Amrine commanded. Two of the team members stepped forward. "Take the general and his wife to the chopper."

"Roger that, Boss."

Bob turned to me and extended his hand.

"Thanks, Colin," he said. He was obviously still struggling to keep up with the events in progress.

"Don't thank me yet, Bob. I haven't done anything."

"Yes, you have," Kristin said as she stepped forward. "You've given us hope." Then she threw her arms around my neck and hugged me tightly. "Find the bastards who killed my son," she whispered in my ear. "Find them and kill them."

"Count on it," I whispered back. "It's what I do."

She released me, and then she and Bob were quickly hustled away by Amrine's men.

"Now," Amrine said as he turned around to the two OSI agents. "Time's up. Have we made a decision?"

"You can't do this to us," Shaw said. He was trying to sound forceful and confident, and it wasn't working out well for him. His arrogance of mere moments ago had deteriorated into raw fear.

"Don't be stupid, Bill," Otenski said. "They're spooks. They can do whatever they want."

"She's right, of course," Amrine said.

"That doesn't mean I'm going to tell you anything though, asshole," Otenski spat back at him.

"No, it doesn't," Amrine replied calmly. "But your partner will. What do you think, Dave? Taser probes on the balls? That always seems to work pretty well."

"Sounds good to me," Smith said. "Guys? Let's get him in the SUV and get his pants off." He gestured to the two team members behind Shaw, and they roughly grabbed him and began dragging him to the SUV.

"NOOO!" Shaw screamed. "NOOO!"

"Shit," Smith said a few moments later. "That was way too easy. Can I tase his balls anyway, just for good measure?"

"Sure," Amrine replied. "After all, we've got to earn our pay tonight."

***

Thirty minutes later, Amrine, Smith, and I were in the rental car, and we were rolling down US Highway 50 toward Washington, DC.

"Thanks for the ride, Colin," Amrine said from the rear seat. "We wanted to get your buddy and his wife out of here pretty quickly and this keeps the chopper from having to make an extra stop."

"Yeah, thanks," Dave Smith chimed in from the passenger seat beside me.

"No problem," I replied. "You guys provided the car. Seems like the least I could do. This isn't quite the rush that flying in a chopper is, but I'll try to keep it exciting for you."

"No worries there," Smith teased. "We watched you drive down here on the satellite feed."

"Hey, speed limits are for people with limitations," I

retorted. "God gave us a right foot and a gas pedal and the two belong on the floor." I veered into the left lane to pass a slow-moving pickup truck. "So where am I taking you guys anyway?"

"Just up to Signature Flight Support at BWI," Smith replied. "We'll get transport from there. Just take the exit for I-97 when it comes up in a few miles."

"Roger that," I said.

"So obviously our little songbird from the OSI didn't tell us much," Amrine said from the backseat a few minutes later. "We now know your friend the general and his wife were under suspicion of something, but the agents didn't know what. We also know that the orders to apprehend him after he met with you came from the OSI Commander's office, and that's about it."

"Not quite," I said softly. "We also know that they know about me and my involvement."

"Not a surprise," Amrine said. "How long do you think, Dave?"

"Probably since October," Smith replied, turning his head. "We had a lot of Air Force guys in our ops center at Edwards when T. C. was fighting those guys over the high desert."

"I agree," Amrine answered. "October sounds about right."

"Sounds right for what?" I demanded.

"You're a file with them," Amrine said. "They're monitoring you." His tone of voice was completely uninflected. He could have been giving me stock advice.

"Jesus fucking Christ!" I exploded. "They're monitoring me? What the fuck does that mean?"

"It just means you interest them," Smith said, obviously trying to calm me down. "It's something intelligence and law enforcement agencies do. When a particular person becomes of interest, they monitor that person and collect data. Don't be too alarmed. It's actually fairly common. The FBI has literally thousands of people it monitors and so do we. You were a file with us before we hired you for your first job."

"Ignorance is bliss I guess," I said, as my anger subsided. "After that whole business several years ago, the thought of them nosing into my life again makes me a little nuts."

"I understand why, after your last interaction with them," Smith said. "What was it that forced you to retire? Stock transactions on your work computer I think?"

I nodded and gave him a wry grin. Of course they knew the answer to the question. They probably knew more about the whole affair than I did.

"Yes, that would be the computer that I wasn't around when the transactions occurred."

I saw Amrine nodding in the rearview mirror. "I'm surprised they used financial transactions and not porn. Putting porn on someone's computer is the white collar equivalent to dropping a dime bag of cocaine into someone's pocket and then tipping off the cops," he said matter-of-factly. "It's easy to do. It can be untraceable, and it ends the career of the person targeted without any follow-up or investigation. Too bad you didn't know us back then. We could have found the person who messed with you.

"Anyway, getting back to the point, it appears that our buffoons from the OSI were essentially told to bring your friend and his wife in after the meeting with you took place. So someone wanted to know what the three of you talked about very badly. And they probably wanted to know how your relationship with us would play into the equation."

"The connection with Miguel is also interesting," Smith said as he motioned toward the exit for I-97.

I nodded back at him and hit my turn signal for the exit.

"Yes it is," Amrine said. "So why do you think Miguel wants an F-35, T. C.?" He regarded me in the rearview mirror.

"Didn't you say Miguel is heavily involved with the

Chinese?" I asked.

"Yes," Dave Smith admitted.

"Well, if he's into them for any cash, an F-35 would be one hell of a bartering item."

"Sure would help the Chinese with their J-31 program," Amrine said thoughtfully. "That's their copy of the F-35, and it's not doing so well these days."

"And it would put some serious coin into Miguel's pocket," Smith added.

"Well, Colin," Amrine said. "Looks like you'll get to combine personal business and national security once again. You still up for the trip to Luke?"

I nodded. "Sure. A little time back in the Viper might be just the thing."

Smith turned his head to look at Amrine. "Are we going to file the standard ops report about tonight?"

Amrine looked back at him steadily and slowly shook his head. "I don't think so. There's something about this that doesn't smell right to me, and I'm afraid of potential leaks if we go up normal channels. Air Force Intelligence will want to get involved and they're buffoons. And this OSI business has me particularly concerned. I mean, let's say that Barnett's theory is correct and the OSI det commander at Luke is in on this. How does she then manage to spin things so that two agents, assigned to the national headquarters on the other side of the country, show up tonight with orders to detain Barnett and his wife and, oh by the way, they just happen to know T. C. is going to be here? The Patriot Act notwithstanding, you know how hard it is to get surveillance authorization on a general officer. This has to go way up the chain."

He paused for a moment, and I could almost hear the gears turning inside his head.

"You're thinking they might have a source inside the agency," Smith said quietly.

I saw Amrine's square jaw clench in the mirror and he nodded. Just barely. "And it is probably someone who was in that room with us at Edwards. In all likelihood that person isn't aware that there's anything untoward going on. They just pass along the odd tidbit here and there. But as you know, that's more than enough sometimes."

"Well, shit," Smith breathed. "That makes things complicated."

"Yes, it does," Amrine agreed. "Since this has interagency implications, you and I are going to have to brief the head of our directorate personally." He looked at me in the rearview mirror. "T. C., we're going to have to conduct this on the down low for a while. That means we're going to be limited in the support we can give you. At least initially. Hopefully, Bob and your classmate at the Air Force Personnel Center have created a legend that will hold up long enough for you to do what you've got to do."

I looked back at him. "If Tappan is really talking to Miguel on a regular basis, he'll find out it's bullshit sooner rather than later."

"Maybe," Amrine said. "You never know. Don't ever underestimate the power of poor communication. Besides, what's he going to do, cause another crash to kill you? Two crashes back-to-back will get him too much attention."

I smiled grimly. "Not necessarily. A friend of mine was Chief of Safety at Luke in 1999. Do you know how many crashes they had then?"

Amrine and Smith looked at me intently.

"Seven," I said. "And no one did a goddamned thing."

Chapter Five

Contract Day One
Wednesday, June 23, 2010
1530 Hours Local Time
Phoenix-Sky Harbor Airport
Phoenix, Arizona

I noticed the tail they placed on me almost immediately as I turned onto Interstate 10 westbound from the rental car area at the Phoenix airport. Apparently, the two agents in the car were under explicit orders to keep me in sight, because they cut across two lanes of traffic and practically ran a FedEx truck off the road as they attempted to stay with me. Of course, the fact that I had cut across those same two lanes mere moments earlier in an attempt to smoke them out probably didn't help their attempt to maintain a covert observation position. I sighed as I looked at them in the review mirror. They were in the standard government-issued SUV wearing the standard cheap suits, with standard haircuts, and standard dour expressions. I found myself wondering if there was an assembly plant where they stamped these guys and girls out with some kind of generic mold. The two faces behind me were the latest in a series of them today, and it was amazing how easy they were to spot once I knew what to look for. Either they weren't making any attempts to be covert, or they simply weren't very good. My money was on the latter.

After spending the previous day making calls and preparations, I was awarded with a set of travel orders and authorization to purchase a plane ticket at government expense. I was told that the rest of my paper work would be provided when I reached Luke Air Force Base. As part of this process, I spent some time on the phone with a classmate of mine from the US Air Force Academy, Major General Gail Petersen, Commander of the Air Force Personnel Center (AFPC) and a former special ops helicopter pilot. Located at Randolph Air Force Base in San Antonio, Texas, AFPC handled all personnel actions and records in the USAF, which made its commander one the most powerful people in the Air Force. Since AFPC was the organization providing the backstop for my orders and supposed promotion, as well as all the theoretical history between my departure from active duty until the present moment, having the AFPC commander involved was a huge bonus. As we attempted to link up via a secure phone line, I tried to remember what she looked like but no memory existed there. We must not have had any classes together back in the day.

Once the phone link was established, Gail didn't waste any time on preliminaries and immediately told me what had been created for me. She then gave me a link to a secure website and an access code so I could download my orders as well as a synopsis of the records that had been constructed to document my recently created career.

"This is pretty thorough stuff," I told her as I looked the documents over.

"We've had some practice," she said matter-of-factly. "We have to create records and assignments for our Black Ops folks all the time. These records sometimes have to stand up to NSA scrutiny. We know what we're doing."

"I don't doubt it," I said.

"Listen," she said as we began to wrap up the conversation, "Bob is one of my very best friends. He's like the brother I never had, and he was a shoulder to cry on as I went through my divorce while we were on the Joint Staff together. I'd do anything for him. He seems to think you can find out who killed his stepson, and if he's confident in you, then so am I. Besides, from what he told me, you seem to be pretty capable... for a fighter pilot"

"We're an oppressed minority these days," I replied. "Someone has to try to give us a good name. There's something else we should discuss. I'm very grateful for your support, but you need to know that the OSI is very interested in this business, and they appear to be especially interested in me. I wouldn't want you to suffer any collateral damage on my account. They come after anyone, even generals."

"Those bastards can kiss my sun-tanned ass," she said. "They're all a bunch of cowboys. Whose bright idea was it to create a group within our service where people get promoted based on how well they screw over their fellow service members and where enlisted people can investigate officers?"

"Good question," I replied. "But you got my attention with something about a sun tan. You have to tell me, just how does a general go about getting such a tan?"

"By finding very secluded beaches in very secluded locales," she answered without missing a beat. "You should try it sometime."

I called the AFPC webpage up on my computer as I spoke to her, and I clicked on the link for her biography. I was rewarded with a picture of a striking brunette woman in a tastefully tailored service dress uniform. She had deep brown eyes and just the merest hint of playfulness in her official smile.

"I actually have on a few occasions," I said. "But it's always fun to try new places."

"Especially if you have the right company," she replied. "Let me know if you're looking for recommendations. I'd be happy to provide a few and maybe even show them to you personally."

The invitation was unmistakable. I was flattered and just a little stunned. No one has ever accused me of being charming. "That sounds fantastic," I said evenly. "Let me get through this business first. May I call you on the far side?"

"I think you're actually going to need to debrief me in person," she said, "over dinner."

"Yes, ma'am!" I replied. "I'll consider that an order."

She laughed and broke the connection.

***

The trek on I-10 from the airport to Litchfield Road, the turnoff for Luke Air Force Base, took longer than I remembered, largely because the westbound traffic was much heavier than it had been when I'd last lived here eight years ago. As I made my exit and turned north, I noted the black SUV several car lengths behind me, now patiently keeping its distance. I wondered how much they knew and whether their purpose was observation or apprehension. While geographical boundaries typically didn't limit their jurisdiction, once I set foot on the base and put on a uniform, their power over me was virtually unlimited. Especially since my friends in the CIA might be forced to keep their distance. The reassuring weight of the 1911 on my right hip made me feel a little better. My federal carry permit superseded the peacetime firearms policies on a military base, so at least I could remain armed.

I looked out the windows of my rented Chevy Impala at the stores, eateries, and neighborhoods that had sprung up since my departure long ago, and for the first time in many years, I let my mind relive that time. I remembered how much I had loved flying the Viper and instructing students and how much I had hated the politics inherent in the command structure of the base. And then, of course, there was the manner in which I had been forced to retire, which had cast a shadow over my entire career.

I looked at the SUV behind me in the rearview mirror and eyed the two drones who sat in the front seat.

"And all because of idiots like you," I said to them.

The houses and trees on my left gave way to an open field and then a loud roar interrupted my reverie. I looked to my left to see a two-ship of F-16s in close formation. They had just lifted off of Runway 21 Left and were retracting their landing gear in unison as they began the departure for the southern working areas. They were configured for air-to-air, with nothing hanging on them but captive-carry AIM-9 missiles. The dull blue paint of the sleek jets made them clearly visible against the rising desert terrain behind them. I watched them and shook my head in wonder. It was still a beautiful jet. All these years later.

And suddenly, I found myself turning left at the southern entrance gate for the flightline side of the base. The years since 9/11 had transformed the entrance. Gone was the single small guard booth between the incoming and outgoing lanes of Super Sabre Street, the road on which the gate was situated. Now there was a building that covered the inbound lanes, featuring multiple guard booths and the ever-present concrete barriers to hinder assaults by potential terrorists. I patiently waited for the driver of the car in front of me to show his ID card to the guard. After the guard waved the car through, it was my turn. I pulled up to the booth, stopped my car, retrieved my retired ID card, and presented it to the guard. I noticed another change from several years ago. Where once the guard might have been a young security policeman in fatigues with a Beretta 9mm pistol on his hip, the female airman examining my ID wore her Beretta in a quick-access holster strapped to her leg, full body armor, and an M-4 carbine harnessed to her chest.

"What's your business on this side of the base, sir?"

" I'm going to the billeting office."

She nodded. "Do you know where it is, sir?"

"I think so. I was stationed here…" I paused for a moment, realizing that when I had been assigned here, this young lady had probably been in middle school. "A long time ago," I concluded.

She handed my ID back to me and motioned me through the gate.

"Have a good day, sir," she said, rendering a snappy salute.

"I will!" I replied and without even hesitating or thinking about it, I returned the salute.

I smiled as I drove through the barrier maze a few seconds later, amazed that the saluting reflex was still in place. Time was a scary thing. Years had passed and it was as if I had never left the service.

I spent the next several minutes cruising around the base that had been my last duty station in the Air Force. I drove past the southern academic building, the maintenance hangars, the Block 42 simulator building, and the squadron building for the 308th Fighter Squadron.

I made my way down to the 310th Fighter Squadron building, taking careful notice of the cars parked in the operations officer and squadron commander slots in the event I saw them later. If Gail Petersen's folks had done their jobs, the 310th was the squadron where I'd do my VIP checkout in the F-16 and where I'd attempt to find out what happened to Thomas and, hopefully, stop the sale of some of our best technology to the Chinese. It would also be the place where Miguel Hidalgo would know that I was working to foil another one of his plans, if he didn't know that already.

I looked at the glass doors of the building's entrance with mixed emotions. Part of my past was inside of that building as well. The 310th was the squadron I had flown with the majority of the time I had been stationed at Luke. I had been an instructor in the Low Altitude Navigation and Targeting Infrared for Night, or LANTIRN system, and had chased numerous students on low and medium altitude checkout flights, the vast majority of them in the evening. I had loved the flying and enjoyed working alongside the people I had been stationed with. It had been a great life. Back then, the 310th had specialized in night training and in VIP checkouts. In 2008, night training was incorporated into all syllabi, and the 310th lost its unique status and trained all pilots, including basic course students. I had a brief taste of that when I transferred to the 309th squadron, shortly prior to my retirement. B-course students were fun to train, but the night stuff was much more demanding.

I had climbed the standard job position ladder in the 310th when I'd been there, starting as an assistant operations officer and scheduler, then advancing to operations officer with a tour at the wing Standardization and Evaluation Shop in between. When a squadron commander job in Korea became available, I was surprised to find myself in contention for it. But that was before the break-in at my house and the ensuing publicity after I killed the three intruders with a shotgun at very close range.

I put the car in gear and then drove to the north side of the base, around the elongated section of the ramp that extended to the southeast and proceeded up Fighter Country Avenue. As I watched pilots and other assorted personnel come and go from the buildings, I found myself transported backward to that simpler time in my life—a time when life was about flying, instructing, and little else. Reflecting back, I found myself amazed that at the age of forty, I had considered myself "an old guy." Now, at fifty-one, I realized that I didn't really know what "old" was back then.

With my OSI tail at a discreet distance behind me, I continued to aimlessly drive around the base complex. Luke AFB's arrangement was somewhat unique. Most USAF bases had the operational side of the base, where the aircraft were located, and the support side of the base, where all the ancillary services were located, interspersed in the same chunk of real estate. But Luke was an exception. The operational side of the base was located on one end of the base, on the west side of Litchfield Road, while the ancillary buildings, such as the commissary, base exchange, and personnel office, were on the east side of Litchfield Road along with the base housing complex. When I had been here previously, the entire east side of the base had been outside of the secured area and drivers could come and go as they pleased. Now it was fenced and guarded with a secure bridge across Litchfield Road connecting the two sides—another testimony to the changes 9/11 had brought to the lives of people in the military.

I spent several minutes in a parking lot near the approach end of Runway 21 Left and sat there, idling, as several flights of F-16s returned to the base for landing. I watched the sleek aircraft execute their patterns, examining their spacing as they flew up initial, watching how crisply they executed the break and how well they flew their final turns. The one thing I had always loved about military aviation was the discipline of it. The average civilian pilot never learned flight discipline until he or she entered a very structured environment, like the airlines, and many never learned discipline at all. For military aviators, discipline was something that was instilled from the very first day. I smiled as I sat there, remembering the words of my primary instructor in pilot training, Captain Morton, at Sheppard Air Force Base. We were on a training sortie in the

T-37, probably my third hop in the jet, and I was flying. I had been assigned an altitude of 5,000 feet and a cruise speed of 200 knots, and I was struggling to maintain those parameters. Finally, I managed to stabilize the aircraft at 4,900 feet and 195 knots and thought I was doing well, but Captain Morton wasn't happy. He reached across the cockpit and tapped on both the altimeter and the airspeed indicator with his gloved finger to emphasize his point.

I remembered saying something like, "Well, isn't this close enough?"

And from across the T-37's narrow cockpit, he'd shaken his helmeted head.

"No," he said. "We are military pilots. We fly on altitude and on airspeed. There is no substitute."

I had never forgotten those words.

Eventually, I made it to the billeting office, with the black SUV still in tow. Every USAF base has quarters for visiting officers and visiting enlisted personnel, which are essentially government-run hotels. The billeting office is the centralized front desk for the visiting quarters, and it was where room assignments are made. I parked the rental car in the lot next to the building and exited the car into the fierce heat of the Arizona summer. I could feel the perspiration forming under my shirt in seconds.

"It's a dry heat," I said to myself. "Like a blast furnace."

Resisting the urge to wave at the black SUV "discreetly" parked about a block away, I walked to the entry, pushed through the double-glass doors, and entered the lobby of the Fighter Country Inn, going from the air-conditioned coolness of the car to heat of the desert and back into the air conditioning in mere moments. The perspiration on my skin dried immediately, and I felt a slight chill. It was a familiar sensation.

Life in the desert, I thought.

The lobby had been remodeled since the last time I'd been there last and resembled that of a La Quinta Inn or the like with lightly colored walls and ceramic tiles. The reception desk covered the entire far wall and had small tiles on the front of it and a tiled counter.

"Nice," I commented to no one in particular.

Apparently I had arrived in a low point of the workday. There were no other customers in the lobby and a lone receptionist was behind the desk—a young, attractive, twenty-something redhead, clad in a business suit that complimented the lobby's decor. I wondered if she was a civilian or an enlisted woman.

"May I help you, sir?" she asked.

I nodded as I walked toward the desk. The placard on the counter told me her name was Clara Morgan.

"Yes, Clara," I said. "My name is Pearce. Colin Pearce. I believe you have a reservation for me."

"Oh yes!" she said, flashing me a radiant smile. "Colonel Pearce! Welcome to the Fighter Country Inn, sir! We've been expecting you!"

I smiled back at her, silently wondering how they could have been expecting me when I myself didn't know I was coming until less than forty-eight hours ago.

"General Tappan told us to make sure everything was perfect for you!" She looked down at the counter in front of her and found a FEDEX envelope. "And this came for you just this morning," she said, handing the envelope to me.

So Satan was expecting me. That was just great.

"We've got you in one of our VIP bungalows, just down the street and adjacent to Club Thunderbolt. They've just been renovated. They're really nice!"

I looked at her blankly.

"Club Thunderbolt?" I asked. "What's that?"

"I guess it used to be the officers' club," she answered.

"That was a little before my time." She paused for a moment as she looked down at her screen. "Do you have a credit card I can swipe for your room charges, sir?"

"Sure," I said, reaching for my wallet.

"I'm also going to need to see a military ID, sir."

I was about to tell her that all I had was a retired ID with the wrong rank on it, but then I looked at the FEDEX envelope in my hand and had an odd feeling about what might be inside. Without thinking, I tore it open to find a small stack of paper copies of my travel orders and a brand new, active-duty military ID card paper-clipped to the top sheet. There was also a government-issued Visa card with my name on it.

"Well, well," I said, looking down at the ID card. It featured a recent picture of me, in uniform no less, and the rank COL/O-6 next to the picture. "I'll be damned," I said unconsciously.

"Sir?" she asked.

I shook my head and removed the ID card from the envelope discreetly and handed it to her along with the new credit card.

"Thanks!" she said.

Clara was good at her job. In mere moments I'd signed for my room at a whopping $53.25 per night, gotten my key card, and received a schedule for my first day of training, which was tomorrow.

"Is there anything else you need, Colonel Pearce?" she asked as I regarded the paper work.

I looked up at her.

"No, Clara. I'm good. Thanks."

"I hope you have a great stay with us," she said.

"Me too," I said as I turned to go. *But I doubt it.*

***

The VIP bungalows were where she said they would be, just down the street and around the corner. There were two of them, mirror images of one another, with earth-toned stucco walls and gray-tiled roofs. Small, well-manicured lawns surrounded them, and they were backed up to the eastern wall of some kind of patio area of Club Thunderbolt. Mine was the one on the right. I parked my rental car on the side street in front of the bungalow and quickly carried my things inside.

I was stunned by what I found when I opened the door. Clara was right. For rooms in a military lodging facility, they were quite luxurious. The bungalow was probably about fifteen hundred square feet with two bedrooms, two baths, a kitchen with granite countertops, a dining area, and a living room complete with a very large LCD television. The decor was tasteful and coordinated well with the mission-style furniture so common in this area of the country.

I found myself nodding. "This will do," I said to the empty room. "This will do."

As I walked my computer bag over to the table in the dining area, which would double as my desk, I saw an envelope on the center of the dining table, about the size of a thank you card. The front of the envelope had two letters on it: "T. C." On the back there was a small blue flag with one star in the center of it. It was the official stationery of a brigadier general. I opened the card and read the short note inside.

"Dinner tonight at the club. Be at the bar at six or I'll have someone come get you and bring you." It was signed with a single letter—"S"—with two little triangles on top, signifying horns.

"Dinner with the devil," I said to myself.

I threw the card on the table and took my suitcase back to the far bedroom to unpack. When I opened the closet, I had another surprise. Hanging inside the closet were five desert-brown flightsuits, all with the appropriate patches, all with my name on the color-coordinated cloth nametags on the front and all with the rank insignia of a full colonel, an eagle, sewn onto each shoulder. On the shelf above the flightsuits was a blue USAF flight cap with a silver eagle pinned to it, and on the floor were two pairs of flight boots. Apparently, Bob and/or Gail had thought of everything.

***

Sometime later, showered and dressed in a pair of Brooks Brothers slacks, a Tommy Bahama shirt, and Margaritaville boat shoes, I walked through the gate behind my quarters, across the Thunderbolt Club patio and into the main bar of the club. The bar had been remodeled somewhat since I had last been there, like everything else on base, and now featured mirrors, lights, and a distinct art-deco theme. I found a seat at the closest bar stool and shook my head in disbelief at the decor.

"In a fighter bar? Un-fucking-believable," I said to no one in particular.

"What can I get you, sir?' asked the bartender who suddenly appeared in front of me with the seemingly ever-present Spanish accent. He was middle-aged with a slightly pockmarked face, intense dark eyes, and slicked-back hair. I had spent a good part of my adult life in bars and had seen a statistically significant sample of the bartender population. This guy did not fall within the normal distribution.

"Do you have Stella on draft?" I asked.

He nodded, retrieved the required Stella chalice from the cooler in front of him, and proceeded down to the selection of taps to draw the beer.

I took the opportunity to look around the bar. It was early evening on a Wednesday, and the bar was doing a fair business. Several of the tables were occupied and the conversation was lively and animated. On the other side of the bar, several pilots, in the ever-present brown bags, or flightsuits, stood in a circle against the bar, engaging in a heated conversation about the sorties they had flown that day, their hands performing a frenetic ballet of gesticulation as they depicted their maneuvers to one another. I smiled to myself as I watched them, seeing a reflection of myself many, many years ago. I had felt that way once. I wondered where all that boundless energy and enthusiasm had gone.

As my eyes continued to roam, I caught another pair of eyes from the far side of the bar that held mine for a second and then looked away. The eyes were startlingly blue and had peered out at me from under a finely coiffed head of natural blonde hair. It had taken me a few seconds to realize who they belonged to.

What are you doing here, Agent Otenski?

She was attired far less severely tonight, apparently trying to blend into the happy-hour crowd. She wore a blue sundress with a plunging neckline, which revealed quite a bit of tanned décolletage and highlighted her long, toned legs. I wondered where she concealed her weapon. When her eyes found their way to me again, I nodded in greeting and raised my glass in a toasting motion. She responded with a friendly smile and a head nod of her own. Apparently, she didn't care that I knew she was here.

A less cynical man might have allowed himself to be flattered by her presence, but it had been my experience that attractive women rarely came without an agenda of some sort. The only questions were, what was the agenda and how would it be presented? But I found it intriguing that Otenski was here, well out of her region, and that she had not participated in the tail crew that had been glued to me all day.

Are you working alone? I silently asked as I gazed over at her

She began to rise off her chair, possibly to come to join me, but then she froze in mid-movement as the atmosphere in the bar distinctly changed.

Two large men in dark suits entered the room. I looked into the mirror in front of me and studied them. Their movements where fluid and economical and their suits weren't cheap, with the look and fit of something that was tailor made and probably of Italian design. Both men had distinctly Hispanic features and hairstyles that were clearly not in compliance with military regulations. Apart from the fact that one was slightly taller than the other and the shorter one wore wire-rimmed glasses, the two were nearly identical in dress and mannerism. Even though they did nothing to attract attention to themselves, their presence interrupted the undertone of conversation in the bar and an air of expectation developed. The bar crowd had seen these men before.

I glanced at Agent Otenski and saw a surprised frown on her attractive features.

You don't know who these guys are, do you? I thought. *Very interesting.*

The bartender eased his way over and spoke to me, sotto voce. "The two men behind you will take you to see the wing commander."

I nodded slowly as I took my first sip of ice-cold Stella Artois.

"Damn," I said as the smooth lager hit my tongue, "it just shouldn't taste that good." I looked back at the bartender and down at his name tag. "Tell me, Jose, is it common practice in the Air Force these days for wing commanders to have their own civilian goon squad, or is this just a Luke thing?"

The bartender's face showed a moment of incomprehension, indicating the words goon squad didn't register and also indicating that English probably wasn't his first language. "Sir," the bartender said, now with a slight edge to his voice.

"You will go with those men. If you don't go, they will bring you."

I took a moment to consider my options and quickly realized that there was nothing to be gained by making a scene or resisting the current tactics. Apparently, Satan needed to impress me with his power. It was probably in my best interest to act impressed.

"Well, Jose, in the interest of preserving my beer, I think I'll do as you ask. No use in committing alcohol abuse just to prove a point." I rose slowly from the bar, Stella in hand, and put a ten-dollar bill on the counter.

"Keep it," I said.

I turned to the door and walked toward the two goons with a leisurely pace as I took another sip of my beer. I looked at Agent Otenski and winked at her as I made the trip. She wasn't even looking at me. She was still staring at them. I wondered when the OSI-issued smartphone would come out and she'd text or e-mail her boss about what she was watching.

"Gents," I greeted the goons, "take me to your leader."

The taller one on the left nodded silently. Without a word, his colleague with the glasses turned and started to walk down the hall outside the bar, toward the ballroom that was closer to the front of the building. Tall Goon motioned for me to fall into trail. I made a mental note not to allow myself to be manipulated into this "sandwich" sort of formation if a more serious situation developed. As we approached the ballroom's double door, Wire Glasses turned and motioned to the wall next to the door.

"We search you," he said in heavily accented English.

I turned to Tall Goon behind me and handed him my beer. He looked at me strangely for a moment and then took it from my hand. I assumed the spread-eagle position on the wall and let Wire Glasses do his thing.

His hands were quick, firm, and matter of fact. He was very

thorough and not at all afraid to check every nook and cranny. I was glad I elected to come to the bar unarmed tonight. Better to let them think I didn't typically carry. But I longed for some kind of weapon, just for the simple comfort of it. A part of me wished I still needed my cane to walk. The wicked blade inside of it would have made me feel much better.

Glasses stepped back and nodded to Tall Goon.

"So I guess I pass, right?" I asked, regaining my footing and taking my beer from Tall Goon. "You didn't drink any of it, did you? God knows where your mouth has been."

Tall Goon's dark eyes showed red for a microsecond, and then he motioned me toward the door. I walked through and then heard a click as the door shut and latched behind me with the two goons on the other side of it.

There was a moment or two of somewhat ominous silence as I turned to face the center of the room and then the scornful voice from years ago cut the through the air; high-pitched, nasal and loaded with contempt for anything or anyone that wasn't Mark Tappan.

"So what the fuck are you doing on my base, Pearce?"

He was seated at the far end of the ballroom, at one of several round tables that covered the floor area, and he regarded me as I approached him. The thin, dark hair I remembered was plastered to his scalp with some sort of grooming product and revealed hints of spotted and peeling skin beneath. His eyes, dark and recessed, were empty of any sort of feeling, passion, or attitude. They reminded me of the "power on" lights of most electronic equipment. Steady but expressionless. He was seated, so I couldn't see what sort of physical condition he was in, but he looked like he maintained the compact frame he always had—some five feet eight inches – and he still apparently resented the fact that he had to look up to those taller than himself. People like me.

"Well, thanks for the gracious welcome, general," I

answered. "The accommodations and reception thus far have been first rate."

"I only did that shit so I could know exactly where you were," he said impatiently. "How are you here as a full colonel for a TX3 course? All these years later? I thought they threw your sorry ass out of the Air Force."

I seated myself on the other side of the table, across the expanse of blue tablecloth, leaned back, and sipped my beer, grateful that it gave my hands something to do.

"You've seen the orders," I said after a moment.

"They're bullshit and we both know it. You need to tell me why you're really here."

I smiled at him. "I actually don't need to tell you anything, General. You're not in my chain of command. The only thing you need to know is that I'm here for training at your base."

He leaned forward and eyed me closely. If I hadn't known better, I would have actually thought he was a little nervous. There were beads of sweat on his forehead and his hands, now resting on the table, appeared to be shaking slightly.

"I'm not buying it, Pearce," he blurted, the words flowing out of his mouth in staccato, rapid-fire fashion. "Do you hear me? I'm not fucking buying it. Why are you here? Why are you here now? You've got to be up to something." He paused for a moment, apparently searching for the right words for his next question but then, without warning, the words came from his mouth almost involuntarily. "Who the fuck are you working for, Pearce?"

It took a herculean effort to keep my face impassive and to keep my typically smart-assed mouth shut, but somehow I managed.

His voice lowered. "You got MAJCOM approval not only to jump to the top of the TX3 training schedule, in front of a lot of other colonels and generals who deserve that training more than you do, but you also got assigned to the 310th for that training. No one gets assigned to a specific squadron at the MAJCOM level. We make those decisions here."

I took another sip of my beer and allowed him to stew for a few moments.

"I was given my choice of squadrons," I answered after a long moment. "I choose the 310th because it's where I used to be assigned."

Tappan almost fidgeted himself out of his chair. His mouth formed the word "bull" but he didn't utter it. Instead, he glared at me across the table as his nervous fingers drummed its surface. "I don't know what you think you're going to do here, Pearce," he hissed at me, "but you'd better not fuck with my people or my base while you're here."

I looked back at him and took another swallow of my amber nectar. "Or what, general? You'll sic your thugs on me? By the way, how did you get those guys anyway? Are they standard issue for general officers now or just the ones who had to blackmail someone to get selected for their first star?"

I sat back and waited for the fuse I'd ignited to reach its object.

"You low-life son of a bitch," Tappan exploded. "Who the fuck do you think you are talking to me like that? Do you have any idea how easily I could get your ass cli..." he stopped in mid-sentence.

And there it was. Perfect.

"What was that, General? Where you about to say clipped?" I asked with an air of incredulity that I didn't have to work hard to display.

"Court-martialed," Tappan sputtered, "I could get your ass court-martialed."

I took the last swig of my beer and rose to go. "I need another Stella. I think we're done here."

"Where the fuck do you think you're going?"

"Back to the bar. There's a hot OSI agent in there that I

feel like talking to. Maybe I'll discuss our little conversation with her."

Tappan nearly jumped to his feet as if to stop me, and I held my hand up, palm out, to ward him off.

"Do you still drive a corvette?" I asked.

His face registered surprise for a moment. Then he nodded slowly.

"Of course you do. Well, if you need to compensate for something where I'm concerned, go drive your penis replacement machine and be content with it. Because if you try a masculinity demo with me, whether it's you or some of your minions, bad shit will happen. You need to keep that in mind."

Tappan eyed me closely, probably to see if he detected any "tell" that indicated my speech was a bluff. He didn't.

"Are you threatening—" he began uncertainly.

I cut him off.

"I don't make threats," I said. There was no use pretending any longer. "And you know that or we wouldn't be having this conversation."

I turned to go.

"Watch your back, T. C.," he uttered as I left him behind me.

"You do the same, Satan," I replied without turning around. "It will be an interesting few months."

Chapter Six

Contract Day Two
Thursday, June 24, 2010
0730 Hours Local Time
Southern F-16 Academic Building
Luke Air Force Base, Arizona

Déjà vu once again. I was sitting in one of the same classrooms in which I had taken and taught F-16 academics several years ago. The podium in the front of the class looked like it hadn't moved an inch since I stood behind it. The overhead projection screens appeared at the front of the classroom with the enlarged unit patches of the 56th Fighter Wing, 56th Operations Group, and 56th Training Squadron aligned alongside, just as they had back in the day. And the tiered rows of desks, with the veneer finish and attached chairs, looked like they hadn't been changed or updated.

I sat where I typically sat in a classroom, in the back row, near the door, with a squadron mug of coffee in my hand, a government-issue laptop computer on the desk in front of me, and two F-16 checklists and a Luke AFB InFlight Guide resting on the veneered surface next to it. I presumed the binders of paper texts we had used back in the day were now loaded on the laptop. But this element of technological progress notwithstanding, I felt like I had been transported back in time. And the colonel's eagles on my newly-issued flightsuit didn't help with the surreal atmosphere of it all.

I wasn't alone in the class. There were two other colonels in the room with me. One, a short, compact, and curvy brunette female, sat two rows in front of me in the second row, her computer open and the screen illuminated in front of her. Apparently, she had arrived early and had browsed the academic material to acquaint herself with it. At the moment, she was engrossed in her USAF issued smartphone, probably answering e-mails, as we waited for the class to begin. As she tabbed through her device, I couldn't help but notice a distinct but unobtrusive gold band on the third finger of her left hand. The second colonel was an African American man, about my height but wider. He sat in the row between the female and me but off to the side. His computer was on the desk in front of him, lid closed and untouched. He didn't have his head buried in a mobile phone or a book. Instead, he sat there in his chair with his muscular arms crossed, calmly regarding the room without focusing on anything in particular. As I looked in his direction, he turned his head and met my gaze. His dark eyes, initially dull and lifeless, became suddenly alive with interest and he nodded at me in greeting. I nodded back, trying not to let my eyes dwell on the faded but visible scars on his forehead and cheeks.

This guy has seen some action, I thought.

I looked down at the cloth name tag velcroed to his chest and noted that in addition to command pilot's wings, he also wore master parachutist's wings, something that was very unusual in the pilot ranks. My roommate from the US Air Force Academy, Burt Magnusson, had senior parachutist's wings but only because he had been on the Academy parachute team. Master parachutist's wings on a pilot were rare indeed.

His nametag read Brock Black.

"Room, ten-HUT!"

The colonel in front sprang to her feet, like a good officer. Brock and I were a bit more leisurely about assuming the position of attention.

There was a pregnant pause and then the familiar nasal voice from last night uttered the magic words, "As you were."

We returned to our seats as a parade of people entered the room. At the front was a female lieutenant colonel, followed by another lieutenant colonel I knew, a full colonel I didn't, and, of course, God's gift to aviation and the Air Force, Mark Tappan.

"I'm Lieutenant Colonel Sherry McGuire, the commander of the Fifty-Sixth TRS," the female said as she reached the front of the room. Her blonde hair was cut in a short, almost masculine style, but she wore light eye makeup that highlighted her high cheekbones and softened her face. She had a body that bespoke of marathons and triathlons, and her flightsuit fit her precisely. She stood with a very erect, military posture as she spoke. "It's my distinct pleasure to welcome you here and to introduce you to some very important people here at Luke."

She motioned to the man immediately to her right, a short, dumpy man with wisps of hair around his bald head and heavy jowls. "This is Lieutenant Colonel Don Weeks. He's the commander of the 310th Fighter Squadron where you'll be receiving your flying training." Weeks stepped forward and nodded at all of us. I recognized him from some of the briefing material the CIA had provided. He didn't appear to have a speaking part in these proceedings.

"Next we have Colonel Brian Beck, the commander of the 56th Operations Group." Beck was about average height with crisp blue eyes, close-cropped black hair, and boyish features. He looked like he could have been my son—if I had one. He too stepped forward and nodded without saying a word.

"Last, but not least," McGuire said, "we have our wing commander, Brigadier General Mark Tappan. He'd like to say a few words of introduction."

On cue, Tappan strutted to the center of the room in front of the first row of tables like a bantam cock and stood with his hands on his hips. I noticed he had arranged the top zipper of his flightsuit and his crew-necked T-shirt so that a fair amount of gray and black chest hair was visible over the collar of the undergarment. I felt a smirk beginning to form on my lips, and I fought to maintain a blank expression.

He's just so fucking predictable, I thought.

Tappan's eyes went to each of us, just for a moment, as if he was taking our measure, and then he began to speak.

"Welcome to Luke," he said flatly. "We have a mission here, and that is to train the best fighter pilots in the world. For the time you're here, you need to remember that you're students. You're wingmen. You're not commanders," he looked at the female colonel in the front row, "you're not special advisors," he looked at Brock, "and you're not," he looked directly at me, "attachés." He accented the word just enough to communicate his skepticism of the job title to the entire class. "You're wingmen." He paused for a moment, maybe for dramatic effect or maybe to gather his thoughts. It was hard to tell. "You've all been used to being in charge. That's what got you here. Just remember that on this base, my base, you're not in charge, I am. Remember that and we'll get along just fine."

The expressions of the other officers at the front of the room were a study in contrasts. McGuire kept her face professionally composed but her eyes belied both impatience and disappointment with Tappan's words. Lieutenant Colonel Weeks' eyes glowed with admiration while Colonel Beck's eyes communicated that he would have preferred to be anywhere but here.

"Do you have any questions?"

There was silence.

"In that case, perhaps each of you can introduce yourselves and tell us what assignment you're going to and a little about your background." Tappan nodded to the woman in the front.

"I'm Christine Billings," she said. "I just came from a tour on the Joint Staff, and I'm going to be the Commander of the 8th Operations Group at Kunsan Air Base, Korea. I've got about twelve hundred hours in the Viper, mostly Block 50's at Misawa and Shaw." She glanced back at Brock and me. "I go by Lindal," she said with a wry smile. "It's a long story."

Tappan appeared to nod respectfully, but the contempt in his eyes was unmistakable. Women didn't belong in the cockpit in *his* Air Force.

Billings appeared not to notice his expression. She was probably used to such Neanderthal behavior. There were still many males in the aviation community in general, and the fighter community in particular, who didn't think women could perform well in the cockpit, especially in a jet as sophisticated as the F-16. I would have gladly argued that point with them. The most challenging air-to-air engagement I had ever flown in my life was against a female pilot. And she'd almost killed me.

Tappan's eyes moved to Brock's.

"I'm Brock Black," the large man said, in a voice that was quiet, deep, and menacing all at once. "I'm on my way to be the special advisor for fighter operations to the Commander of US Special Operations Command. My last assignment was one I can't talk about. I've got three thousand hours in the Viper. All Blocks. I go by B-Rock."

Tappan raised his eyebrows skeptically.

"All blocks? You mean just C-model blocks and later, right?" I knew that Tappan fancied himself as one of the premier Viper experts in the USAF. He didn't like the possibility that someone might have more experience than he did.

Brock looked back at Tappan calmly and shook his head.

"I've flown every model of the Viper that there is, general, and not just the ones in our air force."

Tappan glared at him for a moment and then turned his eyes to me. His gaze was challenging and contemptuous. I was sure he had read or been briefed on the backstory that Gail Petersen and her folks had concocted for me. He just wanted to hear me tell it.

"I'm Colin Pearce," I said quietly. "I'm on my way to be the Air Attache at our embassy in Brussels. I've been working on special projects with the Air Force Reserve before this. I've got about the two thousand hours in the Viper."

Tappan smirked back at me. It was obvious that he didn't believe a word of it.

"And what do you go by, Colonel?" he asked. The tone of his voice made it apparent to all in the room that he knew the answer.

"T. C.," I said. "I go by T. C."

It was as if I'd said the word "fuck" in church. An instantaneous and stunned silence took possession of the room. The three officers in the front of the room tensed and looked at me with a mixture of respect, fear, and, perhaps a touch of loathing. Christine Billings actually turned around to look at me more closely. Maybe she wanted to see if I was also the Antichrist. Brock Black's mouth opened to reveal a sharp, white smile, and he nodded slightly, as if he'd suspected it all along. And Mark Tappan's eyes shined in triumph, as if he had somehow revealed a significant truth.

"Well," Tappan said after a long moment. "Now that we all know each other, I'll give the stick to Lieutenant Colonel McGuire to get your training started."

He began to walk from the stage area and headed up the shallow stairs between the rows of desks to the exit at the back of the room. He got to the top, just about next to my desk, and then he paused for a moment.

"By the way," he said. "I go by Satan. But I'm really not that evil." He laughed for a moment, as if he was amused at some sort of private joke. "Unless you piss me off, of course."

***

"Jesus Christ, what a fucking asshole."

Brock and I looked up from our lunch in the VIP room at the Thunderbolt Club, both of us somewhat astounded that the words had come from our fellow female student, Christine "Lindal" Billings. The conversation had turned to Mark Tappan and Christine had just enlightened us with her opinion of our gracious wing commander.

"You know what I hate?" I asked Brock. "I hate people who have trouble expressing themselves clearly."

"I know what you mean," he said, crunching on a piece of lettuce. "It's like people who sugarcoat things or who beat around the bush. Just makes it hard to know what they're thinking."

"All right you two," Christine said as she raised a glass of iced tea to her lips. "You asked my opinion of that idiot, and I gave it to you. Besides," she continued with a mischievous gleam in her eye, "I can't beat around the bush. I don't have one."

I nearly spit out my lettuce, and Brock almost choked on an ice cube. When we had regained our composure, a few minutes later, I was finally able to speak.

"You are full of surprises, Colonel," I said. "It's going to be an interesting thirty-nine training days."

We had spent the morning going over the course map for the TX-3 training course we were enrolled in and sitting through the first blocks of academic instruction in the F-16.

The TX-3 syllabus was one of several taught at Luke Air Force Base and was typically used as a "short course" to reacquaint senior officers with F-16 experience with the jet. In this syllabus, we had thirteen ground training days and twenty-six flying training days, the total of which typically took about eight weeks to accomplish. There would be 163 hours of academics in 182 separate lectures, about 40 hours of training in simulators and training devices, and 12 total sorties with about 17 flying hours to finish the course. It had sounded like a long time to me, as the major who gave us our classroom instruction talked us through the course, but now, upon reflection, it occurred to me that it might not be nearly enough time to do what I really came here to do.

Christine, Brock, and I had bonded quickly, as students in an intense course of instruction typically do. Christine, while obviously on the Air Force "fast track" to promotion, was very down-to-earth and self-deprecating. She laughed easily and had a very quick wit. But when it came to the jet, she was all business. She knew the aircraft extremely well and had asked more than one question in class that had required some thought from the instructor.

Brock was much more complicated. He seemed to digest everything without saying or doing anything. His body appeared quite muscular and solid, but he didn't move like a typical muscle head; instead, he was catlike and smooth. On at least two occasions that morning, he had managed to get within arms' length of me before I knew he was there. Like many black men, he shaved his head, but with him it was less a fashion statement and somehow more of an expression of who he was. When we finally shook hands after the first session of class, I'd seen something in his eyes that I knew well—the look of someone who had repeatedly taken the lives of others and had reached that place where he accepted it. He had recognized it in my eyes as well. We understood each other.

"So," Christine said as she finished her salad and pushed it to the side, "I have to know." She looked at me. "Are you *the* T. C.?"

I finished chewing the last crouton in my salad, swallowed it, and wiped my mouth before I answered.

"A few months ago, somebody I respect a lot told me that there was only one of us in the Viper community. So I guess I am."

"Wow," she said. "I never thought I'd actually meet you. I thought you were a myth. There are stories about you all over."

"Hard to believe," I answered. "I'm nobody special."

"Shit," Brock said as he sipped some iced tea. "If the whole business about you in Iraq wasn't enough, shooting down five jets and two B-61 nuclear bombs in the space of about fifteen minutes would make you notable at least. You're an ace in the Viper, for God's sake, the only one in the history of the Air Force."

"It is fucking impressive," Christine echoed. "I read the file when I was on the Joint Staff."

"So much for it being Top Secret," I mused. "Jesus. But if you've read the file then you know one guy ejected voluntarily. That doesn't count."

"Yes it does," Brock said as Christine nodded in agreement, "you were responsible for the destruction of the jet. The fact that you didn't use a missile or a gun to do it doesn't matter."

"It's got all of the general officers in the Viper community with their panties in a twist," Christine said. "They don't want to acknowledge it but everyone knows it happened. Once word got out, they couldn't contain it. The Weapons School guys are petitioning the CIA and NSA for the RMC video from your jet so they can reconstruct the engagements and teach them to students. You're like a fucking legend."

There was silence for a moment. I was stunned. I had no idea that any of this had happened.

"I don't know what to say. You do what you have to do and the training I had, both in the USAF and...before the engagements...was very good."

"Training is one thing," Brock said, "but executing in reality is another. I'll tell you something, I've had my share of engagements in certain places of the world, many of which I can't talk about. But I wouldn't want to fight you. Not for real. From what I know about the engagements, you fight dirty."

"Me neither," Christine agreed.

"Well," I said quietly, as I turned the cloth napkin between my thumb and forefinger. "I fight to win. And in this case, if I hadn't won, a lot of people would have died."

"Which is one of the reasons the generals at the Pentagon are so perplexed," Christine said. "They know that but they also know that it can't be officially acknowledged. There's been talk about recommissioning you so they could give you the DFC or the Medal of Honor!"

"Which is why," Brock said quietly, nodding at Christine, "we know your commission hasn't been sanctioned at the places in the Pentagon where it should have been if it was completely legitimate, because if it had been, there'd be generals swarming all over this place looking for you."

"Which means," Christine continued, "there's something going on."

Damn, I thought to myself. *This was a piece of the puzzle that Gail Petersen and her folks hadn't counted on.*

I sat back in my chair and tried to keep my expression neutral. I had never been to "spy school" so I had no experience with how to divert the topic at moments like this. I looked at them. It was possible one or both of them were working for Tappan and crew, but I doubted it. Brock had his orders to attend this class two months ago and Christine had hers for nearly a year. Both had arrived late the previous evening. As rapidly as my orders to attend the class had been generated,

Tappan couldn't have known they'd be in the class with me. Nor could he have gotten to them in time to threaten them. And looking at them, it was clear that neither one of them would have been a pushover when being threatened. Besides, I was a decent judge of character, and something told me they could be trusted.

"And if there is something going on?" I asked them after a long moment.

Brock and Christine exchanged a glance between them and then Christine spoke.

"We want to help," she said.

Chapter Seven

Contract Day Four
Saturday, June 26, 2010
1000 Hours Local Time
Weight Room, Base Gymnasium
Luke Air Force Base, Arizona

"Cmon, T. C.," Brock said. "You've got at least two more in you."

I didn't share his confidence. The 250-pound barbell felt pretty damn heavy to me, and I was amazed that I had gotten three repetitions with it already. I continued to push upward, trying to contract my pectoral muscles and triceps and ignoring the messages that my body and gravity were both trying to send me. The bar traveled the final few inches upward as I continued to exhale and then, miraculously, my arms reached full extension.

"Now lower it, again, quickly, don't think about it."

I couldn't have held it up there if I wanted to. The bar came down toward my chest with my triceps and pectoral muscles barely able to stop the descent.

"Now catch it," Brock urged. "Don't let it touch."

He didn't need to tell me twice. Proper form for lifting had always been a big deal for me, and one thing you learn very early when doing the bench press, particularly at higher weights, is that bouncing the bar off your chest is bad technique. The bar needs to stop when your upper arms are parallel to the floor so you can avoid damage to your sternum and avoid hyperextending your shoulders. I stopped the bar as my upper and lower arms reached a 90 degree angle and started to push upward.

It barely moved.

"I'm not spotting you, T. C.," Brock said, with a stubborn tone in his voice. "You gotta get mad at that thing. You gotta think about something that really pisses you off."

Out of the corner of my eye, I saw Mark Tappan and his goon squad enter the gym. He was attired in close-fitting designer exercise wear and the civilian goons were in matching black warmup suits. A former gymnast, Tappan liked to show off on the rings or pommel horse periodically and apparently today was a designated show day. It was impressive that he could still do that sort of thing at fifty plus years of age, but the fact that he gloated about it spoiled the effect. A memory of my last time at Luke was keyed in the far reaches of my brain; and for just a moment, the rage flared inside of me. I looked up to find the bar at full extension above me and my arms holding it there with little to no effort at all.

"Jesus, T. C.," Brock said, as he helped me rack the weight. "Where did that come from?" Then he looked over at Tappan and his entourage. "Wow," he said. "Apparently you don't like that guy."

"No love lost, that's for sure," I said, standing up and reaching for my sweat towel. "We'll discuss over adult beverages later."

"I'll hold you to that," he said. He reached over to the nearest weight rack, grabbed two forty-five-pound plates easily and handed me one. "Now let's put some manly weight on this bar so I can get some real work."

Brock, Christine, and I had developed a regular workout schedule. This morning, Christine had done a quick pass through the weight room, where she spent most of her time on the squat rack ("So that's why she's got such a great ass," Brock had said) and then gone on to the aerobics room to work on the elliptical trainer. Brock, like me, was a creature of the iron, and we had come up with a split routine that allowed us to work different muscles on different days. Today was chest and triceps day. We had done legs and shoulders on Thursday, back and biceps the day before. The next day, theoretically, we were due for a rest day. I wasn't sure I believed that would happen. Brock was hard core.

He slid onto the bench and under the 340-pound bar. This was his top set as 250 pounds had been mine, but I expected that he'd be expending less effort than I did. He was significantly stronger than I was but, apart from the occasional ribbing, he was pretty modest about it.

"I just spent a lot of time in far-away places where there was nothing to do but lift weights," he said on Thursday after our first workout. "You haven't had that luxury. But you're still pretty strong," he said. "And you've got a great foundation. We'll kick your ass a little over the next month and see what happens."

And here we were, doing just that.

He looked up at me with an expectant look on his face.

"I don't know what the fuck you're waiting for," I told him. "You didn't spot me. I'm sure as shit not spotting you."

He smiled at me. "Dick!" he said.

"Everyone has to be good at something," I replied.

After the bench press, we hurt ourselves with incline presses, dumbbell flies, dips, and triceps pushdowns for the better part of an hour. Then, after arranging to meet Christine later for dinner, Brock and I made our way to the gym's steam room to sweat the soreness out of our muscles. It had been my idea.

"Haven't done much of this," Brock said. "A lot of the places I've been to, you didn't meet the high side of society in these rooms."

"I spent a lot of time in the steam last year. It helped my muscles to recover a lot more quickly. And since I'm in a lot worse shape than you are, I need this. You can close your eyes if the sight of naked men embarrasses you."

He snorted. "Shit. They're all just going to wish they were hung like me."

I smiled and shook my head. "That's profiling," I said. "There are laws against that shit."

"Maybe so, bro," he replied with a sly grin, letting a little ghetto creep into his voice, "but that don't keep it from being true."

The steam room was tiled and shaped like an L with three levels. It also had a wooden lattice over the floor to keep the occupants from slipping, and wooden slats over the various seating levels. I sat down on the lowest level on the short side of the L, on the opposite side of the room from the door, and leaned against the tile behind me, propping my elbows on the next level. Brock sat in the middle of the second row on the long side of the L, laying his long frame out on the wooden slats and propping his head up with a towel.

"So what's all this shit between you and Satan anyway?" he asked after a few moments. "I could tell the other day that he didn't like you very much."

I had been sitting there with my eyes closed, daydreaming, when he spoke and the words hung in the air.

"The feeling is mutual," I said. I opened my eyes and looked at Brock before I continued. "I was his ops officer," I said, "back in the late nineties, here at Luke. And he didn't like me much, mostly because he didn't get to select me for the position."

"What?" Brock asked. "Was it common practice for squadron commanders to select their Ops Os here?"

"Not at all," I said. "In fact, here at Luke they actually had a board selection process for Ops Os. A squadron commander could ask for whomever he wanted, but all the squadron commanders voted and it was the Ops Group Commander who made the final call. Satan never got over the fact that his fair-haired boy didn't get picked. And he never let me forget it. He made me assign his boy, an idiot by the name of John Barry, to be my assistant DO, and the two of them tried to bypass me at every turn."

"Nice," Brock said. "What'd you do?"

"My job," I said. "And things worked fine. Everyone else on the ops side was loyal to me and nothing happened unless I signed off on it. It infuriated the shit out of both of them, but especially Satan. If you haven't diagnosed it already, he's got the whole Napoleon complex thing going on."

"It's fucking universal and international," Brock said. "I can't tell you how many of them I've seen in third world countries."

"There was another thing though," I said quietly. "A minor little thing."

"Oh yeah? Like what?"

"Well, it was really nothing. Just a teeny little thing." I held my right hand up with my thumb and index finger barely apart to illustrate.

"Well? What was it?"

"I sort of fucked his stepdaughter."

Brock looked at me wide-eyed in disbelief for a moment and then chuckled into the steamy air around us.

"No fucking way," he said, laughing.

"He was married then, to a hot older woman who had a daughter who was twenty-five. I think he married the mother for the money because they didn't last more than a few years.

But the daughter came here to visit mommy for three months while she was on summer vacation from grad school, and we fucked each other the whole time she was here. She was kinky! I could barely keep up with her. I'd go to work in the morning all fuck-flushed, and it would drive Satan fucking crazy."

Brock's laughter turned to guffaws. I could see his chest moving up and down.

"When the three of them came into the bar together the first time and he introduced her, I never thought about fucking her. Honestly."

Brock was now on his side, howling, clenching his stomach.

"OK, so maybe I did think about it. I mean she was so fucking hot, and my dick was ready to roll in from the moment I saw her. Damn good think she wasn't Satan's real daughter, because she might have looked like him and my dick would have gone into hibernation."

Brock was holding his hand out, apparently imploring me to shut up so he could breathe, but I couldn't stop talking.

I looked back at him, shaking my head. "I know pretty stupid, right? But for some reason she came on to me that first night and the fact that it would piss him off was just too good to pass up. She kept inching toward me, and he kept trying to give me these threatening looks from across the room, and every time he did, I'd touch her arm or move closer to her and it was driving him fucking nuts. Finally, she pretty much jumped into my lap and rammed her tongue down my throat. He about screwed himself into the ceiling. It was priceless."

I could see the tears coming down Brock's cheeks. It was an interesting look for him.

"She liked it risky, too. She came to the squadron to have lunch with me once, and I did her on his desk once while he was at a meeting. There was DNA all over the place when we were done. She chased me out of there when we got word he was on the way back into the building and told me she'd clean up, but I'm not sure she did. He probably came back into his office to find cum on his blotter."

"Please." Brock gasped. "Please. You're killing me."

I was about to utter another smart-assed comment when a realization slammed into my brain like a car smashing into brick wall.

"Holy, fucking, shit," I said to myself. "It wasn't a robbery at all."

Brock just looked at me, the mirth fading from his face. "What?" he said. "Care to fill me in here?"

I ignored him for a few moments and recalculated the time line in my head. "Jesus," I said. I leaned my head back against the upper level behind me and exhaled loudly. "I can't believe I didn't put this together until now."

"T. C.?" Brock asked. "What's going on?"

"There's a good story here," I said. "And it starts about nine years ago." I sat up. "I'll tell you all about it over a few beers a little later."

Brock swung his muscular legs over the side of his seat and got to his feet.

"It's going to be a busy meal," he said. "That's two stories you'll have to brief me on."

"It's really just one," I said as I stood. "And they're both about the same idiot, Mark Tappan."

As if on cue, the steam room door opened and Mark Tappan strode in with his two goons in tow. It reminded me of a scene from a movie, the mob boss taking to the steam with his bodyguards beside him—there to protect him against a possible assassination. After what I had just realized, it wasn't too far from the truth. It was everything I could do not to launch myself at him, but even with Brock at my side, it didn't seem like a smart play. With their shirts off, the bodyguards were pretty intimidating, each sporting a combination of sinewy muscles, intricate tattoos, and indented scars. I recognized the tattoos. Some guys in Dallas who hadn't fared well at my hands had the same artwork.

Damn. I thought. *It all makes so much sense now.*

"Enjoying your time on my base, gentlemen?" Tappan asked, his eyes alternating between the two of us.

"So far, so good, General," Brock replied. "No complaints. Yet."

Tappan snorted in response and turned his gaze to me. He stood there in his towel with the steam swirling around him and his thin hair plastered to his sweaty scalp. His body actually seemed to be in reasonable shape with muscles visible beneath the thick mat of hair on his chest, but the angle of his chin and the arrogance he emanated made him look like a little man trying to be big. The fact that he thought he was intimidating made the scene almost comical. I fought to keep the smirk off my face. It was difficult.

"What about you, Pearce?"

"The instructors have been professional and the support structure accommodating, General. I'm with Brock. No complaints."

Tappan nodded and looked over this shoulder at his two goons in apparent satisfaction.

"That's good to know," he said after a moment. "I thought I was going to have to teach you a little respect."

I should have let that go. But I couldn't. It was as if my mouth was under its own power and my brain wasn't part of the process.

"Oh, no one said anything about respect, Satan. We just said the base and the training course were okay."

His beady eyes fixated on mine immediately, and it was as if I could see a small fire ignite behind them. The realization that had occurred to me a few moments earlier was still fresh in my brain and demanding attention. My mouth started moving again before I had the power to stop it.

"So here's a question for you Satan. Were the gang bangers you sent to my house in 2000 supposed to kill me or just rough me up a little? I know you were pissed about me fucking your stepdaughter and you wanted your fair-haired boy to get the Kunsan slot, but I don't know how pissed you really were. Pissed enough to have me killed? Pissed enough to send guys like these," I inclined my chin toward the two goons, "to do your dirty work?"

I watched his eyes widen for just a moment, as if he was trying to recall the event, but then the gleam of knowledge suddenly burned within them and even a hint of arrogant pride. I had my answer.

"Jesus," I said, looking back at him. "You are a sick little shit."

I saw a blur to my left and then something hard and round struck my left leg, just below my knee. The blow was incredibly powerful. I felt a flash of pressure and pain and then there was deep, residual ache, as if my calf muscle was on fire. My leg almost buckled, and my guess was that's what Satan wanted. But I knew something he didn't. My skeleton had been reinforced with titanium, implanted by a gifted orthopedic surgeon, as part of the recovery from the ejection last fall. My bones were stronger than the average fifty-plus-year-old man. In fact, they were probably stronger than those of the average twenty something.

So I kept my footing and apparently pissed him off even more. It was then that I saw the collapsible baton dangling from his right hand. He was rotating the end of it in a small circle, as if he was anxious to use it again.

Brock stepped forward, his eyes burning. "How fucked up is this?" he asked, angrily. "Since when does a star on your collar allow you beat on a lower-ranking officer, General?"

The two goons behind Tappan moved aggressively toward

Brock or as aggressively as they could, dressed only in towels.

Brock smiled at them, and then, more quickly than I would have believed possible, he stepped between them and his hands and knees moved in a series of tight, precise, blows. He took the two bodyguards completely by surprise, and they had no time block or resist. They absorbed multiple blows, bounced off the tiled walls, and fell to the lattice-covered floor in seconds.

Brock looked over at me then at Tappan and shrugged his muscular shoulders. "Seems a little fairer to me now," Brock said. "Seem a little fairer to you, T. C.?" He inclined his head toward Tappan. "Maybe you could go a little Hulk on his ass?"

I was way ahead of him. The rage was already simmering within me and the blow to my leg had set it a boil. The moment I saw that Tappan had been momentarily distracted with Brock's handiwork, I ripped the baton from his hand— working against the thumb as I was taught—and flipped it 180 degrees so that the handle was in my hand. Then I smacked him with it just below his ribcage, about half as hard as I wanted to. I popped him again on the side of the leg where he'd hit me, lighter than I wanted to. He went down as if he'd been poleaxed. His face flinched with the pain, but his eyes flashed with fury and he couldn't keep his mouth shut as he crumpled to the floor.

"You can't...treat...a...general...officer like this...and get... away with it," he said, gasping between words.

"If you can threaten us with your gangbanger goons, then anything goes Satan," I said, as Brock and I walked to the door. I spun the baton in my hand. "Do you mind if I keep this? It seems like it could come in handy."

Brock stepped over the two goons and opened the door. "Coming, T. C.?" he asked. "I think there are some beers waiting for us at that Third Base place."

"Definitely," I replied, stepping over Tappan's legs and

joining Brock at the door. I turned to Tappan. "I know your perverted little mind is already thinking about how you'll get even, Satan. And judging from previous experience, you'll probably be tempted to get those idiots at the OSI involved. You need to think about that real hard. You have no idea what I'm fucking capable of."

I looked down at the little man writhing on the floor and resisted the urge to kick him before we left the room. "By the way," I said, "your stepdaughter was insatiable. I had her in every possible position in every possible orifice and in every possible place." I looked right into the furious eyes. "And she fucking loved it."

Chapter Eight

Contract Day Four
Saturday, June 26, 2010
1800 Hours Local Time
Third Base Bar and Grill, Goodyear, Arizona

"Damn," Christine said later as we sat at a table at the Third Base Bar and Grill, "That's some harsh shit. What in the hell would lead him to believe he could even get away with threatening you guys like that? What would make him think you wouldn't report it?"

"I think we were targets of opportunity," I replied. "He saw us in the gym and since it was just the two of us and he had his goons, he thought could get some information out of us."

"Like what?" Brock asked. "I don't know anything."

"Satan is suspicious about the reason I'm here," I said. "He's involved in some shit he shouldn't be involved in and it's making him a little obsessed."

"Involved in what?" Christine asked. Her eyes looked intensely curious.

I took a slow sip of the huge draft beer in front of me and let the cool, amber Stella Artois cascade across my tongue and down my throat. I thought about what I could tell Brock and Christine without endangering them. Then it occurred to me that if Tappan had been willing to threaten both Brock and I in a semipublic place, there probably wasn't much he wouldn't do. My classmates deserved the truth—or at least a portion of it.

"C'mon, T. C.," Brock said. "I kicked some ass for you today. I at least need to know why."

I grinned at him. "So Tappan being an asshole isn't enough?"

Brock laughed. "Well, yes, but I know there's more. I've never seen a wing commander with his own personal civilian goon squad before."

I took another swig of my beer. "Me neither," I said.

I set the glass down and looked at the two of them. Then I casually looked around the bar to see if there was anyone around us who got my attention. The bar was part of a growing chain that featured a good, male-oriented menu, lots of high-definition TVs, and scantily clad waitresses. It was like Hooters on steroids and so obviously pandered to the male perspective that it made me laugh. But the food was good, the drink selections were extensive, and the service was outstanding. It was my kind of place. The girls were a bonus.

Brock and Christine looked around the bar as I did, each with varying expressions on their faces. Brock looked like he was enjoying the view. Christine just smirked as she eyed the members of her gender on the service staff and the way the male patrons were ogling them.

"You know, I have some lingerie just as sexy as the stuff these girls are wearing," she said. "Maybe I should get a job here."

I smiled at her. "That wouldn't be fair to these poor girls, Lindal. You'd outclass them."

"Plus you'd rake in all the tips," Brock added. "An older woman in great shape like you is way sexier than some young chick with no miles and no seasoning."

"You guys know just the right thing to say," she said, smiling at us. Then she pointed a delicate finger at me. "But you, mister, neatly managed to avoid the question. You need to tell us what is going on here. Or do I need to change into something more distracting to get you to talk?"

"Wow," I said to her. "I didn't know you changing into something distracting was even on the menu! But I was actually looking about the room to see if there was someone I recognized or who looked out of place. Your average OSI agent stands out like a turd in a punch bowl. They just don't blend in, particularly in places like this, which is one of the reasons we're here, the view notwithstanding."

"Wait a minute," Christine said. "You're being followed by the OSI?"

I nodded. "Since this whole business began. My little speech to Satan today was just a diversion to make him think I didn't notice the tail already on me. There's a detail here now. See the two guys, black leather bomber jackets, sitting at the far end of the bar drinking—wait for it—some kind of cola on a Saturday evening with sports on the TV? That makes them OSI or corporate pilots, but that would be an insult to the pilots. Besides, I've seen those two faces in my rearview mirror on several occasions before. Take a look over there. You'll see that they'll refuse to make eye contact."

Brock and Christine took turns casting nonchalant glances in the direction of the two agents. After a few minutes they returned to their drinks, shaking their heads in disbelief.

"Well, they couldn't have made that any more obvious," Christine said.

"No," Brock added. "They sure couldn't."

"Same garb, same expressions, same attitude. No imagination at all." I removed my BlackBerry from my pocket, activated the jamming app, and set it on the table in front of me. "This will keep us from being overheard," I said. I leaned forward. "At this point, there are some things I can tell you and some things I can't."

Brock and Christine both nodded. They understood need to know where classified information was concerned.

"Last Monday, I received a phone call from an academy classmate of mine who asked me to meet him and his wife for dinner. At dinner, he told me a story about his stepson, Thomas Rogers. Thomas was a naval aviator on an exchange tour here, and he was killed in a Viper crash on the Gila Bend ranges a few months ago."

"That sucks," Brock said.

"I agree. And while we all know that this sort of thing happens from time to time, in this case, things appear to be a little different. My friend had a contact on the accident board who had access to the raw data from the crash. It's pretty certain that Thomas's death was not accidental."

"What?" Christine asked, after a few moments. "Not an accident? Was it sabotage?"

I shook my head. "Thomas's aircraft was hit by another member of the flight during the egress from a four-ship, low-altitude bomb run. Thomas was killed instantly. The guy who hit him managed to eject." I paused to sip my beer and look at them then continued. "Before the impact."

I let the words sink in.

"He ejected before the impact?" Christine asked after a few moments. "Like he knew it was going to happen? Holy shit!"

"That doesn't necessarily prove anything," Brock countered. "He might have had fast reactions."

"Damn fast reactions I'd say," Christine added. "I've read a zillion accident reports, and I've never read anything like that before."

"Well, it doesn't help that the guy who collided with Thomas seems to have committed suicide before the accident board could even interview him. And it also doesn't help that my friend's contact on the board seems to have been killed in a hit-and-run car accident about a week after the accident report was published."

"Interesting series of coincidences," Brock said after a few moments.

"If they are coincidences," Christine added.

"It's been my experience that true coincidences are very rare," I said. "But I've saved the best one for last." I looked at both of them intently. "And here's where it gets dangerous. The accident occurred in the afternoon. That morning, Thomas reported a conversation he'd overheard between our friend Satan and the 310th commander, Don Weeks. They were discussing how they were planning to steal an F-35."

I took another sip of my beer and watched Brock and Christine process what I'd told them.

"Jesus," Brock said at last. "Who the fuck would they sell it to?"

"That's the part I can't talk about," I answered, "at least for now."

"I have a more important question," Christine said, tapping the table with a well-manicured fingernail for emphasis. "Who the hell did this Thomas guy report the conversation to before he was killed?"

"That's the really interesting and disturbing part," I said. "He reported it to a lieutenant colonel named Lorna Dahlke who just happens to be the commander of the local OSI detachment."

"So the OSI is in on it?" Brock asked as he sat back in his chair.

"Not all of them," I said. "Or at least that's what I'd like to believe, for now. But we certainly don't know which ones are and which ones aren't. But enough of them are that two agents tried to intercept my friends and me after dinner last Monday and take them into custody on the other side of the country for talking to me."

"Goes pretty high up then," Brock said, staring at his beer.

"So it would seem," I said.

"What happened?" Christine asked. "When they tried to take you into custody?"

"I know some people," I said. "They didn't succeed." I inclined my head backward. "Behind me, parked at a table where she's hoping we won't notice her, is a rather attractive blonde about our age with a skimpy sundress on. Her name is Special Agent Lena Otenski, and she was one of them. Apparently we embarrassed them. She's been following me as well, but I think her agenda is somewhat different. She's almost approached me a few times."

"What the fuck is that about?" Brock asked.

I shook my head. "No idea. I'm just biding my time and waiting to see what happens."

"So how are you planning to get to the bottom of this?" Christine asked. "I assume that's why you're here."

I nodded. "I'll just do what I normally do. Hang around and piss people off until I get some answers."

"You got one part of that right," Brock said, smiling. "You sure do piss people off."

"Like I said before, everybody has to be good at something."

We ordered dinner and it arrived quickly. During the meal, we continued to get to know one another. Brock discussed some of the assignments he'd been on teaching third world nations how to fly the F-16. It seemed to be interesting work, and he apparently enjoyed it. He didn't mention any family except for a ne'er-do-well brother he left back in Chicago. Christine also discussed some of her assignments and some of the things she had learned on the Joint Staff. After three years at the Pentagon, she was excited to get back into the cockpit and be the Ops Group commander at Kunsan.

"Best assignment I had in the USAF was at Kunsan," I

told her. "Everyone there, even the SPs, was focused on the mission. They offered me a squadron commander slot there but things didn't work out."

"Why?" She asked. "Did you not want to go back?"

"I would have gone back in a heartbeat," I answered. "But things started to go bad while I was stationed here, and I just wanted to get out of the Air Force."

"Okay," Brock said. "This is the part I've been waiting for."

Christine shot him a harsh glance across the table.

"It's okay, Christine," I said. "I told Brock I'd tell him all about this."

I briefly recounted what I told Brock earlier about my earlier interaction with Tappan. Christine found my interaction with Tappan's stepdaughter equally humorous.

"You're a dog!" she said, laughing. "Oh my God, you're such a dog."

I shrugged. "You know what they say about dogs. You put a piece of meat in front of them enough times and eventually they'll eat it. No matter whom it belongs to."

"So what's this thing you were asking Tappan about in the steam room, T. C.?" Brock asked.

"That's a bit of a story," I said. "And a story requires Scotch."

I signaled the waitress and ordered three glasses of Glenmorangie Nectar D'Or. She brought it to the table quickly, and I watched her retreat, her well-formed ass overflowing from the skimpy lingerie bottom she was wearing.

"That's what apparently got you into this," Christine said as I returned my eyes to the table.

"Some of it, anyway," I said. "But before I tell you some more of my shit, I'd like to propose a toast." I raised my glass. "To new friends and new adventures!"

Christine and Brock raised their glasses in response, and we all downed a healthy quantity of the sweet, smooth fire of the Glenmorangie.

"I'm not a Scotch drinker, but this is good stuff!" Christine said.

"It's matured in dessert wine casks," I said. "Takes the edge off and almost gives it a sweet aftertaste."

"It is good stuff," Brock said. "But let's get back to the gossip. As I always say, 'If you don't have something good to say about someone, let's hear it.'"

"Okay," I said, sitting my glass on the table. "So here I am, at odds with Tappan over being his Ops O and banging his stepdaughter when this Kunsan opportunity comes along. The odds of me being a squadron commander at Luke weren't great, and I wasn't sure I wanted the job there anyway, too much bullshit to contend with. I told Tappan about the offer, and two days later, three armed Mexican gangbangers broke into my house."

Christine startled. "Oh my God!" she said. "What happened?"

I stared into the amber depths of my Scotch glass and watched the amazing liquid sparkle.

"They didn't make it out," I said.

Brock grinned. "Shotgun?" he asked.

I nodded. "Eighteen-inch Mossberg Persuader with a pistol grip and loaded with double-ought buckshot. I had to bring a professional crew in to clean up the mess. After the local cops and the OSI completed their investigation, of course."

"Ah hah," Christine said. "The OSI. The plot thickens."

I nodded. "Turns out it's not terribly politically correct to kill three Mexicans in a town where they comprise a major voting bloc. The Arizona Republic, which you would think is a conservative newspaper given the state's politics, is actually dominated by liberals, and they ran a front-page story about the attack and about me. And that's when the local OSI started probing into the Iraq business. The OSI det commander, a guy by the name of Alan Turnidge, interviewed me and told me he was going to see me tried as a war criminal and run out of the Air Force."

"Jesus," Brock said. "What a crock of crap! Those guys are imbeciles."

I nodded. "That's that happens when you create an organization where people get promoted based on how many of their fellow service members they screw over," I said. "But it didn't work out for him. There was no evidence and I didn't talk, so they had nothing. They had to drop everything. It totally pissed them off."

"So it ended okay?" Christine asked.

I shook my head. "Not exactly. As I was contemplating the Kunsan command slot, the OSI opened up a new investigation on me for allegedly using my work computer to do financial trading."

"What?" Brock asked. "That's pretty lame."

"It gets better," I said. "I wasn't even sitting in my office when most of the trades took place."

"So your computer was remoted," he said. "Damn. That's pretty fucking hard core."

"They meant business. And the irony is that when the OSI investigated, they refused to consider the fact that my computer had been remoted. They said it had to be me because it was my computer. Now this was several years ago and computers being hacked or remoted wasn't nearly as common as it is today, but they never even looked into it. They didn't even know it was possible."

"Nice," Brock said. "Real nice."

"Anyway, after all that bullshit, I just decided to retire. I didn't want any part of a service that would allow that to happen to me."

"Don't blame you," Christine said. "I guess I've led a

sheltered life."

"You haven't pissed anybody off enough yet," I told her. "Believe me. They play no favorites. Eventually you'll have to stand for something, and when you do, they'll kick your ass out. That's just the way it works."

"Amen," Brock said, taking another sip of his Scotch. "So what about this thing with Satan?"

I looked at him. "Well, guess who got the squadron commander nod when I passed on it?"

Brock looked back at me for a second and then the realization hit him. "His buddy that worked for you? No way!"

I nodded. "Don't you think the events and the timing are a little suspicious?"

"I guess," Brock said. "But how would Tappan have connections to Mexican gangbangers?"

"He does," I replied. "And I can't tell you why or how I know that, but he does. He definitely has connections now. I'm betting he did back then too."

"Jesus," he said.

"H. Christ," Christine added.

"So now maybe you can understand why Satan and I don't like each other very much," I said, then finished the last of the Scotch in my glass. "But there is one more piece in the puzzle that you probably need to know."

"There's more?" Christine asked. "I've run out of expletives!"

"When I was shot down in Iraq, I was leading a search and rescue mission to rescue a downed Viper pilot. Guess who his flight lead was?"

Brock shook his head. "No fucking way," he said.

"Yep," I replied. "Mark Tappan. And when they invited me for drinks after I was rescued myself, the wingman went out of his way to tell me what an idiot his flight lead had been for sticking their noses into that mess in the first place."

"That's how he knew the inside story on your escape," Christine said. "And he would have been the one who told the OSI about it."

"Shack," I said as I signaled the waitress over for another round. "Exactly. But let's not spend the entire night talking about my little Peyton Place here at Luke. The night is young and the Scotch is good!" I looked at Brock. "Perhaps you could enthrall us with some dark and mysterious tales of the third world, B-Rock."

"My pleasure," Brock laughed. "But it's going to take a lot more Scotch."

Chapter Nine

Contract Day Four
Saturday, June 26, 2010
2300 Hours Local Time
Third Base Bar and Grill
Goodyear, Arizona

Brock and Christine had called it a night, and I signaled young Miss Emily, our server, to the table so that I could settle our rather substantial check. With multiple rounds of good single malt, the damage accumulates quickly.

"You're leaving me?" she asked when she arrived, her lower lip extended in a pouty expression. Then she leaned against the bar-height table and rested her elbows on it. I couldn't help noticing that her ample breasts were resting on it as well. She watched my eyes go down quickly and back up again and smiled at me brightly. "I was just coming over to keep you company. Did your friends desert you?"

I nodded and adopted an expression of mock sorrow. "Happens to me all the time. Must be the effect I have on people."

She leaned closer to me and looked directly into my eyes. "I don't think that's the effect you'd have on me."

I smiled at her. "Oh really?" I asked. "And what kind of

effect might I have on a beautiful young thing like you?"

She reached out and put her hand on top of my forearm and slowly ran it up my arm. "I don't know... yet," she said, smiling mischievously. "But I'd sure like to find out. Mature guys like you just totally turn me on," she continued as she squeezed my bicep and released it. "You're never in a hurry, and you know how to treat a lady." She nodded in approval and allowed her hand to travel up my arm to my shoulder.

Part of me wanted to believe that this twenty-something beauty was yearning to bang my brains out. But the sensible part of me wasn't convinced. Whether it was the timing of her approach or the earnestness of it, there was something about it that didn't feel genuine to me. Of course the fact that I was close to twice her age brought a hearty dose of reality to the situation as well.

She snuggled closer to me. "Your body is nice and hard, Colin," she said. "And you've got this whole bad boy thing going on. We could have a lot of fun."

"I'm sure," I said, trying to keep the conversation light as I processed the fact that she knew my first name and yet had not seen my credit card.

"Is that a yes?" she said, seemingly delighted by my choice. She hugged me briefly and whispered heavily in my ear. "I don't normally ask customers out, but I just couldn't help myself with you." Then she kissed me lightly on the cheek and released me. "Can I bring you another Scotch while you wait? I'll be off in thirty minutes."

"I can't wait!" I said.

She smiled and made her way back to the bar. I watched her order the Scotch from the bartender and attend to her other tables.

"Beware of anyone who works for tips," I said to myself as I punched in the passcode for the BlackBerry and opened a text message screen to Dave Smith. "Just a question of time now," I murmured as I turned my eyes to the door.

And that's when they walked in. Three of them. They were somewhat clean cut, casually and fashionably dressed without overdoing it in jeans, boat shoes, and button-down shirts. They should have blended in just fine when they took their seats at a table near the door and ordered a round of drinks from the attractive blonde waitress in the red lingerie set who attended them. They should have looked just like all the other young to middle-aged men who populated a place like this on a Saturday night.

But two things gave them away. First, all three wore button-down shirts over T-shirts. While it wasn't an uncommon look, three guys in a trio all sporting the same style was highly unusual, unless, perhaps, they were gay and trying to make a statement. The fact that such a clothing set up was perfect for concealing a handgun, either in the waistband of the trousers or under an armpit made the coincidence of apparel even more suspect. But the main thing that gave them away was the eyes. They each had the old, cold, lifeless eyes of trained killers. I knew the look a mile away. It was the same gaze I saw in the mirror every morning.

I smiled to myself. It was perfect. Use the hot waitress as bait; lure the clueless middle-aged guy to the parking lot, maybe even get him a little worked up, and that's when the crew takes him.

I typed the text message to Smith.

HIT CREW HERE AT THIRD BASE BAR. THREE MEN PROBABLY WITH HANDGUNS ONLY. BAIT IS WAITRESS NAMED EMILY. H-HOUR IN ABOUT 30 MIN. YOU HAVE TEAM CLOSE?

As I waited for the reply, I gazed across the bar at the OSI crew. They continued to avoid making eye contact with me and appeared to be oblivious to the three assassins seated mere feet from them.

Par for the course, I thought.

As I was looking in that direction, I saw Emily stop by the table where the three assassins were sitting, ostensibly asking them if they needed anything but undoubtedly informing them that she'd been successful at luring me to leave with her. There were smiles and laughs all around as she left the table, and I imagined they were enjoying the thought of a middle-aged man actually thinking that a girl half his age would be interested in him. A smile crossed my faces as I thought of Sarah, at one time a monthly mistress for Bachelor magazine, and the bevy of centerfold beauties who had been at my side while I recovered from the ejection injuries several months ago.

If only they knew.

The BlackBerry vibrated. TEAM INBOUND. ETA 25 MIN. GET HER TO TAKE YOU OUT THE BACK.

WILCO, I responded.

There's nothing like sitting around and waiting to be led to your own death. It wasn't an unfamiliar feeling for me, unfortunately, but that didn't make it any less disconcerting. This was the second time in less than a week that I was performing my designated function as bait for Miguel or his minions; and while the circumstances seemed to be more controlled this time, I couldn't say I was more comfortable with it. I didn't know if the three crew members seated nearby knew about the fate of their predecessors; but if they did, there had to be a hell of a lot more firepower waiting outside. I just hoped the ops team from the CIA had the area sufficiently scoped out or the impending engagement might end up being a disaster.

I watched the clock on the BlackBerry's time display click by as I waited for Emily's shift to end and for our trip to the parking lot. I had time to watch a few moments of a baseball game as well as catch snippets of the lives of those around me as they talked, laughed, and drank. I found myself wondering what a normal life would be like—one with friends, family, someone to go home to, and no one trying to kill me. I couldn't decide if such a life was enticing or boring.

I felt pressure on my arm about the same time as her perfume reached my nostrils and her voice landed in my ears.

"Okay honey," she said. "I'm off! Let's go!"

I looked at Emily's face and took in the beauty that resided there. Her fair skin was unlined and her brown eyes were deep and soulful. A casual observer might have looked at her and seen youthful wonder and inexperience. But to those of us who knew what to look for, the signs of something deeper, something darker were there. There was knowledge behind the shining eyes and a sense of power that resonated in her demeanor. She was a woman used to getting men to do what she wanted them to do, and I had the distinct feeling that I wasn't the first man she had led to a rendezvous that didn't work out well for him. I searched her face for some kind of sadness or regret. I didn't find it.

Good, I thought. *That will make this easier.*

She pressed herself against me, and I used that opportunity to acquaint her with the business end of the Colt Commander, which I had surreptitiously freed from its holster and concealed under my napkin. I pulled her to me with my left arm and placed the muzzle of the pistol directly between her ample breasts. To those around us, the weapon was nearly invisible, hidden from view by the angle of our bodies, the height of the bar table and position of my hand. She looked down at my hand and the pistol and her eyes widened when she saw the hammer was cocked.

"Pretty noisy in here tonight, isn't it?" I asked her.

She looked up at my face, down at the pistol again, and back at my face. Her face became very pale. She nodded slowly.

"I'm not sure how much you know about guns," I said. "But don't let the small size of this one fool you. It shoots a big bullet that will do a lot of damage to your insides and probably won't exit your body."

I looked around the room. The OSI guys were still avoiding eye contact, Lena Otenski was nowhere to be seen, and the three-man team had exited the building. *Surprise, surprise.*

"Funny thing about the sound of a pistol shot," I continued, keeping my tone conversational, "to people who have never heard a real one, their ears won't process the noise as a gunshot unless they actually see the weapon fire. And with the ambient noise in this room, the volume on the TVs, and the fact that your boobs will muffle the noise, if I pull this trigger, there will be a sound no one recognizes coming from a direction they probably won't be able to identify."

It was my turn to look into her eyes. I froze the smile on my face.

"You'll be dead in a fraction of a second, and I'll pretend you fainted. I'll carry you out of here, toss you into a dumpster out back, and be home in time to catch the end of the game. Nobody will miss you for days."

She was trembling slightly now. I could feel it as I pulled her against me.

"Please, mister," she said, apparently forgetting my name in the stress of the situation, "I have a kid."

Her eyes were moist and her lower lip was quivering. She was either a highly skilled actress or this was the first time she had been faced with the possible consequences of her actions. I looked at her and marveled at her naiveté.

"Do you have any idea what kind of people you're dealing with?"

"They were friends of my boyfriend," she said, her voice cracking slightly. "They just said they needed to talk to you about some money you owed them."

Freelancers, I thought. *Local freelancers. You guys have no idea what you're up against.*

"I'm not sure how much of that is true," I said, transforming my face into a mask of stone, "because I'm positive this isn't the first time you've done this sort of thing. But it's important you understand something." I pulled her more tightly against me and against the Colt. I lifted the muzzle of the weapon up slightly so that the blade of the front sight dug into the flesh on the underside of her left breast. I felt her stiffen. "You need to understand that I'll kill you without thinking twice about it," I hissed at her. "I'll kill you if you don't do exactly what I say exactly when I say it." I moved my face a little closer to hers. "Do you get that?"

She nodded a few times, very rapidly.

I looked into her eyes more deeply. "But do you believe it?" I asked.

"Yes," she replied at once. The word was almost a gasp.

"So was the plan for you to take me to either your car or my car? In the parking lot?"

"Your car," she said. "I had to pretend mine was broken."

"So they're waiting for us out front," I said.

"Yes," she answered. "In a van left of the entrance."

The BlackBerry on the table vibrated

"Pick it up and read what it says," I told her.

Emily reached for the device with a quivering left hand and read the incoming message. "It says 'In position.'"

I nodded. "I want you to type a response."

"Okay," she said, her voice barely above a whisper. "What do I need to say?"

I put my head very close to hers so that it looked like I was whispering into her ear. "Type this: 'Hostiles in van left of front entrance. Probably local freelance.'"

Emily's hands began to shake even more as she typed. When she was finished she nearly threw the BlackBerry back onto the bar table, like it was a repulsive insect.

"Not so fast," I said, holding her against me. "He's going to respond."

The BlackBerry vibrated a moment later.

"Pick it up and read it," I told her.

She reached for the device again and held it with her thumb and forefinger. "'Message received,'" she read. "Use emergency exit in back. Will cut power remotely in forty-five seconds."

I nodded at her. "Perfect," I said. "Looks like we're going out the back."

Emily looked at me as if I was an alien invader. "Who are you?" she asked. "Who are these people?" She motioned with the BlackBerry.

"The big leagues," I said, "unlike your three friends." I rose to my feet, keeping Emily against me. "We've got less than forty-five seconds," I said. "And we're going to stay nice and close like this. If anyone starts shooting at me, I promise you'll be the first one to die."

"They're not going to shoot you, mister," she said, her voice just above a whisper. "They just want to talk to you."

I looked into her eyes again and could see no trace of fabrication there. She actually believed what she was saying. God help her.

We walked arm in arm quickly toward the door, working our way between tables as we did so and attracting some odd glances along the way. I hid the Colt between my left bicep and my body but kept it pressed into her side as we walked. It made our gait a little awkward but we arrived at the door in a few minutes.

"But won't the alarm go off if we go through this door?" Emily whimpered.

"Nope," I answered.

A few seconds later, the restaurant went completely dark. I

quickly pushed the bar to open the door and maneuvered the two of us through it. We stepped into the parking lot behind the restaurant, and I pushed the door closed behind us. It had no sooner closed and locked when the building's emergency exterior lights came on.

"Oh my God," Emily whispered. "Those people actually cut the power! How did they do that?"

I ignored her and blinked once or twice as my eyes adjusted to the combination of illumination and darkness. The door where we had exited was about thirty feet away from the kitchen entrance, and I could make out the walled enclosure of a dumpster beyond the kitchen at the far corner of the building. There was a shaded sitting area with a table and chairs about ten feet behind the restaurant and even with the kitchen door. I moved us toward the sitting area so that we could get out of the exterior light illumination and I could text Smith and determine what was happening out front. As we approached the table a few moments later and the detail in the sitting area became visible, I saw the glow of a cigarette and the shadow of the person smoking it seated at the table. The shadow began to move.

"What are you doing with my girl, gabacho?" he asked, rising from his seat.

Gabacho? That doesn't sound good.

I freed the Colt from Emily's body, let it drop to my right side, and concealed it behind my right thigh.

"Carlos! No!" Emily yelled across the few yards between him and us. "He has a gun!"

"Si," Carlos replied as he rounded the table and came toward us. "But so do I. And I bet that old man isn't ready to use his."

He began to raise his right arm, and I could see the glint of light off of a large shiny automatic pistol of some sort.

Before last Monday, I probably would have raised my

weapon to the ready position and tried to talk the young man out of what he was doing. I would have given him some slight benefit of the doubt that maybe he didn't really want to try to kill someone he'd never met and that in doing so he'd lose the opportunity for a full life. But after last Monday, I was in full alert mode. And I was fresh out of good nature and trust where young men with guns were concerned.

I raised the Colt and sighted in on the center of the guy's chest.

"Freeze!" I heard a male voice behind me scream at a timbre that sounded like it was an octave or two above normal for the person projecting it. "Federal agents!"

"Get on your knees!" Another voice shouted. "Hands on your head. Do it now!"

Federal agents, eh? I thought. If they had been FBI or DEA, they would have identified themselves as such. The fact that they said "federal agents" could mean only one thing—they were OSI.

So now I had a nervous potential shooter in front of me and two nervous potential shooters in back of me. I was in a bullet sandwich—a human cross-fire zone.

Perfect, I thought. *Fucking perfect.*

For just a moment, I felt myself transported outside the situation I was in—as if I was viewing it from outside myself, looking down. I could see Carlos's pistol in his hand, trembling, in spite of his bravado, as he pointed it toward me. I could see the two agents behind me, both with their government-issued Berettas out and swinging back and forth from Emily to me and to Carlos, their tiny brains trying to decide on a target but not able to determine who was the greatest threat.

And then there was me, in the middle as always, a gun pointed at me from the front and two pointed at me from the rear. I could almost envision the question mark suspended in air above my head. This was definitely a situation that hadn't been covered in training. I had no idea what to do. If I shot Carlos, the OSI agents would probably open fire. And given the mediocre marksmanship that typified most active duty Air Force personnel and the adrenaline that was undoubtedly pumping in their veins, only God knew where the rounds they fired would land. And if Carlos shot first, a very similar scenario would occur. For just a moment, the training I had experienced didn't kick in and provide me the usual alternatives. I stood there, indecisive, reactive, looking for a cue to guide my response. Even though my finger was alongside the Colt's trigger guard, I could sense the grooved metal of the trigger calling for my right index finger, almost bidding me to target it and fire it, as if it was hungry for something to shoot.

The situation was a stalemate. And for a few very pregnant seconds, the tension grew. The air, already growing heavier with the humidity of the coming monsoon season, seemed to become even weightier, and even more laden with anticipation. I had a brief mental image of dominos all lined up in a pattern that led to nowhere and teetering in anticipation of their expected fall.

And then, almost inevitably, something happened to set things into motion.

"No!" Emily screamed. "Don't kill him!" She came alive in my arms, squirming against me and pushing against me as hard as she could.

At that exact moment, Carlos fired his weapon. I presumed he was aiming at me but apparently, like most people on the wrong side of the law, he'd never had marksmanship practice and his single shot careened off into the darkness. Almost immediately there were answering shots from behind Emily and me. I grabbed her and pulled her to the ground, but as I did, I heard a dull thud come from the back of her head, and

I felt the impact of liquid spray and small bits of hard matter on my left cheek. The fall to the ground took a mere fraction of a second, but it was a lifetime for Emily. She was limp in my arms before she hit the concrete.

The guns behind me continued to fire again and again. There were so many shots, I lost count.

I watched Carlos stagger back under the impact of multiple slugs, although far fewer hit him than I expected. As I watched, a hole appeared in his throat, just below his jawline and arterial blood spurted out under high pressure, in rhythm with his heartbeat. In moments, his white shirt was stained in so many places it almost looked like a bizarre designer pattern. He backed into one of the uprights supporting the roof of the seating area and slowly sat down as the rounds continued to tear into the wood and pavement around him. And then his ass hit the cement and he breathed a long, tired breath as the last air left his lungs. His chin came to rest on his chest, and his weapon clattered to the concrete.

And behind me, almost as one, I heard the telltale sound of two slides on two pistols locking open as the two magazines ran dry. Suddenly, with no warning at all, the rage seized me. I was on my feet, Colt in hand in a second, and I turned to face the two OSI agents. Without thinking, without feeling, I raised the weapon, sighted in on the center of mass of the agent nearest me and pressed the trigger. The small gun barked in my hand and 200 grains of .45 ACP departed the muzzle at 800 feet per second and nearly half a ton of energy. The force of the round lifted him from his feet and propelled him to the concrete, even more dramatically than a similar shot from a bad action movie. The second agent, who seemed very young, fumbled with the magazine he was trying to reload into his pistol, saw me pivot to engage him and dropped both magazine and pistol to make a run for it. He made it about two steps before I shot him in the middle of the back. He too was propelled off his feet by the .45 round and onto the pavement. He landed a few feet beyond his companion.

I walked over to them and looked down at them. They were each trying to gather their breath. It took everything I had not to put a coup de grace shot into their heads.

"We're done out front," I head a familiar voice say from behind me. "They're on their way to a place to be ID'd and interrogated. Then they'll be disposed of." He stepped up alongside me and looked down at the two OSI agents. Out of the corner of my eye, I could see the smirk on his face as he surveyed the men writhing on the ground before us.

"What a mess," he said. "Who shot who?"

"The blood-covered Hispanic guy in the gazebo over there fired a round that didn't hit anything and these two idiots opened up and emptied their magazines at him."

"Can't say I blame them for that," Smith said, "although they don't appear to have hit him that many times."

"One of the rounds they fired killed the girl who led me out here," I said. "Because these fucks have no experience, no trigger discipline, and can't hit the broadside of a barn door."

"That sucks," Smith said. "Collateral damage is a big no-no for real federal agents these days." He looked at me and gestured to the two men on the ground. "So did you put them down?"

I nodded.

"How did you know they were wearing Kevlar vests?" he asked.

I looked over at him as I holstered the .45.

"I didn't," I said.

Chapter Ten

Contract Day Six
Monday, June 28, 2010
1300 Hours Local Time
Southern F-16 Academic Building
Luke Air Force Base, Arizona

I probably should have expected it. You can't shoot two OSI agents without consequences, even if they deserved it and weren't seriously injured. Maybe since an entire day had passed, I thought perhaps they'd be too embarrassed to make an issue of it. But that's the one thing about OSI people. They're not smart enough to be embarrassed.

I had just come back from lunch and had been planning on a few minutes alone in our classroom to review some of the material we had been taught. They cornered me as I came through the academic building's glass doors. There were two of them, of course. One was a dark-haired, mousey-looking guy with glasses, about four inches shorter than I was. The other was a female. She was very intense looking in a black pantsuit and short, cropped hair that looked like she had cut it herself in the bathroom mirror.

"Colonel Pearce," the female said. "I'm Special Agent Lorna Dahlke." She flashed me her credentials in a poor imitation of the manner in which I had seen both CIA and FBI agents display them. "We'd like to ask you a few questions."

This was the agent Thomas had spoken to before he met his death on the fateful day. I fought to keep my face neutral and turned to the mousy one.

"And you?" I asked. "Aren't you going to show me yours too? I think I'm entitled to see it."

Almost reluctantly, he reached inside his coat and produced the standard black credential wallet, taking great pains to keep his right hand free. Apparently, he felt like he might need to have access to his weapon. According to his ID, his name was John Johnson. I wondered if he was as unimaginative has his parents had been.

"Calm down," I told him. "I'm not going to hurt you. Yet."

A brief spark of either hate or fear flashed in his eyes. I couldn't tell which and it didn't matter. I smiled at him.

"Colonel Pearce," Agent Dahlke said, "we need you to step into the conference room." She motioned toward an open door down the hallway.

"Okay," I said. "But my class starts in ten minutes, and I'm going to be in it when it does."

Dahlke kept a noncommittal expression on her face and continued to motion toward the door. I shrugged and walked through it, with her and Johnson at my back.

The room was standard USAF with a government-issued wood table, pictures of former squadron commanders on the walls, and the usual uncomfortable lowest-bidder chairs around it. I had spent time in several similar rooms back in the day. As the mouse shut the door behind us, I naturally turned toward the sound and saw, to my somewhat mild surprise that we had an additional attendee in our little meeting.

Seated in the corner of the room was Mark Tappan with a satisfied smirk on his face.

"Well, isn't this cozy," I said as I sat down. I made a show of looking at my watch. "You've got nine minutes."

"Colonel Pearce," Dahlke began, adopting a tone I'm sure she thought was intimidating, "you are a subject in an investigation." Two of our agents were shot on Saturday night behind the Third Base Bar and Grill in Goodyear and our information—"

I interrupted her. "Would these be the two agents that killed a young girl in the middle of an unnecessary shoot out?"

"Our information indicates..." Dahlke was sputtering somewhat. Apparently she wasn't used to being interrupted.

"My knowledge is a little rusty," I continued, "but as I recall, the Beretta 92SF holds 15 rounds of 9 millimeter, right? And these two agents emptied their weapons, that's about 30 rounds, at a single target without a clear line of fire, killing an innocent civilian in the process. Does that about sum it up?"

Dahlke raised her voice. "Our information indicates you were—"

"I wonder what the headline might be in the Arizona Republic or maybe even in the USA Today?" I said as I sat back in my chair and regarded the ceiling. "'Overzealous Air Force Agents Kill Young Mother in Botched Arrest Attempt?' Or maybe incompetent Air Force Agents?" I crossed my arms and regarded the well-worn ceiling tiles above me. "I can see it now, on the opening monologue of every national newscast in the country. Great publicity for you guys."

"Pearce, we have you—" Dahlke was practically screaming now.

I looked at her bemusedly. "You don't have shit," I said, "because if you did, I would have been in handcuffs on Saturday night. I've been in my quarters, on base, since then and you knew that. You need me to admit to something so you can detain me. And after my last experience with you guys years ago, I'll never talk to you without a lawyer present again." I rose to my feet. "Now if you'll excuse me," I said, "I have a class to get to."

"You can't leave until we say you can leave," Dahlke spat.

"Are you going to arrest me?" I asked. "Please do." I held my wrists out to her. "I'll be out in minutes, and you know who I'll call with my one shot at the phone."

Dahlke's face clouded with anger. It occurred to me then that even with the chopped, pixie haircut and the intensity of her features, she was actually an attractive woman. I've made a strict practice of addressing women professionally in the work environment, but I decided that it might be time to make an exception for no other reason than to piss her off.

"You're kind of cute when you're angry, honey," I said, lightly patting her on the shoulder as I walked around her to the door. "We can talk again if you have anything you want to act on."

"Who were the guys in the parking lot, Pearce?" Satan's spoke, his nasal voice hissing from across the room.

So that's what this is about.

"Who?" I asked, trying to maintain a blank expression.

"The guys in black. The guys who met you there after..." he stopped speaking suddenly, as if he was afraid he'd say something revealing.

"No idea," I answered, shaking my head. "Didn't see anyone myself." I winked at him. "Maybe they were good Samaritans."

Satan jumped to his feet. "You have to turn in that goddamned gun, Pearce!" he commanded. "You can't have a gun on my base."

Where did that come from? Hmmm.

"Gun?" I asked, trying to sound incredulous and not sarcastic. It was a struggle. "What gun?"

"The .45 automatic that you shot my two agents with, Pearce," Dahlke said as she turned to face me with acid in her voice. Apparently I wasn't worthy of basic military courtesy any longer.

"Ah," I said. "And these would be the two agents who killed an innocent girl in a fusillade of poorly aimed pistol fire in a public place who would have everything to gain by fabricating a story to cover their asses?"

Dahlke's mouth opened for a moment but no words came out.

"You guys are your own worst enemy," I said. "You can't do shit here and it's your own fault. Reminds me of a similar time several years ago."

The room was silent for several seconds. Satan quivered in the corner but didn't speak. Dahlke stared at me with daggers in her eyes. The mouse stared at me as well, his hand on his belt, apparently itching to draw his weapon. I smiled at him and issued him an unspoken challenge.

Anytime, pal.

"Very well," I said at last. "We're through here." I went through the door and turned around. "So your two agents apparently lived through the encounter they had?" I asked Dahlke.

She nodded, the fire still in her gaze.

"Kevlar vests protected them?"

She nodded again.

"So apparently their assailant didn't aim at their heads."

Her eyes narrowed. "No," she said. "He didn't."

I turned my face to stone and sent some fire of my own her way. "He won't make that mistake again."

Chapter Eleven

Contract Day Seven
Tuesday, June 29, 2010
1900 Hours Local Time
Wright Bar
Arizona Biltmore Hotel
Phoenix, Arizona

The Arizona Biltmore was a landmark in Phoenix and an expression of the architectural style of the legendary Frank Lloyd Wright. Called "The Jewel of the Desert" when it opened in 1929, the original structure was built with over two hundred thousand Biltmore blocks, designed and poured on-site, which gave the hotel a distinct look that was unlike any other I'd ever visited. While stationed at Luke years ago, I had stayed at the place a few times, partially to escape the barrenness of the west side of the Valley of the Sun in the sumptuousness of the east side. But I also frequented the Biltmore to enjoy the feminine company of a few different members of the Luke AFB population—some of whom were enlisted, some of whom were married, and some of whom were both. My current visit was for other reasons, but I still took time to enjoy the view as I drove up to the hotel's main entrance. The tan, geometrically interconnected blocks were still visible in the facade, and the place still looked every bit as modern as it must have eighty years ago.

I left the car with the valet and strode through the sumptuous lobby and into the Wright Bar, looking for the people I was there to meet. The bar was everything a bar should be, with rich woods, comfortable chairs, a wall full of nearly every liquor imaginable, and formally dressed wait staff. I looked the well-dressed crowd over quickly and didn't find the faces I was looking for. Then I noticed the doors to the Squaw Peak Terrace at the back of the room and headed that way. I was glad that I had changed out of my flightsuit and into a pair of casual slacks and a shirt.

I walked out onto the terrace and once again scanned the faces. The two I was looking for had a table all to themselves on the far left side. The terrace was outside, but the combination of shade and water misters kept the temperature quite pleasant in spite of the prevailing 100–110 degree temperatures of the desert air. And the views of the surrounding mountains were inspiring enough to make anyone do without the generic comfort of air conditioning.

"Gentlemen," I said as neared the table, "sorry I'm a little late, but the crosstown traffic is murder this time of day."

John Amrine and Dave Smith looked up and nodded back at me.

"He missed it," Smith said, inclining his head toward his partner. "He flew a company jet into the Scottsdale airport and missed all of it."

"We need to get the Agency to issue us helicopters at some point, Dave," I said as I sat down. "Our drive time has to be worth something."

"I've got a better idea," Amrine said. "We'll issue you guys jetpacks, like James Bond used to have."

"Wow," I said. "That'd be awesome. Do they actually work?"

"As far as you know," he said, grinning.

A cocktail waitress, clad in an earth-toned dress that hugged her curved body splendidly, sidled up and took my drink order and then disappeared as quickly as she had come. Smith and Amrine seemed to be engrossed in something, so I took the opportunity to ease back into my well-cushioned chair and simply watch the world go by. The hotel had made a name for itself catering to "the beautiful people" over the years, and from the clientele that was within visual range of me, it was continuing to live up to that aspect of its history. Here on the terrace and on the grounds below, designer clothes, tanned legs, and toned bodies abounded. I smiled to myself as I remembered a woman with whom I'd a fiery affair many years ago while I was attending the Army Command and General Staff College at Fort Leavenworth, Kansas, just outside of Kansas City. She had come to visit me at Luke Air Force Base while I was getting recurrent in the F-16 after my tour at the college was over, and we'd shared several days and nights roaming the very grounds. While I wasn't sure what contribution I had made to the scenery at the time, with her model-like body, long, brown hair, and expressive brown eyes, she had definitely been at home in this playground of the beautiful.

"Your martini, sir," the waitress startled me from my reverie as she sat the drink on the table in front of me. The gin was cloudy with ice crystals, just the way I liked it.

"It looks great," I said. "Put it on their tab." I nodded toward Smith and Amrine.

"Already taken care of, sir."

"Thanks."

My eyes were naturally drawn to her superb ass as she walked away. And as my eyes followed her, they found a familiar face nursing a drink at a table on the other side of the terrace. OSI Special Agent Lena Otenski smiled back at me from across the tiled floor. She was wearing yet another sundress. This one was plain white, and it accented her tan skin exceptionally well. She looked good enough to eat, but the fact that she was even there was disturbing.

"Well, shit," I said to no one in particular.

"It's no big deal," Amrine said without looking up from the paperwork he and Smith were examining. "We know she's here. One of our teams picked her up shortly after you left Luke."

"And I thought I was being so careful," I said. "I didn't see anyone tailing me all the way over here. And that's quite a drive."

"She probably planted a GPS tracker on your car somewhere," Smith said. "She wouldn't have had to follow closely at all. In fact, she could have stayed back several miles."

"I wonder what the hell she wants. After the incident at the bar over the weekend, my other OSI tails seem to have gone away. She just seems to stick around. I've see her everywhere: in the bar my first night on base, in restaurants and bars where I've gone to eat, at the club on base when I've been having lunch. Fucking everywhere!"

"She's probably trying to figure out what you're doing here to vindicate herself to her boss," Amrine said calmly.

"Vindicate herself for what?" I asked.

"She and the other agent, Shaw, I think his name was, were suspended after we took General Barnett away from them," he said.

"Which embarrassed her boss rather thoroughly, especially considering she and Shaw were part of a special team of agents who work directly for the OSI Commander," Smith added.

"Whoa. She works directly for the OSI Commander?" I asked, incredulous. "When were you planning on telling me that?"

"Tonight actually," Amrine said as he closed the file and

took a sip of the red wine in front of him. "It's one of the reasons we asked you here, among others." He leaned back in his chair and brushed a lock of his surfer-blond hair out of his eyes. "You know, eventually she's going to try to make contact. When she does, you should humor her. We might learn something."

I snorted. "Me, humor the OSI. That'll be the day."

Amrine shook his head slightly. "I don't think this is about the OSI for her. I think it's about something else." He looked at me as he lifted his glass again. "Put your prejudice aside and listen to what she has to say, Colin. Okay? We're in the intelligence gathering mode now."

"Fair enough," I sighed. "I'll do my best."

"Your best might require some physical interaction," he said with a smirk on his face. "You've had a pretty good track record getting information out of women in a horizontal orientation."

I thought of Sarah for a moment but nodded my head in resignation. "If it comes to that, I'll play along. There's not much use in being faithful to someone I'll probably never see again."

Amrine nodded, apparently satisfied. "So," he said, "tell us what you know and we'll do the same."

"You know everything I know," I said. "And while it confirms a lot, it isn't much. There hasn't been time to find out anything else. Today was day four of the syllabus. We've had a lot of academic classes and an orientation tour of the 310th, but we haven't spent much time there. Tomorrow though, I've got two device training events, both of which will be done in the squadron. I should be able to poke around then."

"Do you know if the F-35 is still there?" Smith asked quietly.

"I don't," I said. "But wouldn't you guys find out about that before I did?"

"Not necessarily," Amrine answered. "It depends on what assets we have in place and what channels that sort of news would go through."

"Wow," I said. "I thought you guys could get your hands on whatever you wanted to."

"In most cases we can," Smith said. "But when other US governmental agencies, like the USAF, are involved, things can get tedious. And when there are military and civilian people in the chain who could lose face if the wrong information is conveyed at the wrong time, it gets even more complicated."

"Anyway," Amrine said, impatiently, "we need you to find out if the F-35 is still there, as soon as you can."

I nodded. "I'll do it tomorrow. I wanted to get a look at the thing anyway." I looked back and forth between the two of them. Both of them had grim expressions on their faces. "What are you not telling me about this?" I asked.

"Our friend in Mexico has been very busy," Amrine said. "Very busy indeed. Seems like the factories and warehouse space he bought around Mexico City have been filling up with several thousand crates and several thousand people, only some of which are Mexican."

"So to the untrained eye," Smith continued, "it looks like he's just adding jobs to the economy of Mexico City. But to trained eyes, like ours, it looks like something else entirely."

"And that would be?"

"Staging," Amrine answered flatly, "for military operations. We've done it ourselves in other places. Several times."

I processed his words for a few moments before the obvious answer occurred to me. "It's a coup," I said in quiet realization. "That's the reason he has factories all around the city. He's got the presidential palace and the capital surrounded."

"We agree," Smith said. "And there's no way he can fund it all himself these days. After the foiled attempts on the presidents last fall, we've been working the DEA to put the screws to him. We know that his cash coffers are at an all-time low."

"Which is why he's got the Chinese involved and why we need to know about that damn F-35," Amrine added. "As you deduced, it's the only way Miguel can pay them. So if we want to continue to enjoy the friendship of the people of Mexico, we need to take action. No F-35, no payment. No payment, no coup."

I took a sip of my martini and enjoyed the sensation of the crisp, ice-cold gin oozing down my throat. "Could Mexico really be that much worse with Miguel in charge?" I asked after a moment or two. "It's already a mess. He might actually clean it up a bit."

"You're a historian, Colin," Amrine said. "How often have leaders who were used to absolute power, in this case, the power of a drug lord, transitioned well to democratic leadership positions?"

I thought about the question, but the answer was obvious. "Never," I said.

"Exactly," he replied. "So with events moving at an increased pace down south and the Chinese investing more money, odds are very high they're going to want their prize sooner rather than later."

I nodded. "Yeah, I guess they will."

Smith regarded me for a moment as he took a healthy drink of his wine. "So after this weekend, what's your verdict about Tappan?" Smith asked. "Is he in on it?"

"No question," I said, "for multiple reasons. First, he attempted to rough Brock and me up in the steam room. Then Brock mentions we'll be at the Third Base Bar and Grill that night and there happens to be a hit team and the required bait in place? If nothing else, that confirms the communications link to Miguel. That hit team at the restaurant on Saturday night was just a little too well planned to be a pop-up contingency."

Smith and Amrine both nodded. "Something else we agree on," Smith said.

I paused for a second to take another healthy sip of my excellent martini. "But there's more. The first night I was in town, he tried to threaten me into admitting I was working for you guys. He seemed very nervous about me being there. Yesterday he tried to get me to say something that would give the OSI an excuse to apprehend me, and then he tried to get me to admit I knew about the team you guys sent to Third Base."

Smith smiled. "Miguel has told him what you can do," he said. "That would make anybody nervous. And after Saturday night, he's seen an example."

"No doubt he told Tappan that if you fuck things up it will be the general's head," Amrine added.

"He's also probably been promised a nice little payoff for all of this, so I'm sure that he doesn't want anything to spoil it," Smith said. "People get crazy when money gets involved, particularly when it's a lot of money." He looked at Amrine. "I'm thinking the bodyguards work for Miguel?"

Amrine nodded. "It would make sense."

"No doubt about it actually," I said, looking over at them. "I saw the goons' tattoos in the steam room. Los Diablos."

"Damn it," Smith said, tapping his pen on the table in an irregular beat. "Those guys keep showing up everywhere—Dallas and now here."

"Don't forget about nine years ago at my house in Avondale," I said. "And there's no doubt Tappan sent them, which means..." I gave them a minute or two to make the connection.

"Jesus," Amrine said after a moment. "That means he might have been in contact with Miguel even then."

"Bingo," I said. "The extent to which they interacted would

seem to be an unknown but the fact that they knew each other is not." I sighed and drank a little more of the cold gin. The hint of lime flavor in the alcohol made it refreshing in the hot desert air. "And yet, even with that link, the team at the restaurant wasn't composed of Miguel's men, they were local freelancers," I said. "So it seems Miguel's forces up here are somewhat limited. Not that it makes a big difference who is tasked to do the shooting." I twirled the cold stem of my glass. "Of course, it also doesn't help that because of the syllabus, everyone knows exactly where I am and where I'll be while I'm on the base. And now they know I'm armed, although Tappan and the OSI tried to get me to admit that too."

Amrine took a sip of his wine. "Odds are high they'll try again," he said. "Although I think he'll keep using contract labor. He's got other things demanding his attention and resources at the moment."

"Great," I said as I took another sip of my drink. "Hey, change of subject. Were you guys able to get any intel on the two other students in my class?"

Smith nodded. "I could forward you pdf copies of their personnel records but that would probably bore you. Here's the gist. The female, Christine Billings, is on what appears to be the USAF's standard fast-track-to-general program, although it seems that she might actually deserve it. She's highly thought of by both superiors and subordinates. The bottom line is that she's a generic and typical USAF officer. She has a few personal issues that are really none of our business but other than that, no surprises there at all."

I nodded. "And B-Rock?"

"A somewhat different story. He's a former Chicagoland gangbanger and Air Force Academy graduate, class of 1990. He was a varsity swimmer and wrestler. Attended the underwater demolition team orientation course one summer while he was still at the academy and got a waiver to attend the US Army Ranger School a few years later when he was assigned to be an air liaison officer for a ranger battalion. He's fluent in Spanish, French, Portuguese, Russian, and Arabic. He's spent a lot of time in his career in black assignments, no pun intended, teaching people how to fly the Viper who shouldn't have it."

"That would explain why he has time in all the various blocks and models of the jet," I mused. "Boy did that piss Tappan off. Someone has more experience than he does. And, more pointedly, someone he's never heard of."

"Of course he hasn't," Amrine said with a wry smile. "It's difficult to develop a rep in a particular fighter community when you don't spend a lot of time in the mainstream or when you work for others from time to time."

I sat back in my chair and just shook my head in amazement as I looked at the two of them.

"Oh my God, he's one of yours."

"Sort of. We tried to recruit him a while back, but he preferred to stay in the USAF. We do borrow him periodically and he seems to like the work."

"And since he doesn't have any family to speak of, he comes without any of the typical strings," Smith chimed in. "Sort of like you."

"So did you guys work him into the class at the last minute to be my backup?" I asked.

Amrine shook his head. "Not at all. Seems to be pure coincidence that he's here, although we knew he was going to be. But his ability to assist may be limited. We need to keep his credentials intact so he can get to his next assignment without getting burned. In addition to his other duties at SOCOM, he'll be our eyes inside the command, which is a pretty big deal since we've never really had that before."

I nodded. "Well, I'm used to working alone."

"Oh that doesn't mean he won't help anyway," Amrine

said, shaking his head.

I looked at them quizzically.

"We'd certainly prefer that he keep a low profile and play along. But he doesn't listen to us sometimes. He freelances from time to time in spite of the fact that it's forbidden and illegal. All because," he looked me directly in the eyes, "he likes a good fight."

I smiled back at him and finished the last of my martini. "I've seen him in action, and I'll vouch for that." I set the glass down on the table. "Are we done here, gentlemen?"

Amrine looked at his watch. "We are," he said. "I have to be back in DC tonight. Dave will stay on site here. Send us an email when you see the F-35. Don't wait a moment. Send us an email right away."

I nodded. "Wilco."

"Colin," Smith said, "one last thing. We wanted to give you something that might even the odds." He handed me a briefcase next to his feet. "You can check this out when you get back to your room. You should probably take it with you everywhere. There are still a lot of independent contractors who'd like to collect the ten million dollars on your head."

I took the case from him while shaking my head in amazement. "Holy shit! I never thought I'd be worth that much. How come I haven't had a veritable stampede of people trying to kill me?"

"Because," Amrine said, "Miguel insists on interviewing anyone who wants to attempt the contract. From what we're hearing, the interview process is apparently pretty grueling, particularly for those who aren't selected."

"Oh really? What happens to them?" I asked.

"He kills them. It would seem our friend doesn't want any cowboys coming after you without his approval. And he doesn't seem to tolerate failure either."

"Wow," I said, taking the case and rising to leave, "I guess the local leader of the group that tried on Saturday night isn't long for this world then."

"He was found this morning," Amrine said, "in the swimming pool behind his house. Or at least part of him was."

I looked at him quizzically.

"They took his head," Amrine said.

"And knowing Miguel," Smith added. "It's probably on a spike somewhere."

"The guy has style," I said. "Medieval style but style nonetheless."

Smith nodded with a grim expression on his face. "Keep that in mind," he said.

Chapter Twelve

Contract Day Eight
Wednesday, June 30, 2010
1500 Hours Local Time
310th Fighter Squadron
Luke Air Force Base, Arizona

"And that wraps up the first UTD session, Colonel Pearce. Any questions on what we did here, sir?"

"Nope," I answered my instructor, an earnest young captain named Harrelson. "I think I'm good, Dan."

"You can call me Hondo, sir. Everyone else does."

"Hondo?" I thought for a moment and then began to nod. "Dan 'Hondo' Harrelson from SWAT, right?"

He grinned. "Yes, sir. My dad loved that show. I've been called that since I was old enough to remember my name."

I looked at him. "Well, you do look a little like a young Steve Forrest," I said. "Hondo's a cool handle. You could have done much worse."

He nodded in agreement. "That's for sure, sir."

I was sitting in an electrically powered mockup of the F-16 cockpit called a Unit Training Device or UTD. It was designed to allow the user to practice checklist procedures and switchology. My hands were resting on the throttle and sidestick controller in the mock-up, and I could feel the old excitement and impatience brewing in me once again. I wanted to be in the real jet. It had been about ten months since I'd fought the battle of my life in a cockpit almost exactly like that one, and all I could think about was strapping the sleek jet to my ass once again and blasting into the wild blue.

"What do you go by, sir?"

I realized that he'd been talking to me, and I had completely tuned him out.

"T. C.," I said as I extricated myself from the device and retrieved my checklist and other gear. "I go by T. C."

He looked at me strangely for a moment, and I realized he had heard the handle but not the associated name. And if what Lindal and B-Rock had said was true, apparently my handle had become pretty well known.

"I hope I get to teach you in the BFM phase, sir," he said with an eager tone of voice. "It'll be fun."

"Yes it will, Hondo. I'd enjoy it. But you'll have to take it easy on me. I'm an old guy."

He nodded with a knowing smile on his face. "I'm sure we could teach each other a thing or two," he said. There was something about his tone of voice that drew my eyes to his. They were hungry. I suddenly realized what some of the gunfighters in the old west must have felt like when their reputations became known. The challenge in young Hondo's eyes was unmistakable. He wanted to be the one who beat the "famous" T. C. in a dogfight.

Jesus, I thought.

"Sounds good, Hondo. Hey, it's been a long time since I was here. Is the 310th's maintenance hangar still out the flightline door and to the left? I'd like to go see some real jets now that I have my line badge."

He paused about a half a second too long before he answered.

"Yes, sir," he said, "but Lieutenant Colonel Weeks is pretty particular about who goes out there. There's a classified program using our facility."

"Oh well," I said with what I hoped was the right amount of senior officer bluster in my voice, "I'm not going to disturb anyone. I'm just going to look around a bit. Do I have you for the UTD tomorrow?"

"I don't know, sir. The schedule for tomorrow won't be posted for about another hour."

"Okay. I'll check back again before I leave. Have a good evening."

He nodded. "You too, sir."

The 310th building ran approximately east west and had a front entrance on Spad Street, the main street on the south side of the base, and a rear entrance on the flightline side of the building, which, coincidently, was the side I had parked on. I walked out of the air-conditioned comfort of the squadron building and into the blast furnace that was the Phoenix valley in midsummer. I deposited my checklist and publications bag into the rental car, which was three slots away from the flightline door. Then I walked west, past the building that used to house the 63rd Fighter Squadron and continued down past the 310th's maintenance debrief facility. Beyond it, at the end of a short taxiway that came from the south ramp area, sat an imposing looking hangar with its large doors shut, in spite of the 115-degree heat.

Determining which hangar housed the F-35 had been a relatively easy process of elimination, in spite of the fact that there had been a lot of construction on the base since my departure eight years ago. While stateside USAF bases like Luke typically operated their aircraft from open ramp areas, I had forgotten just how many hangars and aircraft-size buildings were on the base, even though the ramp at Luke was crowded with all the F-16s assigned to the wing. There was even an entire group of new hangars on the west side of the ramp that reminded me of the hardened aircraft shelters I had seen during my assignments in Europe and Korea. I knew there would have been no way for me to search all of them without attracting attention, especially since most of them were in areas I wouldn't logically have access to. But I also knew Mark Tappan; and I knew he'd want his prize in a central location that was a bit of a showplace. It would also need to be near the 310th building since they were operating it for the tests and evaluations. There was only one hangar that met those requirements; and as I walked toward it, I silently thanked young Hondo Harrelson for confirming my suspicions.

The building loomed in front of me, its facade at a 90-degree angle to the ramp. The massive metal doors were painted in a light tan, complementing the desert-brown paint of the surrounding structure. It was easily large enough to house several F-16s, and I wondered whether the F-35 was the only aircraft inside or if portions of the interior were still being used for maintenance while the "classified project" was underway. I dismissed that thought quickly. There appeared to be very little activity around the building. An active maintenance facility always had people and equipment coming and going on a nearly continual basis. The building looked deserted.

I reached the taxiway leading into the hangar and turned away from it and toward the flightline so I could walk down to the ramp. A few moments later, I stopped next to the red stripped line, which denoted the edge of the secured area, and looked out over the several acres of concrete in front of me. In spite of the late afternoon time frame, the ramp teemed with activity, with the whistling sounds of the Pratt and Whitney P220 engines providing an underlying soundtrack. Jets were starting up, shutting down, taxing out, and taxing in. There were maintenance people everywhere, marshaling the aircraft and working on them. Fuel trucks roamed the ramp looking for jets that needed gas, and weapons troops meandered about as well in smaller trucks pulling trailers loaded with the light blue BDU-33 25-pound practice bombs or inert 2,000-pound bombs and chaff and flare canisters.

There had been one major change to the ramp since my departure though, and that was the installation of metal sunshades above all the jet parking spaces on the ramp. Now pilots could preflight their aircraft and maintenance personnel could work on them shielded from the blistering heat of the desert sun. Every once in a while the USAF demonstrated some common sense. I was glad to see it here. As I stood watching the familiar organized chaos take place in front of me, I felt a lump in my throat that I couldn't explain.

God, I love this.

I sighed. It was time for me do what I had come here for.

I turned and walked down the flightline, paralleling the secure area. On the flightline side of the maintenance hangar, there was a suite of offices at ground level. Judging from the lack of cars in the adjoining parking lot, it didn't seem that there were many people in the place. I quickly decided on a strategy and headed for the nearest door on the flightline side.

It was locked.

Well, shit.

I tried the next three doors on the flightline side with similar results.

I rounded the corner to the western side of the building and was rewarded with a door that was actually still open but swinging shut behind the person who had just walked through it, now out of sight inside the building. I stepped through the door quickly and found myself in a long hallway that ran the length of the office space, with the offices on one side and doors that led into the hangar on the other side.

As my eyes adjusted to the darker surroundings, I saw the security guards about halfway down the hangar side of the hall, dressed in black tactical gear similar to the garb worn by operations teams. They were fully equipped with sidearms in quick-access, thigh holsters and M-4 carbines strapped to their chests. While I wasn't surprised to see that guards were in place, I found it very curious indeed that they appeared to be civilian contractors and not USAF security policemen. I couldn't imagine that the local security police commander would have wanted to miss out on having his people guard an important, classified project.

The two guards were distracted momentarily as they inspected the credentials of the person who had entered the building in front of me, a sergeant in fatigues who apparently had work to do inside the facility. It was only a matter of seconds before they noticed me. Hiding from them would have made me more suspicious, so I did the best thing possible under the circumstances: I acted like I belonged there. I walked up the hallway toward them, taking a few moments to stick my head into each office along the way.

"Hey, what are you doing?" I heard one the guards call out.

Interesting. No military courtesy. No use of the word sir. And the voice was heavy with a Hispanic accent. I suddenly knew who the guards worked for. And it wasn't the USAF.

"What do you mean what am I doing?" I snapped back to the guard as I strode down the hallway to him with all the senior officer swagger I could muster. "Who the hell are you? And who taught you how to address a colonel?"

I stopped in front of the two guards with my hands on my hips and drew myself up to my full height. I still had my flight cap, with the appropriate fighter pilot crush in it, on my head and aviator sunglasses on my face. I stood very close to them, well inside the personal space people naturally expect—especially when those people are armed.

"Why are you guys here? Where are the security police? This is an important project! There should be Air Force people here!"

I saw hesitation in the twin sets of dark eyes in the Hispanic faces before me. They weren't used to being challenged. And I was betting their English wasn't the best.

"Goddamn it!" I roared. "I told Tappan and Miguel that this arrangement wasn't appropriate! I told them we needed Air Force guards for appearances sake. But they didn't fucking listen!"

The guards' eyes widened a bit when they heard Miguel's name.

Perfect, I thought.

"Okay, let me through," I said brusquely. "I've got to see what else has been fucked up here." I pushed them aside, as if they were mere peons, and moved past them to the hangar door.

"Señor," one of the guards said, "you are not to go in there!"

He grabbed my arm as I strode past him.

I stopped and looked down at him with every ounce of intimidation I could find.

"Do you want Miguel to hear about this?" I asked. "Miguel sent me here," I pointed at my chest and then pointed at the door, "to check on you!" I held my line badge, with my photo and name on it, in front of his face. "Pearce is my name. Call Miguel and ask him if I'm supposed to be here! Call Miguel and ask!"

The guard's eyes got wider every time he heard Miguel's name, and I watched him struggle with his responsibility and his fear. As usual, fear won. I looked down at his hand on my arm and then looked back at him. He released me and I walked through the door. I had totally blown whatever was left of my cover. I hoped it was worth it.

I walked down a small hallway to another door and out

into the hangar bay to find a huge black curtain in front of me that ran the entire length of the hangar from floor to ceiling. I nodded to myself. Additional security measures to prevent prying eyes, like mine, from stealing glances. After looking for an opening for a few moments, I walked to the edge of the curtain where it met the hangar door and stepped around it.

And there it was. Parked serenely, all by itself, in the middle of the hangar.

The Lockheed Martin F-35 Lighting II with its dull blue-gray paint barely reflecting the bright hangar lights above. My first reaction at close range was that it didn't have nearly the smooth lines that the Viper did. While it was approximately the same size as the Viper, maybe just a little longer and with a slightly greater wingspan, it looked stockier than the sleek F-16. I knew the F-35 held more gas and also carried most of its ordnance internally, but with the emphasis on radar stealth in its construction, it looked boxier and more angular than its predecessor. And then, as I looked it over closely and examined the size of the fuselage and compared it to the jet's wing area, I shook my head in realization.

"This thing really won't turn for shit," I muttered.

The USAF, demonstrating its usual shortsightedness in the aircraft design process, had produced an aircraft optimized for the premerge, air-to-air fight. The F-35 would have radar capable of identifying targets beyond visual range and weapons, like the AIM-120 Advanced Medium Range Air-to-Air Missile, that would allow it to fire on targets before the pilot ever saw them. But that wasn't the way most air-to-air fights happened. Even in the modern age, fighters still tended to intercept other aircraft and identify them visually before engaging them. And granted, the F-35 was destined to be a multirole fighter, not a solely air-to-air machine, but since the decision had been made to eliminate vectored-thrust engines, the jet had been intentionally deprived of the ability to "turn and burn."

I shook my head in disbelief. The USAF's design bureau had done it again.

"What a bunch of fucking idiots," I said under my breath. "I'm surprised they even bothered to put a gun on the damn thing."

"Sir!" A very concerned female voice rang through the air. "You're not supposed to be here!"

I turned to face the voice and found a well-proportioned major walking across the hangar's cement floor toward me. She had to avoid the F-35's engine, which was apparently on a stand on the other side of the aircraft. Her plentiful brunette hair was piled into a tight bun on top of her head, and she had just the slightest hint of makeup on a nicely tanned face. Two young enlisted USAF security policemen in fatigues followed her. Interestingly, they were unarmed. The badge insignia sewn onto their fatigues was the only clue as to their specialty. I didn't plan to allow them a speaking role in the proceedings.

Before the major and her SPs got within ten feet of me, I confronted her.

"Why are civilian guards responsible for the security of an asset like this, major?" I asked with some colonel-level arrogance. I gestured to the security policemen behind her. "And why aren't these men armed?"

She seemed somewhat taken aback. This was a question she wasn't expecting.

"Who is in charge of security here, major? Who made these arrangements?"

She struggled with the question for a moment and then blurted out the answer I expected.

"General Tappan, sir," she said in a resigned tone. "He gave us very specific instructions."

"As I thought," I said, shaking my head in a show of disgust. "Idiot. The Chief of Staff won't be happy about this."

I turned to make my exit while I was still in charge.

"Sir," the major's voice was almost pleading, "you can't leave until we debrief you. We have to hold you until we speak to the general."

"He knows where to find me, major." I said over my shoulder as I headed for the door. "And I hope he has his shit together before he comes to talk to me."

A few moments later, as I walked briskly to my car, I typed a quick e-mail to Smith and Amrine on the CIA Blackberry.

IT'S STILL HERE, I wrote. AND THEY ALL KNOW I'VE SEEN IT. I'M BLOWN.

The reply came back more quickly than I expected.

ROGER, it said. WATCH YOUR ASS.

"Thanks, guys," I uttered into the stifling desert air. "I needed that."

Chapter Thirteen

Contract Day Nine
Thursday, July 1, 2010
1800 Hours Local Time
VIP Senior Officers' Quarters
Luke Air Force Base, Arizona

I had taken my leave of Brock and Christine for the evening. The schedule for the day had been packed with academics and device training from 0730 to 1630. After that, Brock had kicked my ass in the gym for another hour. As we finished the post-workout stretching routine, I told Brock I was going to take the evening off and spend a little quality time in solitude. The VIP officers' quarters came equipped with gas grills on the tiny patios behind them, and I planned to enjoy a nice steak, a martini or five, and the nonstressful pleasure of my own company.

I took a quick shower and threw on some cargo shorts and a T-shirt. After that, I fired up the grill, prepped the steak, and put some wild rice on the stove to simmer. Then it was martini time. The secret to a great martini is preparation and timing. After executing the appropriate steps, I poured the Bombay Sapphire gin, cloudy with ice crystals, into the prechilled martini glass and walked out to sit on the small patio and watch the desert sunset. The temperature on this particular evening wasn't bad at all; and since the sprinklers were active on the lawn next to me, the hydration effect made the climate on the patio rather pleasant.

I looked at my watch and estimated that I had about five minutes before the grill was ready for the steaks. Plenty of time to watch the world go by and enjoy a little alcohol induced relaxation. Maybe even take a few moments to allow my mind to wander and forget about the events around me.

The first sip of the day's first drink is always something to be relished, and I always looked forward to it. I didn't know if that made me an alcoholic and, frankly, I didn't care. As long as no one was damaged by my actions, it didn't seem to make a difference.

I raised the cool glass to my lips and allowed the iced gin to flow over my tongue and down my throat, shutting my eyes to concentrate on the sensations and to enjoy the flavor of the luscious liquid. I took a good, long drink and then returned the glass to the tabletop as I leaned back in my chair. At the end of the day, it's the little things in life that make it worthwhile.

"Ah," I said unconsciously. "This is the life."

"Care to make me one of those?"

The nasal voice took me by surprise, and I nearly jumped out of my chair and spilled my drink. I opened my eyes to see the incongruous sight of Mark "Satan" Tappan standing before me, on the other side of my table, dressed in Bermuda shorts, a loud Hawaiian shirt, a surfer-style baseball cap, and aviator's sunglasses. He was obviously alone. It amazed me that I hadn't heard him walk up. For a moment, I thought about telling him to pound sand or perhaps a certain part of his anatomy, but the adage about holding one's enemies closer came to mind.

"I guess," I said. "But I've only got one steak, and that's all for me."

He took a seat on the other side of the table.

"Understood," Satan said with the trace of a smile on his lips. It seemed to contort his features.

I rose and went into my quarters' kitchen, taking my drink with me. Fortunately, I had multiple glasses chilled and had left all the ingredients out so I was able to make him a martini identical to my own in just a few minutes and refreshed my own glass with what was left in the shaker. Then I turned the heat down on the rice and went outside to rejoin him.

"Here you go," I said, handing him his drink.

He raised his glass to me. "Cheers, T. C.," he said.

"Cheers to you, Satan," I said as I slid into my chair.

He took a sip of the martini and nodded at me with a pleased expression on his face. "Well done," he said. "This is excellent."

"Thanks," I replied.

He took another drink and looked around the courtyard. "You may not know it, but the renovation for both of these units was completed on my watch," he said. "I supervised the design process and approved all the construction and interior configurations. I even hired a pricey interior decorator from downtown to do the inside." He looked across the table at me. "So how did we do?"

"They're very comfortable," I said. "I've stayed in a lot of luxury hotels and suites and many weren't as nice."

He sat back in his chair with a satisfied expression on his face and took another sip of his drink. "Well, my goal was to make my senior officer visitors as comfortable as possible."

"Well, the logistical arrangements of my stay have been superb so far, Satan," I said. "Other elements, not so much."

He nodded. "Let's talk about that, shall we?"

I eyed him across the table as I took a long, slow sip of my drink. "I'm listening," I said at last.

Satan put his glass on the table in front of him and began

to rotate the base of it slowly on the surface. "You know there was a time when you and I worked well together," he said, staring into the martini glass.

I thought about that. There was a little truth there but that was a long time ago. "Maybe before I was your operations officer," I said after a long moment. "But certainly not since then."

"That whole squadron commander business did get a little crazy," he admitted. "It's possible I overreacted. I do get obsessed about things."

"Really," I said. It was impossible to keep the sarcasm out of my voice.

He looked at me, and his mask of pleasantness seemed to fade away and reveal the lurking hatred underneath for a moment or two. Then, as quickly as it had come, the hateful visage transformed back into its previous pleasant expression. The effect was very disconcerting. It was like he was two people at the same time. Then it occurred to me.

Oh my God, I thought. *He's here to negotiate.*

"We might have the opportunity to bury the hatchet here," he said. "And perhaps come to a mutual... profitable... arrangement."

At that moment, I remembered that I had left the CIA BlackBerry inside on the kitchen island. I cursed myself silently. I was about to hear a partial admission or confession, and I had no ability to reproduce it.

"Do we now?" I said, trying to keep my tone as neutral as possible. "And what might that entail?"

Satan sat back in his chair, took a long drink of his martini, and then stared at me over the glass. "I think we might have a mutual friend," he said, "although, I've known him for much longer than you have."

Son of a bitch, I thought. "Sometime on or prior to 2000, I suspect," I said, "if we're talking about who I think we're talking about."

Satan nodded and grinned sheepishly. It was a most unusual look for him. "I might have had a substance issue in those days," he said. "And our friend might have helped me with that if I allowed him access to certain markets."

I felt simultaneously fascinated and frightened. It was an eerie combination. Satan's candor and the information he was providing was going to force one of two outcomes: my recruitment or my death. There was no middle ground.

"I see," I said because I had no idea how to reply.

"He helped me make my way through the political maze that it takes to become a general officer," he continued, as if he didn't hear me.

"Well, that explains it," I said, unconsciously, and then I instantly wanted to clamp my hand over my mouth.

Satan smiled at me nodded. "I know what you're thinking," he said. "That's how a brigadier general selectee who does a body shot on a drunk enlisted chick at an overseas all-ranks club gets to pin on the star." He paused for a moment, apparently lost in the recollection. "She had such nice little titties," Satan said eventually. "And she wanted it. Like they all do."

Jesus.

Satan looked at me with a hint of pride on his face. "To this day I hold the record for the most time between selection date for BG and pin-on date."

Thoughts and suppositions tumbled through my brain, but only one word escaped my lips. "Blackmail," I said, looking at him over the top of my glass. "I did hear something about blackmail."

"Our friend knows lots of people. And there isn't anyone who can't be bought or threatened into submission. Everyone has their buttons." He leaned forward and looked straight into my eyes. "Everyone."

Shit, I thought. *Here it comes.*

"So apparently you almost got married recently," Satan said, as he rolled the stem of the martini glass in his hand. "I hear this Sarah broad is quite the looker. Wasn't she Mistress of the Year?"

I felt a knot in the pit of my stomach, and the gin suddenly tasted rancid in my mouth.

"And you've got a beautiful little daughter."

Without warning, the rage began to simmer inside of me. I could feel my blood start to warm and my face begin to flush.

"There might be a second baby on the way," Satan said, conversationally. "No visible evidence yet, but it seems she's been seeing an obstetrician."

I fought to compartmentalize the emotional grenades that were detonating inside of me. I heard Satan's words echo, as if we were at opposite ends of a long hallway.

"Now our friend knows that he made a vow to not take action against them himself, but he also knows they could be used as leverage in the event that you were considering something stupid. He could also offer a reward in exchange for certain parts of their anatomy to be sent to you. One at a time."

Satan took the last sip of his martini and set the glass on the table.

"But no one really wants that to happen, so I'm authorized to offer you a deal," he said.

Part of me was fuming and part of me was feeling the effect of raw panic. It took every bit of strength in me not physically tremble.

"Our friend will ensure your girlfriend and your kid or kids aren't harmed and will pay you one twenty-five million dollars. And to get it, you only have to do one thing."

I found I couldn't talk. I wanted to. I wanted to ask him what I had to do to make them safe. I wanted to promise anything. My mind filled with images of little fingers and toes severed from their body.

"What?" I said at last, my voice barely audible.

Satan smiled evilly, apparently content with the effect his words were having. "Walk away," he said, spreading his arms in a gesture of simplicity. "All you have to do is walk away."

He leaned back into his chair with a satisfied expression on his face. "You know, you're not so tough," he said. "Oh sure, you can kick ass and shoot people, but when it comes right down to it, you've got the same buttons everyone else does, and the same weaknesses. That's why I got rid of mine."

"Rid?" I asked. Apparently I was only capable of monosyllables at the moment.

"My wife met with an untimely accident and left me all her money," he said, shaking his head. "And I sold her slut daughter to Miguel for a tidy sum. I understand she's one of the whores on call at his retreat in Baja, Mexico."

He crossed his arms and stared at me.

"But this isn't about me," he said. "It's about you." He leaned forward again. "You need to understand something. We know everything. We know why you're here and we know who you're working with. We know every move you make before you make it. You will not succeed. You'll die and so will your girlfriend and your kid. So you need to make a decision."

I looked back at him, blankly. It was almost too much to process. But in the back of my brain, I became aware of a thread that seemed to be loose: when people try to convince others of something they don't know, they often present too much information or too little. It's always difficult to get the balance right. Now I didn't know where Sarah and Colleen were or what they were doing, but Smith and Amrine did. And while they had kept all the relevant location information from me, as they should have, they would have certainly told me if Sarah was pregnant. While part of that would have been about the camaraderie we shared, it would have also been about something else. It would have been about power. If there had been an additional child, it would have made me even more compliant. It would have given them more power over me.

I was beginning to smell a lie. This was a desperate attempt to get me to back off.

"So come on, T. C.," Satan continued. "You've been the next thing to a mercenary or a prostitute since you retired from active duty. It won't hurt you to be one again. One last time. Just do what you do best. Take the money and walk."

Several possible replies ran through my mind. I had a mental image of the scene in the first Terminator movie when the landlord knocks on the Terminator's door and a list of possible things to say is presented to him by his computer brain. As I recalled, 'Fuck you, asshole,' was the one he chose. I was tempted to say the same thing.

"I'm afraid you've misjudged me," I said, my voice back in perfect control. "You claim to know things that you don't. You think I care about things that don't matter to me. And you're trying to bribe someone who has all he needs." I took the last sip of my own martini and took delight in the fact that the gin tasted good to me once again. "I'm not going anywhere," I said, rising to my feet. "I'm going to stay here and see this thing through for one reason and one reason only."

"You're an idiot," Satan said, getting to his own feet. "You could have had everything, and now you're going to get yourself and everyone you care about killed. What possible reason could justify that?"

"The pleasure of kicking your ass and Miguel's. Feel free to tell him that the next time you speak with him."

Tappan left without saying another word. As soon as he as gone, I went into the kitchen and called Dave Smith. He picked up immediately.

"Mark Tappan was just here," I said.

"She's not pregnant, Colin," he said, reading my mind. "We had a distance mic on the whole conversation. Apparently, you scare the shit out of them. Pretty interesting."

"So she's not…"

"No, she's not, and she and Colleen are in the middle of nowhere. There isn't an obstetrician around her for miles. Once you made the trip to Luke, we moved her to an isolated location to make sure we could keep her safe. Trust us. We've got this."

I breathed a sigh of relief.

"Now go eat that damn steak. And watch your ass. Something tells me this will be a long night. We'll be close by."

"Roger that."

I clicked off the phone and finished my dinner preparations. The steak was predictably good, and the rice complemented it well. As I cleaned up afterward, it occurred to me that I had not heard Satan approach me on the patio and that not being aware of a subsequent approach could be hazardous. I remembered a trick I had seen in a movie and found some spare lightbulbs, broke them inside a pillowcase, and then spread the particles on the back patio outside the door. Then I ensured that all the window shades were down, and I turned on every light in the place. Finally, I checked the Colt .45 Commander and ensured it was ready with a round in the chamber.

The knock at the door came about two hours later, right as I was pouring the night's first single malt, a shot of the Highland Park 12, from a set of miniature bottles I traveled with. The knock was loud and insistent; and if I hadn't been expecting it, I might have actually spilled some of the luscious stuff on the granite countertop.

I unholstered the Colt and headed toward the entry area of my quarters. I went to the far edge of the window, to the left of the door, and peered around the edge of the curtain to verify my visitor's identity. When I saw who was there, my mouth dropped open and I found myself shaking my head.

"Now?" I said. "Seriously?"

I holstered the .45 and pulled my shirt down to cover it. Then I went to the door and opened it cautiously.

"Agent Otenski," I said.

She looked back at me, standing on the stoop in a blue and white sundress and white sandals with blingy rhinestones set into the straps. Her blonde hair was pulled behind her head into a ponytail contraption with strands of it loose and framing her face. Her tan shone in the porch light, and her deep blue eyes were intense. If times had been different and she hadn't worked for the organization I despised, I might have appreciated her beauty and her presence more. As it was, I found I was just annoyed.

"After tailing me for nearly a week, you finally decided to actually talk to me?" I asked in exasperation. "What did it? My boyish good looks or psychic charm?"

"We need to talk," she said with an edgy voice.

"Do you have a warrant or official reason to search these premises?"

She shook her head impatiently and the loose blonde hair waved around her face.

"I'm not here officially," she said, her tone much softer now.

I looked back at her and smiled with mock regret.

"Then you're not coming in," I said, easing the door closed. "The last time I cooperated with the OSI, several years ago, I got my ass kicked for my trouble. I don't plan to make that same mistake again."

"You were set up," she said quickly, with a gleam of knowledge in her eyes. "Back in 2000. I read the report. It's against everything I signed up for when I volunteered for this service."

"No shit," I replied.

"That's not all of it," she said.

I raised my eyebrows at her.

"I know who did it."

"Who?"

"The same guy who suspended me last week after your buddy the general and his wife were spirited away by the CIA."

As I stood there pondering her words, she brushed past me and into my quarters, leaving a trail of very enticing perfume in her wake. She continued into the living room area of my quarters without invitation and seated herself on the sofa.

"Well, make yourself comfortable," I sighed, as much to myself as anyone else. And then my manners kicked in. Better late than never I guess. "I was just going to have a Scotch," I said. "Care to join me?"

She nodded. "Neat please."

"The only way to drink it," I said.

I poured her a shot of the Highland Park and handed her the glass. Then I walked over to the armchair across from her and reclined in it, propping my feet up on the accompanying ottoman.

"These are interesting glasses," she said.

"They're Glen Cairn glasses, designed specifically to enhance the bouquet of the spirit as you drink it. I always travel with a few of them so I don't have to drink out of the glasses in hotel rooms."

She took a sip of her Scotch and seemed to relish it appropriately.

"That's very good," she said. "What is it?"

"Highland Park 12," I answered, savoring the spirit's fruity aroma with my nose in the bowl of my glass.

She nodded.

"I typically drink Johnnie Walker or Dewar's," she said. "I'm not sure I've ever had a single malt before."

"Blended Scotch is generic Scotch," I answered. "It's Scotch for Scotch's sake. Every single malt has its own taste, its own personality, and its own story. Each one is unique."

She nodded again and took another sip.

"So I suppose you were wondering—" she began and I held my hand up to silence her. I retrieved the BlackBerry from its holster and activated an application on it. Then I placed it on the table.

"You can talk now," I said. "I just wanted to make sure no one else can listen."

"Isn't that a little paranoid?" she asked.

"Perhaps. Never hurts to be careful," I responded.

"How does that thing work?" Otenski asked.

"Jams the uplink," I answered.

She nodded.

"So, Agent Otenski," I said, leaning back in my chair. "You have my undivided attention. Why are you here?"

She kicked her sandals off, leaned back on the sofa, and pulled her legs up onto the cushion next to her, revealing quite a bit of tanned thigh and a flash of lacy white panties as she did so. I looked up quickly to find her watching me. Her eyes sparkled mischievously when she saw where I was looking.

"First," she said, "I'd feel a lot better if you called me Lena."

"OK, Lena," I answered, feeling a little embarrassed. "What's on your mind?"

"I've read your files," she said, looking at me intently. "So I know a lot about you."

"Files? Plural?"

She nodded and took a sip of her Scotch.

"The one that began last fall and the one that was sealed many years ago. The first one was easy to get because of the position I hold. The second one was much more difficult to find. If I hadn't played up to the records clerk who has been trying to get into my pants for the last ten years, I wouldn't have been able to read it."

"So why the curiosity in me?" I asked after a moment. "You didn't know who I was before last Monday."

She shook her head.

"Oh, I knew who you were," she said quietly. "Everybody in the OSI knows who you are. Or at least, everybody has heard of you."

I felt myself stiffen. *Well that's fucking great.*

"You'll forgive me if I find that a bit puzzling," I said, trying to maintain my composure. "Apart from bad-mouthing your organization from time to time over the years, it doesn't seem like I've done anything to earn that kind of attention."

"The current commander of the OSI is a brigadier general by the name of Alan Turnidge," she said. "Ring a bell?"

Holy shit.

"The same Alan Turnidge who was the OSI detachment commander here at Luke? Back in the day?"

She nodded. "Two of our agents were in that work center at Edwards Air Force Base last fall. When you, a retired Air Force officer, showed up, working alongside the CIA, the agents reported it of course. Turnidge went ballistic. He placed you on a national 'person of interest' list. He ordered a complete work up on you, full monitoring, and full surveillance. He wanted to know everything about you, and he wanted all of us looking at you.

I took a long slow, sip of the Highland Park, savoring the hints of fruit and honey on my tongue and the long, peppery finish as I tried to get my thoughts in order. Smith and Amrine had never mentioned this.

"But, I never..."

Lena shook her head. "No, you never noticed anything because it never happened. One day after Turnidge gave the order, these two CIA types showed up at his office. One was a blond, muscular guy, really good-looking. The other was tall and slim with sandy hair who looks like he'd kill you as soon as look at you. Sound familiar to you?"

Amrine and Smith, I thought.

"And the order was rescinded immediately. It embarrassed the hell out of Turnidge. It was the first time someone has been made a person of interest and then was removed from the list within twenty-four hours. Everyone in the OSI questioned it. So, like I said, everybody knows who you are. And if that wasn't enough, that business with Miguel Hidalgo late last year sealed the deal. Since that time, we've known that you've had CIA crews around you, watching you 24/7, indicating that you are obviously very important."

"I'm not important," I said quietly. "I'm bait. Miguel has a price on my head so large that a successful assassin could buy a third world country with the proceeds."

"So the crews are what? Backup?"

I nodded.

"So I've been asking myself some questions. How is that you show up in Annapolis to talk to a person my boss has assigned me to apprehend, manage to detect that he is under surveillance, and then call in a CIA operations team that just happens to include the two agents who made my boss look like an idiot to take this person and his wife away? Have I missed anything so far?"

I smiled thinly and shook my head.

"So then you show up here at Luke a few days later, apparently recommissioned in the Air Force as a full-bird colonel. Two nights ago you have drinks with the very same guys who made my fellow agent and I look like rookies and who made my boss irrelevant, and yesterday you manage to sneak into the hangar with the tightest security on base and send the entire wing staff into scurry mode. You're obviously up to something, and I need to know what it is."

I paused to consider a response, but in the moment of

intervening silence, I heard a sound that was distinctly out of place at 9:00 p.m. on a Thursday night near a somewhat isolated building like mine. It was the crackle of broken glass being stepped on.

The same broken glass I had sprinkled on the patio an hour earlier.

I leaped up from my chair with my finger to my lips and reached for Lena's hand. She looked at me questioningly, but said nothing and offered it to me. I pulled her down the hallway and into my darkened bedroom.

"Take your dress off," I said as I removed my shirt and threw it on the floor in the doorway.

She stared at me.

"We don't have much time," I said. I took off my shorts and tossed them on the floor by my shirt. "They'll be coming through the door any minute. We have to give them something to look at. A deception. It might buy us a few seconds." I began stuffing pillows under the bedclothes to simulate our bodies.

I could see the realization dawn in her eyes. She nodded and began to pull her sundress over her head. The lacy white panties I had glimpsed earlier were all she had on underneath. My mind processed a tanned, well-toned body with substantial breasts that any other time would have captured my admiration. She tossed the sundress on the floor near the other clothes.

"My weapon," she said helplessly, as she threw the dress on the floor. "I left my purse in the living room."

"Doesn't matter," I said. "Turn off the lamp on the nightstand on the other side of the bed please."

She nodded and did what she was told. I reached under the bed and pulled out the briefcase Smith and Amrine had given me. There inside lay a Heckler and Koch UMP submachine gun, the successor to the venerable MP-5. I had shot the MP-5 during my recent combat firearms training at First Sight and had put thirty rounds through the center of a silhouette target in about three seconds on full auto. I knew then why so many law enforcement groups and Special Forces teams swore by the weapon. It had minimally felt recoil and no muzzle climb at all while firing. The UMP in front of me was smaller, featured more polymers in its construction, and unlike its predecessor, was chambered in .45 ACP. It also came complete with a long, cylindrical sound suppressor.

I lifted the UMP out of its case and attached the sound suppressor to the muzzle via the weapon's quick-connect mechanism. I folded the skeleton stock out until it locked into place and then loaded a magazine into the well. As I cycled the bolt to chamber the first round, Lena came around the bed and stood next to me, completely unabashed at her near nakedness.

"I should have had this thing preassembled," I muttered as I grabbed the extra magazines and threw the briefcase under the bed. "I knew it was just a question of time."

"I could help," she said uncertainly, "I've been trained."

I shook my head.

"Not against guys like these you haven't," I said. I pulled the 1911 out of the holster and handed it to her, along with a spare magazine.

"Are you familiar with the 1911-model automatic? In .45 ACP?"

She nodded.

"This is a Commander model with a modified magazine, so there are seven rounds in the magazine and a round in the chamber. Go lie down in the tub. If anyone else comes through that door besides me, shoot them."

I motioned to the bathroom with my head and she went in. I squeezed myself into the small space between the nightstand and bathroom wall, checked that the selector control on the side of the weapon was on "auto," and then I eased myself down into a sitting position. When my butt hit the floor, I pressed the stock firmly against my shoulder, sighted through the red-dot aiming reticle and waited.

They were amazingly quiet. I never heard the door in the kitchen open, nor did I hear any footsteps in the hall. There were no random shots fired and no whispers or commands. The first indication I had that they were in the house was when the muzzle of a suppressed submachine gun appeared in the door of my room. I was expecting it, but I still felt my skin crawl when I saw it. The muzzle moved back and forth, at chest level, while its shooter searched for a target in the bedroom. He stepped into the room in crouch and fired a string of several shots into the lumps on the bed.

And that gave me the opening I needed.

I sighted in on my assailant's head and squeezed the trigger on the H & K for a fraction of a second. The weapon tapped against my shoulder as it spewed 230 grain slugs at 650 rounds per minute and the shooter's head jerked repeatedly as red columns of gore exploded into the air around it. He crumpled to the floor loudly and lay still.

Sound suppressors do just that—suppress sound. They are not silencers. In the confined area of my bedroom, the two volleys of suppressed gunfire sounded like several loud "pops" all strung together—unmistakable to someone who was familiar with that sort of thing. My ears were ringing slightly, and I could smell the cordite in the air as I pushed myself up, launched myself across the wrinkled bed, and landed on the floor on the far side. If I was lucky, the next man would think all the shots came from his partner's weapon. I sighted around the corner of the bed just as the second man came through the door to back up his partner. He assessed the situation incredibly quickly and after barely glancing at his partner's body on the floor, he pivoted swiftly and pumped several rounds in the place I had been sitting mere moments ago.

I tapped the H & K's trigger again, and the second man's body reeled with the bullet impacts and he fell through the door and into the hallway. I was on my feet in seconds and through the door a moment later. I found him lying in the hall, face up with his eyes wide open behind the black mask and his chest heaving. While there were several spots where the cloth of his shirt was torn, I could see no blood.

Body armor.

I saw his right arm come up with his weapon, and I placed the muzzle of the H & K against his forehead and squeezed the trigger. The UMP shuddered three times and a trio of popping sounds filled the air. The arm fell to the floor.

I shouldered the H & K and slowly made my way down the hallway and into the entry area. I cleared the other bedroom, living room, dining area, and kitchen as quickly as I could, unsurprised that I did not encounter anyone else. Teams of two seemed to be the standard. But there would be a driver, and I needed to deal with him as well. I slipped out the rear door, pausing for just a moment to think about where the car and the driver would be. Then I made a guess as to where the glass I had thrown on the patio might have ended and attempted to leap over it.

And of course I landed on one of the bigger shards and it lanced into the bottom of my right foot.

"Fuck!" I whispered into the desert air, more in frustration than in pain.

I pulled the shard from my foot and eased my way around the edge of the building to get a view of the street in front of my quarters. It was empty, as I expected. A road would be too visible. The transport would probably be in a parking lot.

I saw the wall separating the yards of the VIP officers' quarters from the parking lot behind the Thunderbolt Club and nodded my head. Perfect. But rather than go over or around that wall, I decided instead to go through the door to the club's patio, and as I opened the gate, I held my breath and hoped I wouldn't attract too much attention clad only in boxer shorts and carrying an automatic weapon. Fortunately, the patio was vacant and the lights turned down. It occurred to me then that this was probably the same route that both Tappan and my assailants had taken. Certainly Tappan and company could arrange to have the patio closed when they required it to be. I worked my way along the east wall of the patio, staying in the shadows as much as I could and then along the south wall in the same fashion. At the corner where the south wall reached the wall of the club building, there was a gate in the wall that led to the parking lot. The odds were high that the car and driver were just outside the gate. I backtracked along the south wall until I found another opening, which contained a space large enough for a dumpster or two and was totally enclosed. There were some containers and receptacles against the wall next to the parking lot, so I climbed up on them and peered over the top of the wall as stealthily as I could.

A late model Dodge Charger was idling there. A Hispanic man who looked to be in his thirties sat behind the wheel. The glow of a smartphone in his lap illuminating his face. Apparently, a text message conversation was occupying his attention. Once again, luck seemed to be on my side.

I edged over the wall on the east side and crawled around to the south side. Then, on my hands and knees, I made my way over to the car, keeping as low to the ground as I could, feeling the warm, rough pavement abrading my knees and hands as I did so. I reached the passenger side undetected and took a long and deep breath. Then I shifted the H & K to my left hand and grabbed the passenger door handle with my right. But at that moment, I spied an empty soda can on the asphalt just behind the car's right front wheel.

I nodded in satisfaction and tossed it over the car's roof to land on the driver's side. It landed noisily, clattering against the pavement. I felt the car shudder as the driver turned in his seat to look and that's when I jerked the door open. He barely had time to turn his head before the stream of .45 ACP slugs tore it apart.

Lena was still in the tub with the 1911 when I made it back to my bedroom a few minutes later after texting Dave Smith and advising him that I needed a clean-up crew. She sat up and gasped when she saw me, a logical reaction to a man clad only in boxer shorts and spattered with blood.

"Are you hurt?" she asked.

"Nope," I replied, "I just got a lot of shit on me. With my luck, these guys are carrying bubonic plague or something."

"How many?"

"Three. Two wet work guys and a driver. I put the driver in the trunk of the car but there wasn't much left of his head, which is why I'm so messy. I just wanted to come back and check on you. I just texted my CIA buddies. There will be a company sanitation crew here in about twenty minutes. You should get dressed."

She nodded as she stood. Then she looked down at the floor.

"Are you bleeding?" she asked.

I looked at my right foot and saw a small pool of blood forming on the tile next to it.

"Goddamn it," I said. "I totally fucking forgot about that. I cut my foot when I went out the back door. I've been tracking blood all over the damn place."

"Sit down," she said, pointing to the toilet. "I'll clean it up and get a bandage on it. I've got to do something to help. I've been pretty useless otherwise."

"Don't sweat it," I replied. "Having people trying to kill you takes a little getting used to."

She looked at me and shook her head with a half-smile on her face.

"Are you used to it?" she asked.

"It doesn't really matter," I replied. "It just seems to be a trend."

She put her hand on the tiled wall of the shower as she stepped over the edge, still clad only in her underpants, which I noticed were of the thong variety as she turned her hips toward me to exit the tub.

I half stepped, half limped to the toilet and sat down on the closed seat. Lena pulled a towel off the rack, folded it double, and placed it on the floor near my feet. Then she knelt on the towel and inspected my injured foot.

"Nice work," she said. "How did you do this?"

"I threw some crumpled glass on the patio to alert me if anyone came across the patio," I said. "And it saved our lives tonight, because that's what I heard before I rushed you back here. In my rush to get to the third guy, I tried to jump across it, but I managed to land on a piece."

"Best laid plans," she chuckled. "Do you have any first aid stuff?"

I nodded. "In the vanity over there. Standard issue with the VIP quarters I guess. They must think senior officers are accident prone."

Lena stood and walked over to the vanity. She retrieved a washcloth and ran it under some hot water. Then she opened the vanity cabinet under the sink and bent over to get the first aid kit, rewarding me with a lingering view of her outstanding, thong-clad ass in the process. I felt my penis beginning to stir under the thin cotton of my boxers.

Not now, I thought.

Lena returned and knelt between my legs; and in just a few minutes time, she had the cut on my foot cleaned and bandaged. A few times during the process, however, her breasts brushed my legs, further stimulating the blood flow in my lower extremities. As she closed the first aid kit and looked up from her work, I was fully erect and straining the fabric on the front of my undershorts. She looked there for a moment and then lifted her eyes to mine.

"What now?" she said, slightly breathlessly.

"Um, I need to get cleaned off," I said, trying to get to my feet. "I've got shit all over me."

"Maybe I can help you with that too," she said.

Lena rose, peeled the thong off, and dropped it to the floor, revealing a pubic mound with the barest hit of blond hair. I stood there and drank in the sight of her nude body, feeling my penis throb against the material confining it.

Lena stepped forward and pulled down my underpants, as if it was the most natural thing in the world. The cotton garment slid down my legs and came to rest around my ankles. My erect member jutted forward, like it was reaching out for her. She reached for it and grasped it firmly with her left hand. It throbbed inside her fingers.

"Wow," she said, licking her lips. "You're really hard. We need to do something about that."

"We don't have much time," I said, trying to keep my heart rate under control. "The cleanup crew will be here in like ten minutes."

She smiled and squeezed my member with one hand as she used her other to guide one of my hands to the moistness between her legs. My fingers made contact with the soft, wet skin of her labia. Then she turned her body, bent over, and guided me into her.

"You won't last ten minutes and neither will I," she said as I entered her.

As it turned out, she was right.

***

Later, when the cleaning crew had finished, Lena and I enjoyed a much less hurried reprise of our earlier activity in the comfort of the bed in my quarters. After we were finished, she lay a discreet distance away from me on the newly changed sheets as we caught our breath.

"I didn't expect this," she said quietly. "But I'm not sorry."

I exhaled with contentment.

"I'm not either," I said. "And if someone had told me nine years ago I'd end up having sex with an OSI agent, I would have told them they were crazy!"

She chuckled in the semidarkness. "I feel the same way where the 'famous' Colin Pearce is concerned. If only my fellow agents in the Commander's Group could see me now."

"Commander's Group?" I asked, already knowing the answer.

"Yes," she murmured contentedly. "There are ten of us and we work directly for the OSI Commander to investigate cases that he thinks require his direct attention."

"Like me?"

"Yes," she said. "Like you."

"So how's that investigation coming?" I asked.

There was a pause and she exhaled loudly. "I got suspended," she said after a long moment.

"Really? Why?"

Lena turned on her side and faced away from me. "Because I told him that we shouldn't be investigating a brigadier general whose stepson died in a plane crash and a retired lieutenant colonel who just might be nominated for the Congressional Medal of Honor."

I rolled up on my side toward her and stroked her bare back with my hand. "Sounds like good advice to me."

"He told me the case had national security implications and that you were 'dangerous' and needed to be watched closely. And then he suspended me."

"So are you working for him here or working for yourself?" I asked gently, my hand finding the underside of her ass and the area between her legs.

"Myself," she said, her voice dreamy. "And what are you doing back there?"

"Just playing," I answered as my fingers found her wetness once again. "You know, your boss is right, Lena. This case does have national security implications."

"Does it now?" she asked as her body began to move with the strokes of my fingers.

"Yes," I said. "Would you like to hear the whole story?"

"In a little while," she said, shifting her hips. "Could you do that a little faster? Yes...just like that."

Her hand found my shaft moments later; and after a few minutes of work with her hands and her mouth, I was hard again. She mounted me shortly thereafter and rode me until she came, furiously, grinding herself onto me again and again. As her orgasm subsided, I rolled her on to her back and took her with equal abandon, eventually emptying myself inside of her as she clasped her legs around me.

"Wow," she said a few moments later as she reclined on the bed in the same position I had left her, on her back with her legs spread. "You're something."

"So are you," I replied, running my fingers up her bare thigh.

"You can tell me the rest of the story now," she said. "I think talking is all I'll be able to do for a while."

I thought for a moment about the conversation I'd had with Smith and Amrine back at the Biltmore and nodded to myself. I rolled over so that I was facing her.

"I will," I said, seriously. "But this is some deep shit, and the CIA guys play for keeps. You've seen them in action. You need to understand that if what I'm going to tell you leaves this room, you'll just disappear. No one will know where you've gone and you'll never be seen again. And odds are I won't know anything about it until after it's been done."

I saw her swallow hard in the dim light of the bedroom.

"I understand," she said. "At this point, I don't know who I'd tell anyway."

I took the next several minutes and outlined the whole business to her, from Bob Barnett's stepson to Mark Tappan and Miguel Hidalgo. When I was finished, she merely nodded as she lay there. As silence set in, I could almost hear the cogs in her head turning.

"Good Lord," she said at last. "No wonder they're trying to kill you."

I shook my head in the semidarkness, and the movement caused her to look over at me.

"What?" she asked.

"I'm not sure they came here just to kill me. If that had been their goal, they would have waited until it was later and I was asleep. You were a target of opportunity. You're part of this now, whether you wanted to be or not. Apparently they think you've become a loose end."

She didn't act as if my revelation surprised her. I watched her as she laid there, her generous breasts moving gently up and down as she breathed and her eyes focused on something only she could see. Even in the dimness, I could swear that I saw a gleam of realization in her eyes.

"I think I stumbled onto the reason Turnidge is working on this with Tappan," she turned to face me. "Your involvement notwithstanding, of course."

I nodded.

"And what would that be?"

Her voice became sarcastic. "Well, you know that one of the things that we in the OSI have excelled in is gathering evidence about extramarital affairs. Great utilization of taxpayer dollars there."

I smiled at her.

"Glad you see it for the foolishness it is," I said.

"No one likes doing that sort of thing," she said, shaking her head on the bedsheets. "But it does produce a certain skill set."

I nodded. "I can see that."

"And you learn to recognize certain things and to read between the lines when you don't have all the evidence."

"I can see that too."

She turned her body to mine, supporting her blonde head on her hand as she did so. I marveled again at her incredible body, the outlines of which were clearly visible in the darkness.

"And?" I asked.

She exhaled in disgust. "So I'm pretty sure that Alan Turnidge is a pedophile, and I'm also pretty sure that he consumes a steady diet of teenage girls."

"Whoa!" I said. "How the hell did you arrive at that conclusion?"

"A couple of things," she said. "Most of which occurred even before I was suspended. The Commander's Group typically works out of the main conference room next to his office. I was in the conference room alone a lot while the other agents were out doing fieldwork, and I think he forgot I was in there because several times I overheard phone conversations he had in his office, even with the door closed, mostly because he talked so damn loud. I'd hear him describing girls, hair color and hair style, eye color, body styles, personalities, clothes, everything. At first I thought he was talking about his daughters or nieces or something like that. But later, I realized he was placing orders."

"That was kind of a leap, don't you think?"

"Not really. If you had heard the way in which he spoke and the details, it just sounded creepy. Besides..." she paused for a moment.

"You followed him didn't you?"

She smiled grimly. "I did and frankly, I wish I hadn't."

"What did you see?"

"There were several nights that I just followed him to his house in Virginia. But there were others where I follow him to a condominium in Crystal City. Shortly after he got there, a teenage girl would arrive and the two of them would stay there for several hours. Eventually, she would leave. And after a discreet interval, he'd leave as well."

"Wow," I said. "That's pretty damning."

"Sometimes the same girl would come back for a few times and other times he'd have a different one every night he went there. He averaged between three and four sessions per week and two to three different girls."

"Jesus," I said quietly.

"It gets better, or worse, depending on how you look at it. The condo is owned by the Onero Consulting Company, which lists its headquarters in Cabo San Lucas, Mexico."

I felt my jaw drop open.

"Yes," Lena continued, answering my mute questions, "Miguel Hidalgo owns the condo and someone he knows or pays is providing the girls, probably through the local white slavery trade."

I rolled over onto my back as I digested what she'd told me.

"There have to be pictures," I said, brilliant conspiratorial mastermind that I was.

"No there aren't," Lena said, chuckling. "There's video."

"Even better," I said.

"Nine years of it," she said. "Starting in 2000, I think. There's a catalog of it in an album that the local det. commander had on her desk when I dropped in to introduce myself, shortly after I got here."

I glanced over at her.

"What can I say, I'm nosy! She left the room while I was in

there and the album was on her desk. We're very meticulous about our filing system in the OSI and this one didn't fit any of the specifications, but while she was talking to me she couldn't take her eyes off of it. So when she stepped out of the room to deal with an issue in the outer office, I stole a glance at it. It was one of those books that have plastic sheets with pockets for DVDs. Every one of them had Turnidge's name on it and a date. There were lots of pages."

"How do you know what was on them?" I asked, even though I thought I knew the answer. "There could have been anything there."

"I took one," she said meekly, "toward the back of the book where it wouldn't be so obvious. I took it back to my room and watched it. I had to stop after about five minutes. It was disgusting."

"Did you watch it on your government-issued laptop?"

"No," she said. "I'm not that stupid."

"No accusation intended. We all do things reflexively sometimes. So did you watch on a personal laptop?"

She nodded.

"Just the other night."

"And that laptop has an Internet connection, does it not?" I asked.

She nodded again.

"Tracer program. Coded into the DVD. If anyone plays it without deactivating the program, the DVD broadcasts its IP address to a collection point. That's how they know you're a liability now."

Lena closed her eyes and snorted in exasperation.

"Oh my God!" she cried. "How could I have been that stupid?"

"And that's why they came for you tonight as well as for me," I said. "If the local det. commander has that video, then Tappan knows it exists, and she and Miguel are using it to get Turnidge to do whatever they want. And they don't want anyone looking too closely into what they're doing here."

She looked at me and shook her head in disbelief.

"What the hell are we going to do?"

"Well, if I were you, I'd run as far from me as you can possibly get so you don't get caught in the typical frag pattern I tend to generate."

"Where does that leave you?" she asked quietly.

"Good question," I said. "When I find out, I'll let you know."

Chapter Fourteen

Contract Day Ten
Friday, July 2, 2010
0700 Hours Local Time
VIP Senior Officers' Quarters
Luke Air Force Base, Arizona

Lena was gone when I woke up, which disappointed me somewhat, because a certain part of me seemed to be expecting another iteration of the previous evening's activity. I rolled over to find she'd left a simple note on the nightstand next to me.

"Decided to take your advice. Thanks for everything last night. XOX, L."

"Great," I said to the empty room.

I lay back on the pillow as I contemplated the events of the previous night. Going from feeling heartsick about the possible assassination of Sarah and Colleen to enjoying another woman in a few hours' time didn't seem to reflect well on any sort of moral or relationship scale. I knew that as much as I cared about Sarah, a part of me had relegated that relationship to the realm of the impossible. And last night had been about doing what I always seemed to do best when I cared about someone—building distance between her and me.

It was about letting her go. Another part of me rationalized that last night was about getting intel and there certainly had been plenty of that. But neither realization made me feel any better.

I stared at the ceiling and sighed. "Normal ops, Pearce," I said to the empty room. "Normal ops."

I looked at the bedside clock and realized that thanks to the activities of the previous evening, I hadn't set the usual alarm. The clock read 7:00 a.m. As my faculties kicked in and my blood began to redistribute itself, I remembered that I had class that morning.

Exactly seventeen minutes later, I was in the rental car on my way to the academic building. For several reasons, I decided not to leave the H & K in my room and had made space for the weapon in the briefcase I carried around. I had to carry it with the suppressor unmounted, but I figured that if I had to use it so quickly that I didn't have time to attach the cylindrical device, survival and not stealth would be the primary issue. I walked into the academic building for the morning session about ten minutes later and made a quick stop in the snack bar to snag a cup of coffee. Interestingly, the 56th TRS had ordered personalized ceramic coffee mugs for the three of us. Mine had the squadron patch on one side and an F-16 silhouette on the other with "T. C." monogrammed underneath. I wondered if that was the standard practice for every VIP class that came through. As I strode into the classroom, exactly three minutes early for the class, I found my two fellow students, Colonels Black and Billings, eyeing me appraisingly.

"Busy night, T. C.?" Brock said with a half-smile on his face.

I felt my eyes narrow.

"Are you sure you're up for today's class?" Christine quipped.

"I'm just fine, thanks," I said slowly.

"Have you gotten enough rest?" she added.

I nodded.

"That's funny," Brock said. "Lindal and I went to a late dinner last night. When we came back, we saw some hot number in a sundress enter your quarters. And then this morning as I was doing my early run, I saw said hot number leave your quarters. So apparently she spent some time there."

I felt my cheeks flush slightly. "That was an unexpected... development," I said.

Brock grinned. "Unexpected that she came or unexpected that she stayed?" he said.

"Came being the operative word in that sentence," Christine added, with a sparkle in her eye. "And hopefully it wasn't a one-time occurrence if she stayed all night."

I looked at them both and shook my head. "What's up with you two?" I asked.

"We're just trying to live vicariously through your exploits," Christine said with a wry smile on her face. "We're just happy that somebody is getting laid."

"So we have a bet about last night that we need you to settle," Brock said, suddenly serious.

"Okay," I said, totally at a loss as to what they could be betting on.

"How many?" he asked.

"What?" I countered. "How many what?"

"Episodes," Christine said, crinkling her nose. I couldn't decide whether she found the question distasteful or intriguing. Perhaps it was both.

"Episodes?"

"Engagements!" Christine said impatiently. "How many times did you do her?"

"Seriously?" I asked.

"Yep," Brock said. "Lindal and I have a hundred bucks

riding on your answer."

My eyes widened. "Wow," I said. "You guys must need some action. Jesus."

"Yeah, yeah, T. C.," Christine said. "C'mon, spill the goods."

"In a minute," I said, smiling back at them. "In a minute. But first I have to know, what exactly were you betting on?"

They looked at me for a moment and then looked at each other. Their expressions became a little sheepish.

"C'mon," I said, mimicking Christine's tone, "spill the goods. What was the bet?"

Brock looked at me and then looked at Christine and then back at me again. For a guy as big and as obviously tough as he undoubtedly was, he actually seemed a little timid.

"Well," he said, looking away, "you're kind of an old guy, like me. So I was thinking... uh... once... maybe twice."

I nodded. "Seems reasonable," I said. Then I looked at Christine. "And you?" I asked.

She peered back at me intently. There was a sensual light behind her eyes that seemed to peer into my soul.

"I was thinking more," she said. "Like three to four."

I laughed. "Very flattering," I said, nodding, "if not a bit unrealistic. I am over fifty years old."

Brock turned to her and held his hand out.

"See?" he said.

I smiled at him and inclined my head at Christine. "Pay the woman," I said.

His head snapped around to look at me. "What?" he said.

"Her answer was more correct than yours," I said simply.

"More correct?" he asked. "More correct? What the hell does that mean?"

I shrugged. "She was closer."

"Closer?" they both asked nearly in unison.

"Yes, closer." I said.

"But not exactly correct?" Christine pressed.

I shook my head. "Not exactly," I said.

There was a moment of silence as the two of them looked at each other and then back at me.

"So what was the real number?" Christine asked after a long moment.

I paused to consider my phraseology for the reply.

"Five," said a voice I knew from the back of the room. "And knowing T. C., it probably would have been six if she hadn't left before he woke up. He really needs to learn to turn off the recording app on the BlackBerry we gave him. All that activity made the tech guys a little hot."

We turned to see John Amrine and Dave Smith walking through the door. Amrine, who had spoken, had a wry smile on his face. Smith shut the door behind them.

"But don't be too impressed," Amrine continued. "We've got him on this drug regimen that has all sorts of interesting side effects."

"I need to get some of that," Brock murmured.

"Damn," Christine added. "Lucky girl."

"Hey, guys," I said. "Fancy meeting you here."

"The landscape has changed a little, T. C.," Dave Smith said, almost apologetically.

"Apparently so if you guys are making a public appearance," I said slowly.

"Did you get a chance to look at the faces of the two guys you wasted in your quarters last night?" Amrine asked.

Brock and Christine seemed bewildered now, Brock a little less than Christine because he had worked with these two before, but still, the two of them looked at Smith and Amrine and then back at me and then back to the two CIA officers. The expressions on their faces made it clear that they weren't keeping up.

"No," I said. "I was too busy shooting. Thanks for the UMP, by the way. Awesome weapon."

"Thought you might like that," Smith said, smiling.

"I just assumed they were Hispanic," I said. "I assumed Miguel sent them. The driver was Hispanic."

Amrine shook his head. "Understandable," he said, "but incorrect. They weren't Hispanic. They were Chinese."

It took a moment for the ramifications of that revelation to hit me.

"Wow," I said. "The Chinese are getting impatient. They're going to do it soon, aren't they?"

Smith and Amrine nodded in unison.

"Monday," Smith said. "All three of you will probably be airborne on your first transition flight when it happens. And one of you will have to help us stop it."

***

Later, Brock, Christine, and I were somewhat quiet over lunch. Our usual banter and interaction seemed to have been sidetracked. Smith and Amrine had spent the better part of an hour briefing the three of us. How they managed to displace the required academic schedule and instructor without attracting the attention of the TRS leadership remained something of a mystery. That reality seemed to be heavy in the air around us. I stole glances at Brock as we ate. He seemed impassive. After he understood Smith and Amrine's presence in the business at hand, he accepted it. Christine's reaction was quite the opposite. This was her first exposure to life in the shadowland. And she seemed to be having difficulty understanding it.

"Who the fuck were those guys?" she blurted out at last. "And how in the hell did they know all that shit?"

Brock looked at her with a half-smile. "Language, Colonel Billings, language," he said.

"Please," Christine said, unamused, "I'm a fighter pilot, not a priss." She looked at me. "So those are the two guys that got you involved in that business last fall?"

I nodded. "It's a long and very boring story, but yes, they're the two who recruited me. I guess they're my handlers now."

"Are they worth a shit?" she asked. "The stakes just got pretty fucking high here. And just how did you get on the wrong side of a Mexican drug lord?"

I speared a chunk of chicken and a piece of lettuce with my fork and then looked back at her.

"Do you remember that business last November with the shootout near Catalina Island?"

"You mean the assassination attempt against the two presidents? Of course! It dominated the news for two weeks!"

I nodded at her as I put the food in my mouth and chewed. "We worked together on that," I said a moment or two later. "They know what they're doing. I'd be dead a couple of times over if it hadn't been for them."

I was looking down at my plate and getting some more salad on my fork when I felt both their eyes on me. I raised my head and looked back at them.

"What?"

"It was you in the T-38," Christine said quietly. "You were the one who stopped the attack."

"Jesus, man," Brock said respectfully. "How fast were you going when you punched out?"

"I'm not exactly sure," I said, looking down at my plate again. "The last time I looked at the airspeed in the HUD it was increasing through 500 knots."

There was silence for several moments. You don't have to explain the dangers and injuries of a high-speed ejection to fighter pilots. Thanks to numerous briefings, safety reports, and egress training sessions, they knew exactly what could be expected.

"Listen," I said, trying to move the conversation on, "what you need to keep in mind here is that these two guys are really good at their jobs, and they've kept me alive on multiple occasions. If they have intel that says the F-35 will move on Monday then it's good information and their plan to have at least one of us airborne when the jet moves is a good one. All we have to do is follow the jet to the border, get confirmation, and the F-22's from Holloman will do the rest."

Brock looked at me.

"How can they be so certain about the time?"

I thought for a moment, and Joe Sanchez's face popped up in my mind's eye. Joe was a DEA deep cover operative who had been working for Miguel Hidalgo for several years. He and I had exchanged intel during my last encounter with Miguel. He was now one of Miguel's right-hand men. Odds were quite high that he'd overheard a conversation.

"They have their ways," I replied. "I don't like to think about how they gather the information. That's all the really secret shit."

Brock and Christine nodded.

"In the meantime, since nothing is going to happen until Monday, it would be good if the three of us got off base and out of town for the weekend," I said. "In the event someone comes looking for me or us."

Christine's face went slightly pale.

"Do you think they'll come after Brock and me?" she said, her eyes wide.

"I don't know," I said, "but better safe than sorry. Besides, we could use a class getaway." I looked over at Brock. "What do you think?"

"Sounds great to me," he said. "Are you going to bring that UMP gun with you?"

I nodded. "Seems like the prudent thing to do."

"You got any other weapons?"

"Yep. I have a Glock .45 and a 1911-style .45. I have trouble deciding what to wear some days."

"Then I'm good. Let's head up to Sedona. We'll get three rooms at one of those nice hotel/spa places, sit by the pool, and drink some beer." He eyed Christine. "You in, Lindal?"

She smiled. "A long weekend by the pool with two hot guys? Is that a trick question?"

Chapter Fifteen

Contract Day Ten
Friday, July 2, 2010
1735 Hours Local Time
Somewhere on Arizona Highway 179
On the Way to Sedona, Arizona

"So what exactly is a sanitation crew?" Christine asked from the backseat.

We were in my rented Chevy Impala, had just exited off of I-17 and were now winding our way toward Sedona up Arizona Highway 179. I remembered the road well, having traveled it many times while stationed at Luke. It was refreshing to see the scenic vistas once again. I was glad Brock had recommended Sedona as a place to stay the weekend. It was one of my favorite places on earth and the incredible beauty of the town and its surrounding terrain had tended to calm me when I went there many years ago. I hoped it would have the same effect this time.

Christine sat sprawled in the backseat of the Impala, nursing a large cup of Red Bull energy drink that she'd liberally spiked with vodka after our last rest stop. Brock and I rode up front with our weaponry within easy reach.

"Hello?" Christine said from the backseat. "Mr. CIA

Operative, what's a sanitation crew?"

"They're the guys who clean up after messy events," I said. "And the other night was the first time I'd ever seen one in action."

"So they clean up dead bodies and that sort of thing?"

"Yes," I answered. "But it goes further than that. You know that commercial for the company that cleans up your home or business after a fire or flood?"

"I do!" Christine said merrily. "We had to use them on our house at Shaw once. ' Like it never even happened' is their motto."

"Think that by an order of magnitude," I said. "When these guys are done, there's not only no trace visible to the eye, there's no trace that even the forensic evidence folks will find. Carpet is replaced, plaster is repaired, and the cleaning agents they use would never pass the muster of the EPA folks. They were in my quarters for a little over an hour, and when they were done, everything looked completely normal—even down to the worn color of the paint on the walls."

"So what happens to the bodies?" Christine asked. Her voice was barely above a whisper.

"Well, apparently, they're identified and then disposed of."

"Disposed of? How?"

"Lye, most likely," Brock said calmly as he regarded the road in front of us. "A human body will completely dissolve into liquid in a vat of lye. Once everything is reduced to liquid, they just need to pour the remains somewhere."

"That's an interesting piece of knowledge," I said, glancing across the car at him. "How did you acquire it?"

"Some of the places I've flown the Viper have been run by governments that weren't exactly stable," he said. "When political opponents clash, the losers often need to be taken care of."

I nodded. "I see."

"I feel so fucking sheltered," Christine said. "All I've ever done is fly the Viper in normal places doing normal things. I mean, I've been to war in it, but I've never done anything... weird like you two."

"I was just like you until about a year ago, Lindal," I said. "And trust me. This abnormal shit is overrated."

"That's the truth," Brock said. "Speaking of abnormal, you've seen them haven't you?"

"Yes," I replied, "black Crown Victoria, about four or five cars back since we left the base. You'd think they'd use a car that's a little less conspicuous."

"This car is clean, right?"

I nodded, remembering the GPS tracker I had removed a few nights ago. "I swept the car the night before last and swept it again this morning."

"You know," Brock said, "it might be convenient if these guys weren't allowed to follow us all the way to our destination."

"I agree. You have any ideas?"

He nodded. "We'll pull a little trick I learned from some of our friends in the Middle East."

"You've got the lead on the right, I'm supporting."

"And what am I supposed to be doing?" Christine asked from the backseat.

"We're going to need you to look gorgeous and dead," Brock answered. "And if required, we may need you to shoot one of these guys."

I saw her eyes widen in the rearview mirror.

"Sorry I asked," she said.

***

Twenty minutes later, we had driven several miles up a side road, out of sight of Highway 179, and pulled the car onto the gravel shoulder. We left Christine in the backseat of the car with her head resting on the seat back. Her designer T-shirt was spattered with the contents of some fast-food ketchup packets. Some quick work with a pocketknife created the appropriate holes in the shirt to fool the eyes of those who would look in. Brock and I positioned ourselves in front of the car and behind it, using some of the huge boulders as cover, and waited for our followers to appear.

They didn't take long.

The black Crown Victoria made its appearance after just a few minutes. It slowly cruised by our car, the faces of its occupants barely visible behind heavily tinted windows. It went up the road and around a bend, apparently turned around, and then came back.

I felt my phone vibrate in its holster.

There was a text message from Brock. THIS IS IT, it said.

The car was moving much more quickly this time. It sped up to the side of our car and skidded to a halt. Instantly, three men piled out of it with submachine guns in their hands. One went around the front of the car and another went around the back. The third one, apparently the leader, approached the car from the side and investigated the scene we'd created for him. I watched him cock his head slightly, and then he opened the rear door and leaned into the car.

And that's when Christine's cell phone rang. Right on cue, the attackers turned their heads to look at the source of the sound.

From my vantage point, I watched Brock literally materialize from his cover and take his man down with a movement of his hands that was so fast I couldn't have told anyone what he'd done. I sighted the UMP over the top of my boulder and fired a split second burst at the man nearest me. In contrast to the confined environment of my quarters, the popping sound of the suppressor was much less pronounced in the great outdoors, and I doubted it was audible more than a few yards away. As the near man's body jerked with the impacts of the bullets, the driver exited the car, and I shifted my aim point to him. I targeted his body and let go with a long burst to ensure I nailed him. I saw a few holes open up in his body, less than I expected, but he doubled over obligingly and collapsed to the ground next to the car, out of sight. Apparently though, he had forgotten to shift the car into park, and it began to slowly roll forward.

In the meantime, the attacker who had stuck his head into the backseat found himself confronting the business end of a Glock 36 wielded by a woman he thought was a corpse. He paused for just a moment and then attempted to lift his weapon. But he never made it. Brock reached around his head and broke his neck in an effortless display of speed and strength. The last attacker crumpled to the ground.

"B-Rock?" I called. "The car is rolling."

Brock sprinted after the car, leapt in, and got the Crown Victoria stopped. Then he backed it up to shoulder behind our car and shifted it into park.

"Damn, T. C.," he said as he exited the car. "You sure made a mess of these guys."

"Had to be sure," I replied as I disconnected the suppressor from the H & K. "Besides, this thing shoots so damn fast it's a little hard to turn it off. Funny though."

"What?"

"It didn't feel quite the same as it did the other night for some reason."

"Every combat situation feels a little different," he said hurriedly. "Anyway, in the trunk with these guys?" he asked.

I nodded back.

"Seems like the thing to do."

"Let me guess," Christine said as she crawled out of the backseat of our car. Her hands were shaking as she handed me the Glock 36. She reached into the backseat, retrieved her drink, and took a long pull from it. "The next call is to the sanitation crew, right?"

"Yep," I said. "Only this will be a lot easier to deal with than that business in my quarters." I looked at Brock. "After we get these guys loaded, we're going to need to drive the car quite a bit further up the road."

"Yes," he said. "I'll transmit a GPS location to your boys. We can't have the local yokels discover the car before the crew gets here."

It only took us a few minutes to get the crew's bodies into the Crown Victoria's spacious trunk.

"Damn good thing they didn't come after us in a Subaru or some shit," Brock said as we tossed the last one in.

I regarded the faces before we shut the trunk lid.

"No one of the Asian persuasion in this group," I said. "They all look Hispanic to me."

"What do you think that means?" he asked.

"I don't know," I replied. "Maybe Miguel is trying to save a little face. Maybe he's trying to prove he can handle it without any help."

"Could be," Brock said. "Do you think they'll try again while we're in Sedona?"

"Well, they'll have to find us first; and I've got an ID and some credit cards that aren't me, which I'll use to pay for expenses. As long as we don't use our own cards, don't walk around too much, and stay off our cell phones, we should be okay."

Brock nodded and tilted his head toward Christine who had returned to the Impala and was sitting in the passenger seat, staring blankly ahead.

"Think she can deal with this?" he asked.

"She's a fighter pilot," I answered him. "She'll be fine."

He nodded.

"Should be," he said.

I closed the lid of the trunk and looked at his clothes and down at my own.

"Moving bodies is messy business," I said. "We're going to need to get rinsed off before we try to check into a hotel."

"We'll find a car wash," he said. "Get the majority of it off. We'll change while we're there."

"You have done this before," I said.

He grinned. "Maybe once or twice."

"I don't know about you, but I need a drink."

He inclined his head to the car again. "I think we all do."

***

About two hours later, we were sipping drinks on the patio at the Amara Resort and Spa with a view of the grand rock formations of Sedona around us. I was nursing an outstanding martini, Brock was drinking vodka and soda, and Christine was drinking her ever-present Red Bull and vodka. I wondered how an energy drink and a depressant, such as alcohol, mixed in her system. She had remained mute since we'd found a place to stash the attackers' car and left the side road. Brock and I hadn't been that talkative either. He seemed to be content to ride along in silence. It wasn't a tense silence or even an awkward one. And he certainly didn't act as if what we'd just done troubled him. He just didn't mind not talking. I liked that.

"It's a lot more personal when you see them die," Christine said at last.

I nodded. "As fighter pilots, we do the killing from a distance, with weapons that let us stay well away from our targets and victims," I said. "There was a story that I heard a long time ago about Richard Bong, our highest scoring ace in World War II. I don't know whether it's true or not. The story goes that while Bong was waiting for the transport that was going to take him out of the theater and back to the US after his last mission, the airfield he was waiting at was attacked by a few Japanese planes. An American plane shot down one of the Japanese planes. And since the Japanese found it dishonorable to use parachutes, the Japanese plane crash-landed very near to where Bong was standing. He watched the Japanese pilot burn to death in front of him, and the sight turned him into a blubbering mess. He had never made the connection between shooting down an enemy plane and taking an enemy life before, but on that day, he got it. From that point forward, he was ruined for combat. It was just as well that he was transferring back to the States."

I looked over at Christine. "How many combat missions have you flown?" I asked.

She shook her head, and I could see wetness in the corners of her eyes. "I don't know," she said, "a couple of hundred."

"And how much ordnance have you dropped on live targets?"

She shook her head again. "I was flying Wild Weasel missions mostly, so I didn't drop a lot of ordnance."

"But," I pushed gently, "you've had no doubts that, at times, you've fired something or dropped something and people have died."

She looked down at her drink. "Yes," she said.

"It's one thing to kill people," I said. "It's another to actually see the human cost." I reached over, took her hand, and squeezed it. "Today you saw the cost. That's not a bad thing. It will make you understand and respect what we do a lot more. It will make you a better leader."

Brock was nodding from his chair. "Very true," he said. "I've worked for a lot of yahoos who didn't get it."

She squeezed my hand in return and I released hers. The hotel had provided us with a nice selection of bar snacks at our patio table, and I grabbed a handful of assorted nuts and popped a few of them into my mouth.

"The rooms here are quite nice," Christine said in a voice that was straining to be cheerful. "This was a good selection."

"I was here a few times but that was many years ago," I said. "They've renovated since my last visit and obviously maintained the standard. This is one of the best places in Sedona. And tomorrow, you can do the whole spa, massage, facial, manicure and pedicure regimen, if that's something you enjoy, all courtesy of the US government."

She smiled meekly. "Sounds like fun. I may be a fighter pilot but I'm also a woman, and I do like that sort of thing."

"I thought you might," I said, smiling back at her. "And it's awesome that you can maintain your femininity and your edge in the cockpit." I raised my glass at her. "Your husband is a lucky man."

"I guess," she said, looking away at one of the huge scenic rock formations in the distance. "We don't see much of each other. He's in the astronaut program, so it seems he's always in training."

"Training for what?" Brock asked. "We ain't got no rockets for him to go up on."

"He's training to go up on the International Space Station," she said. "They ride up there on Russian launch vehicles."

"He's going to ride on Russian shit?" Brock said, aghast. "They can't make anything that's worth a damn. Hope he makes it!"

I shot a glance over at him but he ignored me.

"I guess I do too," Christine said quietly.

"So, Miss Christine," I said after taking a long sip of my martini. "I need you to enlighten me. What's the story behind your handle, Lindal?"

Christine blushed slightly, and Brock leaned back in his chair with a huge smile on his face.

"That's a story I'd like to hear myself," he said.

She smiled demurely and took a long drink of her Red Bull and vodka. "Well, you know what it stands for, right?" she asked.

I shook my head. "Not at all."

She smirked at me. "It started when I was new in the Viper. There weren't very many female fighter pilots in those days, so we used to keep to ourselves. One day we had a squadron gathering in the officers' club and one of the more obnoxious and sexist pilots in the squadron said he didn't think women could drink like fighter pilots and he'd like to see me do a drink called a blow job."

Brock nodded. "A shooter made with Bailey's and amaretto with a little whipped cream on top. Definitely a chick drink but very tasty."

"I was familiar with the drink," she continued, "but I told him I'd do him better. I'd do five blow jobs and not even use my hands if he could do the same with five bottled beers."

"And what was the object of the bet?" I asked.

"I'm not sure there was one," she said. "I just wanted him to leave me alone and shut up."

I nodded.

"So we lined up the beers and the blow jobs on the bar, and we each went to work. I had a little bit of an unfair advantage, because my sorority sisters and I used to do a lot of those in college. I could even stick my tongue in the glass and get all the cream out of it nice and sensually. It used to drive the guys in our big brother fraternity crazy."

I grinned at her. "I bet it did!"

"Well, I made a bigger and bigger production out of each drink and kept doing them more slowly and more sensually with a lot of tonguing and lip smacking and soon everyone was rooting for me. Someone said it was like watching Linda Lovelace, the chick from the movie Deep Throat, in action, and they started chanting 'LINDA, LINDA,' and that turned into 'LINDAL, LINDAL.' I finished my five drinks before he finished the second bottle of beer."

"That's outstanding!" I said. "What a great story!"

She nodded and took another sip of her drink. "I had my official squadron name tag with LINDAL on it by the end of the week. And I wore it with pride."

"As well you should have!" Brock said. "So I have to know. What happened to the guy you were betting against? How'd he take it?"

"Surprisingly, he was okay with it. And we got along well after that. I ended up marrying him."

"Good to hear," I said. "He is a lucky man."

"Maybe," Christine said quietly as she looked into the distance once again. "But he'd probably argue that."

***

Later that night, after many more drinks and some superb cuisine, there was a knock on the interconnecting door in my room. I was typing an e-mail to Smith and Amrine on my BlackBerry, and I put the device aside to answer the door, taking the Colt Commander with me. I opened the door to find Christine "Lindal" Billings standing there in gym shorts and a T-shirt. She looked up at me shyly.

"Can I ask you to do me a huge favor?" she asked.

"Sure," I said. "Name it."

"Can I sleep in here? I'll sleep on the sofa over there if it will make you more comfortable. I just don't want to be alone tonight."

"Fine with me," I said. "But we can share the bed. It's a king. We can stay on our separate sides and everything will be prim and proper."

"I'm not terribly worried about that," she said. "I just don't want you to think I'm some kind of slut putting a move on you."

I smiled at her. "Nobody puts moves on me," I said. "That only happens to the good-looking guys. By the way, I don't typically ask this question when married women want to sleep with me, but I respect you and your husband enough to ask it. Is he going to be okay with this? Are you and he going to be okay with it?"

She shrugged. "He's not the jealous type," she said. "Trust me. He won't mind."

I nodded. "If you say so. Give me just a minute."

I finished my e-mail and then prepared for bed. I plugged everything in to charge and then brushed my teeth. Finally, I began to undress. Christine watched me from the bed. She had doffed her gym shorts before climbing in, and I saw a glance of something black and lacy underneath.

"I hope this doesn't make you uncomfortable," I said, standing there in my undershorts. "I usually don't wear anything to bed, but I'll leave these on tonight for propriety's sake."

Christine smiled at me. "I don't usually wear anything either," she said. "So I'm doing the same thing for you."

"Sounds like a plan," I said.

I made sure the Colt was positioned on the nightstand, and then I turned out the light. I climbed into the bed and made sure I was well away from her on the large mattress.

"Good night, Christine." I said into the darkness.

"Good night, Colin," she replied.

We lay there in the darkness for several minutes, and I could tell that she was restless next to me. She shifted position several times and then exhaled impatiently.

"Something wrong?" I asked.

"I'm going to sound like the neediest girl in the world, but all this shit has got me really freaked out. Can I ask you for another favor?"

"Absolutely."

"Could you hold me for a few minutes? It will help me get to sleep, and I don't think I'll be able to calm down without it."

"Sure, if that's what you want," I said. "How do you want to do this?"

She moved over to the middle of the bed and then turned on her side, away from me.

"If you could just put your arms around me like this while I sleep, it would be perfect."

I moved myself up against her, and she lifted her head so I could put an arm underneath it. Then I placed my other arm in front of her stomach and rested it lightly against her. As if it was the most natural thing in the world, she pushed her body back into me and then interlaced her fingers into mine and pressed my hand into her abdomen, just below her breasts. Her body was both voluptuous and firm against me. I wondered how long it would take my penis to figure out that a mere two layers of thin cloth separated it from an ass that felt spectacular. But that thought became lost as I felt the rhythm of her breathing and the tremors that were shaking her body.

She sniffled just a bit, and I realized she was crying. I squeezed her in an attempt to comfort her. "Those guys were going to kill us," she said softly. "If you and B-Rock hadn't set a trap for them, they would have."

I nodded, my face rubbing her silky dark hair. "Not much doubt that was the plan," I said, trying to keep my tone as gentle as possible. "You don't send four armed men if your purpose is merely surveillance."

"How do you know so much about this stuff?" she asked after a long moment.

I laughed softly. "When you get thrown into it, like I did, you have to learn quickly if you want to live. I didn't have much choice. Besides, this spring, when I wasn't learning how to fly new jets, I got to spend some time in a few very special classes."

She was quiet for a while as we lay there together. I knew where her thoughts were. We all have our preconceptions of the way the world is supposed to work; and in spite of the cinematic images we may be bombarded with, we don't want to believe that there are people who kill others with no regard at all for the possible consequences. It's like becoming aware of a new force in the physical universe—a force directed at you and one that you can't understand.

"How many people have you killed?" she asked, finally. "Not with an airplane, I mean. How many people have you killed… personally?"

I knew why she was asking. It wasn't morbid curiosity. She wanted to know if I could protect her.

I rolled onto my back and sighed involuntarily.

"I never really thought about it," I said quietly. "It's not like I have a pistol grip with notches on it or something like that."

I began to do some mental math, but then I stopped the calculations as I became aware of something that surprised me. In spite of the rage that I had struggled with throughout my entire life, last night in my quarters and then today on the empty road, I had killed several men and felt no emotion at all. There was no rage and no high. Instead, there was the cold satisfaction of a job well done and a businesslike resignation about the logistics of the clean up afterward. Apparently I was getting used to killing. And it was equally apparent that I didn't have a problem with it. Whatever conscience I may have had was long extinct. I couldn't decide if that was good or bad.

"Huh," I said unconsciously.

Christine turned her body so she was on her back but facing me slightly. She continued to hold my left hand pressed against her. Even in the darkness, I could feel the pressure from those deep, brown eyes. She needed an answer to her question.

I propped my head up on my right hand and looked down at the outline of her face and the dark hair that surrounded her head on the pillow. Her breasts, the outlines of which were clearly visible under the thin white T-shirt, rose and fell with her breathing and the peaks of her nipples were discernible, even in the semidarkness.

"I'm not sure," I said, forcing my mind into a platonic place. "But it's into double digits. I don't consider that a badge of honor, by the way. It's just a function of the circumstances I've found myself in."

"I know," Christine said. "You can be a killer. But that's not what defines you."

I opened my mouth, but before I could talk, Christine spoke again.

"It's your eyes," she said, quietly. "They give you away."

"What?"

"When I first met you, in the classroom, your eyes were warm. They actually seemed to sparkle." She swallowed, and I saw her throat move in the semidarkness. "But today, on the road, they were hard. Cold. Almost lifeless. It was like you were a different person."

I nodded. I knew what was coming next.

"At first, I thought that made you exactly like those men who came after us, but the more I thought about it, the more I realized it wasn't true."

I raised my eyebrows at her. That wasn't what I was expecting. "And what made you think that?"

"Because apparently you have a warm side. You can be cold when you need to be. But you're not all the time."

I shook my head in wonder at her words. "Without trying to sound rude, how can you possibly know that?"

She raised her left hand and touched the side of my face.

"I just do," she said, tenderly. "Just like I knew you could have sex with the woman in your quarters more than once or twice. It's like I know you somehow."

The touch of her fingers on my skin was electric, and I felt the warm tingle of arousal in my extremities. My member began to engorge; and since it was pressed against her leg, it didn't seem to be something we could ignore.

But fortunately, we did.

"Were you successful in protecting the last woman you were with?" Christine asked. "Before last night I mean."

I gave the question some thought and then nodded.

"For the most part," I said. "There was a little back and forth but she was alive at the end, and the guys who were trying to kill her paid the price."

Her hand dropped to my shoulder.

"What did you do to them?"

I looked down at her. "They don't call me T. C. for nothing," I said, quietly.

She tensed beside me. "You cut their throats?"

"Yes."

"Instead of shooting them or something? Why?"

"Without boring you with an extended discussion of my psychological baggage, the short answer is that I wanted to."

"You wanted to cut their throats?" Even in the dim light of the room I could see her eyes widen. "Why?"

I shrugged. "They had caused a lot of people a lot of pain. They needed to die and die badly. Bullets would have been too quick. They needed to suffer. They needed to feel their lives ebbing away from them and be powerless to do anything about it. They needed to feel like their victims. But even more importantly, they had fucked with people I cared about."

She seemed to accept that explanation, and she dropped her hand to my right bicep.

"How did you feel about it?" she asked quietly.

"Good," I said, matter-of-factly. "I wanted to punish them, and I enjoyed watching them die."

"Because they messed with people you cared about."

I nodded. "Among other things."

She moved her left hand to my back and began to pull me down to her. "Let's see if I can get you to care about me that way," she said, her voice suddenly breathless.

I stiffened my upper body to stop the descent to her lips.

"Christine, you don't have to do this. I already care about you, and I'll protect you in any way I can. I don't want to come between you and your husband."

She shook her head on the pillow and chuckled.

"You won't be. He's gay. I found out about five years after we got married. I've been his beard so he doesn't attract attention while he's in the astronaut program. And," she let go of my left hand and reached over to grip my erect penis through my underwear, "the last time he came to bed with one of these, he had just watched Gladiator with Russell Crowe."

Christine, Brock, and I spent a great weekend together. And every moment we could be alone, Christine and I made love until we were both sore. It was rare that I had the opportunity to compare two women and their performance in bed so directly. Lena had been proficient and technically skilled, but for her it was totally about the sex. She liked having orgasms and was happy to use me to get them. Christine was different. She craved the togetherness—something she had been lacking for a very long time. The sex we enjoyed was an expression of the togetherness and that made it engaging on every level and intensely pleasurable.

Late Sunday afternoon, as I regarded her bikini-clad body basking in the sun by the pool, I could feel a tenderness toward Christine taking root inside of me—the usual precursor to the feelings that ensued. I should have told her to stay away from me. I should have warned her about what happens to those

who get close to me.
But Miguel and his men took care of that for me.
Because on Sunday night, when she went back to her room to change clothes for dinner, they took her.

Chapter Sixteen

Contract Day Twelve
Sunday, July 4, 2010
1950 Hours Local Time
Somewhere on Interstate 17
On the way to Luke AFB, AZ

"Goddamn it, John!" I yelled into the Impala's Bluetooth phone system. "I told you I don't know exactly what happened! She said she was going back to her room to change, and when she didn't come back after about thirty minutes, Brock and I went to check on her. When we got to her room, the door was unlocked and she was gone."

"Easy, T. C., easy." Amrine's California surfer-boy tone came through the car's speakers. The calmness of it infuriated me. "We just got online with this. What makes you so sure she was taken? Couldn't she have just left to go shopping or something?"

"No way, John," I shook my head vehemently, even though I knew Amrine couldn't see me. "She knew the deal. She knew she needed to stick by Brock and me. She hasn't been out of sight of either one of us all weekend."

"I'll vouch for that," Brock chimed in. "T. C. and I been sticking to her like glue." He looked at me across the car and smiled slyly. "And T. C. been sticking to her in a big way."

"You and the ladies, T. C.," Amrine said. I could imagine the smile on his face.

"Yeah," I said in exasperation, "me and the goddamn ladies. In this case, I think it may have done more harm than good. I think that's one of the reasons they took her."

"Could be," Dave Smith said. Apparently he was conferenced in on the call. "Maybe they're thinking of using her as leverage."

"Possible," Amrine replied, "but unlikely. It's more likely they got wind of our plan to follow the F-35 tomorrow and they wanted to reduce the odds by 33% that a body would be available to do it."

"You know what this means, John," I said. "It means that there's a mole somewhere. They obviously knew the plan and obviously knew where we'd be. And I've got no idea how they figured out the hotel thing out. We wasted the one team they sent after us. How'd they track us down? I was using the fake ID and credit card you guys gave me. There should have been no trace of us up there."

Amrine actually chuckled.

"So you're wondering how the most powerful drug lord in the western hemisphere is able to track the location of a particular car in a state where most of the blue-collar labor is Hispanic? Did I hear you right?"

I pushed myself back into the driver's seat and pounded on the steering wheel in frustration.

"Jesus," I said. "You're right. I can't fucking believe it. What was I thinking? It probably only took him a phone call."

"Don't be too hard on yourself, T. C.," Dave Smith said. "Honestly, it didn't occur to us either until this afternoon. By then the team was probably already in place."

"What sucks even more is that we don't know where they're taking her," I said.

"To one of Miguel's warehouses in Phoenix would be my guess," Amrine said. "He's got several, and he'd want to keep her somewhere that was completely under his control."

I could see Brock nodding in my peripheral vision.

"Any chance you can narrow it down some?" he said. "I think T. C. and I would like to pay those boys a visit tonight."

"We have a source we can ask, but his availability is limited," Amrine replied. "Until we can talk to him, you two need to stick with the mission. Both of you are scheduled for your TR-1 rides in the PM go tomorrow. Mass briefing will be at 1500 local time. Takeoffs will be at 1715 and 1730 for B-Rock and T. C. respectively. You both need to be airborne on time. Our information is telling us that the F-35 will move during that same time frame."

"Hey, John," I said, with a tinge of sarcasm in my voice that I couldn't contain, "how is it that now we have specific intel on when this jet is going to move when the other day you couldn't even tell if it was in the hangar without me getting eyes on it?"

There was no response, and the answer to my question became apparent in the ensuring silence.

"I must be new," I said. "You were using me to smoke them out."

"We needed to do something," Amrine said flatly. "Things weren't moving. You know as well as anyone that the best way to shake someone out of their game plan is to show them something they weren't expecting. They weren't expecting you."

"And if the team on Thursday night had been successful in dealing with me? How would that have suited your plans?"

I glanced across the car to see Brock smiling at me. "Welcome to the jungle, babe," he said.

"No shit," I replied. "So all these machinations of yours aside, what about the mole? You've obviously got one or

Christine wouldn't have been taken."

"Duly noted," Amrine said. "It's a good question. We obtained the scheduling info through a source we have 100% confidence in and that source is highly discreet."

"But you were seen on base," I said. "Lena told me that everyone in the Turnidge's office knows who you guys are, which means that nearly everyone in the OSI knows who you are. If they are watching me, they're watching you. I bet someone in the OSI made you."

The silence in the car was different than it was before. "You may have something there, T. C.," Dave Smith said, obviously saving his partner the embarrassment of admitting it. "If they saw us with the three of you and they're aware of what's going on, that's a possibility."

"Bet on it," I said. "The two of you and I are like legends in the OSI these days. They know us."

Another pause.

"What makes you this curious is why they only took one of us instead of all of us if they wanted to stop the mission," Brock said. "Your hookup with Christine notwithstanding."

"That's easy," I said. "Airspace."

He looked at me across the car with his eyebrows raised in curiosity.

"Didn't you ever do any scheduling in your flying career?"

He shook his head.

"If all three of us are flying TR rides at the same time, at least one of us would have to do the area work in the southern range airspace, down by Gila Bend and adjacent to the Mexican border. Now that there are only two of us flying, they can schedule us both in the northern airspace and keep us out of the way without making it apparent that's what they're doing."

"So how are we going to be able to follow them if we're in the wrong place?" he asked.

"We'll just have to rely on our CIA friends to tell us when the F-35 is airborne, and then we'll make our move to follow it. Can you guys tell us that?"

"Yes," Smith said. "We'll call you on your auxiliary radio and tell you when it has lifted off."

"That's only part of the problem though, T. C.," Brock said. "We're flying D-models tomorrow. Two-seaters. How do we bring our instructors in the backseat along with us on this little chase when they might not want to come along and/or might work for the bad guys?"

"We've got that covered," Amrine said over the phone. "Just make sure they drink something about ninety minutes or so before takeoff."

Chapter Seventeen

Contract Day Thirteen
Monday, July 5, 2010
1725 Hours Local Time
Arming Area for Runway 21 Left
Luke Air Force Base, Arizona

I guided the F-16 into the parking slot in the arming/precheck area with some gentle pressure on the rudder pedals and smoothly brought it to a halt with the digital brakes, raising my hands reflexively as the jet stopped rolling. In my peripheral vision, I could see Brock pulling into the slot immediately to my right, his hands also raised as he brought his aircraft to a halt. The precheck, done just prior to takeoff, was a standard in fighter aviation. When the jets were clean, with no ordnance mounted on them, as ours were today, the precheck consisted merely of the ground crew looking the aircraft over for hydraulic or fuel leaks or panels that were not secured. If our jets had been carrying ordnance, this is where the crew would have pulled the arming wires for the bombs and missiles and removed the safety pins on the cannons. It was a nice reminder for me that I wasn't sitting in the cockpit of a business jet on this clear Arizona afternoon, but instead I was strapped into a fighter—an airplane that was designed to kill. I found myself smiling under the soft plastic of my oxygen mask.

Brock and I kept our hands in view to show the ground crew that our hands weren't in proximity to the sidestick controller or throttle, so that the ground crew members could move around and under the aircraft with confidence. Hydraulically powered flight control surfaces, like the elevator slab or flaperons in the F-16, could deflect with such force that they could maim or kill someone working under them if the controls were manipulated at the wrong time.

"Ready to do this, Hondo?" I asked my young instructor over the intercom.

"Shh...sure, T. C.," he said, his voice heavy with sleep. "Ss... sorry. I'm feeling kind of out of...it for some reason."

"No worries, Hondo," I said, eyeing his slumping head over my shoulder. "It happens to the best of us sometimes."

Amrine and Smith had been right on the money with the timing of the drug they had given Brock and me. The little shot of liquid into young Hondo's preflight Diet Coke had done the trick, and he was now nearly unconscious in my backseat.

The crew finished their inspection of my aircraft, and the crew chief saluted me smartly. I returned the salute and the three fatigue-clad enlisted troops scurried over to Brock's jet. His instructor pilot seemed to be sluggish in the backseat as well. I wondered what the two guys were going to think when they woke up and found out they had been along for the ride when two Vipers were commandeered.

The ground crew completed their inspection of Brock's jet quickly and saluted him as well. I looked over at Brock, tapped the earpiece on my helmet, and held up three fingers, silently commanding him to change his UHF radio to the locally programmed Channel 3, the tower frequency. He nodded back at me.

I punched the COM 1 button on the F-16's up-front control

console, the numeric panel just below the head's up display, hit the 3 on the panel and followed with the ENTER button. Then I keyed the mic switch on the throttle to speak on the jet's UHF radio.

"Boiler check," I said.

"Two," Brock replied.

"Luke tower, Boiler MARSA Angel, number 1, Tanks Departure."

Brock and I weren't technically in the same flight today but by using MARSA—military accepts responsibility for separation of aircraft—we could fly in the same formation and provide our own deconfliction. We had briefed it this way last night, knowing our IPs wouldn't be able to say much about it.

"Boiler MARSA Angel, Luke Tower, runway 21 left, wind is 220 at 10, cleared for takeoff. Change to departure."

"Boiler MARSA Angel, wilco." I released the mic button and spoke over the intercom. "Check your seat armed, Hondo." I moved my ejection seat handle into the ARMED position and waited for a moment or two for Hondo to answer me. "Hondo!" I spoke a little more loudly. "Check your seat armed!"

"It's... it's armed, T. C.," he said sleepily. "Good...to...go."

"Thanks, Hondo," I said. *Now go back to sleep.*

I released my brakes and gently applied power to get the jet moving, while making sure my throttle was back in the idle position as I made the 90-degree turn to exit the arming area, a precaution to ensure that the F-16's powerful exhaust didn't blow ground crew members or equipment all over the ramp. Brock and I taxied onto the 10,000 foot runway, each of us centering our jets in the middle of our respective sides of the surface. Looking down the long, gray pavement in front of me, I could almost sense the steam rising up from the concrete in the sweltering desert heat. Once again I found myself transported back in time to the hundreds of training sorties I had flown here so long ago. The barren mountains on the south side of Interstate 10 beckoned to me now as they did then, as did the terrific blue Arizona sky, unmarred by the usual thunderclouds of the July monsoon season. I exhaled softly into my oxygen mask and felt the familiar excitement begin to rise inside of me as I brought my jet to a halt. As Brock stopped next to me, just down my wing line, I twirled my left finger in a circular motion to give him the "run 'em up" signal and then tapped my helmet and showed four fingers. He nodded back at me. I advanced the throttle to 80 percent RPM and allowed the engine instruments to stabilize as I switched the UHF radio to local channel 4, the radar departure frequency. I looked back over my shoulder at Brock, and he nodded at me again, indicating he was ready. I gave him a thumbs up and nodded back at him.

"Boiler check," I said into the oxygen mask's mic.

"Two," he replied crisply.

I released the Viper's brakes and smoothly advanced the throttle to military or MIL power, 100% engine RPM without afterburner. In spite of today's hot temperatures, Brock and I had elected to take off without afterburner, even though we were carrying an external fuel tank on the D-models we were flying. We suspected we'd need the extra fuel to chase down the F-35 and even a few hundred pounds of gas might make a critical difference.

The RPM gauge settled at 100% and the nozzle gauge indicated 0-20% closed. In fighter engines, while RPM, the speed at which the engine turned, was important for thrust, the nozzle or aperture setting of the engine was nearly as important for as the nozzle closed, exhaust velocity increased radically. The Viper rolled down the runway, the nose gear bouncing slightly on the grooved runway. As the jet accelerated. I checked my airspeed at the planned distance to ensure that the jet was performing as advertised and disconnected the nosewheel steering with a button on the sidestick. A few moments later, I applied back pressure to the sidestick controller. The Viper's nose slowly tracked upward, and the main gear left the concrete a few seconds later. Once we were safely airborne, I retracted the jet's landing gear and retarded the throttle to ninety eight percent RPM to give Brock some excess power to catch me. Then I keyed the mic button.

"Luke Departure, Boiler MARSA Angel, airborne," I glanced at the altitude display in the head's up display or HUD, "passing 2,500."

"Boiler, Luke Departure, radar contact. Climb unrestricted to the block, 17 to 19 thousand."

I nodded to myself. The controller had graciously allowed us to disregard the 6,000 level-off restriction on the departure, which was always a pain to comply with, especially in a jet that climbed like the Viper did. I glanced at the Viper's DME display to begin my turn to the west, amazed once again that in a jet as technologically advanced as this one was we still had to rely on basic navigational aids to execute instrument departures. Any business jet I had flown would have had the departure loaded into the lateral navigation system, and the pilot would have just used a steering cue to stay on track. I smiled to myself. The trade-offs in military aircraft design were more apparent to me now after a second career in business jets. Cutting-edge technology to kill things was standard, similar technology to reduce the pilot's workload during non-tactical phases of flight, not so much.

I adjusted my pitch attitude to maintain the briefed airspeed of 350 knots in the climb-out so I could provide a stable platform for Brock to rejoin upon. Looking to my right, I saw him exactly where I expected him to be, slightly low and on the inside of my turn, on a plane of motion that was directed underneath my jet and not into it. After taking a ten-second delay on the takeoff, he had used a combination of airspeed overtake and the angular advantage of cutting me off in the turn to wind up just off my inside wing. As he slowed into position, I pushed at him with my open hand to indicate he could stay in a wide, or route position, for the remainder of the climb-out, instead of coming all the way into fingertip position with its requisite three-foot wing tip to wing tip spacing.

We leveled off in the 17,000–19,000 altitude block and changed our radios to the working frequency for the Gladden/Bagdad Military Operations Area complex (MOA), the airspace to the northwest of the base where most of the training air work was accomplished. The MOA was divided into several subareas. On the schedule, Brock and I had been assigned to separate parts of the airspace, but we had already decided to stay together in the southwestern portion of the area. Typically, the areas had altitude caps in the mid-to-high 20's, but we had arranged a higher altitude block with Albuquerque Center so that we could climb up and conserve some fuel. We were actually fortunate to be flying D-model jets that day, because with the external 300-gallon tank mounted on the jet, we'd have about 800 pounds more fuel than a clean C-model.

And I had a feeling that every pound of gas would matter today.

"Tango Charlie and Bravo Bravo, this is Delta Sierra." Dave Smith's voice came through very clearly on the Viper's AUX radio. "How do you read?"

"Loud and clear from Tango Charlie," I said in response.

"Five by five for Bravo Bravo," Brock's voice intoned.

"Let's push secure fill three," Smith said.

I entered the appropriate settings on the up-front control to get the jet's AUX radio into the secure mode and made sure that fill three was selected. The required crypto "fill" wasn't usually provided for TR missions, but somehow Smith and

Amrine had worked some of their strange magic.

"Any word on the package?" Brock said on the now-secure frequency, his voice slightly clipped by the encryption algorithm.

"Negative," Smith's voice said, obviously disappointed. "Doors aren't even open yet."

"Great," I said. "Once they do get them open, there will have to be a dog and pony show before they even launch. We might not have the gas for this, Delta Sierra."

"Noted," Smith replied. "We gave some thought to trying to arrange a tanker for you guys but thought it would be too conspicuous. How long can you hold?"

I looked down at my fuel totalizer and my fuel flow indicator. I had set the power at about 2500 pounds per hour to maintain reasonable flying airspeed at our altitude, and I was barely making 230 knots calibrated airspeed.

"Two hours, if we're really lucky," I replied. "And that won't give us much gas to chase him down with."

"Roger that," Smith said grimly. "We'll keep you informed."

We spent the next hour "hanging on the blades," flying a maximum endurance, minimum airspeed, racetrack pattern over the southern border of the area. Brock kept his jet in a loose trail position, about 3,000—4,000 feet back, weaving back and forth across my six o'clock as necessary and using geometry to get where he wanted to be instead of throttle. I kept expecting another flight to check in on the working frequency and attempt to use the airspace in which we orbited, but the 310th's late afternoon sorties apparently had sole access to the working areas due to the time of day in which they were scheduled. There were no other jets from other squadrons that were airborne, let alone needing airspace. I found myself also wondering when Luke Arrival Control would call us and ask us when we intended to land. At that point, we were well past the typical duration of a transition sortie.

I looked down at my fuel totalizer—about 3800 pounds remaining. I then used the display management switch to select the horizontal situation display mode on my right multifunction display and slewed my HSD cursor over the green image of Brock's jet. AE01 3.6 appeared at the bottom of the screen. Brock had 3600 pounds remaining. Technology was a wonderful thing. In the "old days" that would have required a radio call or a visual signal.

"Delta Sierra, this is Tango Charlie," I said as I keyed the mic for the AUX radio. "About one hour left now and that doesn't leave us anything to do the mission."

"Standby," Smith's voice was clipped over the radio. "Looks like the doors are opening."

I felt the familiar surge of adrenaline in my blood, and my chest tightened underneath the straps of my harness. It was show time.

"He's not being towed out," Smith said. "The jet's already running. He's coming out under power."

"Would have hated to be in that hangar," Brock remarked over the AUX radio. "Pretty damn noisy."

"Like starting in a hardened aircraft shelter back in the day," I replied.

"Yep," Brock replied. "Just like that. Louder than shit."

"He's rolling," Smith continued, "rolling fast. He must be taxiing at like thirty knots or so. Jesus."

"He's late for something," Brock said, echoing my own thoughts.

I nodded in mute assent. "Yes he is," I said to myself over the intercom. "But late for what?"

"He's at EOR for 21 left," Smith said a few minutes later. "Pretty long EOR check for a clean jet."

I had a vague idea about this, but there was another question demanding attention.

"Any idea who's at the controls?" I asked, even though I knew the answer.

"Hard to tell. He's got the canopy down, his oxygen mask on, and his visor down."

"You got a source watching the wing commander's office?" Brock asked. It was as if he was reading my mind.

"Manning is limited," Smith sighed. "We've got electronic measures in place."

"Where's his car?" I asked. Satan and his 'Vette were inseparable.

"Damn," Smith said. "Not sure we got a tracker in place on it. He keeps the goon squad around it nearly all the time."

"If he's in the cockpit, the car will be in or around the hangar," I replied. "It's just who he is."

"We have a small ops team taking the hangar," Smith said. "The car's not outside the hangar."

"You know it's him," Brock said over the AUX radio. "He wouldn't trust anyone else with this."

"And I'm sure he wouldn't want to split the paycheck, either," I said. "Besides, there are manhood issues at stake here."

"Hey, he's taking the runway," Smith said. "You guys need to get moving."

"Roger that," I replied. "B-Rock, let's go BUSTER, reference 170." I advanced the throttle to MIL power and banked the jet up to make the turn to a heading of 170 degrees. The Pratt and Whitney engine spooled up quickly underneath me, and I felt the familiar push in the middle of my back as the jet's thrust rapidly increased. "Are you monitoring any of the ATC freqs? Do you have any idea what departure he's on?"

"Standby," Smith said. "Checking." There was a pregnant pause as Smith consulted who or what was his information source. "The Nordy One," he said after a moment or two. "He's been cleared to 6,000 feet."

"Perfect," I said, "we're going to have to come out of the Class A airspace and stay below 18,000 to avoid freaking the FAA out, but we can monitor his progress without revealing ourselves too much."

"Stay up there," Smith said. "We've coordinated your movements with Albuquerque Center. You can stay as high as you want as long as you want. They'll move the airliners around you guys."

"It's good to be the king," Brock muttered over the AUX radio. "Damn good."

The Nordy departure was used to transition aircraft from Luke AFB to the southern working areas, particularly to the Gila Bend airspace and range complex. It funneled aircraft over the fix for which the departure was named, Nordy, which was nineteen miles southwest of the base.

"Let's make Nordy the bull's-eye, B-Rock," I said.

"Way ahead of you, T. C.," Brock replied.

I loaded the fix into the F-16's modular mission computer via the up-front control and instantly the cursor on my radar display showed the magnetic bearing and distance from Nordy as I moved it over the display with the slewing button on my throttle. I placed the cursor so that the display read 030/20 and rolled the elevation control knob for the radar, the EL STROBE, down to center the scan at 6,000 feet. The display was clean with none of the small white video squares that indicated an aircraft-size return.

"Looking northeast of bull's-eye at six thousand. Clean there," I said into mic, somewhat puzzled.

Fortunately, Brock wasn't thinking inside the box like I was.

"Contact bullseye 050 for 10," he said over the AUX radio. "Tracking southwest at 30,000 and he's hauling ass."

I had made the assumption that Satan would play by the rules and fly the departure as published. He had quick-

climbed to FL 300 and was headed southwest at high speed.

"Son of a bitch," I muttered into the intercom. "Come on, T. C. Wake up."

I quickly slewed my radar up to the same altitude and found the contact Brock had called and put my cursors there. The faint squares of video immediately illuminated with the brightest one on the southwest side, indicating the direction of travel. I resisted the urge to push forward on the Target Management Switch or TMS on the sidestick and put the radar into situational awareness mode or SAM. That would command the F-16's APG-68 radar to direct a momentary beam of radar energy on the F-35 and track the F-35 while the radar searched for other targets. But in spite of the small dwell time, it would also activate the F-35's radar warning receiver and alert the pilot that we were onto him.

"What do you think, B-Rock? Range-while-search or TWS? I don't want to tweak his RWR gear any more than normal."

"I'll try TWS," Brock said. "As long as the radar has other targets to look at, the dwell time shouldn't exceed the threshold to alert him." TWS was the radar's track-while-scan mode. As long as the target didn't maneuver aggressively, Brock would be able to follow every movement it made almost as well as if he was tracking the jet.

"Nice to fly with someone who's actually trained and current," I said with a chuckle. "I'm going to float to the right, try to push up to tactical left side."

"Roger," he replied.

The F-16's sidestick controller was incredibly sensitive. Almost without my commanding it to do so, the aircraft banked to the right slightly and began to turn. I rolled out of the turn a few seconds later with my nose 30 degrees right of our intended course. I looked over my left shoulder and saw Brock's jet moving up on my left side about 6,000 feet away. As he approached line abreast, I turned back to the left, back to course, and Brock and I were in a standard tactical spread formation. The F-35 was now about twenty miles south of us at 30,000 feet.

"He's walkin' away from us," Brock said. "He's doin' 400 knots cal. If we don't push it up we'll lose him."

I looked down at my fuel totalizer. It was down to about 3,000 pounds. Then I looked over at my fuel flow indicator. 7500 pounds per hour. We had about twenty minutes of fuel at that throttle setting and speed.

"Damn," I said into the intercom. Then I keyed the mic to talk on the AUX. "If we push it up much more we're not going to have enough gas to find a piece of concrete to land on," I said. "We can let him walk away from us. As long as we can verify he crosses the border that will be enough. Do you confirm that, Delta Sierra?"

"That's confirmed, Tango Charlie," he answered. "We don't even need that much. The F-22's are airborne out of Holloman. They're supercruising in at FL 550. They'll be here in about twenty minutes. All we need is the F-35 pointed southbound at high speed and within ten miles of the border to prove intent."

"Roger that," I said. "You better launch some rescue choppers as well, because I think B-Rock and I are gonna be jumping out of these things."

"I've got Gila Bend on speed dial. They'll know you're coming."

I nodded to myself. Gila Bend Air Force Auxiliary Field was due south of Luke by about forty miles and east of our track. I hoped it would be close enough. I had no desire to punch out of another jet after my last experience.

Interstate 8 flashed by 25,000 feet underneath us, the four lanes of asphalt barely discernible against the brown desert landscape below. The parallel ranges of the Mohawk Mountains and the Growler Mountains lay ahead, twin fingers of rock reaching for the land to the south. In the distance, I could see the glint of water from the northern end of the Gulf of California. Mexico was getting closer by the second. I glanced down at the moving map display on my right MFD and then to the left at the radar. Then I did a little mental math.

"He's about thirty miles from the border, Delta Sierra. How far out are the Raptors?"

"That checks, Tango Charlie. Standby one."

"Damn," I said to myself. "He's not stupid. He would have thought about this."

"Bad news, Tango Charlie," Dave Smith's voice was tight with frustration over the crackly AUX radio. "One of the Raptors had an electrical issue and had to return to Holloman. The other is still about fifteen minutes away."

"That's too far," I said. "They'll never get here in time. Are they going to be able to pursue him into Mexican airspace?"

"Negative," Smith replied quickly.

"Shit," I said. "We've got to do something to make him turn."

"Our ops team just cleared the hangar; it's empty," Smith said. "The red 'Vette is there."

I shook my head in frustration.

"Motherfucker," Brock said. "He's going to get away with this."

"Hey, B-Rock," I said, "I've got an idea. Get ready to run."

"Copy that, T. C., what are we doing?"

I smiled under my oxygen mask.

"We're going to test Satan's threat and systems knowledge," I said. "Lock him up."

"Two," Brock said.

I put my radar cursors over the F-35's radar return and pushed the TMS switch on the sidestick controller forward twice. The APG-68 radar went into single-target-track mode, and all other returns on my radar display disappeared. My radar was now bombarding Satan's jet with a highly focused beam of radar energy.

"Targeted," I said over VHF.

"Two's sorted," Brock echoed.

Now Tappan's jet had two radars on it. Radar warning receivers in jets work like their counterparts in cars, only on a much more sophisticated level. When a radar signal is received, the processors examine the frequency of the energy, its pulse width or pulse duration, how many pulses are received per second, and several other parameters. Those parameters are compared against a database, and then the appropriate symbol is displayed in the cockpit to tell the pilot what radar is looking at his or her aircraft. Since specific radars are usually associated with specific aircraft or surface-to-air missile systems, that symbol usually takes the form associated with those aircraft or aircraft of that genre. Additionally, in both the A-10 and F-16, the RWR would generate a tone in the pilots headset based on the pulse recurrent frequency or PRF of the radar, the amount of pulses received in a second. That was usually the first indication a pilot had that his aircraft was being targeted. Depending on the type of radar and threat level associated with it, the tone could sound extremely urgent in the pilot's headset and there wasn't a much more urgent sound than having your jet locked up by two air-to-air radars wielded by jets that could fire deadly radar-guided missiles.

Now it was up to Satan. If he was actually conversant with the systems on board the aircraft, he'd know he was being targeted by a couple of F-16's and not something more sophisticated and he'd light his afterburner and attempt to run. Even if Brock and I had been armed with AIM-120 AMRAAM missiles or "Slammers" as they were affectionately known, trying to shoot a fleeing target in the tail at our current range would have been a waste of tax dollars. The kinematic range of the missile would have been stretched and there was a high probability that the missile would run out of energy before it reached its target.

But I was betting on two things: Satan's ignorance and his ego.

His ignorance would force him to react, because he wouldn't know the jets targeting him were F-16's that were probably unarmed. And his ego would want one more fight to make a name for himself before he left the USAF and the country for good.

"C'mon asshole," I said, staring into my display. "Turn for me."

And then two things happened. One of which was good and one of which wasn't.

I saw the white video square in my radar display that represented the target being tracked begin to rotate to its left. It looked like we had succeeded in getting him to turn. That was good.

But then the radar image disappeared. And that wasn't.

"Fuck!" I said, staring into my radar.

And then several thoughts began careening around inside my head. I remembered that stealth aircraft regularly retracted their antennas and deactivated their radar transponders when they went into combat mode. Up until now, Satan had done none of that, so his jet had been easy to track. But apparently he had just gone into combat mode, and even the APG-68 could no longer see him. But there was something else. The F-35 had spent a long time in its end of runway or EOR check—something that normally happened only when jets were armed with live ordnance. And then the vague idea I'd had earlier became concrete in my brain. Unlike the F-16, the F-35 carried some of its air-to-air ordnance internally to keep the aircraft stealthy.

"Delta Sierra, when Satan was in EOR did he open any

weapons bay doors?"

"Wait one," Smith's voice said.

"Fuck that," Brock said over the radio, "we may not have one."

"And where's that damn Raptor anyway?" I added.

"Affirmative on the doors, Tango Charlie. He's armed."

"Shit!" I exclaimed into radio. "B-Rock, let's abort out left! We're out of here, Delta Sierra. You're going to have to get the Raptor pilot's radar on his last known position."

I shoved the throttle over the detent into afterburner, banked up to 120 degrees, my wings past perpendicular with the horizon, and I smoothly applied back pressure to the F-16's sidestick controller. As the nose began to come around, my headset filled with a radar tone I had never heard before. It varied constantly in both pitch and tempo and did not repeat.

"Electronically scanned in both height and azimuth," I said to myself. While I had never received a formal briefing on F-35 capabilities, I had read of its radar, the APG-81, an AESA or active electronically scanned array radar, with no moving parts. It had a stationary platform with over 1,000 transmit and receive modules and a receiver and exciter modules, offering extreme frequency agility. While I had no idea of its ultimate capability, the demonstration video I'd seen on YouTube had shown the radar tracking 23 targets in 9 seconds.

I glanced down at my RWR screen and watched as the system tried to display several different symbols but eventually gave up and displayed nothing at all.

Satan was now tracking my aircraft. And he was undoubtedly tracking Brock's as well.

Brock was already turning. He was below me and to my left as my nose came around. From God's perspective above, our flight paths looked like twin fishing hooks, Brock's slightly behind mine. Then, I as I continued my turn and lessened my bank angle, I looked over my right shoulder and high, where I expected Satan's jet would be.

And I saw something that filled me with dread: two thin, white contrails, like twin fingers of death, reaching for Brock and I.

"Missiles are in the air, B-Rock! Missiles in the air!"

I had less than a minute before impact, so I had to make a quick decision. If we both maintained the same spacing and headed in the same direction, we were making Satan's targeting problem very easy. But if we split and headed in different directions, we just might make it a little more difficult.

"Continue, B-Rock," I said. "Make sure Lindal's okay. I'm going to try and throw this idiot off."

"What are you going to do, T. C.?" Dave Smith's voice came over VHF.

"Something incredibly smart or stupid," I said as I rolled the Viper inverted and the brown desert terrain filled the canopy above my head. "I'm about to test the limitations of the APG-81."

I applied back pressure to the sidestick controller and pulled the nose of the aircraft down below the horizon, pointing it at a group of rocks in the middle of the valley below. I was trying to do two things to Satan's radar. First, I was going to try to give it a vertical sorting problem. Conventional radars scanned in v-shaped pattern in height when viewed from the side; and the closer to the scanning aircraft, the more narrow the "v." I was trying to get out of the bottom of the V of the scan. I didn't know if an AESA radar suffered from the same limitation, but I was hoping there might be a logic issue I could exploit. The other thing I was trying to do was place my flight path directly perpendicular to Satan's. All pulse-Doppler radars had problems with targets that had the same closure rate as the ground, and by flying perpendicular to him, I had effectively made my closure rate to his aircraft equal to the mountains around me. I had no idea if the APG-81 would be fooled by my actions but without chaff or countermeasures loaded aboard my aircraft, it was all I could do.

I accelerated toward the terrain below me, the airspeed on the jet's head's up display rapidly increasing through 600 knots.

"I sure hope you've lit the wick and are running like a scalded rabbit," I said over the AUX radio.

"Don't you worry about me, T. C.," Brock said. "If he launched a Slammer at me at that kind of range, it would have to have another stage to reach me. Watch your own ass."

"No shit," I said to myself as the detail on the desert floor below me became clearer.

The radar altitude display in the HUD had the jet passing through 10,000 feet. I had just a few seconds before I began to pull the Viper out of its dive and recover to level flight or it was going to be a crumpled heap of metal with my backseater and me inside it. I did some quick mental math and rolled the jet so that the top of it was facing south. Then, I saw 5,000 feet radar altitude go by, and I strained as hard as I could and pulled the sidestick controller back smoothly and swiftly. The Viper's digital flight control system operated as advertised, and the slab deflected at a rate that put 6 g's per second on the airframe. I felt the crushing force as 9 g's enveloped my body and once again, I smiled through the pain. There was just something about g on your ass that made you feel alive. I leveled off at a few hundred feet above the rocky terrain with about 550 knots of airspeed. I pushed the throttle up to full MIL power and glanced at the fuel totalizer: Eight hundred pounds, the level at which Viper pilots typically declared "minimum fuel." And I was in the middle of fucking nowhere.

"Did you make it, B-Rock?" I said on the AUX radio.

There was a burst of static in response.

"Great," I said over the intercom.

And then there was a bright flash of light behind me and a thump that felt like a huge hand had slapped the back of the aircraft.

"WARNING, WARNING!" said the stern female voice of the Viper's onboard monitoring system. At nearly the same moment, the red engine FIRE light illuminated in front of me, just under the glare shield.

The Viper didn't have a fire extinguishing system, and it carried its fuel in the fuselage, just in front of and above the engine—where the fire was. There wasn't much time before the jet would explode.

The Slammer that Satan had launched had found my jet; and while my maneuvers might have confused the radar in the F-35, they apparently didn't fool the radar in the AIM-120's nose, which had gone into terminal guidance mode and had managed to track me through my little Hail Mary maneuver.

The jet began to vibrate around me, and I reflexively pulled the throttle back and over the detent into the OFF position even as I pulled the nose skyward. More altitude under your ass when you ejected was always a good thing. The hydrazine-powered emergency power unit kicked on with a high-pitched whine as the engine rolled back, providing hydraulic power for the flight controls and electric power for the flight control computer.

"Mayday! Mayday! Mayday!" I transmitted over the AUX radio and then over UHF. "Boiler 01 is punching out about thirty miles south of I-8 in the Mohawk Valley. Two souls on board." I was surprised how calm my voice sounded.

I released the throttle and the sidestick and gripped the yellow ejection lanyard between my legs.

"You're such a dumbass," I said over the intercom.

And then I pulled the handle.

Chapter Eighteen

Contract Day Thirteen
Monday, July 5, 2010
1915 Hours Local Time
Somewhere in the Mohawk Valley
Arizona Desert

The ejection sequence in a modern fighter is a true marvel of engineering brilliance. In literally a fraction of a second, the canopy departs the aircraft and the ejection seat travels up the rails under rocket power. In this case, since I was flying a two-seat D-model, the rear seat left the aircraft first but the delay wasn't discernible to me. It felt the same as it had the two other times in my life when I'd ejected. One moment I was sitting in the jet pulling the handle, and the next moment I was hanging under a parachute as it floated down to earth. And yet, thanks to the miracle of temporal distortion, I remembered every small event during the ejection sequence distinctly. I remembered the muffled "pop" as the charge ignited, which separated the canopy from the jet. I remembered the instantaneous rush of the wind as the canopy departed and the cockpit was exposed to the 250-knot airflow around the jet. I remembered the roar of the rear cockpit's seat firing and traveling up its set of guide rails. I remembered the impossible acceleration as my seat fired and began its own ascent. I remembered the feeling as the gyros in the seat corrected the trajectory to ensure the seat traveled directly upward and then the charge behind my head fired, which released the parachute and propelled it up and away to allow it to open as quickly as possible. Then there was the tug on my shoulders as the parachute opened and the tug on my lap as the seat separated and fell away.

And there I was, hanging in the desert air and floating down to the rough terrain below. It was suddenly and surprisingly very quiet, except for the whine of the Viper's EPU, which was still audible as the crippled jet began to arc back to the earth, about a mile south of us. I looked around me to see how my rear-seater had fared. He was just behind me and below me, drifting toward the dirt road that lay under us. I was grateful for that. The desert in Arizona was mostly rocks, cacti, and hard earth. Landing in the wrong place could be damn uncomfortable at best and fatal at worst. I looked down to see myself drifting toward the same road, and I pushed my feet and knees together and prepared for the parachute landing fall that awaited me. Above a few hundred feet in altitude, there isn't much ground rush when you're falling by parachute, but the last few hundred feet can throw an inexperienced jumper into a panic if he or she isn't ready.

I had accomplished five jumps while I was at the USAF Academy and earned my parachute wings. That and an untimely ejection over Iraq had given me some idea of what to expect when I hit the earth. The trick was not to look down but to keep your eyes on the horizon. I pulled my right parachute riser to ensure I stayed aligned with the road and focused on the horizon at the far end of the valley. Behind me I heard a clunking sound as my rear-seater made contact with the earth, and then a few seconds later, a small thud sound as my survival kit, hanging from a fifty-foot lanyard, hit the ground below me.

Then it was my turn.

Five points of contact: balls of the feet, side of the calves, side of the thighs, butt, lower and upper back. My feet hit and I pulled down on my risers and twisted my body to the left. The hard earth smacked into the side of my body and a cloud of red dust rose up around me. And then I found myself looking up at the sky. Training is a remarkable thing. Even as a gust of wind inflated my parachute and attempted to pull me off the road and into rocks around me, I reached up to the Koch release fittings on the harness and lifted and pushed them. The parachute detached and was gone.

I struggled to my feet, knocking the dust off me as I did so.

There was a sickening sound of rending metal, followed by a muffled explosion. I looked to the south and saw a flash of flame and then the inevitable black smoke from where our Viper had impacted.

"Damn," I said to myself. "I sure hope Satan or Miguel are going to get the bill for that one."

I looked around to find Captain Hondo. It didn't take long. He was lying just off the road about twenty meters away. I quickly pulled the lanyard on my survival kit toward me and then detached it so I could grab the kit itself. Then I slithered out of my parachute harness and threw the survival kit over my shoulder. I walked over to where young Hondo lay and at first he didn't seem to be any the worse for wear after being involuntarily ejected from a jet while he was unconscious. But then as I drew near, I could see that the lower part of his right leg was at a physiologically impossible angle from the upper part.

"Shit, dude," I said to him as I walked up. "I am so sorry about this."

The drugs I had given him earlier were wearing off. He was conscious and grimacing with pain. His eyes looked at me with an odd mixture of confusion, anger, and another emotion that I couldn't quite define. He opened his mouth to speak, but I held a hand up to silence him.

"We were shot down by another jet," I said. "And that's all I can tell you. I'll need to get you back to Luke, and then I can fully debrief you."

There was no shock or surprise on his face.

"You're going to hate me, but we're going to need to straighten your leg and get a splint on it."

He nodded at me.

I looked around us to see if I could find anything straight and stiff to devise a splint, and I took stock of our surroundings for the first time. We were literally in the middle of nowhere. The road we were on could barely be called that, it was more like a trail with a pair of tire-shaped ruts in the dusty brown desert; undoubtedly a route for the illegal alien trade or the drug trade or both. A sea of various forms of cacti and boulders surrounded us. The hard ridges of the Mohawk and Growler Mountains lined the horizons to the west and east respectively and to the north and south. As far as the eye could see, there was only more desert. I walked down the road for several yards and realized that there was a barbed wire fence paralleling the road a few yards away. It consisted of three runs of wire attached to a series of thin upright posts about three feet above the earth. I circumnavigated a large boulder and a cactus that was twice as tall as I was and made it to a section of fence that was unencumbered by flora or rocks. A sign on the fence warned me that the US Bureau of Land Management owned the land and the fence and that trespassing was unauthorized.

"I'll bet that sign really keeps 'em out," I muttered.

A few kicks and shakes and I managed to free the fence from two posts. Then I pulled, pushed, and kicked the metal posts until I could pull them from the packed desert floor.

My flightsuit quickly became stained with sweat. I knew the dangers of heat stroke and dehydration in a desert environment, so I retrieved a water bottle from the pocket of my anti-g suit and drank it as I returned to Hondo with the two metal posts and a plan for his splint.

When I reached Hondo after walking the several yards back down the road, he'd managed to roll up part of his parachute and placed it underneath his head so that he could stay prone but keep his head elevated without effort. His face was streaked with sweat and contorted in pain. His right leg looked a little less disjointed than it had previously, undoubtedly a result of his change of body position, which explained the pain in his face as well.

"Did... did you call anyone on your radio?" he asked weakly.

I shook my head. "I haven't even gotten my radio out," I said. "I wanted to get you taken care of first."

He looked up at me, uncomprehending.

"If we get your leg straightened out, your pain level will go down substantially. Then I'm going to get a quick shelter built to get you out of the sun. After that, we'll worry about contacting rescue. Assuming our ELTs went off when we ejected, they should be homing in on our position right now anyway."

ELTs were emergency locator transmitters installed in the survival kits built into our seats. Upon ejection, they broadcasted a nonstop beacon signal on the guard frequency.

"I called them," he said, spitting the words out through clenched teeth. "They said there's a chopper in the air."

I nodded. "That's great," I said, almost absently. "The smoke from the Viper crash should lead them right here."

I knelt next to him and placed the two metal posts on each side of his mangled leg. Then I removed my survival knife from the kit and cut off the lanyard that attached him to his survival kit at both ends. I coiled it up next to the two posts.

"Okay," I said as I grabbed his right foot. "Here's the sucky part." I looked at his face for a moment. "You're not a hardcore Democrat are you?"

He shook his head with a confused expression on his features, as if to say, "What does that have to do with anything?"

I looked at him and smiled. "You know why Monica Lewinsky voted Republican in the last election, right?"

He shook his head again.

"Because the last time she had a Democrat, it left a bad taste in her mouth."

He smiled tightly and that was when I pulled his lower right leg out from the break and pivoted it to bring it into alignment with his upper leg.

"Holy fucking shit..." he said and fainted.

***

About fifteen minutes later, I had his right leg rigidly splinted between the two metal posts and tightly wrapped with the lanyard material from his survival kit. I had recovered my parachute, cut the cords from the canopy off at the risers, and tied the cords to boulders and cacti that were around the side of the road. Hondo was now totally in the shade and the white, orange, and green parachute was nearly fully extended. The large, round shape indicated to anyone flying nearby that there were people on the ground underneath. As I tied the last cord off, I could hear the faint whop-whop-whop sound of a helicopter in the distance.

"The cavalry is coming, Hondo," I said as I made the final knot. "And just when I was making things a little homey here."

I ducked under the canopy.

"Did you hear me, Hondo?"

As my head cleared the edge of the nylon parachute, my eyes made contact with Hondo and I found myself looking down the barrel of a Beretta 92SF 9mm automatic. Standard USAF issue.

"Well fuck," I said, "not you too." I shook my head in exasperation. "That's not a USAF chopper coming for us is it?"

The whop-whop-whop sound was getting louder. And it was coming from the south, the direction of Mexico, not the north.

Hondo shook his head with a triumphant smile on his face. "They knew what you were going to do before you ever did it," he whispered through his teeth. Even with his leg splinted, the pain he was enduring had to be intense. But he couldn't resist gloating.

"They told me you were going to try this." Then he frowned at me. "That was totally lowlife spiking my Coke like that."

I shrugged.

"They're coming for you," he said. "And I'm going to hand you over."

I just looked at him and shook my head. *It was the young and stupid ones who never learned.* "How much is he paying you, Hondo?"

The whop-whop-whop was getting very loud now.

He smiled indulgently. "One million," he said. "One million bucks. Tax free and all mine."

"And let me guess, they gave you a small amount up front and promised the rest on delivery?"

He stopped smiling and glared at me. He didn't answer, but he didn't have to. I knew what the terms would be.

A Sikorsky S-76 helicopter circled us, obviously looking for a place to set down.

"I hope you enjoyed whatever it was that you spent the down payment on," I said to him as I turned to face the chopper.

I could have probably overpowered him, taken the gun, and run but what would have been the use? I was in the middle of the fucking desert, and they would have caught me easily. If I tried to shoot it out with them, they would cut me to pieces. I had no choice.

The sleek S-76 sat down in the middle of the road, about twenty yards away, kicking up a huge cloud of dust as it landed. Through the haze I saw the doors on both sides open and two armed men emerged from each side, clad in black tactical gear with M-4 carbines shouldered and at the ready position. They approached me cautiously, and on a command from the leader, they raised their weapons. I took my cue and slowly dropped to my knees, faced them and away from Hondo, and interlaced my fingers behind my head. The weapons came down.

They encircled me a few moments later. And as the cold plastic of the zip ties went around my wrists, I looked over my right shoulder.

"Good-bye, Hondo," I said.

"Good-bye? What the—"

A three-shot burst from one of the gunmen finished his sentence. He didn't even utter a last gasp.

Stupid fucking kid.

"Colin Pearce," said a heavily accented voice.

I looked up to see Joe Sanchez looking down at me. He was a DEA agent and we knew each other, but he was playing his role as Miguel's right-hand man to the hilt.

"Miguel sends his regards."

I felt a hard thump on the back of my head. There was a flash of light and then there was nothing.

Nothing at all.

Chapter Nineteen

Contract Day Thirteen
Monday, July 5, 2010
2330 Hours Local Time
Miguel's Encampment
Sonora Province, Mexico

The act of regaining consciousness is an odd and unpredictable process. I had experienced it several times in my life, and I had never "come to" the same way twice. This time, before I became aware of my surroundings, I became aware of the words of Edgar Allen Poe sliding around inside my brain with an eerie resonance.

> You are not wrong, who deem
> That my days have been a dream;
> Yet if hope has flown away
> In a night, or in a day,
> In a vision, or in none,
> Is it therefore the less gone?
> All that we see or seem
> Is but a dream within a dream.

As my brain recalled the last events it remembered, the

realization that it had all been a dream would have been welcome. But the hard, painful pressure of the zip ties digging into the flesh of my wrists reminded me that it was not. I was on my back on a military-style cot, and my hands where singly bound, one to each side of it where the canvas fabric was clear of the aluminum joints in the middle. My feet were also singly bound with some sort of cord, one to each side of the cot and at the end of it where the ends of the supporting frame protruded from the fabric. Of course, I couldn't see any of this because my eyes were closed, but after spending a fair amount of my Air Force life lying on one of these structures in basic training and in numerous deployments, I knew a cot when I felt one.

The climate was dry, so we were still in a desert environment, but the temperature had dropped significantly, which indicated that it was night, we were at a higher altitude, and in an area of limited man-made development with no concrete or asphalt to absorb and radiate the heat. Poe's words began to recede in my brain as I became aware of voices around me. I kept my eyes shut and my body motionless.

"What are we waiting for?" Mark "Satan" Tappan's abrasive, nasal voice cut into the air around me. "Let me kill his ass."

"Miguel wants him alive." It was Joe Sanchez's voice, playing his part with heavy accented English. A former Navy Seal, he could speak it with no Hispanic inflection at all. I realized that I had totally forgotten his cover name.

"Can't we fuck him up a little then?" I pictured Satan licking his lips in anticipation.

"Miguel wants him as we found him," Joe said.

"Too bad. This guy's an arrogant asshole," Satan continued. "He always thought he was just a little smarter than everyone else."

I couldn't resist the entry.

"Not everyone else, Satan," I said, opening my eyes, "just smarter than you, which isn't a challenge. Even for me."

My eyes processed the desert camo fabric above my head. I was in a tent at the end of a row of several cots. Joe was standing over me next to the cot, his muscled physique clad in black tactical gear with an assortment of firearms, knives, and other implements strapped to it. Alongside him stood Mark "Satan" Tappan in his dusty desert camo flightsuit with a matching desert camo campaign hat on his head that he seemed to have brought with him to complete the outfit. I couldn't help noticing the prominent star of his rank on the center of his hat. Even as a criminal, he still wanted to be treated like a general.

"It wasn't too smart lighting me up with your radar and then getting your ass shot down now was it?"

"You just can't get decent help these days," I said. "The damn Raptors from Holloman were supposed to blow your ass out of the sky. They just didn't get there in time I guess. It's too bad really. I was hoping to see pieces of you decorating the desert."

"One Raptor made it Pearce. I shot it down. I guess the guy didn't come expecting a fight. He got a Slammer in the face for his trouble and now there are pieces of him and his jet decorating the desert."

Damn, I thought. *That sucks.* Something prodded me in the subconscious. It was getting to be a frequent feeling.

"Well, apparently Miguel is coming up here to get all medieval on you," Satan said, grinning hideously. "He's bringing this huge guy called Ramon to do the dirty work. I've heard stories about him. I was hoping to stay and watch him work, but I've got my own work to do."

"Let me guess," I said. "In addition to stealing the jet, you're going to make sure it gets to the Chinese intact and then provide them instruction and a full debrief on it. After that, you'll live happily ever after on the generous payment package Miguel has arranged with the Chinese."

His eyes narrowed. Joe's face stayed impassive.

"How the fuck did you know all that?" he demanded.

I closed my eyes and sighed. "I have friends in high places," I said.

"They're not doing you much fucking good now," he said with a sneer. "And they didn't do you much good earlier. We totally knew what you were going to do and when you were going to do it. You pushed our time line up a little bit, but we knew every detail of your plan."

That part was a bit disturbing. They had seemed a step ahead of us. I wondered what that meant. The answer was somewhere in my head, but I couldn't grasp it yet. It was like having a word on the tip of your tongue but being unable to say it.

Then my brain did allow me a thought. "Why the hell aren't you flying the jet out of here?" I asked. "It's night. I'm sure there's some JP-8 or Jet-A gas around. You could stay all stealthy and no one would ever see you."

He was silent, but the fire in his eyes indicated that he was dying to tell me. Then I thought it through and he didn't have to. There was only one way he was going to get an F-35 to the other side of the world undetected: via ship. That meant the place had to be somewhere reasonably near the coast and not too deep into Mexico given our helicopter flying time.

It also meant that Smith and Amrine knew where I was. Even if my BlackBerry had been taken from me, its GPS transponder would still be signaling my position—even if the battery was out and it was "deactivated."

Almost as if he sensed my thoughts, Joe Sanchez reached into the pocket of his fatigue pants and removed my BlackBerry. He glanced down at it and then gave me a barely perceptible nod.

"You better go get busy, Satan," I said. "You don't have much time."

He looked at me and then looked at Joe. Joe shrugged at him as if he didn't know what I was talking about. Then he stormed out, shaking his campaign hat–clad head.

"How long before they get here?" I mouthed to Joe even though there appeared to be no one around. Distance mics and listening ears seemed to be everywhere these days.

He held up a hand with five fingers, clenched a fist with it, and opened it with five fingers again.

Ten minutes.

"Just you." He mouthed back at me.

I nodded. Then I pointed at him and shook my head.

"You can't be here," I said, silently.

He nodded back at me. A knife appeared in his hand, and he set to work cutting the zip ties at my hands and feet on the underside of the cot where they wouldn't be visible to someone looking down on me. Then he reached into a pouch and retrieved a Glock pistol with a long, cylindrical suppressor attached. He ejected the magazine to show me it was full and then racked a round into the chamber. He bent down, slid the weapon under my right thigh and adjusted it so that an observer wouldn't detect it.

"Five minutes," he said softly into my ear after he finished placing the weapon. "Then take the guards out and go out the back of the tent where the flap is tied down." He indicated an area to my right and toward the rear of the enclosure.

I nodded.

"There's a parking area immediately behind the tent. Go to the far side and wait for one of the ops team to find you. The sign/countersign is Cabo/Wabo."

I smirked. Sammy Hagar's brand of tequila. Couldn't stomach the stuff myself, but the name was catchy.

"Got it," I whispered.

He rose, and his face transformed into the mask of his cover character. He spit out a command in Spanish and two guards with AK-47s and desert-style fatigues scurried into the tent. As he was giving them instructions, a third fatigued figure entered the tent and interrupted him. A debate then appeared to ensue, and while I didn't understand, the gist of it was clear. The new figure, with dark eyes and bushy mustache, wanted to be in charge of guarding Miguel's prize, and the two men worked for him, not Joe. Joe shrugged and motioned to the tent as if to say, it's all yours and then walked toward the cloth door. He stole a glance back at me, and as the three guards talked among themselves for a moment, he gave me a quick nod.

Thanks, Joe, I thought. *One versus three. Great odds.*

It was a painful five minutes. The mustached head guard came over to look at me and apparently to tell me how superior he was based on the tone of his voice and the contempt in his manner. He even kicked my cot once or twice to prove has masculinity. His teeth were brown and yellow, stained with tobacco, and his breath, even from a few feet above me, would have given Dentine a run for its money. At first I stared up at him blankly and uncomprehendingly, which wasn't a struggle, since I didn't understand a damn thing he said. Eventually though, I tired of his grandstanding, smiled at him brightly, and spoke a few of the only Spanish words I knew.

"Besame el culo," I said in my best Spanish accent.

His face turned red faster than a Chicago traffic light. Like an uncontrolled eruption, a stream of guttural Spanish began to flow from him along with a fine mist of tobacco-stained saliva. He kicked the cot again, hard, and the legs on the side nearest him, lifted an inch or two off of the hard-packed dirt and then returned to the ground with a mild thump.

And then the zip ties on my hands and the cord on my foot nearest him rolled off of me and onto the dirt silently.

We both saw it. He stared for a moment, the lack of comprehension on his face clearly evident as his limited brain processed what he was seeing. Then his eyes grew wide as the Glock appeared in my right hand and the long, black suppressor aligned with his face. He began to open his mouth in warning and fumbled with the flap holster on his hip with his right hand.

I pressed the Glock's trigger and the suppressor made its characteristic popping sound—barely audible above the noise outside the tent. Mustache's right eye disappeared in a fountain of blood. As he crumpled to the ground, I leapt off the cot and pushed him toward the two guards at the door of the tent. His body impacted the guard on the right as both men struggled to understand what was happening.

The guy on the left never had a chance. I steadied the Glock on the area above his flak vest and pressed the trigger just as I had been taught a few months ago. I felt the recoil as the first shot detonated and then slowly released the trigger just to the point where the mechanism reset under my fingers, and then I pressed again. The two bullets dug into his upper chest and throat, and he pitched backward against the tent's entrance.

Meanwhile, the guard on the right was recovering from his surprise and bringing his weapon to bear. The Glock's trigger reset under my finger again, and I swung the weapon to the third guard, centered the muzzle on his face, and pressed the trigger. A red hole appeared just above his left eye, and he stood there for a second, looking at me, before his brain stopped providing commands to his body. Then he dropped his weapon, crumpled to the ground, and lay still.

I waited there for a moment, feeling the blood surging in my veins and reveling in the unexpected high. I had not felt this in my previous interludes on this venture but now it was here. I felt, totally and completely alive. It was intoxicating.

Voices from the outside of the tent interrupted my reverie,

and I moved to the rear of the tent and outside through the flap Joe had identified. I found myself behind a row of pickup trucks and assorted all-terrain vehicles and made my way between the two directly in front of me, using the shadows generated by the vehicles for concealment. I slipped between the two vehicles and paused when I reached the front of them, squatting down so my head was not above the level of the trucks' hoods.

I peered around the front of the vehicles and looked left and right. There were minimal people in the area. Light streamed from a tent about seventy-five feet to my left and raucous laughter came from within. As I watched it, a man staggered out the front flap of the tent turned to his left, walked a few more steps, and then urinated, noisily, into the dirt next to the tent, farting loudly in the process. He yelled something to the men in the tent in a belligerent tone as he relieved himself, and voices from the inside responded in like fashion.

I took the opportunity to move across the hundred yards of open ground to the vehicles on the other side, keeping as low as I could. My foot scraped some rocks in the dirt and farting man turned around slowly as his intoxicated brain took in the sound and attempted to locate it. I ducked behind a row of fifty-gallon drums and lay still, watching him closely through a gap between the two drums farthest along. I could see him look across the open area between the rows of trucks, but his gaze didn't seem to dwell on any one location; and soon he returned to his task, fastening the fly on his fatigues before he returned to the tent.

I moved to the vehicles on the other side of the park, slid between two trucks, and sat down against the rear wheels. I was where I was supposed to be. Now I just had to wait for the good guys to show up and try not to attract any attention.

There was an odd sort of tranquility as I sat there, listening to the raucous conversation and laughter coming from the tent I had noticed earlier and the sounds of people walking and talking in the distance but most noticeably from the blanket of utter silence that surrounded it all. Here I was, in the Mexican desert in the middle of nowhere with a clear sky and sparking stars above, among a group of people involved in an enterprise that could change the balance of power in the world. People who would have sooner shot me than given me the time of day, but I took a moment to appreciate the still beauty of the night sky and the gentle sound of the wind brushing the desert foliage.

"Remind you of Cabo?" asked a soft, familiar voice, very close to me.

"Hello, Dave," I whispered in return. I stayed absolutely still, well aware that at least two Special Forces types would have their rifles sighted in on me. "Aren't you getting a little old for this special ops insertion shit? Wabo back atcha, by the way."

"Not when it involves one of my assets," he said, slapping my shoulder playfully. He made a motion with his hand, which I assumed put the other members of the team at ease and then moved up alongside me. "The chopper's about a click to the west. Can you take it on foot or are you injured?"

"I can walk," I said. "But aren't you going to plant some explosives or do some interdiction shit? The F-35 is here and so is Tappan. Apparently Miguel and Ramon the Stone will be along any minute now."

"Ramon the Rock," he said, correcting me. "I guess we really didn't get him at the rest stop a few weeks ago. Damn that guy is hard to kill," he said, shaking his head. "The gun that knocked him down back in Maryland was a .338 Lapua Magnum, probably the most powerful rifle cartridge in the world and fired by one of our best snipers. He swears he hit Ramon dead center. I don't fucking believe it." Smith sighed and looked around us. "And yes, we'd love to kill all these fuckers, but we don't have the assets in place to do it. We were barely able to scramble the assets to come and get you. If there hadn't been a Delta team deployed to Fort Huachuca that we could commandeer, I'm not sure we'd even be here. But I think we've got some time." He pointed to a place to our right, beyond the truck park. "They've got the F-35 under a large canopy about 1200 meters north of here. We caught a glimpse of it on the IR sensors on the way in. We can't even get close enough to it to see if they're taking it apart. But they'll have to if they want to truck it to the coast. And that's going to take a while."

"Hmmm," I said, wondering. I didn't share his optimism on the time line. "Do they have a ship in place?"

Smith nodded in the semidarkness. "Out in the Gulf of California. It's pretty far to the south, a big freighter with a hold large enough to conceal a dozen F-35's. Not of Chinese registry of course, but belonging to a shadow company with roots in Panama." He motioned for me to stand. "C'mon, Colin. We gotta get moving."

"Panama?" I asked as I got to my feet.

"Panama is to ship registration what Switzerland is to banks. Not too many questions, limited oversight, no safety inspections."

My head was spinning a little. I glanced around us in the parking area and couldn't help but feel that there was something we were missing. I just wasn't sure what.

"You know, Tappan was really in a hurry tonight. Shouldn't you guys try to grab him so we can question him and find out what's going on?"

Smith shook his head sadly. "Not enough time. We need to get out of here before the Mexicans figure out we've been here. They're still a little touchy about the whole Santa Catalina business last fall."

"So you came all the way down here just to get me?"

"Of course," Smith said. "We couldn't let Miguel get to the bait quite yet. We still need you to lure him onto our turf."

"Always nice to be loved," I mused.

"You should see what we do to the people we don't like," he said.

"I'll take your word for it."

One of the Delta commandos appeared at Smith's shoulder and motioned toward the direction of our apparent egress.

"Ready to move?" Smith asked.

"Yes, sir," I responded.

"Cool," he said. "And keep your finger off the trigger of that Glock. If you accidentally discharge it and give away our position, these Delta Force guys might kill you without asking permission."

"They'll have to get in line," I said.

Chapter Twenty

Contract Day Fourteen
Tuesday, July 6, 2010
0215 Hours Local Time
310th Fighter Squadron Ramp
Luke AFB, Arizona

The MH-60 helicopter touched down quietly on the concrete very near where Satan had hijacked the F-35 hours earlier. After discharging Smith, the Delta Force team, and me, the huge machine lifted off into the desert night and lumbered off into the southern sky.

"How in the hell do they make them so quiet?" I asked as the helo disappeared.

"From what I understand, it's the shape of the blades," Smith replied. "Keeps the tips from going supersonic. That's what generates most of the noise."

"Makes sense," I said.

"Speaking of making sense," Smith said, "are you sure this plan of yours will work?"

"Assuming they've got some folks working the swing shift, it should," I replied. "If we want to make sure we get that thing tonight and keep a low profile doing it, this is probably our only option. You and your people are just going to have to make the right phone calls to make sure I don't get shot down flying back into the US at high speed and low altitude."

Smith nodded.

"By the way, good catch on them moving the F-35 by helicopter extraction," he said. "We were in and out of there so fast I never noticed there weren't any large trucks in the camp. If we hadn't been able to get that satellite imagery, we might have never put those pieces together."

"It wasn't only the lack of trucks, there is also no real road structure in the area," I said. "Even if they got the thing out on the road with large trucks, they'd have to drive east, away from the water, then south through that big town I can't remember the name of."

"Hermosillo," Smith said.

"And many miles farther south to that deep water port in the other city I can't remember the name of."

"Guaymas," Smith said, shaking his head. "Did you not pay attention in geography class?"

"Not in that area of the world. Anyway, helo extraction is the only thing that makes sense."

"It will take a big ass helicopter," Smith said. "An F-35 weighs something like 30,000 pounds, even when it's empty."

"I saw a video of a Russian Mi-26 carrying an airliner on YouTube," I said. "And you know what else?"

"What?"

"The entire Mi-26 project was a Chinese-Russian cooperative venture."

"Jesus. Aren't you king of the obscure facts?"

"Obscure perhaps, but relevant," I said. "Now," I continued, walking toward the 310th's maintenance headquarters building, "let's see if we can find some ambitious technicians who are a little underworked tonight."

"Shouldn't we just go to a hangar and see if we can round up a crew?" Smith asked. "It seems like we're advertising going to their HQ."

I shook my head. "It would take too long, and they'd all find out anyway. Maintenance people gossip. It comes with the job description. The best way to control the dissemination of information with them is at the source. The main maintenance operations center on base, or the MOC as they call it, will know all the maintenance work going on all over the base. But the 310th will have a smaller version of that which we can take over and persuade the folks there to do what we require. Odds are high they're the only ones who are working this time of night anyway."

There were multiple lights on in the 310th building, indicating there were people inside working. As we approached the doors, the Delta team leader, a lieutenant who looked young enough to be my son, came alongside us and whispered in a low voice.

"Clear the building first, sir? It's standard procedure."

"I don't think so, Lieutenant," I replied. "In this case it might cause more attention than we need. I'm pretty sure I can talk my way into the building. You guys can follow, and we'll collect the personnel and hold them in one room until we're done with what we need to do here. Fair enough?"

"Yes, sir," he said. "Your call." His tone of voice indicated he didn't approve of my plan.

I reached the doors. "Give me about five minutes and then follow me in," I said. "It'll take me that long to find their control room. You should bring anyone you encounter along the way with you." I looked at Smith. "You might want to get some imagery of that ship. I'm willing to bet you'll find a big ass helo aboard her."

Smith nodded, and I went through the double glass doors.

The building was standard USAF: tiled floors, nondescript brick walls, and the usual official propaganda hanging everywhere. There was no one in the offices immediately to my left and right as I entered, so I turned to the right down a long hallway and headed toward the end. The building was all but deserted. Even for a squadron that flew at night every day of the week, the majority of the maintenance work would still be done during the day. The required logistical support simply wouldn't be available at night. I hoped that wouldn't impede what I had in mind.

About halfway down the hall, I heard conversation and radio traffic through one of the metal doors to my right. I put my ear to the door for a moment or two and listened. I had found what I was looking for. I tried the doorknob, and much to my surprise, it was unlocked. I opened the door slowly and stepped inside the darkened room, leaving the door ajar. The room was about twenty feet long by ten feet wide and lit by the glow of computer screens and a large LCD display hanging on the far wall. The desks were arranged in rows facing the LCD screen with one desk in the back, overseeing the operation. On the screen, tail numbers of jets were displayed with maintenance status, configuration, and work underway in a spreadsheet-like configuration.

The master sergeant at the desk in the back put his coffee mug down as I entered and looked at me with a tired and overworked expression on his face.

"Can I help you, sir?" he asked, not hiding his annoyance. He wasn't used to seeing pilots on his turf, especially not in the wee hours of the morning.

"I hope so, Sergeant," I said quietly, walking toward him.

He remained in his chair and swiveled so it was facing me. Then he raised his mug and took a long sip, clearly indicating he thought his coffee was more important than I was.

I reached him and bent down so that only he could hear me.

"I need a fully fueled Block 42 jet loaded up with two 370-gallon tanks, a nav pod, a targeting pod, an ECM pod, two live AIM-9s, two live AIM-120s, and two live Mark 84 LGBs. And I need it done within an hour and with only a few people knowing about it."

His eyes widened behind the coffee mug, and he slowly lowered it as his mind processed what I had just told him Of course, the Glock in my hand probably didn't help his ability to comprehend the situation.

"This is a matter of national security, and I don't have time to explain or ask permission from the higher-ups," I said. "You're going to have to take my word for this and make it happen."

"But..." he stammered. "There's no authorization for this. I can't just order a crew to load a jet like that. There are forms and requisitions that have to come first."

"Oh, I think you can do it," I said, hearing the door open behind me as Dave Smith and the Delta team came in. The five of them stood behind me in black tactical gear with automatic weapons in the ready position. Smith produced his credentials, which had the letters CIA displayed clearly on them. "And I'm betting these guys can encourage you."

The sergeant stared dumbly at us. It was clear he was having trouble assembling the pieces.

"Listen to me," I said, looking at his name tag, "Sergeant Wilson, your idiot wing commander just stole an F-35 and is about to sell it to the Chinese government. We need to make sure that doesn't happen and right now, this is our only chance."

For a moment, Wilson continued to stare. Then he nodded slowly and spoke without taking his eyes off of us.

"Anyone got an air-to-ground jet configured for 2,000-pounders in their flight that's MR and available tonight?" he called out to the room.

A couple of heads looked up from their screens and nodded.

"With a nav pod on it as well?" I added.

There were blank stares from across the room. The sergeant made a helpless motion with his hands.

"We don't use them anymore. Everything's medium altitude with NVGs," he said.

"Well shit," I said, "just when I was counting on a little technology to give me a break. So no TFR and no FLIR anymore?"

Wilson shook his head. "Not for years."

Smith was looking at me.

"TFR is terrain following radar. It was developed for the F-16 when we were going to fight the next war at low altitude. When I was here in the late nineties, the 310th used to instruct it because even though the US Air Force didn't use low-altitude tactics any longer, other F-16 users did. It was very cool. Set it and forget it, and the jet flies itself down to like 100 feet. Now I'm going to have to fly manually using NVGs, which I've never used. But it doesn't seem like I have any choice."

"They're very intuitive, once you get used to them," Smith said.

"It is what it is, I guess."

"So are we still doing this?" the sergeant asked.

I nodded. "I'm going to need someone to let me into 310th ops, get me some life-support gear, and give me the short course on NVGs," I said.

Wilson inclined his head toward one of the men seated at a computer console.

"It's your lucky day. Jenkins there works egress and can get you into the building. He also can get you hooked up with gear and NVGs."

"Great. I'll need a little mission planning time as well."

"We'll have the jet loaded in about an hour," Wilson said. He turned to the group in front of him. "Get me the jet, two live GBU-10s, two AIM-9X's, two AIM-120s, a weapons loading crew, and a fuel truck and have them meet me at south EOR." He looked back at me for a moment. "Tell them to keep it quiet and tell them to hurry."

The men in the front of the room set to their tasks.

"I'm sending them to the south end-of-runway inspection area—a lot fewer prying eyes down there," he said. "I'll supervise it myself."

"Sounds good," I said.

"Is there a chance Tappan might be in that F-35 when you lay these four thousand pounds of high explosive on it?"

"Probably not," I said. "But he'll definitely be nearby."

"I hope so," Wilson said. "I never liked that son of a bitch."

Chapter Twenty-One

Contract Day Fourteen
Tuesday, July 6, 2010
0330 Hours Local Time
End-of-Runway Inspection Area, Runway 03R
Luke AFB, Arizona

The last weapons loader was rolling away from the jet when Smith and I arrived at the EOR area with my hastily assembled mission materials, newly loaded data transfer cartridge, and borrowed life-support gear. The members of a CIA ops team were in position around the jet, ensuring that the weapons loaders and maintenance personnel weren't disturbed in their work. They formed an ominous-looking ring of black, shadowy figures as they stood just outside the portable lights that had been brought to the EOR to provide illumination for the work to be done. As we drove up in the USAF truck, Smith gave them some sort of hand signal that seemed to relax them.

I barely noticed.

"It'll be fucking sunrise in two hours," I muttered as the truck braked to a halt.

"Enough time?" Smith asked.

"It'll have to be," I said. "Less than two hours to find the damn place, get some laser-guided bombs on target without getting noticed by the Mexican Air Force, and get back across the border before I'm engaged by our own forces when I return."

"Hopefully you'll get there before the helicopter does," Smith sighed.

"Speaking of not offending the Mexican government, this isn't going to make us any friends in Mexico City. Do you guys have the firepower to cover an international incident if I have to shoot down the helicopter to stop the transfer?"

Smith shook his head in the darkness. "I don't know," he said.

"You might want to start working on that, Dave."

Smith's cell phone buzzed and he raised it to his ear as he looked at me.

"Sometimes it's easy to forget how smart that son of a bitch Miguel is," he said.

"He didn't become one of the most powerful drug lords in the world by being stupid," I said. "He's a planner."

"Smith," he answered the phone. I could hear Amrine's voice coming through the line. He sounded agitated. "Airborne?" Smith asked. "Already?"

I stared at him.

"And what else? You've gotta be fucking kidding me." There was a pause. "Yeah, I'll tell him. Out here." He clicked the END button.

"It's worse than we thought." he said. "We didn't see the helo on the ship because it's airborne, en route across the Gulf to the encampment area. The ship is steaming north to shorten the return flight, but apparently they launched the helo early. Your escape must have alarmed them."

"The route is about 275 nautical miles down there from here. At 540 knots ground speed, I should have bombs on target in just over thirty minutes."

"There's more. The imagery didn't pick up just one helo,

it picked up three."

"Three?"

"One large one, possibly a Mi-26, inbound from the west. But there are two more moving in from the Mexican Air Force Base at General Ignacio Pesqueira García International Airport at Hermosillo."

"And?"

"They look like Mi-8s."

I felt my throat go dry. "Gunships?"

He nodded. "That's what the imagery seems to indicate."

"Great," I said.

The Mi-8 Hip was one of the most widely manufactured helicopters in the world, and while it was designed to carry troops and/or cargo, the gunship version was heavily armed indeed, with 12.7mm machine guns, 57mm rockets, and antitank guided missiles. Some versions had been outfitted with air-to-air missiles.

I slid off the seat of the Air Force pickup and into the heat of the desert night.

"You better keep the covert rescue folks around," I said to Smith. "I might be costing the US government another F-16 tonight. And have standby crews in place to meet me at Davis-Monthan Air Force Base and Gila Bend. If I have an issue, I'll put down at one of the two places."

He looked at me and nodded. "Just try not to shoot at them unless they shoot at you first," he said.

"Right," I said. "And since when have I ever complied with standard rules of engagement?"

I didn't wait for an answer and turned to my jet, which was parked in the glow of the floodlights, bristling with armament. There were two MK-84 2,000 pound bombs in place with the laser-guidance assemblies installed—technically known as GBU-10s. I would have preferred the more aerodynamic GBU-24s but those were all deployed to operational units. I smiled grimly to myself. Four thousand pounds of high explosive and metal landing in Miguel's encampment was certainly going to leave a mark. I only hoped I could release the bombs and guide them to their target without getting my ass shot off by the gunships that were now in play.

But if the gunships wanted to dance, I had prepared for that. The jet was also loaded with two AIM-120 AMRAAM radar-guided missiles, one mounted on each wing tip, and two AIM-9X Sidewinder missiles, one on station 2 and the other on station 8, just inboard of the wing tips on the left and right sides of the jet respectively. The AIM-9X was apparently a much more capable missile than the AIM-9M that I had last used in the USAF. It was also more capable than the Python 4s I had used last year. When I had asked the instructor in one of our weapons classes to compare the Python to the 9X, the young major's eyes had positively gleamed.

"Think BMW 6-series vs a Lamborghini," he had said. "They're both fast and they can turn well, but the Lamborghini is way out of the BMW's league."

"Gun full?" I asked the crew chief as I headed for the cockpit ladder and handed him my nav kit, DTC, and helmet.

"You bet, sir," the tall blond staff sergeant replied. "510 rounds of PGU-28 API/HEI. You're ready to rock and roll!"

"You know," I said as I clipped the crotch straps on my parachute harness, "I think I'd actually prefer a lullaby."

The crew chief looked at me, uncomprehending.

"Never mind," I said, taking the items back from him and climbing the ladder.

And as I shut the canopy, after starting the engine moments later, the right word came to me. "Waltz," I said to myself. "I think I'd prefer a waltz. But I'll probably end up in a mosh pit."

***

Ten minutes later, the Pratt and Whitney PW-220's afterburner lit, and I felt the familiar kick in the middle of the back as I rolled down Runway 21 Left and launched into the dark Arizona sky. As soon as the gear was retracted, I canceled the afterburner and allowed the jet to drift up to 1500 feet above the ground as I banked left toward the first point on my hastily assembled route into Mexico. The mountains and ridges south of me were barely visible in the moonless night; but as I flipped down the NVGs and activated them, they became nearly as apparent as they would have been in the daylight, the green glow of the goggles notwithstanding.

I briefly thought back to the preflight conversation I had with Sergeant Jenkins as he helped me find a helmet and set of googles. "What can you tell me about using these things?" I asked.

"The one thing I hear the pilots talk about all the time is the lack of depth perception," he said. "There's no peripheral vision so your depth perception is messed up."

I had nodded.

"Other than that, they're killer. The pilots say that they can see some infrared in them, but if there's the slightest ambient light, you can see nearly like its daytime. Just be careful of light in the cockpit, because excess light can blind you. Use the NVG setting on the lighting panel."

"So no checking my map in flight, I take it?"

"You can look under the NVGs and turn a light on and check it, but don't do it through the googles. You'll hate yourself."

"I hate myself already," I said to the empty cockpit now as the jet continued its descent. I was about to attempt one of the most hazardous maneuvers ever created for a one-man fighter—the self-designated low-altitude loft LGB delivery—without even the protection of a terrain following radar. It didn't help that I hadn't done it in over ten years.

"You sure know how to pick 'em, Pearce," I muttered into the intercom. "You may not even hit the target but at least there's a high probability you'll kill yourself."

I leveled the F-16 off at 700 feet above the rocky desert terrain just as I reached the first turn point, a small hill west of the Estrella Mountains and about fifteen miles south of the town of Buckeye. I turned the aircraft toward the next waypoint, pushed the throttle up to MIL power, and watched the fuel flow stabilize at about 8900 pounds per hour. The airspeed crept up to just over 500 knots and the jet began to demonstrate the mild rocking and yawing behavior it manifested with the dual 2000-pound bomb payload. The sensation of movement I felt in the cockpit reminded me of riding a horse over uneven terrain. I smiled under the soft plastic of the oxygen mask.

"The old Mark 84 dance," I said. "Nothing like it."

The motion was annoying but not significant, and I ignored it after just a few moments. Instead, I peered through the NVGs and attempted to discern the terrain beyond. Thanks to the quarter moon suspended in the cloudless desert sky above, the topographic detail I could see was impressive. Ridges, mountains, rocks, and arroyos were clearly visible, as were man-made features such as roads and buildings. Anything that generated light, like a houses or vehicles, stood out starkly from the terrain around it. I was also glad to see that the NIGHT setting for the HUD allowed me to see the HUD symbology without overamping the NVGs.

"Damn," I said to myself. "I might actually be able to do this."

The decision to ingress at low altitude had been made for us. In spite of the fact that the F-16 was certified to 50,000 feet, the jet didn't like to get much higher than the mid-20s, especially when it was loaded with ordnance. And ingress in the 20s was out of the question because of the traffic density and radar coverage in that altitude regime in southern Arizona/northern Sonora.

So I was stuck.

While I didn't have to drop down to extremely low altitude until I approached the border, I allowed the jet to gradually descend to 500 feet to get a better feeling for manually flying the aircraft at low altitude on the NVGs and was surprised to discover it was just about as benign as flying during the daytime.

I saw the glow of the town of Gila Bend and the USAF Auxiliary Field just south of it off my right side as I passed abeam a break between two ridgelines. The second point in my route was twenty nautical miles ahead—about two minutes. So far, so good. I was on course, and the Block-42's GPS navigation system was functioning flawlessly. Now all I needed was an exact set of longitude and latitude coordinates for the target, and apparently we needed a satellite pass to get them.

"Any time, Dave," I said into the dark cockpit.

I glanced up to see the cars on Interstate 8 in the NVGs and then seconds later, the freeway passed under the nose in a blur as I headed south into the Barry Goldwater Range Complex. My route was to take me just east of the Eastern Tactical Range. For a moment I wondered if there would be any other jets working low altitude attacks on the range. But then I realized that I was more likely to have an encounter with a Customs and Border Patrol aircraft than another F-16 at this hour of the morning. Since 9/11, the CBP had been granted patrol access to the Barry Goldwater Range Complex and spent the evenings looking for the inevitable human trail of illegal immigrants.

I looked on the navigation display in the HUD. Miguel's camp was twenty-three minutes away. Time passes quickly—nine miles per minute at 540 knots. And there wasn't much of it left.

"Tango Charlie this is Delta Sierra," Smith's voice crackled on the auxiliary radio.

"Go, Delta Sierra," I answered.

"Satellite feed shows Mi-26 about fifteen minutes out. Gunships are north and south of the target, facing inward in a protective formation. At your current speed, you should have bombs on target while the Mi-26 is slinging the load."

"Copy that," I said. "Any word on the target coordinates?"

"They've hidden it," Smith replied. "There are several tents or canvas structures that could conceal it. Apparently they're waiting until the last minute to reveal it. You know what that means."

"Affirmative," I said into the mic.

They know we're watching them, I thought, shaking my helmeted head in the cockpit. *And they know I'm coming.* I pounded my left fist on the canopy.

"Where the fuck are they getting this shit?" I yelled into the intercom.

I made the slight course adjustment to stay on steering at point three and headed toward my last waypoint inside the United States, just a few miles north of the US-Mexico border. The air was eerily still as I sliced through it at 540 knots. There was no buffeting and no turbulence at all, as if the atmosphere was holding its breath to allow for my passage. I wasn't sure I cared for that thought. Since I was out over the flat terrain for a few moments, I flipped the NVGs up and regarded the brilliant desert sky with the stars shining above me like myriad candles. Flying a fighter—being alone in a complex machine at high speed and low altitude—created a sensation that transcended mere existence. It was as if you were one with the universe at that point in time. I flipped the NVGs down and watched the green-illuminated ground go underneath me so rapidly that it appeared as an emerald blur.

The perception of speed was surreal. And then I could see the outline of the small mountain I had selected as turnpoint three ahead.

The target was fifteen minutes away.

I took the small mountain down the left hand side of the jet and it vanished into the darkness. A few miles ahead of me, I could see vehicular traffic on a small road that was nearly perpendicular to my flight path. It was the only indication of the US-Mexican border in this part of the country.

"Some boundary," I said to myself.

The vehicles glowed brightly against the dark desert landscape and from my vantage point they were easy to see— something that gave me hope for my task in the target area a few moments from now. There was a single vehicle moving at high speed, followed by two larger vehicles apparently pursuing it.

"Somebody else is in a little trouble tonight," I murmured.

They were about to get the scare of their lives as a completely blacked out F-16 roared over them at 540 knots.

The vehicles shot under the nose, and I had to fight the urge to look back over my shoulder to see if either vehicle had run off the road.

And then I was immersed in the total darkness of the sparsely populated province of Sonora in northern Mexico. The rocks and ridges were still visible, and I was grateful for the illumination of the waning moon as I headed southbound. The next turnpoint was a road intersection just west of a small town. As much as I trusted the GPS and the inertial navigation system, I wanted some reassurance that the navigation system was accurate before I lofted two 2,000 pound bombs into the air without seeing the target. The intersection was a precise fix. If the nav system got me there, all would be good.

"Tango Charlie, Delta Sierra." I found myself wondering how I could hear Smith so clearly beneath a mountain range in Mexico.

"Go, Delta Sierra," I said, gently easing the nose of the jet skyward.

"Target coordinates. Ready to copy?"

I looked under the NVGs and hit the buttons on the F-16's up-front control unit to bring the correct waypoint for the target up in the small display.

"Go ahead," I said.

He read me the latitude and longitude, and I typed them into the Viper's nav system. Then I had him read them again so I could verify my entry. Finally, I read the coordinates back to him.

"Good copy," Smith said when I finished. "The target is dead center in the complex. They must have moved it right next to the truck park."

"Roger that," I said. "Where's the Mi-26?"

"Just a few minutes out. What's your time remaining?"

I looked at the clock in the HUD. "About eight minutes," I said.

There was silence for a few moments. I could feel Smith thinking. "Hopefully that will be soon enough," he said at last.

"Where are the two Hips?"

Another pause. Smith was undoubtedly looking at a satellite feed. "One is about two clicks south of the target and the other is about six clicks northeast."

Blocking the egress, I thought. I keyed the mic. "Delta Sierra, Tango Charlie. I'm probably going to have to take at least the one on the northeast down," I said. "He's blocking my egress route. I'll be going nose to nose with him as I try to guide the bombs in."

"As required," Smith said after a long moment. "Do what you have to."

"Roger," I replied. "I'll call you off target."

"Copy that," Smith said. "Out here."

I looked back through the NVGs just in time to see a mountain looming before me, the pattern of the rock clearly visible in the green glow NVGs.

"Son of a..." I said and promptly almost killed myself.

My gloved right hand automatically applied aft pressure on the sidestick controller to bring the Viper's nose up and avoid hitting the rocks in front of me. The F-16's digital flight control computer responded quickly, but I had to ensure that I didn't exceed 5.5 g's so I didn't over stress the laser-guided bombs I was carrying. The jet began to track upward rapidly. But I was behind the power curve. As my anti-g suit tightened around my legs and clenched against my stomach, my vision in the NVGs tunneled down so that I could only see about a quarter of the field of view, and I could feel myself becoming light-headed.

I was losing consciousness.

I hadn't had time to get into my anti-g straining maneuver before applying aft stick and now I was paying the price.

The anti-g straining maneuver has been likened to bearing down while having a bowel movement. The pilot breathes in quickly, tightens his torso and legs, and pushes the air in his lungs down as far as he can, with the objective of increasing his intrathoracic blood pressure so the blood in his head stays there and keeps the brain conscious. If the pilot is well into the maneuver when he applies g, he stays conscious. If he applies the g before he gets into the maneuver, he may never catch up. There had been numerous g-induced loss of consciousness (GLOC) casualties in the Air Force that proved that point.

But I bore down as hard as I could and tried to keep the remaining blood in my head as the jet continued to climb to clear the ridge in front of me. The rock was beneath the aircraft now, and I had no idea about whether I'd clear it or not. I continued to fight to stay awake and tried to stay focused on flying the jet.

Then suddenly there were stars in front of me and the earth was retreating below.

I relaxed, took a deep breath, and then rolled the Viper onto its back to pull the nose back down to the rocks. I had cleared the ridge and stayed alive but that was likely to be the easiest hazard I would face tonight.

As the jet returned to low altitude, I peered through the HUD to check the position of the video diamond that indicated the next turnpoint. To my relief, the diamond lay directly on top of a road intersection that was clearly visible in the green glow of the NVGs. The Viper's nav system was doing its job. Next stop was the last point prior to the target, the initial point or IP.

The target was four minutes away.

I went through the cockpit and ran a quick FENCE check, making sure the jet was ready to drop ordnance and not emitting any signals or lights that would lead to its untimely detection. I ensured the chaff and flare dispensers were armed, actuated the MASTER ARM switch and used the DOGFIGHT switch on the throttle to toggle through the air-to-air and air-to-ground master mode variations I had programmed into the Viper's avionics, verifying that correct modes and weapons were called up in each position. They were. So far, I was set. I went back into air-to-air mode and placed the DOGFIGHT switch back into the center position, bringing the navigation mode back up again. Then I exhaled slowly, rotated my neck to work out the kinks in it, and I settled back into the Viper's 30 degree inclined seat as I peered through the green glow of the NVGs at the world beyond.

In the distance, just under ten miles away, one minute or so at my current speed, I could see the green waypoint diamond in the HUD overlaying the small hill that was the initial point I had selected. The target was about one minute and forty-five seconds beyond that. I could feel my pulse quickening. It was nearly time to rain death from the air once again. I just hoped I didn't die in the process. I punched the air-to-ground button on the up-front control with my left thumb. In the HUD, a vertical line became my steering cue; and in the right multifunction display or MFD, the imaged infrared world seen by the targeting pod became visible. The tracking gate, the area denoted by the crosshairs in the display and where the laser designator would be focused, was parked directly on the IP, indicating that it was cued to the correct position. I was tempted to try a test slew of the tracking gate with the circular switch on the throttle, but I didn't want to screw up the cueing for the target.

The small hill of the IP flashed under the nose in a green blur. I rolled the jet up and turned it about twenty degrees to the right to center the flight path marker in the HUD on the vertical steering line.

"Delta Sierra, Tango Charlie is IP inbound," I said into the mic. My voice was dead calm on the radio. The words from Ozzy Osbourne's I Don't Wanna Stop ran through my mind.

Mama don't cry I just wanna stay high

I like playing with danger and fear...

"Copy, Tango Charlie," Smith's voice responded, breaking me from my reverie. "The big helo is still in the hover."

I nodded grimly as I clicked the mic button twice in reply.

"Not for long," I said in the intercom.

I looked into the HUD and noted the word "ARM" displayed. I rechecked that both stations 3 and 6 were ready to dispense weapons and that the bomb fuses were ready to arm. All seemed to be set. I ran through the low altitude loft procedure in my mind again.

"Lift, loft, roll, pull, roll-out, slew," I said to myself. "Oh yeah and try not to hit the ground on the recovery to low altitude. I'd kill for a TFR right now."

In the days of training for the Cold War and the self-designated loft, the pilot toggled the terrain-following radar off for the loft maneuver but then reengaged the TFR as the jet was descending back to low altitude and relied on the TFR to auto level the aircraft off at low altitude, allowing the pilot to concentrate on slewing the targeting pod to the correct aim point so that the laser-guided bombs would impact in the right place. Tonight, I would have to slew and recover the aircraft manually. And if I didn't, I'd be a smoking hole in the ground. At that point, creating an international incident would be the least of my worries.

The large, 50-milliradian circle flashed in the HUD, signaling that I was reaching maximum range for the pull-up. On cue, a horizontal line appeared on vertical steering line below the flight path marker and began to travel upward. That was the pull-up cue. When it reached the flight path marker, it would be time to lift the nose. Only seconds to go now. I peered through the HUD into the blackness to see if I could make out where the square of video was that should be overlaying the target. At low altitude with terrain between the target and me, there wouldn't be much to see; but it was always a good thing to do for orientation purposes.

But instead of terrain or the target, there was something else entirely.

The NVGs revealed a glowing shape in front of me that seemed to be blocking my way. At my altitude no less. I felt a sudden tightness in my stomach.

"What's up with these fucking NVGs?" I wondered out loud.

And then my mind processed the image in front of me, and I realized what I was seeing.

"Jesus Christ!" The words came out of my mouth unbidden.

My eyes converted the glowing, amorphous shape into something I recognized, and I found myself nodding. "These things really do rock," I said into the intercom. I glanced under the googles and down at the infrared display from the targeting pod to confirm my suspicions. The clear video from the imaging infrared sensor cleared up any doubts.

I was looking at one of the Mi-8 attack helicopters.

The large machine looked like a hovering insect, and it was bristling with rockets, missiles, and God knew what else. But as my mind connected the neurons to refine the image, I could see it wasn't pointed at me but was instead oriented inward, watching and guarding the pickup operation in the flat area beyond.

"You should have been farther east," I said to the glowing mass in front of me. "Then you might have survived."

Then my reflexes took over. I toggled the DOGFIGHT switch on the throttle outboard with my left hand and pushed the target management switch on the sidestick controller forward with my right thumb. The radar boresight cross appeared in the HUD, directly over the helicopter. The Viper's radar operated as advertised and almost immediately went into single-target-track mode.

"LOCK, LOCK," the Viper's female voice reminder system informed me, and instantaneously the suppressed whistle of the AIM-9X on station 2 was audible in my headset as the missile's seeker head was slaved to the radar.

My left index finger tapped the UNGAGE button on the throttle, and the sound changed from a growl to a high-pitched whine, indicating the seeker was locked on the heat source in front of me. I glanced down at the designated launch zone display in the lower right side of the HUD to verify that I was in range to shoot and was astounded to see how much above minimum range I was.

"What a missile," I said to myself as I found my right thumb found the "pickle" button on the sidestick and pushed it.

And then I almost went blind.

The AIM-9's rocket motor ignited and the missile shot out from under the left wing faster than a bottle rocket leaves the ground, leaving a trail of bright fire its wake. Seconds later, it slammed into the Hip and must have hit a fuel tank or some ordnance on the helicopter because a huge fireball immediately erupted in the night sky.

The infrared display in the NVGs bloomed white hot in front of me and nearly seared my eyeballs. At the same time, the eruption of light gained the NVGs down and the light amplification virtually ceased. Almost instantly I had spots in my eyes and could see nothing but blackness in front of me.

"Jesus Christ!" I screamed and flipped the NVGs upward, hoping that I had retained enough vision to still see the symbology in the HUD.

I toggled the DOGFIGHT switch downward to call the air-to-ground mode back up and blinked my eyes to try to see around the bright spots that were fluctuating in my vision. As my vision focused, I could see that the pull-up cue was above the flight path marker.

"Shit!" I spat into the oxygen mask. "I might be out of fucking time!"

I centered the flight path marker on the steering line and smoothly but firmly pulled aft on the Viper's sidestick controller as I found the pickle button again with my right thumb and held it down. The jet's nose lifted smartly skyward. As I peered into the HUD, I could see the fiery glow of the burning Hip reflected on the HUD combining glass. The dying helicopter was sinking to the ground beneath me. As the flight path marker approached the pull-up cue, I hoped the F-16's modular mission computer could still make the physics work. A moment or two later, the flight path marker reached the cue, and I gently pushed forward to keep the marker centered on the horizontal line.

"C'mon baby," I murmured into the intercom. "Let 'em

go."

If the Viper's modular mission computer couldn't solve the problem, there would be no release indication, and I'd be forced to turn away, get some more spacing from the target, and then try a reattack—something I wasn't thrilled about. If the lessons of Vietnam, Iraq, and Kosovo had proved nothing else, they had proved that "one pass haul ass" was the best way to survive. Reattacking the same target after the bad guys knew you were in the area wasn't just stupid, it was often fatal.

After an eternal moment or two, the flight path marker flashed and I could feel the twin "thumps" underneath me as the two LGB's were ejected from the bomb racks. I immediately rolled left to 135 degrees of bank, grunted into my straining maneuver, and applied back pressure on the sidestick, pulling the Viper's nose back down to the ground. I now needed to slew the targeting pod to the right target, and I had to be wings level before the video view of the target was unobstructed. I was sure that I had released the bombs well inside of optimum range, so I had no idea how much longer they would be in the air before they impacted.

The nose came down rapidly, and I stopped it at about five degrees of descent angle as I rolled out of the turn. Then I looked down into the right MFD's targeting pod display to see what was there.

Nothing. Absolutely nothing. The display was dim and nothing was visible.

"Fuck!" I screamed into the intercom. "How did that get messed up?"

I had two LGBs in flight and right now they were destined to hit the dirt and do no good at all.

Then I remembered something from one of my academic classes about the targeting pod having both a TV and IR capability. Instinctively, I pushed the TMS button on the sidestick to the right and the left MFD was instantly filled with the IR image once again. Apparently I had bumped the TMS switch during the previous few seconds.

"Nice work," I said to no one in particular.

The targeting crosshairs rested on an open area in the middle of several tents. But the cold, dark outline of the F-35 was clearly visible at the top of the display.

"It's being lifted," I said to myself. "Holy shit."

The Mi-26 was raising the jet off the ground.

I used the round slew button on the throttle to move the cursors up and onto the F-35 and hoped like hell that the bombs could manage the energy to get there. LGBs were ballistic objects and their maneuverability was a function of the energy imparted to them when they separated from the releasing aircraft. While they could often still hit their targets if the trajectory required less energy (i.e., lower or closer than anticipated), increasing the elevation of the target might place the LGB in a place where it didn't have the energy to correct and would miss the target by impacting below it.

I slewed the crosshairs upward and waited. The bomb time of fall indicator in the MFD indicated that I had seven seconds left. I switched back to narrow field of view and attempted to keep the crosshairs on top of the F-35 as it moved steadily upward. It amazed me that seven seconds was taking so long. And then, as I moved the crosshairs up in one more adjustment, the bottom of the Mi-26 came into view in the targeting pod display, the underbelly of the helicopter alive with infrared energy in contrast to the cold metal of the F-35.

And then the bombs impacted.

The MFD display went instantly awash in a flash of bright, white heat. When the initial flash diminished, there was nothing left to see in the display, just pieces of metal and flames.

"Jesus," I said involuntarily.

"ALTITUDE! ALTITUDE!" The insistent female voice in

the F-16's reminder system yelled at me.

I instinctively applied back pressure to the sidestick controller and leveled the aircraft out about 300 feet above the ground. Then I started a slow climb back to 500 feet and flipped the NVGs back down again, hoping they were still operative. The green landscape came back into view, and I could see the next ridgeline to the north several miles in front of me.

"Tango Charlie, off hot," I said into the mic.

"Copy, Tango Charlie." Dave Smith's voice sounded in my ear. "Target destroyed. Helo and target are down. Great jo..." His voice stopped in midsentence as he apparently examined something on the feed in front of him. "Missile!" He screamed a second later. "Missile behind you!"

Years of USAF training builds reflexes that are useful. I was into my straining maneuver and into a right "break" turn immediately, at eight g's, my wings nearly perpendicular to the horizon and my left hand pulling the power to idle.

I knew what had happened. The other Hip helicopter, which had deployed to the south, had headed north during my attack and had managed to get within air-to-air missile range of me. Yet another thing I had failed to take into consideration. Reflexively, I hit the countermeasures dispensing switch on the sidestick controller and pumped several decoy flares into the night behind me. I felt a thud somewhere behind my jet and saw quick flash in the sky in that same vicinity. The missile had detonated behind and beyond me. I glanced down at the glare shield, warning light panel and engine instruments. Everything seemed normal. Nothing had hit my jet.

The right thing to do then would have been to return to my egress course and get my ass north of the border as quickly as possible. But the blood had begun to boil in my veins. I rolled out of my turn, shoved the throttle into MAX AB, and pulled aft on the sidestick. The Viper shot skyward, and I kept pulling the nose back until the jet was nearly vertical. The trick to fighting a slower, more maneuverable adversary was to take your airplane somewhere he couldn't go. The Hip could do many things, but it couldn't go vertical.

I looked around and behind me and attempted to locate the Hip. It was simpler than I expected. He was a few miles behind me, the glowing infrared signature standing out against the dark desert background. I grunted in acknowledgment, checked the HUD to make sure I still had about 300 knots airspeed and then began to pull the Viper onto its back, very gently. The nose tracked smoothly over and, after apexing at about 6,500 feet above the ground, I continued to pull the nose below the horizon.

"What are you doing, T. C.?" Smith inquired over the secure auxiliary radio freq.

I ignored him and allowed the familiar rush to take possession of me.

I pulled the Viper's nose to the helicopter below me and rolled the aircraft upright as I activated the DOGFIGHT mode and called the boresight cross up on the HUD. My right thumb went forward on the TMS switch.

"LOCK! LOCK!"

I considered uncaging the other AIM-9 just then but decided against it. Instead, I put the small circular pipper or "death dot" of the air-to-air gunsight over the helicopter's cockpit, waited until the slant range was equal to about 6,000 feet, and opened fire.

RRRRRRRRRRRRRR. The M-60-A1 Vulcan cannon shot fire at 6,000 rounds per minute and the 20mm PGU-28 rounds closed the gap between me and the helo in a fraction of a second. They chewed the cockpit up completely, probably killing the pilots instantly. But I wasn't done. I held the trigger down and ripped into the huge helicopter with 20mm slugs until the gun was empty, just a few seconds later. The flash from the cannon was behind the cockpit so it didn't overamp my NVG vision; but the slugs themselves created a white trail of destruction across the night and impacted with fearsome effectiveness, tearing the machine apart. The Hip stubbornly refused to explode though. As I recovered from my dive and began my turn back to the north, the helo sank to the desert floor and settled there, without a hint of sparks or light. I wondered if anyone had survived. The bloodlust inside of me was distinctly unsatisfied.

"Tango Charlie headed north," I said into the mic. "Reverse route."

"Roger Tango Charlie," Dave Smith's voice said with a tired resignation. "Did you really have to do the last one?"

"You bet your ass," I said. "Miguel had it coming. I hope he was on the damn thing."

Then I glanced down at the fuel totalizer.

"You might want to ensure that the folks at Gila Bend are awake. I don't think I'm going to have enough gas to make it back to Luke."

"Roger," Smith replied.

"And by the way," I said, "can you get me a ride back up north?

***

About thirty-five minutes later, after an uneventful landing on Runway 35 at Gila Bend, I taxied the Viper to the transient aircraft ramp. The crew chief was a civilian, probably older than I was, with a gaunt face and a gray ponytail. He looked like he had been awakened from a dead sleep, as he probably had been. He went about the tasks of pinning the gun and remaining missiles. His demeanor changed significantly as he realized that the aircraft had released and fired live ordnance in its flight. He finally pinned the emergency power unit and gave me the signal to shut down. I pulled the throttle over the detent into the OFF position and hit the switch to raise the canopy. Then I removed my helmet and took a moment to regard the stars in the wide-open desert sky above me. They looked far away, lonely, and magnificent.

"You need to appreciate this shit, Pearce," I whispered to myself. "Because some day that luck of yours is going to run out."

The standard Viper ladder appeared over the edge of the cockpit, and I made sure that the ejection seat was disarmed and pinned. Then I collected my DTC, kneeboards, charts, and helmet, stuffed it all into my borrowed helmet bag and handed it to the crew chief.

"What kind of mission were you on, sir? We didn't even know anyone was flying tonight, let alone that they were carrying live ordnance."

I shook my head.

"I'm sorry chief," I said. "I'm afraid I can't talk about it. There will be some folks here in a while to debrief you though. The less you know the better."

The old veteran nodded slowly. "Not the first time I've experienced that," he said. "I worked F-4s and Vipers in the day. I know the drill."

He took my helmet bag and vanished down the ladder. I took a few more moments in the cockpit of the jet and peered up again at the night sky

Eventually I disconnected myself from the aircraft and slowly climbed down the ladder. After releasing my harness straps and fastening them outside my legs, I walked around the mighty machine one more time and ran my gloved fingers over the coarse aluminum skin. I felt the familiar lump in my throat once again. This jet wasn't just a machine I flew. It was a fucking part of me.

Out of the corner of my eye, I saw a black suburban come

through the gate at the side of the ramp and drive over to the jet.

"That was quick," I said to myself.

As I watched, B-Rock emerged from the driver's side of the car with a huge grin.

"Hey, hero!" he said playfully. "So add three helicopters and an F-35 to your total?"

I grinned tiredly back at him.

"They were in the wrong place at the wrong time."

"That happens around you a lot," he said, shaking his head.

"Just lucky I guess. So I take it you're my ride?"

He nodded. "Yep. It's a dirty job, but someone has to do it."

"When will the team get here to deal with the jet?" I asked. "Do we have to wait for them?"

"They'll be here in a flash, and we're cleared to press." He glanced at his watch. "Besides, the one guy in the tower, the crew chief here, is the only one awake on the base. They're not going anywhere. And we need to move. It'll be daylight soon."

"Okay, Okay," I replied. I turned to the old veteran crew chief who had been listening to the conversation. "Mister," I looked at his name tag, "Connors, in a few minutes, some plainclothes people will arrive to debrief you. It won't take long. They'll probably tell you something like we were never here."

"I wish I wasn't, sir. My cot was a lot more comfortable."

I nodded and shook his hand. "Have a great night or morning or whatever it is."

"You too, sir."

I threw my helmet bag in the backseat of the suburban. Then I doffed my harness, survival vest, and anti-g suit and threw them back there as well. I climbed into the front passenger seat of the suburban and closed the door.

"Home, James," I said.

Brock nodded and handed me a miniature of Macallan 12.

"A little Scotch for your journey?"

"You, sir, are a gentleman and a scholar and there are damn few of us left." I unscrewed the cap. It seemed a little easier to open than they normally did but my tired mind didn't focus on it. Instead I downed the luscious spirit in one gulp.

"Cheers," I said, somewhat belatedly. "I needed that."

"There's more in the bag in the back if you want it," Brock said.

I settled myself into my seat and buckled my seatbelt.

"I think I'm good," I said.

My eyelids suddenly felt like bricks, and I found I couldn't keep them open.

"Your call," Brock said.

"Hey, B-Rock," I said, my mouth barely able to form the words, "I hope you don't mind if I sleep...a...little."

"No problem, T. C." I heard him say the words from some distant place.

And then, a few moments later, as my mind lost its battle for consciousness, I heard Brock's voice again, talking to someone else.

"I've got him," Brock said. "Tell Miguel."

Then the world went away.

Chapter Twenty-Two

Contract Day 15
Wednesday, July 7, 2010
2300 Hours Local Time
Somewhere in Phoenix, Arizona

"Colin?"

It was a female voice. And it seemed to be very far away. I was having trouble processing it. My brain seemed so clouded and dense.

"Colin? You've got to wake up. We don't have much time."

Much time? I wondered. Much time for what? The voice seemed closer now. I became aware that my wrists and ankles were uncomfortable. Very uncomfortable. Burning in fact.

"COLIN!"

The voice was insistent now. The cobwebs in my brain stubbornly refused to clear. Images came rumbling into my mind in haphazard order: there was the ejection in the desert, the brief stay at Miguel's camp in Mexico, the trip to Sedona, and Brock and I dealing with the guys that followed us. Something about that wasn't right. Christine's kidnapping. Brock said he'd look after her when they went back to their rooms to change for dinner. Then there was the landing at Luke in the helicopter. Brock wasn't around when we planned the mission. He wasn't part of the ops team. How did he know I had shot down three helicopters?

And then there were the words I heard before I'd passed out in the car.

"I've got him. Tell Miguel."

My eyes shot open in an instant; and my brain cleared so fast, it nearly gave me vertigo. All the leaks and issues from the previous several days zoomed into focus.

"Jesus!" I hissed. My voice was barely audible. "He's one of them!"

I became instantly aware of why my wrists and ankles were uncomfortable.

My wrists were handcuffed above me and my ankles were anchored beneath me. My weight was supported by the balls of my feet, barely making contact with some sort of iron plate. I glanced upward and downward in disbelief. The handcuffs seemed to be standard police issue, and they were anchored to a large iron screw eye that had been twisted into the side of a wood joist above. Below a length of reddish hemp rope was wrapped around my ankles and tied to 100-pound Olympic barbell plate with YORK painted on it. A part of me was bemused that a piece of iron from a factory in Pennsylvania had come so far just to piss me off.

"What is this?" I said to myself. "The fucking Middle Ages?"

"It may be," the female voice said from close by, "before they're done with us."

The sound startled me.

I turned my head to find Christine Billings hanging in a similar configuration next to me. She was clad in the same clothes I had last seen her in, a pair of tight white shorts and a coral-colored tank top. Her brunette hair was tangled and greasy, and her skin was smudged in many places. I couldn't tell if the smudges were from dirt or bruises.

"Fancy meeting you here," I said. "How long have you—"
She interrupted me.

"That whole Sedona ambush thing you guys did was staged," she said quickly. "Those are the same guys who brought me here. Brock let them into my room."

I nodded in realization. "I was just thinking that something didn't seem right," I said. "The gun I used didn't feel the same way it had when I fired it that night in my room. And the guys I shot didn't seem to have quite as many holes as they should." The conclusion was obvious. It had been loaded with blanks.

Christine nodded. "If Brock tries to act like he's on our side, you know it's bullshit, right?" she said.

I nodded again as I looked over at her. Despite the grease and the dirt and the smudges, Christine still looked beautiful. It was just a damn shame that we were both probably going to die here. I attempted a smile. "So have you been hanging around this whole time?"

She smiled thinly and shook her head. "No, I haven't. We were both cuffed in separate rooms until about an hour ago. Two of those guys who brought me down here brought you out here first and then me. This huge guy I hadn't seen before was ordering them around. His arms where all covered with tattoos, and he was wearing some kind of leather vest with these silver things all over it."

"Ramon the Rock," I said. "Just great."

"Who is that?" Christine asked, her eyes growing wide with fear.

"He works for Miguel. Apparently, he's a real bad dude."
Christine swallowed hard. "How bad?"

I looked at her, hanging by her wrists and trying to be brave. I wondered how much I should tell her.

I took a few seconds to look around as I gathered my thoughts. We were in the center of an open space between two rows of covered pallets loaded with God-knew-what.

There were a few incandescent bulbs suspended from the unfinished ceiling above us. Around the edges of the space, beyond the pallets, there were large pieces of machinery against the outside walls, lying in the shadows. Shapes were hard to detect, but there was order in the arrangement of what I could see.

"He's Miguel's chief enforcer, whatever that means," I said after a long moment. "Miguel uses him for special projects. Like me, apparently."

"Great," Christine answered. "So now we're in some abandoned warehouse in the middle of nowhere waiting for him—"

"It's not abandoned," I said, intentionally interrupting her.

"What?" she said, surprised. "What are you talking about?"

"There's no dust," I said. "Look around you. We're in the desert. It's the dustiest place known to man because there's no humidity in the air. If this had been abandoned, there'd be dust everywhere."

Christine cocked her head, looking at me in disbelief. "Who gives a shit!" she said, her voice was starting to crack. "We're here and they're coming to do—"

"And we're not in the middle of nowhere," I said, interrupting her again. "Miguel is a businessman. If he has warehouses, they're in places where he can make use of them. The man is many things, but he's not wasteful. We're probably somewhere in downtown Phoenix, in a neighborhood where the locals are loyal to Miguel and chase away gringos who ask too many questions."

"It doesn't matter!" she replied, fighting for control. "This is like the worst scenario we ever prepared for in resistance training. It scared the shit out of me then and it scares the shit out of me now. I'm fucking terrified! What the hell are they going to do to us?"

"Not the way you had envisioned dying for your country?"

I asked.

She shook her head fiercely. I could see the panic on her lovely features and the moisture in her eyes.

"Well, given Miguel's line of work, it's a pretty sure thing that he's had some practice at this sort of thing."

"Thanks," Christine said, choking on the word. "That makes me feel a lot fucking better."

As I looked around us, over the pallets, which were about five feet high, I could see many places against the walls of the space that were deep in shadow and easily large enough for one or even several people to lurk, just out of sight, even a person as large as Ramon the Rock.

"Anyway, why would they leave us all alone here? What the hell are they waiting for?"

"They didn't leave us alone," I said quietly. "It's an old interrogation trick. Remember that from SERE training? The longer they make you wait, the longer the tension builds. The longer the tension builds, the easier it is for them to scare the prisoner into talking."

"What are you talking about?" Christine asked, totally lost.

"Why don't you guys come out of your little hidey holes," I said, raising my voice. "You've heard all you're going to hear from me without a little elbow grease. If you want me to talk, at least do me the respect of beating it out of me."

There was a pregnant pause for about thirty seconds or so, and then I could hear some rustling in one of the shadowed areas in front of us. After a long moment, the two members of Tappan's personal goon squad stepped out into the dim light from around some pallets to our left front. Instead of suits, they were wearing jeans and sleeveless leather vests. The more typical biker garb contextualized their tattoos, which I had noticed previously.

"Los Diablos," I said. "Again. Damn."

"Those are the guys who brought us out here," Christine

said. "Who are Los Diablos?"

"One brigade of Miguel's army. They're a large motorcycle gang that works for him based out of Nogales, Mexico, but they operate all over since our government refuses to control the border. These two guys are actually Satan's personal goon squad, the ones Brock and I encountered earlier. But some others came into my house ten years ago, I told you that story. I also ran into three more in Dallas a few months ago."

"What happened," she asked, still staring.

"It was me or them, and I'm still here," I said quietly. "I bet they don't deal well with the death of one of their own—or several of them."

Christine turned her head to look at me, lost in the moment. "Several of them?"

I nodded.

"How?"

I began to answer but then a voice we both knew chimed in.

"They underestimated him," said Brock Black's voice, as he stepped into view from the shadows in front of us. "Like a lot of people."

As he spoke and I turned my head toward the sound, I saw Ramon the Rock materialize from the darkness next to Brock, almost dwarfing him. Ramon seemed to glide between the two closest pallets and stop in the clear area before us, ducking his head so as not hit the nearest hanging lightbulb. I dangled from my bonds and stared at him, mouth agape.

Ramon was probably the largest human being I had ever seen in close proximity, and I realized that in our brief exchange at the rest stop a few weeks ago I had not gotten a sense of scale. Then, he had stood in the back of the pickup truck, hunched over the Barrett rifle. Now, before me, the scale was Brock, who was as tall as I was, but broader. Ramon made Brock look tiny. He was at least a foot taller than Brock was and easily twice as wide. The leather vest he favored seemed to be straining to contain the pectoral muscles underneath it. His arms were as large as my legs and his legs were impossibly huge. As I regarded the sinew in his arms, I saw that the tattoos there matched those of the other two men who had showed themselves earlier, and I winced unconsciously.

"You're Los Diablos too?" I said. "This just keeps getting better."

Brock uttered some words in Spanish, obviously translating. Ramon answered, not taking his eyes off me.

"He's the national president," Brock said, without intonation.

I stared at Ramon's face, which was ringed in a corona of incandescent light from the bulb behind his head. His expression was one of curious intelligence, and the dark eyes gazed at me thoughtfully but hungrily, as if I was his prey.

I turned to Brock. "So how does it feel to be a fucking traitor?"

A moment of still silence ensued. I could see Christine tensing beside me.

When Brock answered, his voice was strangely quiet. "We don't always get to choose the best path, T. C.," he said. "You of all people should understand that."

He had me there. I myself had ended up being one of the good guys more by accident than by design.

"What the fuck happened to you then?" I asked him. "You seemed like a decent guy."

The eyes in the dark face seemed determined but sad. "Shit," he said simply. "Shit happened."

Ramon said a few words in Spanish and Brock answered him. Both of them looked at me while they spoke.

"Why the fuck aren't you dead?" I asked the huge man, interrupting their conversation. "I put at least seven bullets into you, and I saw a CIA sniper put you down with a big ass rifle."

Brock translated and Ramon answered him with a wide grin and gleaming eyes.

"He says he is protected by the Blessed Virgin," Brock said, obviously fighting to keep any tone of disbelief out of his voice. "He says he cannot be killed until his purpose is complete."

So huge, determined, and fucking crazy, I thought. *Wonderful.* "And let me guess, part of that purpose is to kick my ass?"

Brock seemed to sigh slightly before he shot the Spanish at Ramon. The huge Mexican shook his head at me while he answered Brock's query. Then Brock delivered the verdict with Ramon watching my face as he spoke.

"Actually, he came here to kill you," Brock said.

Ramon spoke again and his eyes narrowed. Brock's eyebrows lifted and he translated.

"Miguel couldn't be here to watch. Ramon says he sends his regrets."

"He was in the second helo after all, wasn't he?" I asked.

Brock translated the words and Ramon nodded and his eyes grew cold. He spat a reply at Brock.

"He's asking why you didn't leave after you destroyed the large helicopter and the jet," Brock said.

"The second helo shot at me," I replied. "It pissed me off."

Ramon turned to look at one of Tappan's henchman who had stepped out earlier. The shorter one with wire-rimmed glasses was eyeing me hungrily and looking back and forth between Ramon and me. Ramon smiled at him, inclined his head toward me.

"Es tuyo, Pablo."

Pablo practically leapt from where he was to a position directly in front of me, less than a foot away. Ramon spoke again and the Spanish rolled off his tongue smoothly. His voice was sibilant and the sound of it mesmerized me.

"You could have easily outrun the missile and still left," Brock said. "Why didn't you?"

"Like I said, it pissed me off."

"Pablo," Ramon said, while Brock was still speaking.

Abruptly, I felt a blow on the left side of my head. The impact knocked my head sideways, and my vision went momentarily dark. When it began to clear, there were specks of light, like stars, sparkling in my field of view. My mouth felt wet, and there were loose particles inside my gums. My jaw felt like it had been realigned. Pablo stood before me with a crooked grin on his face and his arms at his sides. I never saw his hand move.

Ramon spoke again, calmly, insistently. Even though I couldn't understand Spanish, I knew the question. "Why didn't you leave?" Brock's voice asked. "Just fucking tell him, T. C."

"What do want to hear?" I asked him, spitting a piece of a tooth on the floor between Pablo and me. "That I wanted to kill your boss?"

Brock spoke to him and Ramon spoke to Pablo, and another blow came to the same side of my face. My head bounced off my arm on the opposite side. I couldn't believe I stayed conscious through it. My vision came and went, and I spit the rest of the tooth out. I grinned at Ramon through the blood that was now dripping from my mouth.

"I did want to fucking kill him. I was hoping like hell he was in that second chopper. That's why I used the gun instead of a missile. I was hoping to split his ass apart with a stream of 20 millimeter. But apparently I didn't succeed because you're fucking here."

Brock translated, and as he spoke, Ramon nodded at me with a satisfied expression on his face. He put his massive hands on his hips and the muscles in his biceps seem to be trying to burst through his skin. His posture of superiority was unmistakable.

"You didn't kill him," Brock said. "Apparently Miguel was injured, seriously injured. But he's going to recover. They moved him to some retreat he has in Baja California."

Images of the place from the last time I was there flashed through my mind. I realized that I had never seen the master suite in the place and didn't know where he'd actually be in the huge hacienda.

"And he sent you to do his dirty work?" I asked, looking back at Ramon. "I'm surprised you have a job after your whole team got wiped out by some dumbass, middle-aged pilot with a .45 automatic and you got your ass flattened by a CIA sniper."

As Brock translated my words, Ramon's smile grew even wider. His teeth were perfectly white and perfectly even, an obvious product of expensive cosmetic dental work. Apparently the huge man had a vain side. He responded with a long and elaborate explanation. Brock listened, shaking his head in admiration at what he was hearing. Finally, Ramon finished speaking and Brock interpreted.

"They were coming to get you anyway, you just happened to come to them. The entire crew had come off a boat that came up the Chesapeake Bay. The goal of their mission was to take you out and to see how much of your CIA backup they could smoke out. Judging by what he said and what I know, they did pretty well. They even had a crew watching you at the restaurant in Annapolis."

We totally missed them. And they saw Smith and Amrine and the whole team show up. Jesus. The conversation I had with Lena Otenski echoed in the back of my head. The connection between Alan Turnidge, the OSI commander, and Miguel was apparently alive and well.

Ramon was watching me closely, apparently regarding the cogs in my head as they turned. He spoke quietly but insistently. Brock's voice reached my ears a moment later.

"You should have stayed out of this," Brock said. "The plan to steal the F-35 had been in place for months. You should have stayed out of it."

I shook my head in defiance. "He killed the son of friend of mine. But I would have come anyway. It had to end this way."

The blow came to the left side of my stomach this time, like a pile driver smashing into my abdomen. With no warning of its arrival and no ability to tighten my muscles in anticipation, Pablo's fist buried itself into my side. I could almost feel my internal organs collapsing into one another and a huge quantity of vomit shot up my esophagus like a geyser. As the warm fluid reached my mouth, I could see Pablo step backward to avoid the spray. I refused to give him the satisfaction though and, I forced the vile fluid back down into my stomach.

There were more words in Spanish and then I heard Brock's voice again.

"Miguel would have ensured no one but you died," Brock said. I could tell he was fighting to keep the disbelief out of his voice. "But by prying into his affairs again, you put everyone you care about in danger."

I raised my face and opened my mouth to speak. Blood and bile where now dripping from my lips, but I didn't care. "Bullshit." I said. "He's a bloodthirsty fucking lowlife. He would have killed everyone anyway."

Even as Brock began to translate, Ramon's face became hard. Then he spoke again. As Brock translated, his voice became quiet and tight.

"Everyone you care about will die because of you: your friend next to you, the general and his wife, the OSI agent you slept with, and the woman, Sarah Morton, and her child. They will all die. It is just a question of time."

I had a brief mental image of a row of coffins, the last one barely a third the size of the others, and the thought filled me with despair and fury at the same time. And there wasn't a damn thing I could do about it. The rage within me, an ever-present companion, rose to a boiling point and then even higher. I could feel the hot blood within me, searing my veins from the inside and filling me with an anger that was fueled by my helplessness and my guilt.

"Se le puede cortar ahora, Pablo," Ramon said.

Pablo grinned and drew a long silver knife from somewhere behind his back with his right hand and presented it, allowing the highly polished blade to sparkle in the incandescent light.

The rage inside of me was suddenly focused. *Knife,* it said. *Get the knife.*

My body responded without my willing it, and my back and bicep muscles, stronger than they had been in a long time, engorged with my boiling blood and began to slowly but inexorably pull against the screw eye holding my handcuffs to the beam above me.

"Looks like a pretty fucked up plan from where I'm standing," I said, with a voice I didn't recognize. "Now that I've blown up the F-35, your boss doesn't have a damn thing to give to the Chinese. He's out of luck and out of money. I hope he's got enough guys at the hacienda to defend against a couple of SEAL teams, because they're probably already en route to kill him."

"You didn't stop shit, Pearce," Mark Tappan's nasal voice said as he stepped into view. "Your boy Brock and I are on our way to get the real jets. Two of them. The first one would have been a nice bonus but it was only ever meant to get you guys to show your hand after you survived that business in Maryland."

"The gang's all here," I said. "I should have known that if your goon squad was around you'd have to be close by, Satan. Here for the show, are you?"

"I'm here to watch your ass die!" Satan exclaimed, his voice on the edge of hysteria. "I couldn't get it done ten years ago, so I'm sure as shit not going to miss it now!"

The rage and adrenaline were surging through my body and I could feel the screw eye above me bending with the tension I was placing on it. The blood was roaring in my ears so loudly that I could barely hear the dialog between Ramon and Brock.

Brock said something to me that didn't register completely. The words "how would they know" rang through but I didn't process anything else. The screw eye above me was opening, and I could feel the handcuff chain moving downward. Fortunately, the screw eye was on the back side of the joist above me so no one else could see it.

Almost in slow motion, I saw Pablo twirl the knife in his right hand and draw his right arm up and back in preparation for some kind of slashing or stabbing attack.

Knife, said the rage again. *Get...the...knife.*

"How... know... Miguel," Brock's voice hit my ears from a million miles away.

"Espere un momento, le golpeó de nuevo Pablo," Ramon's voice commanded.

Pablo drew his left arm back, as if he was preparing to hit me again. I couldn't believe that I actually noticed it this time. Then the arm began coming forward, slowly, purposefully, and forcefully.

He's too late, the rage said.

I know, I said back to it.

The handcuffs slid off the screw eye, and I brought the chain down around Pablo's right wrist. As soon as the metal made contact with his skin, I crossed my wrists underneath his to tighten the chain, and I pulled him toward me as hard as I could. With his right arm up and his weight displaced in midswing, he was on the wrong side of the motion dynamics equation. He came forward quickly, and I pivoted to my left and put my legs in front of his shins. He fell head and torso first toward the hard cement floor. He attempted to break his fall with his left hand, but as he fell, I slid around his body and drove my knees into the center of his back so that his face was driven into the concrete. As he impacted, I pulled hard against his right wrist and felt his right arm move in a direction that should have been impossible. I heard a dull "snap" sound somewhere in the back of my mind. His fingers let go of the big silver knife and somehow it wound up in my right hand. Without even thinking, I twirled the knife in my fingers so that the blade was against his wrist. Then I pulled my hands apart underneath his wrist and severed his right hand. Warm arterial blood sprayed all over me and the rage drank it in, reveling in the feel of it on my skin. The severed hand fell and as it hit the cement floor, I saw it come to rest against the 100-pound weight attached to my ankles. I impatiently sliced through the rope just as I felt Pablo begin to move underneath me, trying to use his left hand and right stump to get back to his feet.

I grabbed Pablo's hair with my left hand and slid the blade of the large knife in front of his throat with my right.

"No..." the words barely escaped his mouth before the blade sliced into his skin. Whether it was the keenness of the blade or the firmness of his tissue or the rage-induced strength remains a mystery, but in short order, I held Pablo's head in my left hand.

Only a few seconds had passed.

I stood and faced the remaining member of the goon squad, Ramon, Brock, and Satan, all of whom appeared to be glued to the floor in front of me. I tossed Pablo's head to the floor before them.

"Next," I said.

That seemed to spur them to action. Satan, ever the

example of stalwart courage, scurried off into the darkness like a cockroach fleeing the light. The remaining henchman dove inside his leather vest, presumably for a concealed weapon.

"No," Ramon said in a smooth, sibilant voice. "Él es mío."

The huge Mexican drew a knife of his own, nearly identical to mine, and grinned at me as he flexed his massive shoulders. "He estado esperando por esto," he said.

"Federal agent! Freeze!" commanded a female voice from the shadows to our left. It took me just a moment to process it. Lena Otenski?

Several things happened at once.

The remaining goon squad member pivoted and tried to bring his weapon to bear; but several pistol shots rang out from Lena's direction, and I watched him writhe with the impacts and fall to the floor.

Ramon did something with his right hand and threw his knife in the direction of the shots. Then he said something in Spanish to Brock that I couldn't hear over the ringing in my ears from the gunshots and the two of them vanished into the darkness as well. I fought the urge to chase them and sliced the rope securing Christine's feet.

"Nice work, Lena!" I said. "Now if you're carrying a set of handcuff keys that will be perfect."

"In the pocket of that one," Christine said, inclining her head to Pablo's headless corpse. "Right vest pocket I think."

I retrieved the keys and a pistol and returned to Christine.

"Lena?" I called over my shoulder. "You can come out now. There were two more but I think they left."

I unlocked Christine's arms. As soon as she was free, she backed away from me as if I had the plague.

"What the hell are you?" she asked.

I watched her, unconsciously twirling the knife in my right hand. "That's the usual reaction," I said after a moment.

"Colin?" Lena Otenski's voice called from somewhere in

the darkness. "I need...I need some help."

Before I could stop her, Christine disappeared into the darkness toward the voice.

"Great," I said under my breath. "Hopefully this isn't some kind of fucking trap."

"T.C.!" Christine called a few seconds later. "Get over here!"

I made my way to the sound of her voice and found her kneeling by the prostrate figure of Lena Otenski lying on the cold cement, still clutching her government-issued Beretta. Ramon's knife was buried in her abdomen, nearly up to the hilt, and there was an ugly dark stain on her shirt just above the waistband of her pants.

"I got him, Colin," she said, coughing up some drops of blood. "I got him good."

"You did, Lena," I said, taking her hand and placing her gun in my pocket. "We'd be dead if it wasn't for you."

"T. C.," she said, looking up at me through cloudy eyes. "They call you T. C."

"Do you have a car, Lena?" I asked.

"Yes, T. C., a black Dodge Charger parked on the next street over. Keys are here." She padded her right front pants pocket.

I retrieved the keys and handed them to Christine. "Hopefully we won't see anyone else outside and hopefully there's a hospital nearby. I'll carry her. You drive."

"No one's outside, T. C.," Lena said. "They... try... to... make... it... look... normal."

I lifted her up, surprised at how little she weighed in spite of her height. Christine, pistol in hand, pushed open the double doors and led us into the warm desert night.

I had been wrong. We weren't in a barrio-style neighborhood at all. We were in a modern industrial park, and Miguel's building looked just like all the others: a nondescript warehouse-like structure in muted off-white.

"Wasn't... ready... for... this," Lena said, her voice rasping against my chest as we rushed to the car.

"You did great," I said. "Everybody gets shot from time to time. I've been shot like four times or something like that."

"So...much...blood," she said. "So...much...death."

"How did you get here?" I asked her.

"Following...Brock. Watching building...Saw Tappan arrive... trying...to...get closer...when you cut..."

We reached the Dodge, and I put Lena in the backseat and got in with her. Christine got into the driver's side and started the car.

"I've got no idea where we are! How can I find a hospital?" she asked.

"Lena? Where's your phone?"

"Purse," she said weakly. "Trunk."

Christine hit the remote control for the trunk, bolted out the side of the car, and was back with the purse in seconds. She retrieved the phone, turned it on, and we were on the way to Phoenix General Hospital in a few moments.

I held Lena's left hand with my left hand and reached over the seat to Christine with my right.

"Phone please."

She handed it to me.

I dialed Dave Smith's number.

"Smith," he answered after several rings.

"It's T. C."

"T. C.! Holy shit! We've been looking all over for you! Where the hell are you?"

"On my way to Phoenix General. Lena Otenski rescued Billings and me from a pretty gruesome scenario but got a knife in the gut during the process."

"Damn," he said.

"There's more."

"I'm listening."

"Miguel has been working us from the very beginning. This latest F-35 thing isn't the main effort. Tappan plans to steal two more F-35s, and he's not going to be doing it alone. He's got help and you'll never guess who. Brock Black."

There was a long, pregnant pause. I could almost hear the gears turning in Smith's head. He was putting the pieces together just as I had.

"Son of a bitch," Smith said at last. "Didn't see that one coming."

I hung up and found Lena looking up at me through eyes that were barely open. There was a half-smile on her lips.

"Now I know," she said.

"Know what?" I asked.

"Why they call you T. C."

Then her eyes closed.

Chapter Twenty-Three

Contract Day 16
Thursday, July 8, 2010
0550 Hours Local Time
Phoenix General Hospital
Phoenix, Arizona

"She's in serious condition," the young Indian doctor said with an accent that sounded like he had grown up in Brooklyn instead of New Delhi. "We stopped most of the bleeding but there may be hemorrhaging in some of her internal organs. We'll know more in a few hours."

"Do you think she'll make it?" I asked.

He shook his head and exhaled. "No way to know just now. That blade was huge and it did incredible damage inside her body."

He looked between my face and Dave Smith's.

"I'm sorry I don't have any better information."

"Doctor, with no offense intended, is there a better hospital in the area to take her to?" Smith asked. "One that might increase her chances?"

The doctor smiled sadly.

"No offense taken," he said. "But you've got the first team here. This is the best trauma center in the state, and I'm the lead surgeon. If anyone can save her, we can."

Smith nodded. "Fair enough," he said.

"Now if you don't mind, gentlemen, I'll get back to my other patients." The doctor turned away for a moment but then turned back to me.

"If she makes it, she owes her life to you," he said. "It was smart of you not to remove the knife. It kept the bleeding down. And the CPR you gave her on the way here kept her alive until we could treat her. Nice work."

I nodded back to him. "Seemed to be the thing to do at the time," I said. "She had just saved my life. I owed her."

The young doctor smiled and nodded in return. Then he turned and went down the aisle to another bed where a nurse was urgently summoning him.

Smith and I turned to look at Lena. She lay on the trauma bed with wires and tubes of every kind connected to her. A nurse stood over her with an iPad and a stethoscope, monitoring the displays. Lena seemed to have shrunken somehow. She looked very small and frail.

"Damn brave woman," Smith said.

"She needs a guard, Dave," I said.

Smith nodded. "We'll have two men on her and constant surveillance," he replied. "I'm not sure if anyone will come after her, but we won't take the risk."

"Did your guys find anything at the warehouse?"

Smith shook his head. "You mean other than a buttload of supplies to make crystal meth and two dead gangbangers?" he asked. "Nope, not a damn thing. But the DEA is having a field day with the place."

"So we don't have any idea where Satan and B-Rock are or where they're going."

"Not at the moment," he said.

"Well shit," I said. "Tappan said the first F-35 was a side show. He said they were going to get two more jets. I didn't see any others at Luke when I was there. Where the hell do you think he'll get them?"

Smith shook his head in response.

We had been at the hospital for several hours. The medical staff had treated Christine and me for our wounds and provided us with access to a shower and clean surgical scrubs. The scrubs felt good after my torn and bloody flightsuit.

Smith and I walked down the row of beds, through a set of glass doors, and into a small waiting area with a few chairs, a sofa, and an LCD TV mounted on the wall. Apparently big watches were for sale on the shopping network during the wee hours of the morning. Christine was dozing on the sofa when we walked in but sat straight up when the doors clicked closed.

"Relax, Colonel Billings," Smith said. "We've got guards posted."

"Sorry," Christine said, her voice groggy. "It's been a long night." She looked at Smith and me. "How is she?"

"Not in the clear yet," I said.

"I never thought I'd be grateful to an OSI agent," Christine said.

"That makes two of us," I said. I sat down next to Christine on the sofa. "Did you hear anything these last few days?" I asked. "Anything at all? The slightest thing might be useful. We both heard Satan say they were going to get two F-35s to take to Miguel, but I can't figure out where he thinks they're going to get them. There aren't any more at Luke."

"I didn't hear much," Christine said. "They didn't exactly have conversations in the room where they were holding me."

"I guess not," I said. "Damn." I looked at her and shook my head. "This business about B-Rock is really fucking with my head. I totally thought I had him figured out. He felt like one of us."

Christine nodded.

"How long was he there?" I asked.

"He brought you in very early Tuesday morning," she replied. "As far as I know, he hung around in one of the other rooms until Tappan and that big Mexican guy..." She shivered as she remembered him. "Showed up. They came after dark on Wednesday. He came in and checked on me a few times. Brought me food, took me to the latrine, that kind of thing. He didn't talk much."

"Wow," I said, as I rubbed my eyes. "So I was unconscious all that time?"

She nodded quickly. "They kept coming into the room and injecting you with something," she said. "It was like they were afraid of you." She looked over at me with a mixture of respect and fear in her deep brown eyes. "Now I know why."

"They pushed me too far," I said, looking at the floor, "with all that talk about people dying because of me. I sort of snapped."

Christine nodded. "Yeah you did," she said. "I was waiting for you to turn green and bust out of your shirt."

It should have been a funny remark but it wasn't. The rage had enabled me to do some crazy things in my life. But the consequences were never pretty. And I never felt good about it afterward. I was grateful for Smith's silence. There was a lot of input he could have added to that conversation.

"So even after Ramon and Tappan arrived, you didn't hear anything?" Smith asked.

Christine started to shake her head then stopped as she seemed to recall something. "No, but I did see a text message on Brock's phone after I came out of the latrine. Before they arrived," she said.

Smith and I both looked at her.

"There were three words I could see, 'photo,' 'shoot,' and 'base.'"

"Base photo shoot?" Smith asked. "What does that mean?"

"Might be a PR thing," I answered. "But I don't see what

it would have to do with the F-35s." I turned to Smith. "Do you know if Tappan still controls Luke?"

"No. The USAF is wise to him after he took the F-35 and thanks to the F-22s we needed to scramble to try to get him. And news about your little sortie into Mexico has been burning up the intel reporting chain. We had to answer some USAF inquiries on that one as well."

"So what you're telling me is that even if there was another F-35 on Luke, the odds are high he wouldn't be able to get it out of there without setting off major alarm bells."

Smith nodded. "Definitely not."

I looked over at Christine, and she had Lena's phone out and was looking at an Internet browser window.

"I think I found something," she said. "The Luke Base paper is online, and they're saying that there's a photo shoot scheduled for tomorrow in front of the control tower and F-35s from the Edwards Flight Test Center are flying in for the shoot."

"Well then he won't be able to get to them," I said, satisfied. "If the jets are on Luke, he's done."

"Hang on, Tex," Christine said, still reading. "The jets are making a stop to do some other pictures and accomplish some ground training before they come to Luke."

Smith and I stared at her. Christine looked up from the phone.

"At Gila Bend."

"Jesus," I said.

"What's the big deal?" Smith asked. "It's a USAF base. Miguel wouldn't go after it there, would he?"

"Dave, it's a postage stamp base, with hardly any staff, near a very small town, literally in the middle of nowhere. And it also lies near the north end of one of the largest corridors for illegal immigration into the US. Miguel could easily take it over for the time required to steal to those jets."

"Damn, damn, damn," Smith said, as he tapped his right hand idly. "Looks like I need to get John and our local ops team in the loop. And I keep hearing you say jets, not jet. Why would they steal more than one?"

"Because they can," I said. "They've got two pilots. And while Brock hasn't flown one, he's a pretty smart guy, and I'm betting he can figure out enough to get it airborne and across the border. Double the bounty for Miguel."

Christine nodded. "No doubt," she said. She looked down at the phone again. "Oh shit." she looked up at Smith. "What's today?"

"Thursday the eighth," Smith said.

"I was afraid of that," Christine said. "I got the date wrong. Being up all night does that to you. The photo shoot at Luke is this morning and the one at Gila Bend is before that. The jets should probably be getting to Gila Bend any time."

"Damn!" Smith said. "We need to move!" He ripped his BlackBerry from its holster, called up a number, and hit the send key.

"Bart?" he said, "Bruiser. We've got a situation here!"

Christine and I listened as Smith described the situation to John Amrine. His sitrep was detailed, concise, and complete. It took him about two minutes.

"I agree," Smith said. "A reinforced ops team. No telling how many men Miguel will send to take over the base. And we might want to recruit some local SPs from Luke as well."

There was a pause as Smith listened. I could barely hear Amrine's voice over the speaker, but I made out the word 'intercept.'

"I'm thinking F-22's again," Smith said. "Can Holloman get a two-ship here ASAP?"

Another pause.

"What do you mean there's a base exercise?" Smith exploded a few moments later. "Don't they have any preconfigured jets they can scramble? They can do that supercruise thing and be here from Holloman in like a half hour or so."

Amrine's voice barked again in the speaker. Smith looked at me.

"I'll ask him," he said.

"Uh oh," said Christine. "I think I know what they're going to ask you to do, and I don't think you're going to like it."

"I rarely do," I said. I looked at Smith. "You want me to try to stop them, don't you?"

Smith smiled grimly and nodded.

"Do I have time to make a quick phone call?"

***

Ten minutes later we were in a Sikorsky S-76 medevac helicopter, cruising over the Phoenix suburbs at a few hundred feet. Looking through the pilots' windscreen in the front of the helo, I could see the runways of Luke AFB in the distance.

"Are you okay with this?" Smith asked.

"Do I have a choice?"

"You can always say no."

"I think we both know I'm not that smart."

Smith smiled at me. "Very true."

"So you're really gonna do this?" Christine asked in disbelief. "You're going to fight two F-35s in a Viper?"

"Doesn't look like there are any other options," I said. "Besides, Satan can't know the jet that well, and Brock has never flown it before. How hard can it be?"

Christine shook her head.

"You're an idiot," she said. "That jet has technology that is way beyond the Viper's. They'll see you coming a long way off and nail you before you get to them."

"If the jets are even armed," I said. "And I'm not sure they'll have a lot of time to use the technology. And I'm also thinking they'll be busy while I'm trying to sneak up on them," I said.

Christine looked at me. "Doing what?" she asked.

"Dealing with the decoy."

"Decoy? What decoy?"

I looked at her and smiled.

Her eyes got wide for a moment.

"Okay," she sighed after a long pause. "I guess this is why I make the big bucks."

***

As the helo crossed Avondale, I could hear one of the pilots coordinating for entry into Luke AFB's airspace. Smith sat directly behind them and gave them the instructions and authentication codes they needed to enter. He glanced over his shoulder at me.

"310th ramp, right?" he asked.

I nodded. "Anywhere they can find a space to set down. You made the calls right?"

Smith nodded and turned to speak to the pilots.

"Quick flight brief?" I asked Christine.

"Sure," she said.

We developed a quick game plan that we could implement once we got airborne. We'd launch and get some spacing between us. Then she'd find Satan and B-Rock and get their attention on her so I could sneak up on them and get them turning. After that, it was going to be more about luck than anything else. But I was used to relying on luck. It hadn't let me down so far.

"So both jets will have 370 gallon tanks and a full gun," I said. "But mine will have two AMRAAMs and two AIM-9s. We wanted to get your jet uploaded too but there wasn't time. I hope that will be enough."

"You need to get them to bring you a JHMCS-modified helmet," Christine said.

"A what?"

"A joint helmet-mounted cueing system helmet," she said.

"Oh yes, I've heard of them," I said. "They were supposed to be introduced later in the course for old guys like me who hadn't flown with them. Helmet-mounted sighting system, right? "

Christine nodded. "Yep. And it rocks."

"Any adaptation issues?" I asked. "I'm not exactly going to have a lot of time to get used to it."

"Nope," Christine said. "It's very intuitive. Like having the HUD display projected on your visor. Only now instead of just appearing in front of you, it appears everywhere you look."

"Great SA builder, I'm sure," I said. "But what good will it do me in a fight?"

"You know how when you went one circle with a guy, you'd end up across the circle from him and wish there was a way to put ordnance on his jet?"

I nodded.

"Now you don't have to wait. With the JHMCS and the AIM-9X, if you can see him across the circle, you can kill him. The missile is cued to your eyeballs and the AIM-9X can hack the corner. It's a helluva missile."

"Damn," I said. "That's awesome."

"But wait," Christine said, "there's more."

We spent the next five minutes with her talking and me listening. When she was finished, she must have seen a look of disbelief in my eyes.

"Damn," I said.

"If you hit the merge with one of them, beak to beak, do the maneuver," she said. "It works. I promise."

I nodded at her. "I believe you. But still, damn."

"There's one catch though."

"What's that?"
"It's takes a continuous 9-gs and the onset is a bitch."

Chapter Twenty-Four

Contract Day 16
Thursday, July 8, 2010
0730 Hours Local Time
310th Fighter Squadron Ramp
Luke Air Force Base
Glendale, Arizona

The helicopter landed between the edge of the secure area and the first row of aircraft at the 310th FS ramp—very near the location of the hangar where Tappan had hidden the first F-35 earlier. Two jets waited for us in the last two parking spots under the awnings near the end of the row, surrounded by a cordon of armed security policemen. The canopies on the two Vipers were up, and the aircraft crew chiefs stood next to their aircraft, maintenance forms in their hands. Several other ground personnel stood around the two jets, apparently very eager for our arrival. I did notice that one jet had the missiles on it that we had asked for and that there was a blue USAF Step Van parked between the jets, probably with our flight gear inside of it. There was a black Chevy Tahoe parked there as well, which I presumed held John Amrine and whatever CIA personnel he had with him.

"This will be interesting," I said to Christine as I exited the helo. "I'm not sure I've ever had a reception crew like this."

We ran to the step van and jumped into the back of it. Inside, two USAF life-support technicians had a full suite of gear for both of us. Flightsuits, boots, anti-g suits, survival kits, harnesses, and helmets. Neither Christine nor I had on anything but the scrubs we received from the hospital staff; but the thin material slid well into the flightsuits, and we were both dressed in no time. Fortunately, the life-support folks had remembered to bring boot socks. Christine gave me a brief helmet orientation.

"You strap in normally but you'll have another cord called the HVI cord that you'll need to route under your left riser strap and plug into the QDC which is on the left side of the cockpit. There's an HMCS rheostat near your left knee, by the gear handle. That's how you turn it on and adjust the brightness."

"Do I have to program it?"

She nodded. "I'll talk you through that and the alignment process after engine start."

"Got it."

"One thing to remember, this helmet is heavier than the one you're used to. Make sure you have your head in the right place before you lay into the g or you'll be sorry."

"Cool. Thanks."

We both finished dressing, and Christine clipped the chest strap on her harness as she looked at me with a grim expression on her face.

"Do you really think you can do this? Kill two F-35's in one Viper?"

"If I can get them turning, yes," I said. "Before we left the hospital, I gave a friend of mine at Edwards a quick call. I told him that I was working on something and that I needed him to answer one question and not ask anything in return. I asked him if he knew he was going to get into a turning, visual fight, would he rather be in an F-35 or a Viper."

"And?"

"He said the Viper. No question."

"I just hope I can give you the time to get there."

"Me too," I said. "We're both going to need be lucky and good this time."

"It seems like the last time we did something together, we were," she said, smiling. She looked up at me with a tender expression on her face, and for a moment, I thought she was going to kiss me. But then her eyes became distant and the expression ran away from her face.

"Good hunting, T. C.," she said.

"Same to you, Lindal."

***

Fifteen minutes later we were airborne and headed south. As we crossed over I-10, I did a gentle 360-degree turn to get spacing behind her and then set a more westerly course as I dropped down to 500 feet above the ground. I turned the helmet rheostat on and the symbology instantly appeared in front of my eyes. It wasn't a complete HUD display, but most of the information was there and what was more important, it stayed in front of my eyes no matter where I moved my head. I then moved the DOGFIGHT switch on the throttle to the outboard position and the diamond-shaped symbol that represented the AIM-9X's field of view appeared in my vision.

"Damn," I said, "this is unfucking believable."

As I flew southward, I experimented with how far left, right, and above the nose I could move my head without losing the missile reticle display. The angles that the missile was capable of were astounding. Air-to-air missiles are complicated pieces of equipment and the AIM-9 "Sidewinder" was no exception. Born in the late 1950s and extensively used in the Vietnam

War, the first AIM-9's were only capable of guiding to a target where the seeker could detect hot metal, making them a rear hemisphere weapon only that required the attacking jet to be behind the target aircraft. Then in the early 1980s, the AIM-9L was introduced with a seeker that detected and guided to a target's fuel plume, making forward aspect shots possible and allowing an attacking aircraft to lock on and shoot a target from nearly any angle, if the target's infrared signature was large enough. The AIM-9L was followed by the AIM-9M, a missile that used the same seeker technology but had logic built in to reject decoy flares that a target might dispense. The AIM-9M was the mainstay of the USAF short-range, air-to-air missile inventory for over ten years. But as capable as it was, the AIM-9M suffered from two significant limitations. The missile's seeker head was mounted on a gimbal platform that only allowed it to look about 40 degrees off the longitudinal axis of the missile, and it was programmed with arming logic that prohibited it from making any turns until it was nearly 2000 feet in front of the launching aircraft. In a turning visual fight, either one of these limitations created issues, but the combination was crippling. Essentially, one aircraft had to get behind the other or had to be able to nearly get its nose on the other before the AIM-9M was useful. So the F-16's internal 20mm Gatling gun was the chief weapon in a tight, turning fight.

It appeared that those days were over.

As I moved my head in ever-widening circles around the nose of the aircraft, the AIM-9X missile reticle stayed with me, stubbornly centered in the HMCS's field of view. I could even put my head against the seat's headrest and look directly above me, and the reticle was still there. I had no idea how much degradation the missile would suffer under g, when the laws of physics would limit its performance, but what I saw was impressive enough.

I was speechless and grateful.

"Tango Charlie and Lima Lima, Luke Approach. Push to tactical frequency is approved."

I keyed my UHF radio. "Tango Charlie copies. Push Net 3."

"Lima Lima." Christine's voice came over UHF.

We had agreed to use the UHF "Have-Quick" radio in a full wartime frequency-hopping mode to keep B-Rock and Satan from listening in on our conversations. I punched the appropriate numbers into the Viper's up-front control or UFC and waited for a moment for Christine to do the same. Then I keyed the UHF mic again.

"Tango Charlie," I said.

"Lima Lima," Christine replied. I could hear the soft "clickety-click" in the background as she answered, indicating her radio was indeed hopping frequencies as designed.

"Tango Charlie, Lima Lima, Darkstar has you both loud and clear."

Darkstar was the ground control intercept or GCI radar at Luke AFB. Normally used for training missions only, Smith had managed to have it manned at short notice for today's action. We couldn't rely on air traffic control radar to find B-Rock and Satan. The wavelength and update rate of air traffic control radars, even approach control radars, wasn't able to detect the F-35. It was highly probable that the GCI radar, even with its shorter wavelength, higher frequency, and faster update rate, wouldn't be able to detect them either. While I didn't expect that B-Rock and Satan would be stupid enough to leave their radar transponders on, I was hoping that they might not retract their radio antennas and provide some angled surface to reflect the GCI radar.

"Tango Charlie and Lima Lima, Delta Sierra." Dave Smith's voice was over UHF now. I was positive he was sitting next to the GCI controller in the facility. This little escapade was probably going to give the controller something to think about for years. He certainly wasn't going to be able to talk about it. "Previous reports are confirmed, Gila Bend is not, I repeat not, under USAF control. We have a team heliborne and headed toward Gila Bend for reconnaissance and action."

"Copy that, Delta Sierra," I replied. "Are Satan and B-Rock airborne yet?"

"Unknown, Tango Charlie," he said without hesitation.

I felt a moment of optimism. If we caught them on the ground at Gila Bend, stopping them would be a lot easier. I should have known better. A few moments later, Smith's voice cut through the airwaves again.

"Tango Charlie, Delta Sierra. Ops team reports ramp empty at Gila Bend."

"Shit," I spat into my oxygen mask. "Figures." I keyed the mic. "Any idea when they got airborne?"

"Negative, Tango Charlie. But it can't have been more than a few minutes ago."

"Any idea of their initial heading?" Christine asked.

"Negative as well, Lima Lima."

I tried to put myself in Satan's place and tried to predict how they would attempt to leave US airspace. The inevitable direction was south of course, but they'd know we'd be looking for that, and they couldn't know that we didn't have any Raptors to chase them. I didn't know much about the Raptor's radar but I knew enough about the way the USAF designed aircraft to know it probably had some capabilities that the F-35's didn't. So if they thought F-22's might be a possibility and the Raptors would be coming from Holloman AFB, New Mexico, and they didn't want to head south initially, that left only one direction for them to proceed. West.

And as if on cue, the GCI controller's voice cut through the silence on UHF.

"Darkstar has a group, bullseye 260 at 20, headed southwest at angels 30." The bullseye was Gila Bend itself today and the target aircraft were west, southwest of it at 20 nautical miles.

Gotcha, I thought.

"Darkstar, Tango Charlie, any range traffic in that area right now?"

"Negative, Tango Charlie. Range airspace is closed per government order."

I smiled under my oxygen mask. Leave it to the CIA to take no chances. Smith and Amrine had just simplified our targeting problem considerably.

"Cleared to commit, Lindal," I said over UHF. "Get them turning, but if they disappear off your radar and look like they're coming around, get the hell out of there."

"Roger," she replied crisply.

Although she was several miles ahead of me, I knew where she was on my air-to-air radar, and I watched the video square that represented her aircraft start a hard turn to the west and begin climbing. On the horizontal situation display, on the right MFD, I saw the symbol for her jet—a green circle with the number 2 in it, begin to track in the same direction. And then, as I looked though the HMCS, I saw a small green circle with the number 2 in it, rising and turning across the visor in front of me.

"This is way too much, SA," I said to myself, marveling at the technology. "Way too much SA."

I pulled the nose of my aircraft toward the contacts.

"Atta girl," I said over the intercom. "Let's get 'em."

Her jet didn't have any missiles but they wouldn't know that and would be forced to react if she could light them up. While we initially had our suspicions about whether Satan and B-Rock's jets would be armed, I had a sneaking suspicion they would be. Satan wouldn't leave something like that to chance; and even if he had to bring the missiles, bullets, and personnel with him to Gila Bend, he would have ensured it.

He probably still had some loyalty in the munitions troops somewhere on base.

I pushed the Viper's throttle forward into MIL power, 100% RPM without afterburner, and watched the nozzle close. The airspeed increased slowly and steadily past 500 knots calibrated airspeed and on its way toward 600. I used the EL STROBE knob on the throttle to raise the center of the radar's scan pattern and then I used the slew control on the throttle to move the cursors to the area where Darkstar had called the contacts. The bullseye readout on the radar display confirmed the cursors were in the right place.

Nothing there.

I wasn't surprised. The Viper had a good radar but, it was never designed to detect and track a target as stealthy as the F-35. Nose to nose with another Viper, initial radar hits weren't observed until somewhere between 18-22 nautical miles and that was with an intake for the radar to look down and spinning compressor blades to reflect energy.

"Darkstar, group now bullseye 255 at 30, high, headed southwest."

"Lima Lima, hits there 30,000, tail."

"Good girl, Lindal," I said into my oxygen mask. "Now light 'em up."

"Lima Lima targeted, single group, bullseye 250, 33, 30,000, tail."

Christine had her radar into the group now for sure. She must have closed the distance between them and her jet very rapidly.

"Tango Charlie copies."

"Darkstar copies."

I moved my cursors to the altitude and position of Christine's latest radio call. Still nothing. Then I bumped my radar down from 80 to 40 mile scale and made sure my elevation scan was precisely centered. Two squares of inverse video appeared on the green screen of my display. I was about nineteen miles behind them.

"Lima Lima is locked," Christine's voice came over UHF with just a bit of an edge on it.

"Tango Charlie copies."

While this was not precisely correct brevity code terminology, it was a radio call we had briefed. Christine had just gone to single-target-track on her target, and her APG-68 radar was now bombarding one of the F-35's with pulse-Doppler energy. It was a repeat of my ad hoc tactics a few days ago, and I hoped it wouldn't end the same way. At least one of us was armed in this bait-and-switch scheme of ours, but until I got within "turning and burning" range of Satan and B-Rock and I could open fire, we were taking a huge risk.

Now it was just a question of whether we could get them turning and stop their departure to Mexican airspace.

"C'mon fuckers," I grunted into my oxygen mask. "Turn and fight. You know you want to."

The seconds crawled by. My jet was eating up desert and airspace at about ten miles a minute, and with every moment the distance to the Mexican border and the time to stop Satan and B-Rock from getting there were shrinking.

I stared at my radar display and the two squares of inverse video and silently willed them to maneuver. All our efforts were for naught if these two didn't change their direction and react.

The barren desert terrain raced by underneath the Viper, nearly a blur at the speed the jet was traveling. The open, blue desert sky seemed to mock us with its emptiness.

"C'mon goddamn it," I whispered into the intercom. "C'mon Satan, you know you want to fight. Turn that fucking airplane."

"Target maneuvering through south," Christine said, the radio call startling me a little. I could tell she was trying to keep the emotion out of her voice. "Now bullseye 245, 35, 30,000, beam."

"Darkstar same."

"They took the bait, T. C." Her voice was upbeat over UHF.

I grunted in approval. "That's what I'm talking about."

I brought my eyes back inside the cockpit and looked down at the radar display, moving my cursors to the position Christine had just called.

And there was only one square of video there. It was possible that my radar was simply having difficulty tracking the stealthy F-35 but something more insidious occurred to me.

What if?

My mind ran through a number of possibilities, none of them good. Then the obvious reason hit me between the eyes.

Holy shit!

"Darkstar, Tango Charlie, number of contacts in the group?"

There was a pause that seemed to last forever but was only a few seconds.

"Darkstar, one contact in that group. One contact only!" The controller's voice was a little higher now. He knew what that meant.

"Lima Lima, abort out now!" I said over UHF. "Abort out now!"

"Negative, Tango Charlie," she replied. "Group is staying beam aspect. I repeat beam aspect."

Jesus. I felt a chill pass over me and goosebumps rise on my arms. *We're being played.*

"You're only seeing one of them, Lima Lima!" I shouted over UHF, as if raising my voice would make it travel faster over the airwaves. "You're only seeing one! Abort out now!"

I was ten miles behind the F-35 she was targeting and closing steadily. My cursors still showed it there, flying nice and straight and level at 30,000 feet, making its leisurely fucking way to the Mexican border. A perfect sitting duck.

Gotta be Brock, I thought. *No way Satan would trust him to be anything but the bait.*

My Viper was flying at just over 600 knots calibrated airspeed now, as much as it could do without afterburner in the heat of a July morning in the desert. I was barely sub-Mach, and I knew it wouldn't be fast enough. I felt the despair and anger rising inside of me once again. If Brock was playing decoy and his jet was the one we were seeing then that meant Satan was...

I keyed the UHF mic as I felt my guts twist inside of me. "Lindal," I screamed into the mic on UHF, "he's coming after you! Satan's coming after you!"

"No joy," Christine replied, indicating she didn't see an attacking aircraft. "Lima Lima no joy!"

I didn't know what to tell her to do. I had no idea of the orientation of Satan's jet to hers. For the first time in my life, I was in a command situation where I had no idea what to say.

And then I saw the fireball. It appeared in the brilliant blue desert sky above me and to my left, impossibly orange and impossibly yellow, followed immediately by the inevitable cloud of black smoke.

There was no sound.

From the distance I was from the explosion, I could actually see pieces of the aircraft emanate from the cloud and sparkle in the morning sky. It was like a Daliesque painting creating itself against the blue heavens.

And as if to echo the harsh reality, the circles representing Christine's aircraft vanished from both my HMCS display and from the horizontal situation display on the right MFD.

Christine's jet was gone.

And so was she.

Just like that.

There probably was a time in my life where I would have registered the fact of her destruction coldly and dispassionately and locked it away into the recesses of my brain so I could pursue the mission, coldly and effectively, like the machine I was.

But not today.

"Fuck!" I screamed into my oxygen mask as I pounded the canopy with my left fist. "Fuck! Fuck! Fuck!"

Satan you son of a bitch! He was the one who would have known how to direct this engagement. He was the one who would have known how to stow the antennas and actuate the weapons systems on the jet. And above all, he was the one who would have wanted to prove the point.

"I'm coming for you, you evil motherfucker," I said into the oxygen mask as I shoved the Viper's throttle into MAX AB, full afterburner. "I am fucking coming for you."

First things first though.

I was five miles behind Brock's F-35 at 615 knots and 500 feet AGL or above ground level. I smoothly pulled into about four g's and raised the nose of the sleek Viper into the vertical. The nozzle swung open, and I felt the familiar kick in the middle of my back as the burner lit. The terrific blue desert sky surrounded the Viper's sleek gray-blue nose and way above me, in the distance, over 30,000 feet above me, I saw the tiny speck of Brock's F-35. The gray jet was barely conning, generating contrails, the white trails of mist making it easy to acquire—something that I was sure was no accident. I wondered if Satan thought I'd be coming after him single ship. I wondered if he thought that his work for the day was over.

But I wasn't counting on it. He'd been too resourceful.

I placed my radar cursors on the remaining square of inverse video to verify Brock's altitude and position. Then I keyed the UHF mic.

"Darkstar, Tango Charlie, engaged bullseye 240, 40, 30,000 tail."

"Darkstar copies."

"Darkstar, Tango Charlie, Lima Lima is down. I need you to tell me about even the slightest radar contact you detect between my current target and her last known position."

"Tango Charlie, Darkstar copies. Currently clean between you and last known position of Lima Lima." There was a pause, and I could sense the GCI controller pausing. There was no brevity code in the USAF lexicon to express one's condolences. "Darkstar, rescue alerted," he said a few moments later. "They'll find her, Tango Charlie."

They'll find what's left of her, I thought, shaking my head, *if there are pieces big enough to find.*

As the climb continued, my airspeed began to decrease. I checked my fuel totalizer and verified that the two 370-gallon external tanks were empty. I selected the SEL JET or selective jettison mode of the stores management system and pushed the weapons release button, jettisoning the two wing tanks into the sky behind and below me. The Viper, now relieved of the weight and drag of the empty tanks, seemed to bolt upward like a thoroughbred eager for the challenge of the waiting contest.

The gray outline of Brock's jet grew in my HUD. I was through 10,000 feet now and his jet was just over three nautical miles above me. I rested my thumb on the DOGFIGHT switch and pondered the weapons delivery mode I'd use to shoot him down. The easiest thing to do would be to lock him up on radar—at that range the F-35's stealthiness would be no defense—call up the AIM-120 Slammer, and shoot it into Brock's jet at point blank range. The deadly missile would tear his aircraft to shreds and probably kill him. It was the closest option that was a sure thing.

And yet I hesitated. There was something about Brock's

treachery that wasn't sitting well with me. Satan needed to die. Brock I wasn't so sure about. At least not yet.

The Viper continued skyward. The airspeed continued to bleed down, although at a much slower rate than before I jettisoned the tanks. I was slowing through about 320 knots as I passed through 18,000 feet mean sea level or MSL. Brock's jet was two miles away. I pushed the DOGFIGHT switch to the outboard position and called up the AIM-9X in the HMCS.

The missile seeker head whistled in my ear as the seeker detected the infrared energy coming from Brock's jet. Almost unconsciously, I tapped the gain knob on the throttle and uncaged the seeker head. A high-pitched whine filled my ears. The AIM-9X was locked on and ready to go. My thumb hovered over the pickle button on the sidestick but my brain wouldn't let me push it. At that range, the Sidewinder would do as much damage to Brock's jet as the Slammer might have. And I might need both of them to fight Satan.

24,000 feet and 280 knots now. I had to make a fucking decision.

"Well shit," I said to myself as I recognized the only remaining option. "Not the smartest thing to do, Pearce."

I pushed the Target Management Switch or TMS forward on the stick and put the Viper's APG-68 radar into boresight mode with the cross in the HUD superimposed over Brock's rapidly growing jet.

"LOCK, LOCK," said the sexy female voice in my ear.

The circular pipper appeared in my HUD, centered on the underside of Brock's jet and the analog slant range display around the pipper indicated my range to Brock's jet was decreasing through 5,000 feet. I had a fraction of a second to make the shot happen before he reacted and maybe kill his jet without killing him. And also to avoid killing myself since my jet was on a collision course with his. I thought about pulling the power to idle and even deploying the speed brake to slow my closure but dismissed the thoughts quickly. Speed was life. And I needed to keep as much of it as I could.

I tapped the right rudder pedal gently and yawed the Viper's nose slightly to the right, which also moved the pipper to the middle of the F-35's stubby right wing. As soon as it stabilized, I squeezed the trigger on the sidestick controller for the barest fraction of a moment and 20MM high-explosive incendiary bullets spewed out of the Viper's internal M-61A1 Vulcan cannon at the rate of about 100 per second. Without waiting to see if the bullets hit home, I rolled slightly and pulled the Viper's nose to right as hard as I could—and barely missed the right wing of Brock's jet as it erupted into flames.

One down one to go.

I wanted to check and see if Brock had successfully ejected but I needed to get away from there. Fast. Satan was going to be able to find me easily enough with all the technology at his disposal in the F-35, but I didn't need to make it easier for him by orbiting a fire in the sky. I rolled the Viper over onto its back and watched the barren desert fill the canopy below me. Then I applied back pressure to the sidestick and smoothly pulled the jet's nose down to the earth.

"Darkstar, Tango Charlie, kill one F-35," I glanced at my radar display, "bullseye 237, 40, 30,000."

"Darkstar copies!" I heard an enthusiastic "yes!" in the background as the GCI controller released the mic button.

"Don't get too excited, Dave," I said into the intercom. "That was the easy part."

I had the Viper nearly pointed directly at the desert floor below, and I pulled the throttle out of afterburner and into idle. Satan was probably looking for me with his radar, but I wasn't going to help him with a huge infrared signature of my own. Besides, the jet would accelerate rapidly with gravity, "God's g," helping it, and I needed to save some gas. I checked my fuel totalizer as I descended through 20,000 feet. It read

5,000 pounds. Still plenty of gas to fight with.

"Where are you going, T. C.?" The nasal voice reached my ears over UHF. It gave me chills and pissed me off at the same time. For a moment, I was at a loss as to how he could have discovered our Have-Quick net, but then I realized I was also monitoring 243.0, the UHF guard frequency. I hit the button on my UFC with my gloved left thumb to allow me to talk on guard.

"I'm not going anywhere, Satan," I said, keying the mic. "I'm going to stick around until I scatter your hair, teeth, and eyeballs all over southern Arizona."

"I call that bold talk for a man in a last generation airplane with a last generation radar," he teased. "You might as well be blind. I'm going to kill you before you ever even see me."

"Well, that's the sort of cowardly shit you specialize in, Satan. Sneaking up on people or sending others to kill them."

I applied back pressure to the sidestick and leveled the Viper at 15,000 feet as I brought the throttle up to MIL power. Satan was arrogant but he wasn't stupid. If he was toying with me, it was because he wanted to distract me. He wouldn't want to kill me at long range, assuming he even had a Slammer on board. He wouldn't even want to kill me at short range with an AIM-9. He'd want to make it personal. He'd want to do it with the gun so I'd have a few moments to contemplate it before I died. And to do that, he'd have to get close. Close enough for me to see him.

I toggled the UHF back over to the Have-Quick net as I searched the sky around me. Visually acquiring any aircraft when it's nose on to you is difficult. But visually acquiring a modern fighter, an aircraft designed to be hard to see, when it's nose on is nearly impossible.

"Darkstar, Tango Charlie, anything?"

"Negative, Tango Charlie." The disappointment in the GCI controller's voice was plain. "Darkstar clean."

I started a 3-4 g left turn and set up a scanning pattern to the inside of the turn, where a fighter that wanted to use a gun would have to appear. Air-to-air gunnery, even in modern fighters, was still subject to the laws of physics and the principles that were established in the very first aerial combat in World War I. For a tracking gunshot, the only kind that Satan could be sure would kill me, the only kind that would give him the satisfaction he needed, he had to be in the same maneuvering plane as my aircraft, close enough to be in range for the shot, with his nose in lead, that is pointed ahead, of my aircraft.

I briefly reviewed what I knew about the F-35's internal cannon. I remembered that it was a 4-barreled 25mm gun with a rate of fire of about 3,300 rounds per minute, about half that of the 20mm M61-A1 on the Viper and it also only carried about 120 rounds of ammunition internally, as compared to the Viper's 510. But the slower rate of fire and smaller ammo capacity might not be much of a disadvantage if the 25mm packed more energy than the 20mm PGU-28 rounds. I couldn't imagine that, but I had to consider that it was possible.

But there was something else about the F-35's gun that I couldn't remember, something that was gnawing at me.

I began to scan small sectors of the sky to the inside of the circle, pausing to let my eyes focus on each sector long enough to detect any movement and then move to the next. As I moved my eyes from sector to sector, I found myself longing for some kind of optical detection system, something that would help my eyes find a target without the use of the radar. And then, as I scanned the sky through the symbology imposed on my vision by the HMCS, I remembered it's most important feature.

"You're an idiot," I said to myself over the intercom.

I toggled the DOGFIGHT switch to the outboard position

and the diamond of the first AIM-9's seeker head appeared in the display, the audio tone of the missile making the low whistling sound typical of ambient IR energy in its field of view. The small field of view of the AIM-9 was like searching the sky through a soda straw, but it was better than nothing. And it wasn't a catchall. If Satan came at me from high to low, odds were he'd have his throttle at idle to control his overtake, which would reduce his infrared signature; and if he came at me from low to high, while his power setting would be higher, he'd have the warm desert terrain behind him which could cause his infrared signature to be masked in the ambient energy of the ground below. But it was better to have the AIM-9 seeker looking than not.

So I continued my scan. Pause eyes, focus eyes, look, wait, move eyes. Back and forth across the airspace inside my turn, like the raster scan of an air-to-air radar, across to the left, down one level, and back to the right. Down one level and back to the left. Again and again. My eyes weren't detecting anything, and the AIM-9 seeker wasn't either. It was frustrating. I knew he was out there, but I couldn't see him.

"Goddamn it, Satan," I whispered into the intercom. "Where the fuck are you?"

As the moments ticked by, the anxiety slowly increased inside of me. I was betting everything that Satan would perform in the predictable asshole fashion that I had envisioned. He had a lot on the line. Maybe he had the presence of mind to be a little more deliberate, to be a little more careful. He had already lost one F-35, he couldn't afford to lose a second. And in spite of his arrogance, I knew he respected my dogfighting ability. We had fought one another numerous times back in the day. And I had kicked his ass every time.

I tried to get inside his head. What would I do if I wanted to kill someone with a gunshot but get them into a predictable flight path and hopefully in a low energy state before then?

The answer was so obvious it stunned me.

"Tango Charlie, Darkstar, single group, single contact BRAA 269, six miles, coaltitude, head!"

"You've been out of the game for too fucking long," I said to myself.

The best way to make a target predictable for a guns attack is for the attacker to shoot a missile at it, an infrared missile, at close range. The defending pilot is forced to reduce to idle power to reduce his heat signature while he executes a high-g break turn that bleeds his energy off at an extremely high rate. In less than 360 degrees of turn, if the attacker keeps the pressure on, the defender would typically be in a predictable, low rate turn with little energy left to maneuver.

Darkstar's warning meant that Satan had opened the F-35's weapons bay doors to shoot a missile, an action that I presumed happened automatically but would also add sharp edges to the F-35's radar profile and make the jet easier to detect on radar. As I looked back over my shoulder, I saw the fireball of an air-to-air missile headed my way, with a wispy trail of smoke behind it. And beyond the missile, I saw the angular frontal profile of Satan's F-35 about two miles back, low and on the outside of my turn.

The next few actions happened automatically, even reflexively, and they saved my life. I mechanically pulled the throttle to idle with my left hand and rolled the Viper with my right. As I applied the side pressure to the stick, I deployed chaff and flares with the countermeasures dispensing switch on the sidestick. I stopped the roll with my vertical stabilizer pointed directly at Satan's jet and then inhaled, got into my straining maneuver and pulled aft on the sidestick as hard as I could. The horizontal stabilizer/elevator or slab, at the aft end of the jet, went to its g-commanded deflection instantaneously, and in a second and a half, the Viper was into 9g's and turning at 25 degrees per second.

In the "old days" of dogfighting, or basic fighter maneuvers, BFM as we called it in the USAF, before fighters had thrust to weight ratios of 1:1 or greater and high-g limits, aircraft fighting one another made rather extensive use of out-of-plane or vertical maneuvering to find the turning room they needed to control their overtake. In the age of modern fighters like the F-15 and F-16, out-of-plane maneuvering wasn't necessary, because overtake could be controlled by speed brakes and massive engines and turning problems could be remedied with extra g and harder turns. This led to fights that were very flat with very little out-of-plane maneuvering. It also led to pilots who spent their entire careers in jets like the Viper, guys like Satan, who had very little practice in maneuvering or thinking out of plane. Unfortunately for him, I had learned to fight in the A-10, one of the most energy-limited jets in the modern era, and the vertical was my friend.

In any BFM engagement, the goal for the defender is to neutralize the attacker, and the first step in that process is to get the attacker to change his game plan, which was exactly what I had in mind for Satan.

Rather than give him a horizontal turning problem to solve, I gave him a vertical one and got some help from gravity, God's g, to maintain my energy and give me additional g. I rolled past his plane of motion and oriented my lift vector downward. As I began the 180 degree turn in the vertical, essentially a split S maneuver, I watched the AIM-120 Slammer that Satan had fired lock on to one of the bundles of chaff I had dispensed and guide it to a harmless flight path that was well behind and above me. The missile's lack of correction and lazy flight path confirmed what I thought might be true: Satan had shot the missile without locking it on to me. He had shot it ballistically for one reason and one reason only: to get me to turn. And now he was getting what he wanted, although probably not quite the way he wanted it.

As the Viper's nose came around, I forced my head back in the headrest, fighting the ten g's of Viper turn plus gravity and looked up to watch Satan's jet, now above me, travel from well in front of me to a point aft of me, so he could begin the turn into my circle. The HMCS felt heavier on my head than a conventional helmet, but the symbology I saw through the visor was reassuring and the diamond-shaped reticle of one of my AIM-9Xs made me feel even better. Satan might have come to this engagement expecting me to throw away the heavy artillery and fight him one-on-one with the gun, like some sort of fucked up Hollywood movie finale, but I didn't have time for that shit. I flexed my neck muscles to rotate my chin upward as the Viper turned under max g while I struggled to get the HMCS faceplate over Satan's jet as the Viper's nose continued around the circle. Rivulets of sweat began to run down the sides of my face as I grunted through my straining maneuver, and I could feel the pressure in my chest and thorax as I fought to stay conscious under the relentless pressure of the g.

And I smiled through it all. I loved this shit.

The diamond in the helmet visor reached Satan's jet and the rate of my turn held it there. I could hear the AIM-9X seeker head whistle in my headset as it sniffed Satan's infrared signature, and I remembered a phrase one of my Viper instructors had taught me back at Luke many years ago.

"Time to let the big dog eat," I said to myself. My left index finger hit the UNCAGE button on the throttle and immediately, the first AIM-9X's missile seeker whined in my ear. Without thinking about it or assessing the angles and range, my right thumb found the pickle button on the sidestick and punched it.

The AIM-9X swooshed off its station underneath the left wing. I couldn't see it because of the angle of my head and vision, but I heard it depart the jet. And as my jet continued to turn and Satan's F-35 sped to its turn entry point, I watched the missile enter my field of view from the bottom and burn through the air toward Satan's jet. The missile left a trail of white, wispy smoke in its wake, which contrasted starkly with the blue sky above, and the small fireball of flame at its stern added an ominous certainty to its trajectory—as if it couldn't miss its target. The path it was traveling left no doubt that it was guiding on the F-35, and I found myself mesmerized by the physics the missile was displaying. It seemed impossibly maneuverable.

Satan, apparently surprised by the fact that I had fired on him, had a battle of his own to fight. Now it was his turn to bring his power to idle and execute some sort of defensive break turn to avoid the impact of my missile. He immediately went into a hard left turn, away from me, and deployed decoy flares.

I stopped my vertical turn while my jet was about 20 degrees nose low to the horizon, shoved the throttle into MAX AB, and pushed forward on the sidestick to put the jet at near zero g. The nozzle swung open, the burner lit, and the Viper leapt forward. For a few seconds, the jet had no weight. No weight meant no lift was required to keep it airborne. No lift meant no induced drag, and no induced drag meant the aircraft accelerated rapidly. It was here that I realized another benefit of the HMCS. I could look over my shoulder, observe Satan as he maneuvered, and through the symbology on my visor, adjust my pitch, and watch my airspeed increase.

Satan was hard into his break turn and decoy flares were pouring out of the rear end of his aircraft as he tried to avoid my missile. As I watched him turn and saw the vapor trail off the tips of his wings, the missile flew behind and beyond him and detonated, extremely close to his aircraft, with a flash of yellow-white flame and a small puff of smoke. He rolled out of his turn and extended away from me, intent on gaining some energy of his own. I continued to watch him as my airspeed increased through 350 knots, then 400, then 450. When it hit 500, I rolled the Viper into Satan, placed my lift vector on his jet, and pulled my nose around to him. Satan saw my wings turn perpendicular to the horizon and began a turn of his own, bringing his nose to mine.

In a few seconds, we were nose to nose, about 12,000 feet apart, racing toward each other, like two aerial knights in a high-altitude jousting contest. I opened and closed my hands on the stick and throttle for a moment to increase the blood flow to them and prepare them for the piccolo drill that was to come as Satan and I fought.

"That was chickenshit, T. C.," Satan said over UHF as our aircraft hurried toward one another. "All I was trying to do was get you to turn so I could shoot your ass. The missile wasn't even locked on. You would have had a fighting chance. Then you had to go throw a missile back at me."

"You get what you give, Satan."

"We need to fight this out fair like men, mano a mano, and all that shit."

"Fuck that," I replied. "I didn't come here to fight fair. I came here to kill your ass and get this over with."

"You always were an arrogant son of a bitch," he said to me. "Fight's on."

"You bet your ass it is."

Our jets were 6,000 feet apart and ripping through the sky with a combined closure rate of well over 1,000 knots—about 1,800 feet per second. In less than three seconds, we would merge. And I was going to try to execute the maneuver Christine had described about an hour ago—a lifetime ago. I checked my power to idle and dispensed a few flares in the event Satan was considering a head-on AIM-9 shot, in spite of his braggadocio.

When jets meet nose to nose in a high-aspect engagement,

there are generally two courses of action. One of them is the classic "two-circle fight," where each jet turns across the other's tail in the opposite direction and the two flight paths, when viewed from "God's eye" or above, look like two separate circles. Before the advent of the AIM-9X and the HMCS, this was the best option in a Viper, because it allowed the pilot to exploit the Viper's outstanding turn rate and preserve the range necessary to bring the older AIM-9M to bear on the adversary. The other option was the "one-circle fight" where after the first aircraft turned, the other aircraft turned toward the first aircraft, in the same direction, and the two jets wound up on opposite sides of the same circle.

I had no idea what Satan was expecting me to do. All I knew was I needed to keep him off balance until he made a mistake. And Christine's maneuver, the 9-g duck under, seemed to be the ticket. I just hoped it worked.

As our jets neared each other, I noticed something peculiar. Usually, in the last few thousand feet of a head-on engagement, the opposing aircraft will settle on the side they plan to pass each other on, left side to left side or right side to right side. But Satan wasn't picking a side. He was pointed directly at me, on a collision course. Apparently he wanted to get me out of my game plan, even at the cost of his own life.

It took me about an extra half second longer to process that than it should have. By then it was almost too late.

"You homicidal son of a bitch," I spat into the intercom as I snapped the sidestick aft.

The Viper leapt into the vertical, like a nimble steed jumping an obstacle.

Thank God for reflexes. As I increased my altitude, I pushed the stick forward and rolled the jet inverted, just in time to watch Satan's jet go underneath me.

First rule of BFM: Lose sight. Lose fight. I wasn't going to lose sight of this asshole. Not even for a second.

Satan's jet went by in some kind of crazy slow motion. It was so close to my Viper that I could see the faint outlines of some of the aluminum panels and the distinct shape of the air-refueling receptacle. I could also see the aperture for the F-35's internally mounted 25mm cannon, and I felt that something tug again at the back of my brain. It was something I had read somewhere but had never paid any attention to. And it was important.

Damn, I thought to myself. *What was it?*

Immediately after our jets cleared each other, Satan rolled his jet to the left and applied the g, his wing tips trailing vapor from the humid monsoon-laden July air over the Arizona desert. Still inverted, I shoved the throttle into MAX AB, rolled to orient my vertical stabilizer in front of Satan's nose, inhaled, pushed into my straining maneuver and wedged my helmet between the canopy and the side of the ejection seat so I could maintain sight of Satan's jet. Then I pulled back on the sidestick controller as hard as I could.

Once again the control slab deflected and once again the g's came on at six per second, and I was into nine g's in no time. I could feel the helmet pressing down on my head and the familiar crushing pressure on my chest. I grunted through my straining maneuver as the Viper's nose sliced through the air at 25 degrees per second. In just over six seconds, my jet was nearly parallel to the ground, and I forced my head off the canopy and back onto the headrest, feeling a muscle twinge in the back of my neck as I did so.

I looked up at Satan's jet now, above and slightly in front of me. He was turning quickly also, but not nearly as quickly as I was. Rather than our jets being parallel or slightly pointed toward each other, as they would be if our jets had compatible turn rates, I had made significant angles on Satan, and my nose was tracking toward the side of his aircraft.

Jesus, I thought to myself. *The F-35 designers sure fucked this up.*

As I stared at the side of his jet through the HMCS symbology and particularly through the diamond of the second AIM-9X reticle, I heard the whistle of the AIM-9's seeker in my ear and was rudely reminded that I still had shit to do. I uncaged the seeker and it immediately whined reassuringly in my ear. I took a second to evaluate the range and angles and decided to let the big dog eat. I punched the pickle button on the sidestick.

WOOOOOOOSH!

The AIM-9 shot off the rail more quickly than my peripheral vision could keep up. One second it was there and the next it wasn't.

The missile flew a much more recognizable trajectory this time, although a much tighter one than I had seen before. I watched the fireball and smoke trail travel a semicircular path up toward Satan's jet. It was guiding perfectly and in just a second or two it was going to hit his aircraft and splatter his arrogant ass all over the Arizona desert. I found myself smiling in anticipation under the soft plastic of the oxygen mask.

But I noticed something different this time. He wasn't dispensing flares.

What the fuck? I found myself wondering. *Even Satan isn't that stupid.*

And then the AIM-9 missed his jet. Completely. It flew a lazy trajectory well above and beyond his jet and then detonated, almost as an afterthought. There was the quick burst of orange flame and then the typical white smoke cloud, which seemed to hang above his aircraft like still art, mocking me.

I felt my mouth open in stunned surprise under my oxygen mask.

"No fucking way," I said to myself.

"You might have the turn, T. C.," said the nasal voice over UHF, "but you don't have the technology."

And then it occurred to me. The jets he and Brock were flying came from Edwards. They were test-bed aircraft.

"Laser IR defense," I said to myself over the intercom. "He's got onboard IR missile defense. Son of a bitch."

But there wasn't time to dwell on that revelation. There was still BFM to do. As I climbed up toward Satan's jet, he increased his bank and oriented his lift vector directly into my plane of motion. I had made angles on him and was at about 90 degrees of aspect, my nose oriented down his wing line, but well below it, and by coming down toward me, he was taking any vertical turning room away from me and seriously complicating my BFM problem. Apparently he had learned something from our last interchange on this engagement. While frustrating, his move didn't surprise me. It was exactly what I would have done. "Nice move, Satan," I mumbled into the oxygen mask.

In this kind of situation, the offender has two apparent choices: go over the defender or under him. I chose the option Satan would be least expecting. Neither.

I released back-stick pressure to stop my climb and even pushed slightly to keep my flight path oriented under his. The nimble Viper responded like the thoroughbred it was, reacting to the subtle differences in pressure on the sidestick as if it was reading my mind. With the jet unloaded, it rolled rapidly and with slight pressure on the stick, I rolled left to a point where I could still just barely see Satan's jet over the edge of the right canopy rail. Then I pulled the power out of AB and pulled back on the sidestick for all I was worth. In about three seconds, my fuselage was nearly parallel with Satan's, and I'd bled off about 80 knots of airspeed.

Now I was parallel with his jet and about 2000 feet away, on the inside of his turn, low and slightly aft of his wing line, nearly co-energy with him, our airspeeds and altitudes almost equal at about 250 knots and 14,000 feet. Up until then, he'd probably expected what he had seen. Hopefully he wouldn't anticipate the next part. I shoved the throttle into AB to keep my energy from bleeding too rapidly and with the jet still under g, I rolled up and around his jet in a barrel roll, trying to fly a greater distance through the sky than he did, attempting to push him in front of me so I could gain a more offensive position.

But Satan was wily, and the F-35 was more maneuverable at low speed and high angle of attack than I predicted. As soon as I started rolling to right, Satan rolled right too, keeping me in sight and denying my attempt to get behind him. My windscreen was filled with the shape of the gray, angular 35, and I could see myself creeping forward on Satan's jet, more toward a neutral position.

I pulled the power to idle and reversed my roll to the left, scrambling to preserve my remaining advantage, but Satan anticipated my move and reversed his turn as well, and we ended up in a mirror image of our previous orientation. Our jets were about 1,000 feet apart now with his jet slightly in front of and slightly below mine, but now we were constantly rolling and starting into one of the two endgame orientations of a visual fight, the rolling scissors, where both aircraft continually rolled around each other in an attempt to get an advantage.

"Nice work, T. C.," the nasal voice said over UHF. "I even let you have the advantage at the beginning and you blew it. The famous T. C. The only Viper ace in the USAF, beaten by some old general in a jet that doesn't turn as well."

I wanted to respond with something insulting and witty, but he was right, goddamn it. I had totally fucked up. Whatever advantage I had left was minor and likely to be gone soon if I didn't do something drastic.

"Aren't you wondering why I chose this particular jet?" the nasal voice taunted, with no sound of exertion at all. It was like all the g we were under wasn't even affecting him. I loved the g, but it was still kicking my ass.

As I looked at his jet fly its corkscrew path through the blue, Arizona sky, and as I commanded my jet to follow his, I focused on the outline of the aperture for the F-35's cannon, just aft and left of the cockpit. And then the piece of information that had been tugging at the back of my brain popped into my consciousness. But before I could contemplate it, Satan spoke again on UHF.

"The F-35 gun doesn't work," Satan said matter-of-factly over UHF, echoing the thought that had occurred to me. "It's a software issue. They awarded the contract to some low-rent software company, and the company couldn't get it fielded. So I'm carrying around about 1,000 pounds of deadweight in this jet. But I'm also carrying something else. A special gift for Miguel. And the Chinese. And I've arranged a demo, just for you."

As I watched him, Satan stopped his roll, as his jet became parallel with the surface. I saw the F-35's horizontal slab rotate down and forward and his jet leapt into the vertical. The engine nozzle on the angular aircraft opened and the orange flame of his afterburner became visible.

"Not good," I said to myself as I stopped my own roll and pulled back on the sidestick controller. He was forcing us into a flat scissors, where we'd be heading uphill with high pitch, high angle of attack, and low airspeed into a regime where the F-16's maneuverability was severely limited.

And as I watched, a small round dome emerged from beneath Satan's jet, just behind the nose gear doors and seemed to lock into place. Then it rotated until it found the spot it needed to be in and stopped.

"What the fuck?" I spat into the intercom.

But in a microsecond, my brain made the connection and I knew what I was looking at.

"Shit!" I said to myself, "How the hell did he get that?"

Another F-35 test-bed system: the Lockheed Martin Laser Turret. Eventually slated to be the crown jewel in the new aircraft's weapons suite, it sat in the box just behind the cockpit where the vertical lift fan was for the F-35B and drew limitless power from the F-35's massive jet engine. It featured built in gyro and atmospheric stabilization mechanisms to allow the beam to focus on targets at several miles in range. My jet, about 1,000 feet away, wouldn't even be a challenge.

I didn't have time to think, and I didn't have time to plan. I had no idea what the laser could do to my jet; but with a fuselage full of target directly behind it, I was thinking it wasn't good. I had to either run away and save my ass or risk letting Satan fry it.

And running wasn't in my nature.

So I selected MAX AB and checked the DOGFIGHT switch in the outboard position, pulling aft on the TMS switch to force the Viper's radar into 10 x 60 vertical scan mode.

Second rule of BFM: Nose position over energy.

I spent every last bit of energy I had to pull the Viper's nose up to his aircraft. I had no idea how long it would take for the laser to meet the parameters it needed to fire, and I needed to get some bullets into Satan's aircraft before it did. But the Viper's digital flight control system stubbornly refused to cooperate and limited the upward movement of the nose, doing its sentry duty to keep me from departing the aircraft from controlled flight. My pitch increased excruciatingly slowly and each second that passed seemed like a small eternity as I watched the dome of the laser turret continually adjust to refine its solution.

"I don't have time for this shit," I said to myself. "I've got to get my nose up there and get some bullets into his ass."

The Viper, now hanging on the pitch limiter due to the high angle of attack, like a stubborn horse, refused to go.

I was screwed. And dead.

But then I remembered something, something that had saved my ass once before. Something that I had been taught by the woman who almost killed me.

I retracted the speed brake as I put forward pressure on the sidestick. As soon as the jet unloaded, I rolled it inverted and reached over to the MPO switch on the left console. The MPO, or manual pitch override switch, allowed the pilot to override the pitch limiter and deflect the slab beyond its normal limits. Unfortunately, the MPO allowed more range in the downward direction than it did upward. Hanging in the straps, inverted, I looped my middle finger in the ring around the MPO and deflected it with my index finger. Then I pushed on the sidestick and the nose tracked roughly downward, like a horse fighting the reins. Since I was inverted, the downward motion of my jet was actually upward motion in relation to Satan's jet and to the surface of the earth. The moment my nose began to move, I saw a flash of light go just under the canopy and felt a yaw moment in the rudder pedals under my feet.

"Jesus," I said into the intercom. "He almost burned my rudder off."

I wasn't going to allow him another shot. I continued to push forward on the stick as I held the MPO switch down. But the stick was more sensitive than it normally was and it tracked through his jet and suddenly I was looking at the top of his aircraft through the top of my canopy. And I saw that the contour of the top of his jet had changed since I had last seen it.

There was another laser turret on the top of his aircraft as well.

Holy shit!

As I watched, the dark dome swiveled and the eye-shaped aperture on the side trained itself on my jet. It was almost surreal—like a scene from a sci-fi movie. And if I hadn't read the article on the developing technology in an aviation industry magazine recently, I'm not sure I would have believed it. But there was no doubt it was real and it was happening and I was about to get blasted. Again.

And there wasn't much I could do about it, inverted, out of energy, and almost out of ideas.

Unconsciously, I released the MPO switch, kept the jet unloaded and tried to roll it to the right to put the bottom side down and the top side up. The Viper was stubborn and almost listless in my hands, trying to obey my commands in the confines of its digital flight control laws in a high angle of attack environment that it had never been designed to operate in. The jet rolled slowly, painfully slowly, and the earth and sky seemed to creep around the nose sluggishly as the Viper fought to right itself. I could feel the buffet of the turbulent airflow created by the nearly stalled condition around the aircraft as it rolled, and I found myself gritting my teeth in anticipation as the wings slowly rotated through 90 degrees of bank on the way to level flight.

"You can do it, baby," I uttered into the intercom. "You can do it."

Then there was a bright flash of light and the last three feet of my left wing was severed from my airplane.

With the loss of lift on that side, as well as the loss of weight from the AIM-120 AMRAAM on the wing tip, the Viper immediately began an uncommanded roll to the left. The digital flight control system was now in a situation it had never been programmed for, and it seemed to give up trying to keep the Viper longitudinally stable. Due to my lack of airspeed, the roll rate wasn't nearly as fast or disorienting as it could have been, but it almost didn't matter, because

I couldn't seem to stop it. I tried to apply right sidestick to counter it, then right rudder, then both inputs at the same time, but the jet continued to roll.

Then, as I watched the rotating mosaic of brown desert and blue sky in my canopy, I saw the nozzle on Satan's jet wind open a little wider and the afterburner flame grow longer. Then he slowly began to accelerate away from me. I shook my head in sick realization. He had the power to pull away from me all along. This whole engagement had been about setting me up and playing to the famous Pearce ego.

"Idiot," I said to myself in the intercom. "No. Make that fucking idiot."

"Nice airshow you're putting on back there, Pearce," said the evil voice over UHF. "Are you enjoying yourself?" There was a maniacal chuckle. "This isn't exactly how I planned to end you, but it will do just fine."

Fuck you, asshole.

"I figure you've got a few more turns before the nose drops, the airspeed increases, and it wraps up into that roll real good."

Damn, I thought. *He's right. Once the speed increases, the roll rate will increase. And if I don't have the control authority to stop it—*

"Oh you might be able to stop it and get control of the jet, but I'm betting you'll be puking your guts out by the time you get sufficient airflow to counteract the roll. And besides, I'll be hanging around with another couple of missiles to blow your jet into pieces if it doesn't break apart by itself."

The earth and sky continued to alternate in my canopy and instead of staying at one point in space like it did when the jet was in an unloaded roll, the nose of the Viper transcribed an irregular circle in the sky, a circle that was slowly shifting downward.

And then I noticed something.

Satan's F-35 was in the middle of the circle, which meant that if things stayed constant for a few more turns, he'd pass through the upper arc of the circle—and directly in front of my nose.

The switch actuations happened without me even willing them. I checked the DOGFIGHT switch in the outboard position and pressed forward on the TMS switch on the sidestick. The boresight cross appeared in the HUD in front of me.

The Viper continued to rotate through its lazy roll, but as the nose continued to shift downward, the roll rate began to increase.

"Some radar tricks now, T. C.?" said the arrogant nasal voice. "And what good will that do you? You'll never get any bullets into me with your nose tracking around like that."

The boresight cross went just over the top of his jet as my jet made another revolution.

"C'mon, baby," I whispered into the intercom. "You can do it. One more turn."

"And you know with the virtual vision technology in this jet I can actually see you through the back end of my jet, even though you're below me. It's fun to watch."

"You forgot something, Satan," I said to him over UHF, fighting to keep my voice under control as my jet continued to roll.

"Oh I don't think I did, T. C.," he said cheerily. You've shot your AIM-9s and your gun is useless if you can't stop the roll."

"I guess you weren't paying attention when we were fighting," I said. "I still have one more present for you."

"You mean the one Slammer you have left? I did the operational test on that thing! It'll never separate cleanly while you're rolling like that!"

"But," I said, suddenly remembering a film I had seen in pilot training, "what if I stop the roll?" I grabbed the Viper's landing gear handle with my left hand and shoved it into the down position.

"Keep dreaming, T. C.," he replied smugly. "Keep..." His voice trailed off as he watched.

In seconds, the Viper's landing gear deployed and the jet's flaperons moved to the down position. The change in the jet's center of gravity generated by the gear deployment and the addition of drag on the underside of the airplane slowed the roll immediately. And a little right sidestick, enhanced by the extra lift of the deployed flaperons, stopped it completely.

"What the f..." I heard Satan's voice over UHF; he must have forgotten to release the mic switch.

"LOCK! LOCK!" said the luscious female voice in my ear.

I rotated the DOGFIGHT switch inboard to the MISSILE OVERRIDE position and the circle of the AIM-120 AMRAAM's seeker head immediately centered itself on Satan's jet. I checked the designated launch zone display in the lower right part of the HUD and noted that the massive missile's minimum range criteria was satisfied. I was 6,000 feet directly behind him, and he was moving away, tail aspect to me. It was perfect.

"It won't work T. C.!" Satan's voice had just a little edge in it now. "The ECM on this jet will keep the missile..."

"We'll see," I said to myself, and I punched the pickle button.

Unlike the AIM-9, which races off the rail in a microsecond, the AIM-120 takes a second or two before it leaves. And when it does, it sounds like a freight train. The huge missile roared off the right wing tip station with a vengeance and tore through the air toward Satan's jet, trailing the typical orange fireball.

I had to hand it to him though, he was fast.

Satan banked up and pulled his nose into the vertical in a classic orthogonal roll. The AMRAAM attempted to correct to his flight path but the missile was still accelerating and was just clearing the minimum arming distance from my aircraft before it began to maneuver. Still, the huge missile did an admirable job of hacking the corner and flew just under and past Satan's jet before it detonated with a huge orange and black flash. The force of the blast actually moved Satan's jet upward and toward me, and I saw pieces of both metal and composite separate from the aircraft. Almost immediately, the F-35 began to trail red hydraulic fluid and white smoke.

I slid my throttle forward into min AB and allowed my jet to accelerate toward him. I rotated the DOGFIGHT switch into the outboard position and watched as the EEGS gunsight computed a firing solution for Satan's jet. Ordinarily, with my landing gear down and the other aircraft at full power and maneuverability, I would have never been able to catch him. But he was suffering now. His jet was low on energy because he had not gotten away from me quickly, more intent on watching the show than increasing his speed or his altitude. With the high g and aggressive climb required in the orthogonal break, he had bled off the energy he had. Now his jet was damaged and he was descending, slowly, right in front of me. Since he had turned nearly 90 degrees to my flight path, my airspeed, 250 knots, was almost pure closure. And as I quickly crossed the distance between us, I could see him frantically trying to push buttons and flip switches in the cockpit. I was just behind his wing line and closing to 3,000 feet of range when I saw his head come up and stare at me for the first time. I could see his left arm repeatedly cycling the throttle in an attempt to get his afterburner to light. The nozzle opened and closed in response to the attempts but didn't stay open and no orange flame appeared.

I found myself smiling under my oxygen mask.

"You can run but you can't hide, Satan," I said over UHF.

"You lucky fuck!" he replied with a sneer. Even in a crippled airplane with a 20mm cannon pointed at him, he still had attitude. "I had your ass! I had your ass!"

The EEGS's gunsight had settled and the circular "death dot" had appeared. I raised the Viper's nose gently and smoothly to place the pipper right over the cockpit and pulled my power back into MIL. Then I watched the analog range indicator, a clocklike dial, retreat in its circular path as the distance between our jets decreased.

"You almost did," I agreed. "But that was then and this is now. And I've got just over 400 rounds of 20 millimeter that's looking for a home."

"Is that supposed to scare me, T. C.?" Satan said. "Is that supposed to scare me into confessing something?"

The range between our jets had closed to 1,500 feet. My right index finger was twitching. It was everything I could do not to pull the trigger on the sidestick.

"Do you expect me to talk?" Satan continued.

The immortal exchange between Sean Connery's James Bond and Gert Frobe's Goldfinger flashed through my mind.

"No, General Tappan," I said over UHF. "I expect you to die."

The range was 1,000 feet now, and I actually had enough detail under the pipper to decide what part of Satan's outline I could place the death dot on. Uncommanded, my right index finger found the trigger and was gently resting upon it.

"Then fuck you," Satan replied. "And when Ramon and Miguel find your slut chick and bitch daughter, fuck them too."

The rage took me. Instantaneously. My eyes saw red and the blood sang in my veins. In the distance, over the Have-Quick net, I could barely hear Dave Smith's voice saying something about what information Satan might provide. But I could feel my heart beating in my ears, and the words he was uttering didn't register or matter.

I placed the pipper precisely on Satan's helmeted head

and pulled the trigger.

The M61-A1 spat 20mm rounds at about 100 per second, and the inside of the F-35's cockpit transformed into a shredded mess of Plexiglas, blood, and gore. I then pulled the pipper left as I continued to fire and ripped into the jet's fuselage and held the trigger down until the gun emptied.

"And fuck you too," I added as the gun went dry.

Satan's F-35 began a slow turn, down and away from me, and flames began to seep through the cracks in the jet's outer skin. I banked to the right to get some separation from the crippled aircraft. The flames reached the fuel tanks a few seconds later, and the jet suddenly exploded with an orange and red fireball and the usual black cloud that was a typical of a petroleum-based fire.

It reminded me of the fireball that had been Christine's jet and Christine just moments ago. A lifetime ago.

"Damn," I said into my intercom as I turned the Viper north. "What a fucking waste."

I toggled my radio back over to the Have-Quick net and keyed the mic. "Darkstar, Tango Charlie. Kill the other F-35."

"Tango Charlie, Darkstar," said the young controller's voice, obviously relieved. "Glad you made it. What can I do for you?"

"I need a vector and frequency for Gila Bend. And tell them to have the emergency trucks ready. I'm not one hundred percent sure I can land this thing."

Chapter Twenty-Five

Contract Day 16
Thursday, July 8, 2010
0913 Hours Local Time
Gila Bend Air Force Auxiliary Field
Gila Bend, Arizona

With 1200 pounds of fuel and a jet with landing gear hanging, my landing options were limited. Gila Bend was my only choice and so for the second time in just a few days, I found myself on final approach to the Air Force Auxiliary Field's 8,500 foot runway. The Viper seemed to be handling predictably with the landing gear and flaperons deployed. And with the slow speed maneuvering I'd experienced earlier, I didn't expect any controllability issues in the landing flare.

"Tango Charlie One Emergency," the controller's voice came through on UHF, "Gila Bend Tower, check wheels down, cleared to land Runway 35. Emergency vehicles will be standing by."

"Roger," I said. "I shouldn't need them but thanks." The landing habit patterns were reemerging for me. I checked that the gear handle was down and the landing gear down indicator lights illuminated. I checked that the landing light was on and glanced at the hydraulic gauge. "Handle's down, three green, good pressure, light's on," I said to myself. Then I keyed the mic. "Tango Charlie One Emergency," I said, "gear down, full stop."

From there it was a mechanical process. I flew the 2.5 degree pitch ladder in the Viper's HUD to threshold of the runway, put the flight path marker over the pitch ladder, and pulled the throttle back to keep the angle of attack at 11 degrees. In a fighter, airspeeds on final were guesses. Angle of attack told the pilot exactly what the wing was doing and was far more accurate. I maintained the descent and the speed until the runway overrun went under the nose, then I retarded the power to idle and lifted the Viper's nose up slightly. The jet touched down gently a few moments later, and I held the nose up in the aerobrake for several seconds and then flew it down to the asphalt.

"Still got the touch," I said to myself.

On most military bases, the arming and de-arming areas are located just off the runway adjacent to or on a taxiway that was parallel to the main runway. But at Gila Bend there was no parallel taxiway and the arming and de-arming areas were attached to the runway at the northern and southern ends. As I slowed the Viper and approached the de-arming area near the departure end of Runway 35, I noticed a vehicle that I wasn't expecting. There was the usual USAF pickup truck that the arming crew traveled in, but there was also a black SUV in standard government configuration.

I nodded to myself as I slowed the Viper to taxi speed, about 10-15 knots, and began to turn into the de-arm area. *Dave must have left some folks here to secure the place,* I thought.

I taxied the Viper onto one of the painted yellow lines in the de-arm area and stopped when signaled by the sergeant who was in charge of the de-arm crew. His eyes widened a bit when he saw the extent of damage to my aircraft, and I grinned under my oxygen mask.

If you only knew.

As the jet stopped, I raised my hands and let the de-arm crew descend upon my jet to pin whatever was left to pin as well as to secure and pin the Viper's hydrazine-powered emergency power unit. As I watched sergeant's face, I saw something there that was out of place. Most of the time, arming crew chiefs watch their people closely while they're under the jet and have no other expression on their faces other than one of concentration. But the expression on this guy's face conveyed something else. He was edgy—and scared. I felt my eyes narrow behind the shield of the HMCS helmet.

There was something else going on here.

A few moments later, the arming crew cleared my aircraft, and the chief signaled me to shut down the jet. I shrugged and did what I was told. I also noted that the emergency vehicles had returned to their alert locations, without me, the pilot of the emergency aircraft, releasing them.

I had no sooner gotten the canopy open and my helmet off when the ladder appeared over the side of aircraft, and shortly after the face of OSI Special Agent Lorna Dahlke along with a very nasty-looking compact 12-gauge combat shotgun.

And it was most definitely pointed at me.

"No fucking tricks, smartass," Dahlke said. "We have a mission here."

I stared at her for a moment and unconsciously shook my head as I packed the HMCS into my helmet bag and removed my gloves. After I stowed the gloves and my checklist into the bag, I put the bag in my lap and kept both of my hands wrapped up in the bag's cloth.

"Tappan's dead," I told her. "I blew his ass all over the Arizona landscape. And both F-35's are also part of the local desert scenery. Whatever mission you might have had is fucking history."

She smiled crookedly. "I never took orders from Tappan," she said, "only from my uncle."

The expression on my face must have conveyed my surprise.

"That's right," she said, her eyes gloating in triumph. "My real name isn't Dahlke, it's Diaz. Miguel's my uncle. He's the one who paid for my college and got me my commission after I had been in the OSI for three years. He said he needed his favorite niece to help him from the inside."

I could sense the pieces of the puzzle dropping into place. *And he's the one that's using you to control the OSI commander, Alan Turnidge. Jesus.*

"So what do you intend to accomplish now?" I asked. "Tappan's dead. The plot is foiled. Miguel is toast, because he can't pay the Chinese. What in the hell do you possibly hope to help him with?"

She shrugged and the crooked smile on her face broadened. "He just wants you dead, and I'm happy to oblige." She actually winked at me.

"You need to get in line," I said. "You're not the first, and you won't be the last."

As we'd been talking, I had been sliding my hand into one of the long, outer pockets of my helmet bag and working my fingers around the grip of the Colt Commander that I'd left in there. Lorna had been so intent on telling me how much shit I was in that she hadn't noticed. My fingers worked themselves around the rubber grip and my finger found the serrated face of the conditioned trigger.

"We'll, I'm going to be the one today," she said, with a slightly maniacal glint in her eye. "I'm going to kill you right here, in the cockpit of this fucking jet. The famous Colin Pearce, shot by a woman in the airplane he uses to prove his fucked up masculinity."

My thumb found the Colt's rounded hammer and I slowly

pulled it back.

"Are you now?" I asked, raising my eyebrows. Then I raised my voice. "You're going to kill me? Right now in front of everybody?"

She couldn't help herself. She had to look over her shoulder to see if anyone had heard. She did it quickly, very quickly.

But not quickly enough.

Because as she turned, I reached up with my free hand and pushed her off the ladder as hard as I could. She had time to turn her head to me and register surprise before her head disappeared over the side of the aircraft. The F-16 cockpit isn't that high off the ground—only about six feet or so. And when someone is standing on a ladder, their feet are just a few feet off the ground. But that's far enough to fall when there's hard pavement below, especially when a loaded weapon is involved.

The muffled crunch of Lorna hitting the pavement and the roar of the shotgun blast were nearly simultaneous. Then there was a pregnant, ominous silence. I stole a glance over the side of the jet and saw what was left of Lorna Dahlke lying on the pavement below. Her body was intact, but her head and face were decimated by the blast of her shotgun at close range. Apparently Agent Dahlke wasn't following proper procedure and had her finger on the trigger instead of alongside the trigger guard. What a surprise.

"That left a mark," I said.

As I watched, Dahlke's two OSI cohorts ran to her side and looked down on her remains. One of them turned his head to the side and vomited onto the pavement next to her. The other, the same guy from the conference room just a few days ago, looked up at me and reached back to his right hip.

I produced the .45 and aimed at him over the side of the Viper's canopy rail, pulling the gun's hammer back into the fully cocked position.

"Please," I said, imploring him. "Please give me an excuse.

I've wanted to kill one of you motherfuckers for about nine years now."

He seemed to consider it for a moment or two. But then discretion became the better part of valor and he moved his right hand back into plain sight. Then he signaled his partner, and the two of them retreated to their black SUV and left the gory remains of their boss on the tarmac. In moments, they had backed up, turned, and were on their way.

I gathered my gear and, keeping the Colt in my hand, exited the cockpit and went down the ladder. The crew chief appeared at the base of the ladder, patiently waiting for me. After my feet hit the ground, I placed my helmet bag on the pavement and then unfastened my harness straps from between my legs and refastened them on the outside of my hips.

"You fucked this jet up pretty good, sir," the sergeant said, his face now assuming a carefree expression. "I hope the other guy got it worse."

"They did," I said simply. "This not bothering you?" I asked him, inclining my head to the remains of Special Agent Lorna Dahlke.

"Get real, sir," he responded. I did two tours in Afghanistan and one in Iraq. This is nothing. Besides, those OSI fuckers are assholes."

***

An hour later I was in a CIA SUV and headed northbound, back to Luke AFB. Dave Smith was driving, and I was in the front passenger seat. John Amrine sat in the back. I had the oddest feeling of déjà vu.

"Miguel is finished," Amrine said as the SUV shot up Arizona Highway 85 on the way back to the Phoenix valley. "Tappan's dead, the F-35s are history, and he doesn't have money to pay the Chinese. We've already intercepted communications that indicate the Chinese know what's happened and are getting ready to withdraw.'

"Couldn't they just take over without Miguel?" Smith asked. "The Chinese have deployed enough men and equipment to completely control Mexico City."

I saw Amrine shake his blond head in my peripheral vision. "Mexicans are funny about that sort of thing," he said. "They're a very proud people. Their government is a mess. Their economy is in shambles and drug cartels run the country. But without a Mexican figurehead to rally behind, they're uncontrollable."

I looked back at him.

"Oh believe me," Amrine said, smiling at me with just a touch of irony on the surfer-boy features. "We've looked at it in every possible permutation. We'd love to take control of Mexico. It would solve so many problems."

I nodded at him. "I hear that," I said. "But Miguel isn't finished." I paused for a moment to let the words sink in. "He may be out of money, out of influence, and perhaps even out of prestige, but he's not finished."

Amrine looked at me quizzically.

"How good is your Mexican history?" I asked.

Amrine looked at me and shrugged. "Decent," he said. "We have been doing quite a bit of research of late."

Out of the corner of my eye, I saw Dave Smith smile.

"Miguel claims to be a descendant of Antonio Lopez de Santa Anna," I said, "the guy who maintained political power and influence in Mexico after losing the Texas Revolution and the Mexican-American war."

I saw a lightbulb go on behind Amrine's eyes.

"He's not done until he's done," I said.

Amrine thought for a few moments and then he nodded. "What do you have in mind?" he asked.

"We need to go after him," I said.

Amrine smirked at me, and Smith looked at me in disbelief.

"There's no fucking way," Smith said after a few minutes. "Especially with the breakdown in US-Mexican relations after the business last fall and your strike on his camp earlier this week. We'll never get the mission approved through CIA channels."

Amrine nodded. "He's right. The agency has just about worn out its welcome in Mexico. Besides," he said, "we don't even know where he is."

"And even if we did," Smith added, "we'd never get approval to operate inside Mexico again. John and I are lucky to have our jobs after the strike you made."

"I know where he is," I said. "And I even know some people who might want to help me get him."

***

About an hour later, Smith stopped the SUV in front of the OSI detachment headquarters at Luke Air Force Base.

"Seriously?" Smith asked as I opened the SUV's passenger door.

I nodded at him. "Most of these guys are assholes and the concept and institution is fucked up," I said. "But one of them risked her life to save me, and I'm hoping there will be a few other believers who want to do the right thing."

Amrine looked at me and nodded with a sage expression on his surfer-boy features. "You're smarter than you look, T. C.," he said.

I laughed at him as I exited the SUV. "I get that a lot," I said.

I walked down the sidewalk from the curb to the front door of the OSI detachment headquarters with a cacophony of emotion playing inside my head. I remembered the walk I had made so many years ago and how that had ended. I violated one of the principal pieces of advice that the first sergeant of the 310th Fighter Squadron had told me at the time.

"Don't matter whether you're innocent or guilty," he said, "don't talk to them fuckers without a lawyer."

And he had been right. I had answered their questions. I had tried to be cooperative. And it had backfired in my face and everything I'd said had been used against me.

Never again.

But today was different. Or at least I hoped it would be.

I stopped in front of the metal door set into the brick building and looked up, contemplating the impossibly blue desert sky above me. The air around me was blast furnace hot and even a little humid with the July monsoon season rolling in. I could feel the sweat inside my flightsuit, but I could also feel a little chill at the back of my neck. It was an odd juxtaposition.

I entered an alcove, sheltered on three sides by USAF-issue beige brick, and I pushed the doorbell-like button on the side of the metal entrance door.

"May I help you?" a disembodied male voice from a speaker answered, the words echoing in the small space.

"You can," I said, matter-of-factly. "My name is Colin Pearce. You know who the fuck I am. Let me in."

There was only a second or two of delay, and then a buzzer sounded and the door unlatched. I grabbed the warm metal handle on the door, opened it, and stepped into the reception area inside. The drab, grimy space was empty except for a few cheap waiting-room chairs, a window that looked like a bank teller station in a questionable neighborhood, and another metal door that led to the inner sanctum of the building. There was also an obvious closed circuit TV camera at the top of a corner of the room by the wall with the window. I didn't know whether the camera was a decoy or the real thing and I didn't care. I stepped into the center of the reception area, looked up at the camera, and put my hands on my hips.

"Dahlke was Miguel Hidalgo's niece," I said. "And your commander, General Turnidge, is a pedophile, which you can confirm by looking at the notebook you'll find somewhere around Dahlke's desk. Dahlke was working with Tappan to steal F-35s for Miguel so he could sell them to China. And Dahlke was also blackmailing Turnidge on Miguel's orders to ensure you guys looked the other way. Now you don't have to take my word for it. I've got two friends in the CIA who are outside and who will vouch for all of this." I looked intently up into the camera. "Your organization has a lot of shit on its face right now." I paused and shook my head in near disbelief of the words I was about to utter. "But I'm offering you an opportunity to clean some of it off," I said. "Now who's game?"

Chapter Twenty-Six

Contract Day 18
Saturday, July 10, 2010
0115 Hours Local Time
Special Operations C-130 Hercules
30,000 feet over Baja, California

It had been a long time since I had sat in the back of a C-130. At least twenty years or so. I had ridden in a few of them during Operations Desert Shield and Desert Storm—several lifetimes ago. The canvas bench seats felt the same as they had then. The aluminum tubes that ran along the front of the seats felt the same behind my knees as did the cargo netting behind my back. The dull vibration of the airframe felt the same, and the low-pitched hum of the four turboprop engines through the foam earplugs in my ears sounded the same.

It all felt the same.

And none of it felt the same.

Instead of a flightsuit or a dress blue uniform, I wore black fatigues and combat boots. I had an Airborne Systems MC-6 tactical parachute strapped to my back and a matching reserve parachute strapped to the front of me. There was a rucksack clipped to the harness with weapons and several magazines of ammunition secured inside. And, of course, there was also the helmet I was wearing, a version of the same HGU-55 helmet I had worn for nearly my entire flying career in the USAF and, attached to it, the same oxygen mask I had worn as well. The mask was clamped to my face and I was breathing pure oxygen because the C-130 was unpressurized.

We were prebreathing for a HALO jump into Miguel's hacienda. HALO—high altitude low opening. We were going to jump out of the C-130 at 30,000 feet, and fall for approximately two minutes, and then open the chutes at about three 3,000 feet. I was the center jumper in the ten man stick.

The rest were an OSI special ops team.

Or so I surmised. There may have been SEALs or Delta Force members along with a few OSI personnel who specialized in counterintelligence. I didn't know and I didn't care. They and the C-130 had shown up in the evening after my appearance at the OSI detachment at Luke. There were nine of them, seven men and two women, and they were cool, collected, and apparently competent. Each one shook my hand firmly and introduced himself/herself professionally without saying their names, ranks, or titles. They showed appropriate deference to my rank and displayed no OSI-style attitude at all.

The briefing had taken place in the very same OSI "interview" room I had been interrogated in years ago. Smith and Amrine had provided the imagery of Miguel's hacienda, and I had provided the interior detail since I had been there before. The CIA also supplied some infrared time surveillance to help to discern the number and schedule of the roving patrols.

"What's the mission?" the team leader had asked. He was a young-looking blond guy with a crew cut, a square jaw, and piercing blue eyes. He had introduced himself with two words: 'Number One.'

"Simple," I had replied, looking him right in the eyes.

"Find and kill Miguel Hidalgo."

He nodded, as if the answer was exactly what he'd expected. "Anyone to extract?"

I felt my mouth moving to say "no" but then a conversation Tappan and I had played itself through my mind and I paused. But then I doubted what I was thinking. I was just there, like eight months ago. And I hadn't seen her.

Or had I? There had been a glance on one of the walks I'd been permitted to take without escort or accompaniment. Had I seen her? Walking out of one of the bedrooms? Without proper contextualization, it's very difficult for the brain to process images that it knows. At the time, I hadn't recognized her. I hadn't been prepared to recognize her. But it was highly possible she was there.

"Well?" Square Jaw asked.

I nodded. "One. Maybe." And then I thought about Brock. Could he be there as well? I shook my head involuntarily. If he was, there was no guarantee he was on our side. In fact, if he was there, that would confirm the fact that he wasn't on our side. "No. One will be it, if she's even there."

"Copy that," he answered. "We'll have a special ops MH-60 orbiting off the coast. It will land on the tarmac in front of Miguel's hangar twenty minutes from the time we hit the ground. We're not going to have much time for anything extraneous."

"Noted," I said.

The mission brief began then. Four members of the team would deal with the exterior guards and defenses. The other five members of the team, plus me, would take the house.

"Who can we expect on the inside?" Number One asked.

"Ramon the Rock will probably be there," Smith had said. "Are you familiar?"

Number One had shaken his head.

"Out of the country during our last operation against

Miguel last year," Smith said. "He's six foot eight and 300 pounds of mean hombre. I personally saw him take a chest shot from a .338 Lapua Magnum inside of one hundred yards and get away."

Square Jaw's eyes actually widened slightly. "Jesus," he said. "We didn't bring an elephant gun as part of our standard package."

Smith looked at me and I smiled back at him. "We may have already sort of taken care of that," he said.

Square Jaw shrugged. "It doesn't matter. Any man will go down if you put enough lead into him."

Then Square Jaw addressed his team and briefed the mission to the rest of the team, including the drop zone, the jump, the rendezvous on the ground, the tactical plan, and contingencies. It was thorough, professional, and took him all of about fifteen minutes. I paid close attention, although I didn't understand much of it. When it was over, he looked across the table at me.

He addressed me. "How many jumps do you have?"

"Five real ones," I had said. "And three ejections."

His eyebrows raised at the last bit. "How fast?"

"Two of them were below 300 knots," I said. "One was well above 500."

He nodded and allowed himself a grim smile. Apparently I had passed some kind of test. Although I was surprised he didn't have that information already. The OSI seemed to have compartmentalization issues also.

What followed was an instruction session on how to use the MC-6 and a discussion of the timeline of a HALO jump. They decided, among themselves, that I'd jump solo, not in tandem, and that I'd jump in the center of the stick so they could keep an eye on me and give me some coaching if I needed it. They also asked me to describe the inside of the house and the probable location of Miguel.

I drew a rough sketch of what I remembered. There was the large great room, the long staircase, the bedrooms upstairs, and the study downstairs.

"I never saw the master bedroom when I was there the last time," I said. "But it will be at the back of the house so that it has an ocean view and will be either downstairs near the study or upstairs above it. My money is on downstairs, because that would place Miguel farther from any guests who might be in the house and also closer to his study."

Square Jaw nodded. He then proceeded to discuss how the entry team would go about clearing the house, a discussion that I was left out of. It seemed they didn't think they'd need my help. For my own part, I didn't particularly care. All I wanted was to see Miguel die. And if we could get Ramon the Rock in the process, that'd be a bonus.

The red light in the C-130's cargo hold came on, indicating we were nearing the drop zone. The nine members of the team released their seatbelts and stood up. I stood up as well, donning my gloves as I did so. The inside of the aircraft was unpressurized yet had remained warm, thanks to the airplane's heating system. But the normal air temperature at 30,000 feet, at the standard lapse rate, was about -46 degrees Celsius and about -51 degrees Fahrenheit. Pretty fucking cold. So in a few minutes, when the cargo ramp was opened, it was going to feel like the arctic in the transport's cargo hold. Fortunately, as soon as we jumped out, we'd accelerate downward at 32 feet/second squared, so our time in the cold of the upper atmosphere would be very limited. It was a good thing. The fatigues we were wearing weren't made of heavy material, and given the temperatures we were likely to encounter on the ground in Baja California in July, heavier clothes would have only gotten in the way.

"Six minutes!" One of OSI team members yelled, one of the females, holding one hand with five fingers and the other with one finger up to ensure the message was received by all of us in the cargo hold. I noticed she was plugged into the ship's intercom, listening to the flight deck crew. That made her designated jumpmaster for this flight. Even with just her eyes visible above the oxygen mask, there was something about the coffee-colored skin that made her familiar. Her eyes were piercingly blue and the combination of eyes and skin color was quite memorable. I didn't remember getting a good look at her earlier and wondered why I had not done so. She was the sort of woman men pay attention to.

We all lined up, one behind the other, in two columns facing the aft end of the aircraft. I was the third person in the right column; and as I walked into place, the female jumpmaster came over to me and very objectively checked and pulled at all my straps and buckles, ensuring that they were all secure. Then she keyed the mic in her oxygen mask on the intergroup frequency so that I could hear her.

"Get into the body arch as soon as you can," she said. "Jump when it's your turn, hit the arch, and hold it. If you do, you'll stabilize. You'll probably see some of the other guys roll to get stable but don't worry about that. Just hit the arch and hold it. When you see 3,000 feet on your wrist altimeter, pull your ripcord. And once your chute deploys, steer it like you steered the other chutes you've used. When you hit the ground, do your normal PLF. But it won't be too bad, because these chutes have a slower descent rate than the old ones did. Remember to jettison it as soon as your feet touch the ground."

I nodded at her and was glad she couldn't see me swallow as hard as I did. "I'll do my best," I said.

"We know you will," she said. She almost turned away for a second but then she turned back to me and keyed her mic again. "We're glad to be here," she said. "The boss probably didn't say that but we all are. We want to kick that Mexican asshole's ass."

The frequency she was on was an open channel between all ten of us. After she finished speaking, I looked around and the remaining members of the team were watching us and nodding. Even Square Jaw, at the head of my column, was nodding. I could almost sense his eyes gleaming behind the helmet visor.

"Thanks," I said.

The jumpmaster disconnected and took her place at the end of the line on the left side. She began to shake out her arms and her legs. Some of the folks in line squatted to flex their leg muscles and others bent over to touch their hands to the floor. The atmosphere in the hold was one of calm but intense expectation.

Suddenly, a loud mechanical whine filled the air as the C-130's rear cargo doors opened and the ramp lowered, allowing the frigid air from the outside to fill the open space. Small puffs of condensed air became visible as the members of the team exhaled and the vapor of their breath escaped the exhalation valves on their oxygen masks. The roar of the airflow outside was barely audible through the helmet and the earplugs I was wearing. As I looked out through the doors and over the ramp, I saw that a frail moon dimly lit the night sky. The light seemed to be filtered through some high clouds above us.

"Thirty seconds!" the jumpmaster yelled. "Lights out!"

The dim light that was illuminating the C-130's cargo hold extinguished.

"Power up!" Number One commanded.

I lowered the night vision goggles that were hinged to my helmet down into place over my eyes and activated them with the control knob on the side. As the cargo bay came back into focus, bathed in the artificial green light of the NVGs, I could see the other team members doing the same.

I felt for all my gear once again and verified the position of my ripcord. And for the first time, I felt a small tinge of apprehension. I wasn't really worried with what would happen on the ground. I was more concerned with the jump itself. Ejections were one thing. You didn't really have to think about them. But jumping out of a perfectly good airplane was a different thing entirely.

Another light came on in the cargo bay and the jumpmaster yelled, "Go!" over the intercom. For just a moment, I didn't move. But in the next moment, the training and discipline kicked in and I was out the door and into the cold night air without even thinking about it.

There was no sensation of falling at all. I felt a sense of familiarity from my free-fall jumps at the USAF Academy long ago. When you exit an aircraft with forward velocity, your body initially carries that velocity until your vector of motion transitions to one of pure descent. It felt like I was in a wind tunnel, with currents of air buffeting my clothes and gear. There was also no real ground rush. Although my eyes, through the NVGs, detected that my vertical perspective was changing, it seemed to be almost gradual and not rapid at all. Around me, the members of the team were spread into a perfect formation with just a few feet between us. Somehow I had managed to do just as I had been instructed and arched my body as soon as I exited the C-130. Now I was stabilized and falling, in my place, next to everyone else.

Wonders never cease, I thought.

As I looked toward the ground, I could see the coastline next to Miguel's hacienda beckoning to us from far below, bathed in NVG green. There was the inlet that I remembered and the part of the coast immediately to the north and west where the hacienda sat, with its spectacular view of the Pacific Ocean. When I was there last fall, I had arrived at night, spent my time in the house or in the hangar, and then departed with a quick turn out over the Pacific Ocean. While I knew something about the inside of the house and the hangar immediately to the east, I had no idea about any of the surrounding terrain features. I remembered a huge, immaculately manicured lawn and a Roman-style pool behind the house, and that was about it. But after studying the imagery that the CIA had provided earlier, I saw that the terrain around the inlet and the hacienda was mostly sand and rock with a few volcano-shaped hills. Apparently Miguel had spared no expense to turn his hacienda into a slice of paradise. I wondered if he'd built a golf course somewhere on the grounds.

The drop zone we selected was about one kilometer south of the hacienda, on a narrow peninsula between the inlet and the ocean. The terrain there was slightly lower than that of the hacienda, and we were hoping to make our approach unseen. The infrared video feed provided by the CIA didn't show much activity outside of the hacienda and it seemed, at first glance, that defense and defenders might be limited. I hoped our luck would hold.

"Ten thousand feet," said the jumpmaster in my headset.

I was stunned. We had fallen 20,000 feet already. Time flies when you're plummeting to earth.

"Standby," she said a few moments later. "Pearce, I'll call your pull.'

"Roger," I said weakly.

I moved my left arm from beside my body at a 90-degree angle to above my head at approximately the same time as I moved my right hand to my harness and located the metal ring of the ripcord. I allowed my gloved fingers to wrap themselves around the oval ring and then pressed my hand against my body.

Around me, I could see parachutes deploying and bodies decelerating and being pulled upward. I found I was impatient to pull my own cord. I wanted to stop falling. Looking downward, the ground now seemed impossibly close; and through the NVGs, I could clearly see the outline of individual pools and inlets on the section of coast we were aiming for. I cast a glance at the hacienda. It was barely lit.

I hope they're fucking here, I thought in a moment of panic.

"Pull," said the jumpmaster.

I reflexively yanked the ripcord away from my body and waited for the instant deceleration of parachute deployment.

But it didn't come. I could barely hear a rustling of material behind my head but the parachute had clearly malfunctioned.

"Streamer," said the jumpmaster dispassionately. "You can go for your reserve immediately and risk entanglement or cut your main away and deploy the reserve." She might as well have been reading the local weather forecast.

I glanced at my wrist and saw the digital display counting downward through 2000.

Fuck!

Several things ran through my mind, the first of which was that the OSI might have intentionally sabotaged my parachute. I quickly dismissed that thought, because we had all taken our chutes from the same rack, randomly. But then I remembered watching my fellow jumpers fall to earth during my academy parachuting class and seeing more than one chute malfunction. I also remembered I had seen entanglements when reserve chutes were deployed too quickly.

1200 feet.

I hit and held the canopy release buckles on the harness and suddenly I was free-falling again.

800 feet.

I found the ripcord on the side of the reserve pack in front of me and pulled it immediately. My body felt like it was yanked to a near halt as the reserve deployed. In a wave of déjà vu, I recalled the ejection from the T-38 above Santa

Catalina Island eight months ago and the incredible trauma my body had suffered. My joints, though repaired and healed, sent me several messages of extreme discomfort. Maybe they were warning me not to mess them up again.

I blinked and recovered my vision as the wrist altimeter counted through 200 feet. Apparently I was going to be the first one to the ground. The beach area that was to be our drop zone appeared in front of me, and I barely had time to get my feet and knees together for the parachute landing fall when my boots hit the sand. I rolled onto my side and then onto my back and lay still.

Thin, wispy clouds intermittently covered the moon and starlit sky above me. The NVGs amplified the dim light of the faraway orbs, and the sky looked like a sea of green dots of light. It was an awesome sight. Even with the helmet and earplugs, I could hear the sounds of waves lapping at the sand and somewhere in the distance, the caw of a seagull.

Jesus, I thought to myself. *That was close.*

I rolled up to my knees, unbuckled the harness, and began to slip out of if before I realized that I hadn't disconnected my rucksack. Apparently a little post-jump stress was sinking in.

Come on, Pearce! Wake the fuck up!

A few moments later the parachute harness was off, the rucksack was open, and I was taking care of the first order of business: strapping weapons to myself. I loaded a magazine into the suppressed UMP, charged the weapon, and then slipped my arms and neck through the weapon's harness. Through the helmet's headset, I could hear dull thuds as the other members of the team landed on the beach around me. Then I remembered that I still had the helmet and oxygen mask on.

Oh for God's sake.

I unbuckled the oxygen mask, unsnapped the chinstrap, and extracted my head from the helmet, suddenly aware of how dark the night sky was around me without the benefit of the NVGs. For a moment I forgot how I was going to connect the NVGs to me again and felt a knot of panic in my gut. But then I remembered the hat-like head harness for the NVGs in the rucksack. I donned it, snapped the NVGs on it, disconnected the helmet's radio cord from the transceiver on my belt, and plugged the cord from the NVG harness's integral headset into the transceiver. I seated the headset's earbuds just in time to hear Number One's voice on the frequency.

"Everybody make it? One's good."

The team members answered in order, with me chiming in at number five.

"Stow your gear. We move out in three minutes."

I hurriedly strapped my sidearm into the holster on my right thigh and checked the security of the silenced Colt Commander under my left arm. Then I retrieved my reserve parachute, my parachute harness, and helmet and stowed them in the rucksack for easier carry. The goal, apparently, was to leave no trace of our existence. I looked around as the rest of the team members stowed their parachutes and wondered where my main chute had landed and hoped it was nearby and not out to sea.

A dark, irregular shape lying where the water met the sand caught my eye and I trotted over to it. It was my main chute, soaked with water and tangled in a patch of seaweed that flowed from the beach into the ocean. I quickly wrapped the parachute up in my arms and dragged it over to my rucksack. Then I stuffed the parachute into the sack, noting how heavy it was now that it and the accompanying straps were waterlogged. But as I loaded the still -undeployed canopy into the sack, I noted something odd. There was a single line of parachute cord completely wrapped around the canopy and tied off.

It wasn't my imagination. The parachute had definitely

been sabotaged.

Well fuck, I thought to myself. *That changes things a little.*

I found myself longing for the special CIA Blackberry so that I could type out a quick text to Smith but mobile devices had been prohibited for this mission in the event we were captured or killed.

I felt a presence next to me and looked up to see the female jumpmaster. She was shaking her head, and she moved her mic away from her mouth so that only I could hear her. "I don't know what happened," she whispered earnestly. "I checked every one of those chutes myself!"

"Shit happens," I muttered back. It seemed to be the only thing to say.

She continued to shake her head. "Not like this. Not on my watch. And," she looked around at her fellow team members, "that's the first time I've seen or heard of an MC-6 with a streamer malfunction."

I looked at her with the unspoken question in my eyes. *Who?*

She looked around again and shook her head a final time. Then she reached down and grabbed her rucksack.

"Let's move out," One's voice came over the headset. "Keep your spacing,"

We trudged north with several yards between each of us, up the beach and then onto the small rock formations beyond. Each of us had a weapon at the ready and our rucksacks over our shoulders. As we moved, I found myself thinking of each of the team members and wondering who the traitor or traitor(s) could be. With the exception of Number One, Square Jaw, and the jumpmaster, I hadn't gotten a decent look at any of them. Why was that?

"Stop," said One, "objective in sight. Rally here."

We all moved up and gathered behind a row of large rocks that were about shoulder high. Then we peered over and around the rocks to see what lay before us.

We were at the end of Miguel's expansive rear lawn, which, in spite of his financial troubles, still appeared to be immaculately manicured. There was a large gazebo in the middle of the lawn with a huge chiminea in the middle of it and several comfortable easy chairs around it. Beyond the gazebo was the huge Roman pool and beyond that magnificent southwestern mansion where I had spent a few fateful days last November. Miguel's manias and dreams notwithstanding, his hacienda was a work of art. I found myself regretting the damage that I knew was coming.

Apparently though, Miguel didn't want to let on that he was in residence, so only a few of the many exterior lights were illuminated. Additionally, it seemed that nearly all the curtains in the many windows of the hacienda's ocean-facing side were drawn. A curious occurrence given the view they beheld.

"Pearce!" One said. "You still think the French doors in the back are the best way in?"

"Yes," I answered. "And there are two and possibly three sets to choose from. One set in Miguel's study, one in the great room, and one in his bedroom if it's on the ground floor like I think it is."

"Roger," One answered. "Then that's the way we'll go in."

"Change of plan here. Four and Six, gazebo. Set up an observation and firing position. Stay off freq unless you see something."

"Four copies," said a deep male voice.

"Six copies," answered a female voice with a slight touch of Alabama accent.

"Seven, you, Eight, Nine, and Ten work your way around the front of the house. Deal with any patrols you find and get control of the LZ for the helo. Switch to secondary freq while you're clearing but check in on primary when you're done."

"Seven," answered another male voice.

"Two, Three, Pearce, and I will perform the entry. We'll wait until you're secure before we blow the doors. Don't keep us waiting too long."

"We'll get it done fast boss," Seven replied, and this time there was a hint of Philly accent in the voice. Something about the pronunciation of the letter 'L.'

I smiled to myself. Maybe I had been a linguist in a former life.

"Do you want us to try to cut the main power so you can breach with NVGs?" he asked.

One looked at me and I shook my head. "Miguel will have thought of that," I said. "There will be at least two backup sources of power if I know him. He's spent some time in prison. He'll never allow himself to be surprised again."

"Copy that," Seven said. "We're out of here. Guys, switch to the backup freq."

Four and Six left the shelter of the rocks and worked their way around the ocean side of the formation. Seven and his team made their way around the rocks toward the right and headed toward the front of the house and toward the airstrip.

And One, Two, Three, and I, remained behind the cover of the rocks.

"Lose the NVGs," One commanded. "Stow them in your bags."

We all peeled our NVGs off and placed them in our rucksacks. Then we crouched behind the rocks as we waited for Four and Seven's teams to complete their missions. As we waited, I had a chance to regard two of my team members at close range, even if the light was somewhat dim. The female jumpmaster knelt next to Number One and I had a chance to look at her in profile. I was usually very good with faces but I couldn't seem to place hers.

Damn, I thought. *Where have I seen her?*

Between her and me was the one known as Three. He seemed to be of average height with light brown hair, a normal complexion, and dark eyes. He had a very intense expression on his face as he regarded the scene around us and seemed to be intent on avoiding eye contact with me. His face too seemed familiar. But the feeling was different from the one I had looking at Number Two. With Two, I knew I'd seen her somewhere, it was just a question of where and when. With Three, I didn't think I'd seen his face, but I had seen a face very much like it. And I couldn't seem to remember where or when that had occurred either.

Jesus, Pearce. You have killed too many brain cells with Scotch.

"One, Four," I heard the radio in my headset crackle.

"Go, Four," One replied.

"Observation and firing position established. We detect no movement behind the target or in the adjoining areas."

"One copies. Seven, say status."

There was silence. Apparently Seven was still on the other frequency.

Five more minutes passed. The night stayed silent. There were no alarms, no yells, no screams, and no gunshots. It was quiet. Almost too quiet.

"One, Seven," said the Philly voice. He sounded a little strained.

"Go, Seven."

"LZ secure. One patrol neutralized."

There should be more men here. The thought suddenly inserted itself in my brain. *There were more the last time. Why aren't there more now? Especially with the Chinese... Jesus!*

I put my hand over my mic and half-walked, half-slid over to where One was crouching.

"Do you have an alternate means of egress, other than the

helo pick up?"

I saw One's face take on a surprised and irritated expression. "That's a need to know thing, Pearce," he said. "If we need to..."

I put my face next to his so that only he could hear me and whispered, "Call them. This is a trap. Miguel completely suckered us. Call your other men back. Do it now."

One tilted his head and looked back at me as he processed what I had told him. He seemed to ponder my words for a second and then he opened his mouth to speak. A ragged red hole appeared in the center of his forehead and red, gooey tissue exploded onto the rock behind him. The sound of the suppressed pistol shot behind me was almost an afterthought.

I turned to see Three standing a respectful distance away from Two and me, holding a Glock pistol with a long suppressor on it. The weapon was eerily similar to the one I had used in Miguel's camp earlier that week. As he watched us, Three spoke a few words in Spanish over the radio. Instantly, two massive spotlights on the top of the hacienda illuminated. A moment or two later, the loud, booming report of a heavy sniper rifle cut through the tranquil ocean air, followed a fraction of a second later by a second report. It was the same sound I had heard at the rest stop in Maryland a few weeks ago. And I was pretty sure the same man was standing behind it—none other than Ramon "The Rock" Pétreo. Four and Six were dead. The fates of Seven and his team were uncertain, but I was betting the strained sound of Seven's voice was due to the fact that he had a gun to his head.

"We will go to see my uncle now, Mr. Pearce," Three said, with a gleam in his eye. "He is waiting for you inside."

Holy shit! I thought. *How many fucking relatives does Miguel have?*

"So he is inside after all?" Two asked. "I mean really inside?"

Three nodded, with a triumphant smile on his face. "He knew that Mr. Pearce would come after him. He is in his master suite, surrounded by the most modern medical equipment and many, many guards." He gestured to the terrain around the mansion. "And surrounding the mansion is the entire Seventh Mexican regiment. All loyal to Miguel. All prepared to die at his command."

"And that would be the first floor master suite?" Two asked. "The last set of windows on the left here?"

Three looked at her with impatience. "Yes. Yes. What difference does it make?" he asked. "You'll be seeing it soon. It will be the last thing you see."

"Don't think so," Two said.

The handle of a stiletto knife suddenly appeared in Three's left eye. He took a step or two backward as his brain attempted to cope with the intruder and then his brain stopped working, and the suppressed pistol slipped from his fingers and dropped to the rock. Then he fell to his knees and onto his face. And as his face hit the rock, the point of the stiletto penetrated the back of his skull and the pointed, silver blade emerged into the moonlight.

"I knew I recognized you," I said to the woman.

She smiled and winked at me. "Surprised you did with the facial prosthetic makeup," she said. "But I'm glad. I had to try to look like a member of their normal crew."

"Still Sharona? Or should I call you something else?" Her name, when I had known her the last time, had been Sharona Brown. She was the deadliest woman, maybe even the deadliest human, I had ever seen.

"Doesn't matter," she said, kneeling to get her rucksack. "It seems like you and I are the only two left alive. And we've got a mission to take care of."

"How far out is the strike?" I asked.

She pulled back her sleeve and looked at her watch. "About

two minutes," she said. "And we'll have to designate for it."

"Platform and weapon?"

"MQ-9 Reaper with Hellfire missiles. Low altitude launch and better standoff, also a smaller warhead than a JDAM or laser-guided bomb. Looks a little more like it could have been some sort of random explosion."

"I guess I could ask why I wasn't briefed on all of this, but I've given up trying to understand how you guys compartmentalize information."

Sharona pulled something that looked like a skeletonized rifle out of her rucksack and tossed it to me.

"Laser designator housed in that thing that looks like a telescopic sight. Just aim at the last row of windows and pull the trigger. The laser code is preset."

I offered it back to her.

"You need to do it," I said. "I need to get in that house and look for someone."

She shook her head. "No. You need to do it. Because as soon as you show your head, Ramon the Rock is going to blow it off. I'm going to keep his head down with this." She removed a short rifle from her rucksack and opened the bolt, which was at the rear end of the rifle near the stock and well behind the pistol grip and trigger.

I must have been staring. The rifle seemed so tiny, and I knew Ramon would have his trademark Barrett .50.

She smiled at me. "Size does matter," she said. "But in this case, smaller is better. This is a Desert Tactical Arms Compact Sniper System in .308 Winchester with a twenty-power night scope. It has a twenty-two-inch barrel, just like a conventional rifle, but because the action is set aft and the trigger is set forward, it's shorter than an M-4."

She closed the bolt and I heard the sound of a round being chambered. Then she looked at her watch again.

"Shit. We've got less than a minute." She pointed toward

the right side of the rock formation. "Get ready to lase. As soon as you hear my first shot, head's up and hit your trigger."

"But I need…"

"No time," she said. "Besides, the missile will distract the hell out of them and cause all sorts of chaos. Then we can both go into the house and get whoever it is you want to get."

I nodded and quickly made my way around the side of the rock formation nearest the house. I had no sooner gotten to the edge and peered over the top of it then I heard a "chunk" sound in the rock next to my head and a shard of rock embedded itself into my left cheek. It was then that I heard the low boom of the Barrett rolling over the lawn in front of me as I ducked back down behind the rock.

Ramon had almost killed me.

Then there was another loud booming sound from my left as Sharona opened fire. One of the lights on top of the roof was immediately extinguished. Ramon returned fire. I heard a ricochet or a thud somewhere to my left.

"Here goes nothing," I said to no one in particular.

I edged around the side of the rock this time, placed the stock of the designator to my shoulder and the scope to my eye. I located the last row of windows on the far left side of the hacienda, placed the crosshairs in the low-light scope on them, and pulled the trigger. A small green dot flickered at the side of my field of vision, which I assumed meant the laser was on.

CHUNK!

Another round from Ramon's rifle slammed into the rock near me, and I felt the sting of more shards of rock. I clenched my jaw and held the designator on target. Ramon's Barrett was probably the semiautomatic version, and Sharon's weapon was bolt action. Even if she was really quick, she still wouldn't be able to match his rate of fire.

BOOM!

Sharona's weapon fired a second time. The other spotlight on the roof was extinguished and now the rear of the hacienda was in near darkness again. I felt the oddest need to duck and without thinking, I did so, keeping the designator on target as I squatted.

CHUNK!

The rock immediately beside and beyond where my head had been, mere seconds ago, exploded into a mist of small pebbles and dust. The low rumbling sound made it to my ears again.

Any fucking time, I thought.

In my peripheral vision, I detected a light of some kind, moving very quickly. But before my brain could attempt to identify it, a finger of fire zipped over the lawn leaving a trail of smoke in its wake and slammed into the lower left window of the hacienda. The explosion occurred a nanosecond later, and the lower left corner of the hacienda transformed from a structure into a mass of flying glass, wood, flame, and various pieces and parts of things and people.

"Time to go," said a voice in my ear. "Toss the designator but make sure you have that UMP ready. We'll need it."

I sprang from my crouch, and Sharona and I ran down the edge of the yard, around the pool house, and toward the French doors of the great room.

"How's your throwing arm?" Sharona asked as we ran.

"Good enough I think," I answered.

She handed me a small fragmentation grenade with her left hand as she pulled another one off her harness with her right hand. "Get ready," she said. "We need to do this together."

She stopped me as we reached the side of the pool house, about ten yards from the French doors.

"Pull the pin," she said, as she nonchalantly yanked the small metal ring free with a gloved finger. She could have been twirling her car keys.

I pulled the pin from the grenade with my left index finger and dropped it to the ground, listing to it ping as it hit the pavement.

"Toss it," she said. Without waiting to see if I complied, she wound up and threw a beautiful fastball directly through the middle of the right French door. I watched one of the panes of glass disintegrate as the dull gray sphere sailed through it and into the room beyond.

I cocked my arm and threw a gentle lob that chinked through the second to uppermost pane in the middle of the left door and clattered on the tile floor beyond.

"Oh yes, and the most important part," she said. "Get the hell out of the way."

She pulled me around the side of the pool house away from the doors and pushed me up against the stuccoed wall, pressing her body against mine. For a few seconds, I could feel the warmth of her on my body and her hot breath in my ear. Even through the fatigues, the gear, the sweat, and the grime, there was electricity between us, probably fueled in no small measure by the adrenaline singing through our veins. I put my arms around her and drew her in more tightly against me and she came willingly, putting her hands on both cheeks of my ass and pulling my pelvis to hers.

"We still have unfinished business from last time," she said, with just a hint of breathlessness as she lifted her face to mine.

"We do," I said, bringing my mouth down on hers.
TH-THUMP!

The two grenades exploded nearly as one, and she was off me, getting her hands onto her M-4, and inclining her head toward the doors.

"Let's move, lover boy," she said. "And shoulder that UMP. We'll have company to deal with."

We stepped across the concrete pool deck, now strewn with

wood and glass from the explosions, and toward the now open entry to the great room. As we came through what remained of the doors, I took in the magnificent room again, with its beamed ceilings, rich walls, and sumptuous southwestern furnishings. And of course, there was the bar area, to my right, with the painting of General Santa Anna on the wall, the place where Miguel and I had sipped Scotch together and he'd offered me command of his Air Force, nine months ago.

Times had certainly changed.

Now furniture was overturned and walls were scarred. And there were several bodies lying on the tile near the doors, some intact, others not so much.

"Check left," Sharona said as we came through the door. "Let's make sure the missile did what it was supposed to."

I nodded and we headed down the short hallway to the left.

"Study first," I said as we approached the double doors.

"Roger," she said, pulling a grenade from her harness, arming it, and tossing it though the barely open doors. "Fire in the hole!"

"But what about…" I asked as I flattened myself against a brick wall to the outside of the study.

"Prisoners wouldn't be kept in there," she said as she shoved herself next to me on the wall.

THUMP!

Explosions don't sound the same in person as they do on movies or television. Grenades are often depicted making huge explosions and belching fire and smoke. In the open, the sound is more like a sharp crack and inside a building, with walls to contain the explosion, it sounded more like dull thud.

We came off the wall, and I kicked through the remains of the rich wooden doors and regarded what was left of the beautiful office. The desk was overturned and the windows in the back were shattered. Papers, books and pieces of both covered the floor. But other than damaged furniture and shelves, the office was empty.

"Clear," I said.

Sharona was already moving past me and down the short hallway. Or what was left of it. A good portion of the wall to the left was missing and wall studs and pieces of drywall were all that remained. Chunks of wood, glass, and drywall coated the hallway floor, and there were paintings and knick-knacks strewn about. Here and there, a miscellaneous piece of a human being lay among the debris. I saw some fingers, an eyeball, a piece of black-haired scalp, and even what looked like a tongue. It was amazing how indiscriminate explosions could be.

We stepped through what remained of a large set of ornate double doors and into Miguel's master suite. There was a high-beamed ceiling and a commanding view of the Pacific Ocean through a series of large picture windows. None of which remained intact. There was a small library in one corner, on the wall the room shared with the study, and I wondered if there was perhaps a hidden door between the two. In the middle of the room was a sunken floor which appeared to have been a retreat area with a sofa and a few chairs. The right side of the room was where the bed would have been, with a raised platform and pieces of very high-end furniture lying about.

Now there was only decimation in the huge open space. There were pieces of debris, furniture, wood, glass, and more drywall chunks and dust everywhere. It was as if a giant fist had come into the room and pulverized everything.

I looked around at the devastation. "Jesus," I said. "One hellfire did this? That's not a big missile. The warhead can't be any larger than—"

"It's a thermobaric warhead," Sharona said, interrupting me. She seemed to be studying pieces of wreckage for something. "It works like a fuel-air bomb. Very devastating in enclosed spaces."

"I guess," I said. "I had no idea." I watched her kick a few pieces of debris with her feet.

"What are you looking for?" I asked.

"Well, now that we're here," she answered, "it'd be nice to have some proof we actually got him."

"Good call," I said. "But we probably don't have much time if we're going to complete our other errands."

"So where's the damn bathroom?" she asked, suddenly moving toward the area of the room to the right of where we had entered.

I didn't understand what she was talking about. "Bathroom?" I asked. "What the fuck do you need a bathroom..." I started to say. And then I remembered telling Lena to get in the bathtub back in my quarters when a shootout was imminent. "Oh yeah. If they had time to hide him they would have—"

"Now you're thinking," Sharona said, moving toward what was left of the only other doorway in the room, on the wall near the raised sleeping area.

The double doors were surprisingly intact and they looked formidable. Sharona reached for the door handle on the right door, seemed to think better of it, and then produced a length of parachute cord from her belt. She looped it around the door handle and then stepped back so that she was out of the left side of frame of the door completely. She motioned me to the right side of the doorframe. When I got into place, she pulled on the string and rotated the door handle.

Instantly, as if an "on" switch had been activated, automatic weapons fire from inside the bathroom perforated the door. The firing continued for several seconds. Whoever was on the inside apparently had a lot of ammunition and wasn't afraid to use it. As the firing stopped, the sounds of the last few shell casings hitting the tiled floor on the inside of the bathroom were audible, even with the ringing in my ears from all the loud noises I'd experienced that day. Due to either the accuracy or volume of fire from the inside, there were several holes in the door large enough to put a fist through.

Sharona smiled at me with a gleam in her eye and tossed me a grenade. Then she made a motion of pulling the pin and the mouthed the words "Wait two" and then made a motion of putting the grenade through the door. I smiled back at her as I caught the heavy metal orb and pulled the pin a second after it landed in my hands. I placed it in my left hand, squatted down, and reached over to place my hand just below the nearest hole that looked large enough. I released the spring-loaded handle and counted to two. Then I stuffed the grenade into the hole and dove over to my side of the doorframe.

Inside the bathroom, the grenade clattered to the title, and I heard a voice yell "Joder!"

THUMP!

The doors to the bathroom blew open and debris and dust flew out of the small space.

Sharona didn't wait a moment. She immediately shouldered the M-4 and stepped into the opening. Two bursts of automatic weapons fire followed, both from her weapon.

"Probably overkill," she said after a moment. "But it never hurts to be sure."

I stepped into the doorway next to her and saw two Mexican men, one lying on the floor and the other sitting up against an ornate vanity and sink combination. The bodies of both were perforated with shrapnel in addition to several 5.56 millimeter rounds from Sharona's weapon.

The bodies and debris near the door notwithstanding, the bathroom had seemed to survive the melee thus far and it, like the rest of the house, was beautiful with hand-painted ceramic tile and wood lining the walls and a tiled floor that could have been imported from a monastery somewhere. Immediately to the right was a large shower with several shower heads and benches, and enough room for at least four people.

And in the far corner of the bathroom, on the other side of the vanity, beyond the toilet/bidet closet and a large dressing area was a huge sunken tub.

We walked toward it carefully, clearing the nooks and crannies of the bathroom on our respective sides. As we approached, I saw Sharona palm another grenade and pull the pin, but she kept the loop from the pin around one of her fingers. Apparently, the grenade was the backup plan. As she crept up on the left, I crept up on the right with the UMP against my shoulder and the red dot of the aiming reticle trained on the edge of the tub. Then, as the far wall of the tub became visible, Sharona shuffled her feet loudly and moved forward. I moved forward as well and saw a wiry man with a Beretta pistol lying in the tub and attempting to aim the weapon in Sharona's direction.

I touched the trigger on the UMP and a few rounds of .45 ACP ended his day.

Then we both moved forward some more and found what we were looking for lying in the bottom of his tub, next to the body of his last guardian. Miguel Hidalgo, once the most powerful drug lord in Mexico, lay on an air mattress with both arms and legs in casts and a neck brace on. His once vibrant skin looked like parchment and there were needles and wires stuck into him in too many places to count. Part of his scalp had been shaved off and there was a scar indicating that there had been some cranial surgery, probably as a result of the helicopter crash. And while he looked helpless, his chest moved up and down with regular breathing, and the dark eyes burned with hatred.

He was very much alive.

"So you think you have won, Pearce?" His voice was raspy but steady. I wondered how much effort it took for him to speak.

"I'm not the one who made it personal, Miguel," I said.

"You think," he coughed and grimaced in pain, "you think you can destroy my life's work...my family's life's work...and have it not be personal?"

"I had a mission last fall. That's all. You got in the way. But then you threatened the only two people I really care about. That's when it got personal for me. Until then, you were just a job."

"Just a job," he said mockingly. A wicked smile came across his features. "And that is what I gave to my little brother where you are concerned. A job." He coughed again and there were droplets of blood visible on his dehydrated lips.

His little brother? Ramon was his little brother?

"You see, Ramon, he does not feel things. Everything to him is a job. But where killing people is involved, it is a job that he loves. He lives for it."

"Well, he was on the roof of this house when the missile hit," Sharona said. "He's probably not living much now."

Miguel laughed. It was a horrible sound, both maniacal and hollow at the same time. "You think that killed, Ramon? You cannot kill Ramon," he said. "You cannot kill him, you cannot control him, you cannot stop him. Ramon, he is a force of nature." Miguel coughed again and more blood was visible on his lips. He opened his eyes wide and then focused them on me. "And he will never stop coming. He will come for you and for your woman and for your child. He will never stop coming."

"We'll see about that," I said evenly. "I've got something special for him." I saw Sharona look over at me. "Something very special."

"You will die alone, Pearce. Ramon will kill you last. And he will kill you slowly and make you look at the heads of your woman and child as you die."

The rage took control of me again. But this time it was gentle and subtle. I didn't consciously command the UMP into the firing position but it had arrived there. I didn't consciously place the red aiming reticle on Miguel's forehead, but there it was. And I didn't consciously squeeze the trigger, but the gun was suddenly firing and Miguel Hidalgo's head was disappearing in a cloud of blood, gore, and bathtub tile.

The UMP's action locked open as the magazine emptied, and I looked down at the remains of the man who had placed a ten million dollar bounty on me.

"About fucking time," Sharona said. "That was getting annoying."

I ejected the UMP's empty magazine and inserted a fresh one. "We need to find Ramon," I said as I released the bolt and charged the weapon. "We need to end this."

She nodded and we were out of the bathroom, out of the bedroom, and into the great room in moments. As we made our way alongside the staircase, I eyed the bar area longingly, knowing there were some very fine and expensive bottles of single malt stowed there.

"There's a basement to this house," Sharona said. "Prisoners would probably be held there. We'll just need to search around until we find the right door." She looked at her watch. "We've got about ten minutes until exfil," she said. "We're going to have to do this fast."

"Copy that," I said. "But I've got to spare about thirty seconds to look behind the bar here."

"Seriously?" Sharona asked. "We don't have time for that!"

"There's always time for good Scotch," I said. "And if I remember correctly, Miguel has some of the best."

Ironically, it was the Scotch that saved us.

As I diverted my path to the bar area on the far right side of the room, there was a loud crash behind me. As I spun around and brought the UMP to bear, I was greeted with the sight of Ramon the Rock standing over Sharona Brown, who was either unconscious or dead on the floor beneath him. Apparently Ramon had vaulted the railing lining the walkway on the second floor and landed right on top of her. While Sharona was both fast and strong, she was no match for three hundred pounds and gravity, especially when it made no sound on the way down.

The huge Mexican stood there staring at me, about twenty feet away. I could see the muscles bunched in his tattooed shoulders and the sweat and dust on his arms. His long black hair, normally neatly tied behind his head, was disheveled, and his trademark black vest with silver circles on it was torn and dusty. But there was a purposeful gleam in his eye and a huge knife with a long serrated blade in his right hand.

The distance between us was about twenty feet, and I knew he could close that gap in seconds. I raised the UMP and trained the red dot of the aim reticle on the center of his chest. Ramon looked down at the dot on his vest and actually brushed it with the fingertips of his left hand. Then he looked up at me and smiled.

"You will get one, maybe two shots," he said, with just the barest trace of an accent, "before I reach you and cut your head off like you did to Pablo." He twirled the knife in his right hand.

"So you do speak fucking English," I said. "Then maybe you'll understand this." I smiled back at him. "Your brother is dead. I turned his head into a fucking pincushion. And you're about to join him."

Ramon's face clouded and the smile turned into a deranged scowl. He began to come toward me.

It's amazing how lucid you can be at moments like this—and how alive. I could feel my heart pounding in my chest and even in my ears. I could hear Ramon's booted feet crunching the wood and glass as he came across the floor and imagined

I could feel his breath in the air.

I let go of the UMP's pistol grip with my right hand and shoved my hand downward to the grip of the Magnum Research Desert Eagle .50 caliber pistol that was riding on my right thigh. I felt my gloved right thumb push the holster strap to the side, my index finger slid alongside the trigger guard, and the rest of my fingers went around the grip. Then I began to pull upward.

"Hey, Ramon," I said to the mad Mexican as he closed the ground between us. "I've got something for you."

He responded with something that sounded like a grunt and roar of rage combined and raised the large knife over his head. In mere seconds he'd be upon me.

The heavy pistol cleared the holster, and my arm began to raise it to fire even as my right thumb clicked the safety on the left side of the slide into the FIRE position. As the front sight tracked across the dusty floor and up Ramon's body, it suddenly occurred to me that even if I killed him, he'd still probably bury that huge fucking knife into my chest. I was wearing the standard Kevlar vest, but Kevlar didn't stop knives very well. Especially those propelled by huge Mexicans hopped up on God-knew-what drugs. Strangely, I found I was at peace with that thought. The one thing I did know is that he'd never live to threaten Sarah or little Colleen again. And that was all that mattered.

He was less than six feet away now and the Desert Eagle was tracking up his body, and I was already squeezing the huge pistol's trigger. Ramon's knife hand was starting its downward motion, and I couldn't tell if he was trying to cut my arm or my body. But it didn't matter. His time was up. The Desert Eagle's front sight reached the center of Ramon's massive chest just as my finger pressed the trigger past the sear point. The huge pistol bucked in my hand but stayed on target, and I continued to fire, again and again. The good thing about heavy weapons is that they can tame heavy recoil, especially when they use some gas energy from the cartridge to operate the mechanism like the Desert Eagle did. Even one handed, the weapon recovered beautifully, and it sent seven .50-caliber, three-hundred-grain, armor-piercing slugs through the gaudy vest the immense man wore and into his body, ripping into his flesh and shattering bones.

Ramon reeled with the impacts, and his forward progress slowed to a shuffle as the Desert Eagle fired its last shot and the slide locked open. I was already reaching for a spare magazine as I ejected the spent one, but Ramon was still moving forward, and the knife was still coming toward me.

Focus at a moment like this is critical. You have to concentrate and lock out fear, panic, or anything else that distracts you from the task at hand. I was almost inside of Ramon's reach as I slammed the fresh magazine home into the Desert Eagle's pistol grip. I had retracted my right arm so that my upper arm was alongside my body and the huge pistol was now low and centered on Ramon's abdomen.

But the knife was still coming.

And I wasn't going to be able to get out of the way.

Tiredly, slowly, like a locomotive with too much inertia to stop, Ramon pushed me back against the wall with his left hand and the force of his weight, as he cocked his right arm back to begin a downward slash. I prepared myself for the impact as I hit the slide release on the Desert Eagle and felt it go forward. The reassuring sound of a round getting chambered reached my ears even as I shoved the muzzle of the weapon into Ramon's stomach.

I pulled the trigger on the huge pistol as the point of the knife ripped through the cloth of my harness and the fatigues below it and found my skin. I pulled it again as the knife entered my body on the upper section of the left side of my chest. And I pulled it a third time as the knife buried itself to the hilt in the meat and muscle of my body. I don't know what I was expecting in the way of pain, but between the adrenaline coursing through my body and the sharpness of the blade, there wasn't much—at least not at that moment.

Ramon's face and my face were inches apart; and I could feel his hot, rancid breath on my forehead. His breathing was labored and slow, and his massive chest heaved spasmodically with every intake of air. He leaned against me, as if to gather strength, and I saw him stare at his right hand as if to reassure himself the knife was still in it. Then he opened and closed his fingers to reinforce his grip and his muscles tensed. I knew he was gathering strength to pull the knife out of me and stab or slash me again. And I knew I probably wouldn't live through it. I fired into his abdomen two more times, feeling the heavy automatic pistol recoil in my hand. Ramon turned his head and looked at me with a dazed and drunken expression on his face. His eyes were about half closed but they looked satisfied and even peaceful. Almost in slow motion, the corners of his mouth raised into a slow, exhausted, sick smile. I fired the Desert Eagle once again into Ramon's abdomen, attempting to angle the gun upward as I pulled the trigger. His body barely shuddered with the impacts, and his smile even became a little wider.

"Me muero," he said, pulling the knife out of me with a loud grunt. "But...you...die...first."

The knife came out of me, pulling pieces of my skin with it as it exited my body. Out of the corner of my eye, I saw blood pouring out of the wound and over the harness and the fatigues and down the front of me. I felt detached, as if I wasn't inside my own body—as if it wasn't really me. Maybe it was some kind of defense mechanism. Ramon pushed against me hard with his left hand and reared his right hand back to slash downward once again. With every ounce of strength I had remaining, I raised the Desert Eagle, now feeling impossibly heavy in my right hand, to try to fire the last round into him. More to make sure I killed him than to save my own life. At that point, I wasn't sure it mattered.

But then something odd happened.

In the middle of his motion, Ramon stopped and froze. Like something had startled him. He forced his massive body into a more erect posture and the knife fell from his hand, as if forgotten. His tired eyes registered surprise and then shock as he pivoted slowly to look behind him.

And as he turned, I saw the long shaft of a medieval lance sticking out of his back. It was one of many from Miguel's collections all over the hacienda. And standing beyond Ramon, on the staircase behind him, was Brock Black. He looked worn, dusty, and bloody, but he was alive. And there were two women on the stairs with him, one Caucasian and one African American. They were both dressed in some kind of boudoir ensemble and were as dusty as he was although not nearly as bloody. The Caucasian girl I recognized. And I smiled because I realized she was still alive, in spite of her stepfather selling her into white slavery. Maybe the day hadn't been a total failure after all. As my eyes then regarded the other girl, I knew I didn't recognize her, but she looked familiar. As I looked at her face and then at Brock's, I saw the resemblance.

She was Brock's daughter.

Son of a bitch. That explains a lot.

In the meantime, Ramon stood in front of me with his back to me, apparently staring in disbelief at the man who had just run him through from thirty feet away. The huge man weaved a little as he stood there, the effects of the bullets and the lance finally seeming to slow his body function and his awareness.

There was one thing left to do.

"Hey, asshole," I said, struggling to keep my voice steady and audible.

Ramon turned back around to me slowly, like a man in a drugged state but aware of the consequences to come anyway. As his head came around and his eyes met mine, I forced the Desert Eagle upward and placed the muzzle of the heavy pistol on his forehead.

He blinked and mouthed three words in a voice so soft it was almost a whisper.

"Others will come," he said.

"Say hello to your brother for me," I said and I pulled the trigger.

The Desert Eagle bucked in my hand and the round went through Ramon's head in a microsecond, taking surprisingly little tissue with it as it transited. The huge Mexican's head snapped backward and he fell backward, driving the lance through his body as he hit the floor with the large metal point exiting his body through the garish vest with pieces of bloody tissue hanging from it.

In the meantime, I was sinking to the tiled floor with my back against the wall. I didn't seem to have the strength to stay on my feet any longer. I looked down at my chest and saw blood pouring from the knife wound. The red liquid was gushing forth like a bottle of wine that had been knocked on its side.

Damn, I thought. *Who knew a body could have so much blood?*

As my ass hit the floor, I exhaled heavily. I suddenly felt exhausted. And used up.

Some operative you are. Three missions, multiple gunshot wounds, a high-speed ejection, and now you've been stabbed. You are too old for this shit.

My eyelids felt like lead, and I fought to keep them open. I began to slide sideways on the wall and I found myself longing for the rest that would come after I got horizontal—and the peace. I was ready. Sarah and Colleen were safe. They had to be. Miguel and Ramon were gone.

Others will come.

What the fuck did that mean?

My shoulders slid off the wall and my head was destined to bounce on the tile floor. I closed my eyes and braced for the impact. Hopefully the last one I would ever feel.

But instead, I landed in a silken lap. Surprised, I opened my eyes and saw a familiar face looking down at me with expressive brown eyes framed by light brunette hair.

"I know you," she said.

"I know you too," I said weakly. "Glad you're alive."

Her eyes were glistening. "And I'm free now, thanks to you."

I felt pressure on my wound and transferred my gaze downward to find Brock Black pressing on me, apparently trying to stop the blood flow. His dark face looked concerned, but when he caught me looking at him, he smiled at me.

"You throw a great party, T. C.," he said. "But if you make any spear-chucker jokes, I'm going to have to kick your ass."

I laughed then and coughed up some blood and pieces of tissue. "Wouldn't dream of it," I said. "That was fucking impressive."

"I did the javelin in track and field," he said as he tore pieces of gauze he had retrieved from somewhere and stuffed them into my wound. "Held a USAFA record in it for about ten years." He looked away from me, across the room. "Is she conscious, Natalie?" he asked.

"Yes," a voice answered. "She's coming around now."

A few moments later, two more feminine faces were looking down at me.

"B-Rock," I said, "Meet Sharona Brown. Or that's what her name is this week."

He looked up at her. "We've met. Another time and another place." He looked down at me again. "You need to stop talking." He looked back at Sharona. "Exfil on the way?"

"They'll be here any minute," she said. "MH-60."

Brock nodded.

My eyelids started an inexorable descent. I knew I only had a moment or two before I wouldn't be able to speak any longer. And I had to say something.

"Sharona, Brock saved my life tonight. He's the one who put the spear into Ramon."

"Noted," she said. "I sort of gathered that."

I looked at Brock.

"Thanks for that by the way," I said. "I owe you one."

"It's me who owes you," he said. "You could have blown my ass out of the sky, but instead you only knocked out the airplane. Miguel wasn't terribly happy but I didn't give a shit."

"Maybe when we're done with this, we can have a nice Scotch together and talk about it," I said, as my eyelids finally shut.

"Look forward to it, T. C."

"By the way, there's some great stuff in the bar next to us," I said, smiling. "We need to take some with us."

Then I could hear them talking about me in concerned tones and hushed voices. But soon after, I didn't hear anything at all. I exhaled once, slowly, easily, and completely, and I embraced the blackness that reached for me.

Chapter Twenty-Seven

Sometime in Mid-August
Sometime in the Morning
Somewhere in the Caribbean

I awoke from a short nap on the lounge chair to feel the ocean breeze gently dancing on my skin and the rhythmic sound of the waves lapping at the nearby shore. I didn't know what day it was or exactly what time it was, I just knew it was sometime in the afternoon. As I looked out from under the beach umbrella, the seascape in front of me could have been a postcard; white sand in the foreground, clear teal water in the background.

As far as I could see.

I breathed in the salt air and let it fill my lungs with clean, untainted goodness, wincing slightly as the wound on my left shoulder made its presence known.

I had been there, on the island, for about two weeks. The CIA had paid for a jet and three weeks of rest and relaxation for a companion and me. After a little coordination, the choice of companion had been obvious. Now I spent each day in the company of my lovely partner, with a pleasant interlude in the morning, some breakfast, some exercise, and then the rest of the day on the beach. She spent her time working on her flawless and lineless suntan. And I spent time looking at her amazing body and trying to work through the events after the raid on Miguel's hacienda.

The raid in which I had almost died.

Again.

***

After losing consciousness in Miguel's great room, I had regained it, briefly, on the special ops helicopter as it flew back up the Mexican coast to the United States. All I could recall was the vibration of the machine and the noise of the wind through the open doors. There were flashes of faces around me and movement of my body as gear and clothing were cut away from me.

***

The next time I awoke, I was in a hospital—I later learned it was the Navy Medical Center in San Diego—being wheeled in for surgery. There were masked faces above me with several sets of eyes looking down at me. One of the sets of eyes was set in a dark face and showed impatience and concern.

Brock? What the hell are you doing here?

Metal doors opened, and I was taken into a room with many bright lights and monitors.

"Let's get him under," a commanding male voice said. "We don't have a lot of time."

And then there was a soothing, drug-induced calm and the welcome darkness once again.

***

The next time I awoke, I heard Brock's voice talking

to me. I was so drugged up, I couldn't understand exactly what he was saying but there were words I remembered like "daughter," "slavery," and "manipulated." I remembered looking over at him in my drug-induced haze and being able to tell he was tortured about working for Miguel and what had nearly happened. I had actually laughed at his confession or explanation or whatever he was saying. When he looked up, I grabbed his forearm with my hand and managed to speak a few coherent words.

"We...all...fuck up...Brock," I had said. "I'm...the...last... one... to... judge." Then I looked into his dark, anguished eyes and with all the conviction I could muster with the cocktail of drugs coursing through my veins, I spoke to him again. "You... were... there...in...the...end. That...showed...who...you...are." He squeezed my arm in thanks before I drifted back into the drug-induced never-never land again.

***

I awoke for good sometime later—apparently about a week or so. The damage Ramon's massive blade had rendered to my shoulder and chest was substantial. I was told by the attending doctors at the Wilford Hall that three surgeries had been performed; one in San Diego to keep me alive and two since my arrival at the USAF Medical center in San Antonio, Texas, to try to repair the wound. The doctors told me I would probably regain full use of my left arm. They also told me it would take a while to completely heal and that I needed to take it easy for a substantial period of time. They didn't need to tell me that twice. I was going to put my fucking phone in a vault somewhere so I couldn't answer it.

Smith and Amrine floated into my room a few hours after I regained permanent consciousness.

"Congrats!" Amrine had said cheerfully.

"For what?" I asked. "For managing to stay alive?"

He had shaken his head with the usual Amrine smirk on his face. "Well, that too," he said. "But most of all for stopping what you stopped. The theft of not one, not two, but three F-35's. The damage to national security would have been incalculable."

"Well, it cost enough," I said.

Amrine nodded. "It did. Thomas Rogers and Christine Billings. Not to mention the others who were killed along the way. But, and I know these words can sound hollow at times, at least their deaths meant something. At least they died for a greater good."

"The words don't sound hollow, John," I said. "They're just hard to take comfort from. I didn't know Thomas at all, but the pain on his mother's face was beyond comprehension. And Christine was one of the most special people I ever met. I'm really going to miss her. And I'm sure I'm not the only one." I looked at him. "What happened with her... body?"

Smith had shaken his head then. "There wasn't much left to find, as you can imagine. Pieces of her jet were scattered over several miles. Some biomass has been recovered. Most of it will never be. Whatever biomass is recovered will be positively identified and then placed in a casket and returned to her husband."

"The casket needs to be weighted, Dave," I said.

He nodded. "Standard procedure for something like this," he answered. "I know you're used to it from aircraft accidents, but we do the same thing for covert ops when field agents aren't recovered. There's something about weight in the casket that gives loved ones a sense of closure."

"It's good you're familiar," I said.

"No," he said. "It's not. I'm a little too familiar. Too many lives lost. Too many people I knew. I'm sure you understand."

I nodded. "I do," I said. "Unfortunately." I decided to

change the subject. We needed to. "So what's going to happen with Brock?"

"What do you think should happen?" Amrine asked, leaning forward with a keen look on his surfer-boy features.

"Nothing,' I answered without hesitation.

"But what about him working for Miguel?" Amrine asked. "What do you think about him being a traitor?"

"I'm not sure he was," I said. "I think he was a prisoner. I think he was coerced. I don't think it was voluntary. Besides, he saved my life. That says something."

Amrine smiled and nodded. "We agree," he said. "We're not looking into it and neither is the OSI. We all seem to be in agreement there."

I laughed. "The OSI seeing the big picture? Wonders never cease."

Smith nodded. "It's the truth. After Lena Otenski woke up, we spoke to her and she's on board. We gave her the information you told us about Dahlke's link to Hidalgo and how the two of them controlled Turnidge."

"That's nice," I said. "But what good will it do? She doesn't have any pull."

Smith's mouth twisted into an ironic smile. "She actually does. She might not have mentioned it, but she's pretty high up in the OSI food chain. And between her uncovering Turnidge's pedophilia and rescuing your sorry ass, she's gotten a promotion and a decoration. She vouched for Brock and talked her peers in the OSI out of an investigation. So he's clean as far as the USAF is concerned and clean as far as we're concerned."

I leaned back in my bed. "Well, that's something, I guess," I said. "So what was the deal there?"

Amrine shrugged. "He had a daughter from a relationship a long time ago. She fell in with the wrong crowd and got abducted. He started searching for her and eventually found out she was working for Miguel. Brock being Brock, he thought he could work out some kind of deal with Miguel to get her back and didn't ask for our help or even let us know, in spite of the fact that we've worked with him several times in the past. Well, Miguel ignored him, until Miguel learned Brock was in a TX class at Luke thanks to the late Mark Tappan. The rest, as they say, is history."

"I see," I said. There was silence for a few moments. I thought about how predictable we all could be when people we cared about were involved: Bob and Kristin Barnett with her son Thomas, me with Saran and Colleen, and now Brock with his daughter. Predictability was dangerous, especially in this line of work.

"So there are some questions you're not asking," Amrine said.

I raised an eyebrow at him. "Such as?"

"The aftermath for Miguel's operation and for Mexico," he said.

I shook my head. "You know what? If the Chinese are out and Miguel is dead that's all that matters to me," I said. I looked over at him. "There aren't any other contenders for the throne, are there?"

"Not that we know of," he said.

"Then I'm good."

It was at that moment that she of the cappuccino-toned skin and sensual smile wafted into the room, sans the facial prosthetics. She walked over to my bed, and in front of her coworkers, gave me a warm, lingering kiss that made me see stars.

"How are you doing, hero?" she asked after our lips parted.

"Much better now, Sharona," I said after I regained my awareness of the room.

"I'm glad," she said, smiling at me from about six inches away. "And it's Isabelle. Just so you know."

I looked her over unabashedly, oblivious to Smith and Amrine's presence in the room. "You look none the worse for wear."

She shook her head and smiled tightly. "How's that saying go? Nothing hurt but my dignity. I never heard him and never saw him. He's the quietest human being ever."

"Was," I said. "Was the quietest human being ever."

"Yes," she smiled again. "You saw to that."

"I had help."

She nodded. "But you're the one who paid for it."

"I guess," I said. I looked at the beautiful lineless face and playful dark eyes. "I don't know when I get out of here, but I'd sure like to spend some time—"

She shook her head and interrupted me. "I'll have to take a raincheck," she said. "I actually came in here to fetch these two in addition to seeing you." She looked back over her shoulder at Amrine. "The Shadow just whacked another one, boss," she said. "In Paris this time."

"Goddamn it," Amrine spat. "That's going to piss the director off. All right, reunion time is over. We've got work to do."

Sharona/Isabelle gave me another kiss that made me forget where I was.

"Hold that thought," she whispered, as she got up from my bed.

I could see Smith and Amrine with twin smirks on their faces as she exited the room. I looked at Amrine. "Don't say it," I said.

He chuckled and turned to leave.

Smith walked over to my bed and offered his hand. I shook it.

"Great work again, Colin," he said.

"Thanks," I said. "Maybe one of these days I can actually do some work for you guys and not be shot or stabbed in the process.”

"That'd be a good thing," he said. "But if it's any consolation, the government has something for you." He reached inside his jacket pocket and produced an envelope. "Three weeks in the Caribbean on us, when you're out of here."

"That's awesome," I said. "Thanks."

"And," he said, smiling at me, "it's for two. I thought you could probably find someone you could talk into going."

I looked back at him. "I just might," I said.

***

I spent another three days in the hospital, mostly for observation and physical therapy. By the time my discharge date came around, I was ready to leave, and I was sure the hospital staff was ready to see me go. Fortunately, Smith and Amrine had collected my things from Luke and had them delivered to my room so I actually had something to wear. I had just finished dressing and was in the process of closing up my suitcase when I had my last set of visitors.

"Going somewhere?" asked a familiar female voice behind me.

"I was hoping to," I said, turning around.

She looked better than her picture, with lustrous brunette hair, deep expressive brown eyes, and a playful smile. Even clad in USAF fatigues, her body looked amazing.

"General Petersen," I said, offering my hand. "Glad to meet you in person."

"Colonel Pearce," she answered, looking me up and down. "Glad to meet you also. It seems you came through this in reasonably good shape." Our hands touched and shook but stayed clasped an extra moment or two.

I smiled at her. "I recover quickly," I said, releasing her hand.

The playful smile got a little larger. "We may have to see about that," she said.

"Did you come here for your debriefing?" I asked.

She shook her head. "No, I have another venue in mind for that," she said. "I brought some people here to see you." She turned to the door. "Bob? Kristin?"

Brigadier General and Mrs. Robert Barnett walked into my room, hand-in-hand, both sporting dark suntans and relaxed expressions.

"Looks like a little CIA-provided R and R did you both some good!" I said. "I'm glad."

Bob nodded. "It was like another honeymoon," he said. "It was really good to just disconnect from the world and be together. When we heard the news about the raid on Miguel's hacienda, I knew that had to be you. We got back to the States as soon as we could."

Kristin stood at his side, looking at me intently. I knew the question she was dying to ask.

"Most of them are dead, Kristin," I said to her. "But a few aren't. Satan, Miguel, and the OSI det. commander at Luke are dead. But Don Weeks, the 310th Commnder, and Alan Turnidge, the OSI Commander in DC, are still alive. But they'll both be spending a long, long time at the Military Correctional Facility at Fort Leavenworth. They'll probably wish they were dead after a few years there. And regarding Turnidge, when word gets out that he's a pedophile, odds are high someone in the prison population will stick a shiv in him pretty quickly."

"Which ones did you kill?" she asked after a moment.

I looked back at her, not knowing what to say. I wasn't sure how much, if any, comfort my words would bring to the mother of a dead son.

"Please," she said. "I need to know."

"I killed Satan and Miguel and someone you've probably never heard of, a guy named Ramon the Rock. I had some help with him."

"How?" she asked.

I looked at her quizzically. "How what?"

"How did Satan and Miguel die?"

"Satan died in the cockpit of an F-35. I put about a few hundred rounds of twenty millimeter into him. Miguel died in his bathtub from multiple gunshot wounds to the head."

"Multiple?" she asked, with a trace of a smile on her face.

I nodded. "I had to make sure. It was personal for me too."

"Were they afraid at the end?" she asked. "Did they know they were going die at the end? Did they feel helpless at the end?"

I thought about that for a moment and recalled both scenes briefly in my mind. "They both knew they were going to die, and they both knew they couldn't stop it. Whether they were afraid or defiant, I can't say."

She nodded and looked down at the floor. I could tell that what I told her hadn't been enough. But I had known it wouldn't be from the moment we had dinner in Annapolis weeks ago. I reached over to her and took her free hand.

"Kristin, last year my best friend in the world was killed at the hands of some very nasty people. Bob probably knows most of the details. I killed nearly everyone who had anything to do with it. And you know what?"

She looked up at me with glistening eyes.

"It still hurts," I said. "I still miss him. I'll always miss him. Revenge might feel good in the moment, but when the act is over, the hole inside you is still there."

"I feel like such a monster," she said, her voice cracking. "I just wanted everybody dead. I wanted them all to suffer. I wanted to feel better."

"And now they're all gone, but so is Thomas. And you don't feel any better."

She nodded.

"Welcome to the club," I said. "The pain will lessen over time. But it will always remain. And that's actually a good thing. Because as long as the pain is there, it shows the love is there too. And besides," I said, "there's only one monster in this room."

Kristin released Bob's hand and took a step or two toward me. I offered her my arms and she stepped into them and hugged me tightly. I hugged her back, and we had moment of mutual consolation, the kind only those who have lost someone very close to them can understand.

"Thank you," she said, with her head against my chest.

"You're welcome," I said.

She kept her arms around me for a moment and looked up at me. "Your life hasn't been easy, has it?" she asked.

"Harder than some, easier than others," I said. "I try not to think about it much. That's why I stay so busy."

She smiled and released me. And then, without another word, she turned away and left the room.

Bob looked at me and shrugged. Then he offered me his hand and we shook. "Thanks, Colin. You're right, it won't bring Thomas back, but at least it's some closure for her."

"Stay by her side, Bob. Don't let the demands of work get in the way. Once the closure comes, the grief can get even more raw. She's going to need you."

He nodded. "You're right," he said. "Take care, Colin." He began to turn away but then he turned back. "Or should I call you T. C.?"

I smiled at him tiredly. "I think I've had enough of being T. C. I think I'll just be Colin for a while."

Bob raised an eyebrow at me. "Until the next time of course," he said.

***

And now here I was relaxing on a beautiful beach and watching Gail Petersen rise out of the water like the mythical naiad and walk toward me on the white sand, wearing nothing but a smile, a suntan, and seawater. But even as I drank in the sight of her magnificent body and smiled at the prospect of the coming evening's activities, Bob Barnett's words rang in my ears.

"Until the next time," he had said.

And I nodded to myself in answer.

"You're right, Bob," I said to the ocean air. "Until the next time."

COLIN PEARCE WILL RETURN
IN
THE SHADOW CONTRACT

ABOUT THE AUTHOR

Chris Broyhill is a retired U.S. Air Force fighter pilot who flew the OV-10, A-10, and F-16 while on active duty. He holds a bachelor's degree in computer science from the U.S. Air Force Academy, a master's degree in national security studies from California State University at San Bernardino and a Ph.D. in aviation from Embry-Riddle Aeronautical University. Chris is an outstanding graduate of the U.S. Air Force Fighter Weapons School and is a National Business Aviation Association Certified Aviation Manager. He also sits on the NBAA Business Aviation Management Committee. Chris has flown aircraft and held various leadership positions in aviation organizations for over 30 years. He currently resides in the Dallas-Fort Worth area.